W9-BYA-603

RANDOM
HOUSE
LARGE
PRINT

THE

LAGER QUEEN

OF

MINNESOTA

THE

LAGER QUEEN

OF

MINNESOTA

J. RYAN STRADAL

RANDOM HOUSE
LARGE PRINT

This is a work of fiction. Names, characters, places, and incidents either are the product of the author's imagination or are used fictitiously, and any resemblance to actual persons, living or dead, businesses, companies, events, or locales is entirely coincidental.

Copyright © 2019 by J. Ryan Stradal

Penguin supports copyright. Copyright fuels creativity, encourages diverse voices, promotes free speech, and creates a vibrant culture. Thank you for buying an authorized edition of this book and for complying with copyright laws by not reproducing, scanning, or distributing any part of it in any form without permission. You are supporting writers and allowing Penguin to continue to publish books for every reader.

All rights reserved.

Published in the United States of America by Random House Large Print in association with Viking, an imprint of Penguin Random House LLC, New York.

Cover design: Jaya Miceli
Cover images: (bottle cap) kyoshino / Getty Images Plus; (wheat) CSA Images / Getty Images

The Library of Congress has established a Cataloging-in-Publication record for this title.

ISBN: 978-1-5247-7842-2

www.penguinrandomhouse.com/large-print-format-books

FIRST LARGE PRINT EDITION

Printed in the United States of America

10   9   8   7   6   5   4   3   2

This Large Print edition published in accord with the standards of the N.A.V.H.

to Doris and Esther,
grandmothers who could, and did

CONTENTS

$20,000 1

$31.00 31

$15.00 87

$92.27 121

$40,000 179

$5.00 213

$18.95 289

$100,000 313

$200 349

$57.00 369

$1,020,000 435

THE
LAGER QUEEN
OF
MINNESOTA

$20,000

It was July 5, 2003, and Edith Magnusson's day hadn't been too bad, so far. She'd just taken a strawberry-rhubarb pie from the oven, and was looking for her favorite tea towel, when she saw a grasshopper on the white trim of the windowsill. She didn't like the idea of it sitting there, vulnerable, so she gently poked at the bug with the handle of a wooden spoon. As she'd hoped, it leapt into the yard, and vanished into safety. She felt herself exhale.

Then, she felt terrible. Maybe it just wanted a little vacation somewhere different, and she came along and ruined everything. Edith, for one, never once had been anywhere different, or ever truly had a break of any kind. Then again, she'd never intended to take one. Things were pretty decent where she was, and she didn't ever see the point of bellyaching about the things she couldn't change, especially in a world that never once ran a want ad looking for a complainer.

After all, she had a good job at St. Anthony-Waterside Nursing Home six blocks from her rented two-bedroom rambler in the central Minnesota town of New Stockholm. Edith also had her husband, Stanley, who at that moment was in a Peterbilt somewhere in South Dakota. She had an adult son, Eugene, who was just starting out as an independent distributor for an interesting company called LifeWell, which apparently sold quality household products direct to customers at low prices. She also had an adult daughter, Colleen, who'd gone to college, and even though she had to drop out, had done OK for herself. She married a handyman named Mark, who was a kind man, even if he didn't go to church. They were raising Edith's sole grandchild, a smart, curious girl named Diana, who was somehow almost a teenager already.

If all this wasn't everything a person needed, she didn't know what would be. It was true that she missed the farm where she grew up, and missed her parents for one reason and her sister for another reason, but it was no use dwelling on people and things that were in the past.

Edith was only sixty-four years old, but if she died right then, she would've felt the most important things a Minnesotan, woman or man, can feel at the end of their lives. She'd done what she could, and she was of use. She helped.

But life wasn't done with her yet, and before long she'd come to regard everything that happened before July 5, 2003, like it was all just a pleasant song in an elevator. When the music stopped, the doors opened, and the light first fell in, it was in the form of her boss, a man she liked, running down the hallway at work, smiling, shouting her name, and waving a piece of newspaper in the air like a child.

Edith had worked as a dietary aide in the nursing home's kitchen for thirty-seven years. Her coworkers were mostly hardworking, exhausted, and kind. The hallways smelled like baby powder sprinkled onto boiled green beans, which over the years had become kind of pleasant. Also, everyone agreed that the new boss, Brendan Fitzgerald, who had the benign charisma and calm authority of a TV meteorologist, was the best administrator they'd ever had. He also chain-smoked and only referred to residents by their room number, but at least he was always glad to see Edith, and that day he was the happiest she'd ever seen him since he won fifty bucks playing pull tabs.

Brendan, his slick black Reagan hair gleaming

under the fluorescent lights, held out a copy of **Twin City Talker**, one of those hip newspapers for hip city people. Edith had flipped through an issue once, twenty years ago, and thought it was kind of different, so she never read it again. FOOD ISSUE, this cover read, and Brendan tore it open to a page somewhere in the middle.

"Did you hear about this?" he asked her.

She saw a list with the heading, BEST PIES.

1. Betty's Pies, Two Harbors
2. Keys Café and Bakery, St. Paul
3. St. Anthony-Waterside Nursing Home, New Stockholm

"Our nursing home has the third-best pie in Minnesota," he said, shaking the paper for emphasis.

"Well, that's bizarre," Edith said.

"No, it's not. It's because of number eight's granddaughter. You've seen her here, with the pink hair," Brendan said, pointing to the name in the byline. "That's her. Ellen Jones. Staff food critic!"

"Neat. Well, I'd better get back to the kitchen," Edith said.

"I'm going to get it framed and put in the lobby,"

Brendan shouted. "That's something, Edith! Third-best pie, in the whole entire state!"

Edith had been baking her own pies at work since her first year there, when she noticed that the apple cobbler—purchased pre-made from a contracted vendor—came back in unusually high quantities, some completely untouched, most just one or two bites smaller, some with one bite missing and a moist chunk of the stuff elsewhere on the plate. One resident, a wonderful old stick-in-the-mud named Donald Gustafson, had sent it back with a note reading MAKE IT STOP.

When you see a man falling off a ladder above you, Edith believed, you don't envision your arms breaking. You just hold them out.

Had she known that this decision would one day, decades later, change everything she loved about her life, she still would have done it, because the kitchen at St. Anthony-Waterside was responsible for the last desserts that the residents would likely ever have. If it were up to her, the people in this building would at least have the texture, the taste, or even just the smells of homemade pie once or twice a week, as heaven weaned them from the senses of this world. It's the least a dang person can do.

And, as it turned out, it was indeed up to her.

With the help of a few extra dollars from Brendan and the folks in charge before him (to help subsidize the ingredients) she'd been serving her homemade pies year-round for almost forty years now. Most residents felt that they were pretty decent, if a tad on the sweet side, not that they were complaining.

Edith turned her back to Brendan. "Well, let's just hope it blows over."

"Let's hope it doesn't blow over! This is awesome! You should be proud!"

Brendan still wasn't married and didn't have kids, and as a man in his sixties, at least one of those two things probably was never going to happen, so more than ever, he lived for his job. This was only an unfortunate scenario for Edith when it made her life more complicated, like now.

Of course, Edith had been in the paper before. **The New Stockholm Explainer** ran pieces on Edith every eight years or so, with a headline that was something like PIE LADY STILL SERVING SLICES, along with a picture that always made her look confused and old. She didn't read the articles and never even kept copies for herself. When the phone rang at home around lunchtime the following day, she knew it would be Stanley, and she didn't even think she'd mention it to him.

The man on the other end of the phone wasn't

Stanley, though, it was his boss, The Other Tom Clyde, and she decided that she wouldn't mention it to him either.

"Edith," Mr. Clyde said. "There's been an accident. Now, first, your husband's OK, he just has a concussion."

She knew he was OK. They'd been married for almost forty-four years exactly and she'd know it if he wasn't alive somewhere. They could have sent him to Pluto and she'd know if he made it. But she also knew that this could happen sometime, and soon.

"What did he do now, Mr. Clyde?"

"Well, he drove a truckload of frozen hamburgers into the front of a Hardee's in Sioux Falls. Normally they like their deliveries in the back, so I'm told." Mr. Clyde shared his cousin Big Tom Clyde's dry sense of humor.

"Was anyone hurt?"

"No, thankfully. There's some trash cans and picnic tables that wished they hadn't met your husband's truck, but that's about it." Mr. Clyde sounded a little sad. "I gotta be honest, I think he's hauled his last load, ma'am."

"Well, send him on home," she told him, said good-bye, and hung up the phone.

It was noon, and outside, a basketball belonging to the neighbor kids tumbled into her yard, reminding her of high school. A mayfly beat its papery body against the screen door, delighted to be anywhere. And now, Edith was alone in her home kitchen, slicing fruit, and waiting for her life to change, once again.

The next day, she took Stanley to see Dr. Nebel. En route, Stanley proudly announced that he'd been to Dr. Nebel only once the last five years, as if his ignorance was proof of his perfect health. Only once, despite the fact that they were members of the same Elks Lodge. Who knows how they talked there, but in his small, simple office, Dr. Nebel did not BS around with her husband. "Early onset" was the only term he may have used purely out of kindness. While Stanley was sixty-five, it's always too early for something like this, for both of them. He'd miss the pride he'd felt in his ability to fix his own truck, he'd miss his CB handle—Charlie Brown, which he'd earned because of his perfectly round bald head—and he'd miss the smiling faces he'd gotten to know in places like Casper, Pierre, and Grand Junction.

Stanley would now be home every day, and although his Social Security wouldn't be nearly as much as his paycheck was, with some trimming, they'd get by, if no emergencies or surprises happened. They used to live next door to a fireman who said that he prayed every night for tomorrow to be boring, and she knew exactly how he felt.

That evening at St. Anthony-Waterside, there were four guests in the dining room, about three more than usual for a weekday, but nothing alarming. It simply meant that she had to cut both of the pies she'd made into ten slices, which she hated to do.

Clarence Jones in #8 was one of the residents who had regular guests. His granddaughter Mandy, a pleasant young nurse who wore her scrubs all of the time, had brought her two-year-old son, Zach. With his big eyes and slick hair, he looked like a toddler version of Ugarte from **Casablanca**.

"Congrats on making the list in the **Talker**," Mandy said, even though it was her own little sister, Ellen, who wrote it.

"I'm relieved that nobody seems to have paid it any attention," Edith replied, and turned to Clarence, eager to change the subject. "Isn't it good to see your great-grandson?"

"The kid's a commie pinko," Clarence frowned. He was a tad less pleasant than most of the other residents, but God likes all kinds, and Edith sure tried to as well.

"My grandpa's just mad because he gave my son a bag of gumdrops, and Zach gave them all away already," said Mandy.

"These schmucks don't need 'em. And you know what else is a problem?" Clarence asked, now staring at Edith. "Your slices are getting too small. If I'm going to keep living, I want bigger servings of pie."

"Same," said Amelia Burch, who, at ninety-nine, was the oldest person in the entire county, and so far as Edith was aware, still ate everything, except for pork, white bread, and French fries.

"I'll see what I can do," Edith said, looking over the shining, empty dessert plates in the dining room.

The next day, Edith realized that she was running low on pie ingredients quicker than usual; she knew she should build up the nerve to ask Brendan for more again, but first, she had to demonstrate that she'd done everything she could with what she had. Anyway, their twelve-year-old granddaughter, Diana, would be coming up from Hastings that weekend, so Edith had something more pressing to prepare for. It was a tradition that every year, Diana spent a week with her grandparents right before school started. The difference now is that Stanley would be home with her all day, every day, for the first time ever.

From the kitchen, she saw her husband shuffle toward the door, and pull it open with the brisk, blind excitement of a little kid on Christmas.

"I just thought I heard a car," he said, and took a

moment to stare out into the empty driveway, as if he could will Colleen's old blue Dodge Omni into materializing.

When Diana finally arrived, Stanley took her out for Shirley Temples at the Elks Lodge, bought slices of cheddar cheese pizza at Sven Larsen's new restaurant, The Pizza Man, and over dinner, suggested that they visit that buggy oxbow lake near St. Anthony-Waterside and feed the ducks, if she hadn't already outgrown that kind of thing.

"No, I still like ducks, Grandpa," Diana said, and even if she was indulging them, it was kind of her to extend her childhood for their benefit. When she was little, she was perfectly happy just playing with a pie tin full of orphaned keys and dice, or standing in the hall, staring at the painting of the farmhouse with a different family member in each window, coming up with names for each one. Those days were long gone. Now, it was clear that the highlight of her visit was when she and Stanley went to the video store.

Stanley liked sci-fi, and Diana was evidently now into emotional adult dramas, so, judging by the titles on the spines of the DVD boxes, this made for some unusual double features: **Driving Miss Daisy** and **Krull. Blade Runner** and **Steel Magnolias. Terms of Endearment** and **eXistenZ.**

As far as Edith knew, they would watch the movies back-to-back, and would sit patiently through the other person's choice of entertainment.

Starting around that time, though, her sweet, quiet husband wasn't the same. Before the Hardee's incident, he'd seemed mostly himself, just like two or three petals had been plucked from a bouquet. After he was forced to retire, it seemed like there were entire flowers missing. And now, most of the week, he'd be taking care of their only grandchild, alone.

It could've been much worse, but there were issues. On the Tuesday of Diana's visit, he took a fresh loaf of bread out of the oven and fed it to the ducks. Later, he tried to make canned chili in a pot on the stove and forgot about it until the smoke alarm went off. On Thursday he walked Diana to George Schmidt's used car lot, where he tried to put money down on a used Cadillac Eldorado. Luckily, an employee there who knew them from church called Edith at work, and she ran over and put the kibosh on the whole thing.

It made her a little sad not to blow most of their savings on a car they didn't need. Stanley had always dreamed of buying a Cadillac, but neither of them had found themselves on a path in life where buying a Cadillac was ever going to be likely. She couldn't blame him, because she was sure that to him it felt like his last chance to try.

———

That evening, something even more frightening happened. He not only brought Diana to the Elks Lodge, which they agreed was fine, but he purchased an off-sale six-pack of beer, walked home, and gave her a bottle.

Although Edith thought it was deeply troubling to serve alcohol to a pre-teen girl, the particular kind of beer made her even more upset. It was a Blotz—a brand they'd agreed never to speak of or have in their house. She opened the remaining three bottles and poured them in the toilet, not the sink, to make a point. Diana was crying, and said it was her idea, but Edith knew that the girl was just covering for her beloved grandpa.

The Elks Lodge was in a majestic old brick building in the middle of downtown, and Edith had always thought that someone should knock it down, so she could have a nice view of the river while standing in line at the post office. Sadly, the building was on some kind of historic registry, because in the 1800s it was the town brewery, back when small towns in the Midwest had their own local breweries. As long as she'd lived in New Stockholm, though, the building was home to a dusty antique store called Bygone But Not Forgotten, an evolving array of restaurants, and the Elks Lodge, which non-members had to buzz a doorbell to enter.

When the door buzzed back, she dashed inside before she had a chance to change her mind. The Elks Lodge didn't have windows, so at least none of her neighbors could pass by and wonder what the heck she was doing in there.

As she entered the bar area, everyone within fifteen feet of the entrance turned and looked at her for about two seconds—longer than a glance, but not long enough for a greeting. The place was about half-full, mostly with men, and only one or two people she recognized from work, church, the grocery store, the post office, or anywhere else on her life's petite circuit. The walls had backlit signs for Hamm's, Schmidt, Grain Belt, Blatz, Blotz, and Schlitz, most of which she'd tried once, and that was fine. She used to like a glass of Ripple once in a while, but they didn't make that anymore, and according to a menu posted behind the bar, even a plain old glass of white wine was the same price as a pound of ground chuck, so forget it.

A jukebox was playing that nice Otis Redding song, the one about the dock of the bay. As Edith stood at the bar waiting to be noticed, she heard a line about remaining the same, and it sounded like a good idea.

The bartender was a stout woman with a lot

of makeup, and she seemed to know exactly who Edith was and what she was doing there.

"Oh my God," the bartender said, extending a tanned, bejeweled hand to Edith's arm. "Stanley gave a beer to your granddaughter, didn't he?"

Edith only had to nod.

"I promise we won't sell him off-sale liquor again. Will we, Mort?"

"Nope," said Mort, from somewhere.

"Thank you," Edith replied. The place smelled like pizza, but she didn't see any.

"No, thank you," the lady bartender said, squeezing Edith's arm. This touchy-feely woman obviously wasn't raised here, or if she was, it was by people who weren't. "My mom loves your pies so much. When I visit her, she makes me leave early so she can get a good table."

"It's good pie!" said Mort, from somewhere.

Big Tom Clyde, who Edith knew from church, grinned at her from his barstool. "It was written up in one of them city papers, wasn't it? Best pie in the state, I heard."

"Third best," Edith corrected.

"Well, now," the bartender said, eyebrows raised, as if to say, **I'll be the judge of that.**

"How do we get some of that pie?" Big Tom asked. "You know, I never thought about it before, but can we pay to eat in the dining room with our parents?"

They'd already had four or five guests now

almost every night, since that unfortunate article, and that was as much as Edith cared to handle. "People hardly ever do, but sure," Edith said.

"Great," the bartender smiled. "We'll spread the word."

By the end of the following week, Brendan had to borrow folding chairs from the chapel to accommodate everyone on "Edith's pie days." People phoned to see if she was in the building and inquired after her future work schedule. Relatives who'd never visited the nursing home before were now making regular and lengthy appearances. At least three people called the front desk and attempted to make dinner reservations. A truck driver from West Fargo whose aunt was a resident called ahead to ask if there was parking for an eighteen-wheeler. From then on, a lot of the folks who drove to work had to parallel park in the street.

Less than two weeks after making the list in **Twin City Talker**, after she'd believed it had all blown over, Edith was now making at least four pies for every shift she worked. But it had indeed brought nice things, too. People were visiting in numbers they never had before. The five o'clock dinner at St. Anthony-Waterside had been transformed from a quiet but well-lit thirty-five minutes into a boisterous social event, the kind where people of all ages lingered around tables hours after the sun set and the kitchen closed.

Edith was nervous about how St. Anthony's delicate social dynamics would react to these sudden changes. She'd never spent much time in a nursing home before working at one, but even after almost forty years, it still reminded her of high school. She figured out pretty quickly that there were cliques and popular folks, and the people who grew up there in New Stockholm dominated the social scene, and tended to exclude the people who'd grown up somewhere else. To counter this, she'd brought her children in to visit the residents who didn't appear to have local family, friends, or visitors. There were more than you'd care to guess. The kids loved it too, because neither Edith nor Stanley had parents who were alive, so to them it was like suddenly having a dozen grandparents who spoiled them recklessly with attention and candy. Still, she'd also wanted her kids to bring something to the table. "I'm going to have to teach you two how to play cribbage," she'd told them on the way home.

Now, decades later, visitors were just showing up by the dozens. Within three weeks of the **Talker** mention, her name appeared in the **Star Tribune**: BEST PIE IN MINNESOTA A BEST-KEPT SECRET?; the **St. Paul Pioneer Press**: OUTSTATE NURSING

HOME A CULINARY DESTINATION; the **Duluth News Tribune**: MINNESOTA SLICE: SMALL-TOWN WOMAN SERVES HUMBLE PIES; and, most troubling, **Twin City Talker** again, evidently amending their earlier ranking: MINNESOTA'S TOUGHEST DINNER RESERVATION: EDITH MAGNUSSON MAKES THE STATE'S BEST PIES, AND NO, YOU CAN'T HAVE THEM.

A reporter from the **Wadena Pioneer Journal** got the closest, pretending to be someone inquiring about a room for a relative, requesting a self-guided tour. When she got to the kitchen, where Edith was making pie crust among the steam and stainless steel, she snapped a photo and asked Edith if she brushed the bottom of her crust with egg white to keep it crisp.

Edith saw right through this charade. "I'm not telling any of you people anything about anything," she said, and a burly ex-Marine named Edgar Caquill, who worked there part-time while he was in school for his criminal justice degree, let the reporter know the interview was over, without touching the young woman or speaking a word.

"I don't trust the media," Edith said to Edgar. "They're all trying to make me seem like I'm somebody famous. Thanks for protecting me from those dingbats."

Edgar just nodded at her in reply, and she nodded back.

Brendan Fitzgerald, however, was thrilled. He handled the interviews, framed the press clippings and mounted them in the lobby, and even bought a velvet rope for the lines he imagined would form. And there were indeed lines. Even with Brendan charging non-residents six bucks each for a slice of pie—a ludicrous amount, in Edith's opinion—the orderly rows of nice, hungry people went halfway to the curb.

Helping the staff set up and taking down all these extra place settings, chairs, and tablecloths added time to Edith's day, and she could never seem to do it fast enough. More than once, Edith had to give the stink-eye to some complainer. One night, as she helped set up folding chairs in the hallway, a teenager in a Packers jersey loudly asked how long he had to wait for pie.

Two people in line behind the Packers kid, Big Tom spoke up. "See that woman unfolding chairs? That's who makes the pies! Show some respect for how hard she's working. Dammit, she's just one person!"

"Thank you," Edith told Big Tom.

"I'm sorry," the Packers kid said, unable to look at her when he spoke.

"I'll make sure you get some," Edith replied. "Who are you here visiting?"

It seemed to take the kid a moment to think of an answer. "Uh, Lulu," he said.

Edith shook her head. "Oh, you're one of those," she said, and went back to work.

Since someone had to know a resident to be allowed admission, and St. Anthony-Waterside had become the most-visited nursing home in the entire five-state area, it followed that certain residents who'd rarely had a guest were now entertaining six or seven actual or so-called distant relatives, old friends, and erstwhile neighbors at a table. Lulu Kochendorfer was first to profit from her gatekeeper status, and let it be known that she'd claim anyone as her relative for a mere two bucks a pop. By the end of October, she'd obliterated three once-unbreakable St. Anthony-Waterside records by having fifty-two nieces, forty-nine nephews, and over a hundred grandchildren.

Stanley was still with it enough to be unimpressed. "They're making money off of your labor, hand over fist," he said, turning his fork around in a bowl of buttery spaghetti.

"I've noticed," Edith replied. He'd become more aggrieved than ever, which confused her, because even though they didn't have a lot, she could think of a lot of people who were worse off. "By the way, don't forget that you have an appointment with Dr. Nebel tomorrow morning."

"It's not the end of the world to ask for something you deserve," he said. "It's not like we couldn't use it."

Stanley maybe didn't have the mind he once did, or have access to the checkbook, but she supposed he wasn't wrong. Two months ago, on the day they received both her husband's last paycheck and first medical bill in the mail, it was clear that things were going to be more difficult. She could see that their nest egg would continue slowly draining away, but this is what it was for, right? And it's not like there was much Edith would've done differently. They never did get around to buying a house, sure, but they were able to send their daughter to college, even if she couldn't finish. She didn't regret any family trip or any Christmas gift. But she'd known for a while that for them to be financially stable into old age, more money would have to come in, and it would have to come through her.

"I've got a plan for that, Stanley," she told him, and she did. She just wasn't sure yet if she could go through with it.

She tried not to lie in bed at night and keep herself up wondering about how their lives would be different, if she'd received the half of the farm that was owed her. Their father had always liked Helen more, sure, but he was a fair, reasonable man. Helen had to have manipulated him into changing his will; there was no other explanation. She planned the whole time to be with him at the end. As sick as that old man was, it certainly wouldn't have been too difficult to put one over on him.

Edith and Stanley were no different from their friends and neighbors. Twenty thousand dollars would've made an unimaginable difference in their lives. It was difficult not to wonder, ever since, if Helen ever regretted what she did. Edith only knew that she would never be the one to break the silence between them. If that's how Helen treated a sister, she did not deserve to have one.

Now, while her sister lived high on the hog somewhere, Edith spent Thursday afternoons hovering over the local paper, scanning fine print for the words "part-time" and "evenings." She hoped that there'd still be time every day for her to come home and make meals for Stanley so he wouldn't try to make that LifeWell Iowa-style chili again and burn the house down.

"Don't worry about me," Stanley said. "I don't have to use the stovetop. And if I do, I'm the one who should be making dinner. I'm the one who's home all day."

It was sweet of him to say, but she didn't want him going near anything hot or sharp anymore. He had worked full-time all those years so she only had to work part-time, and now it was her turn to help him. She had to. Besides their children, they were all they had.

She spread the want ads section across the chipped green dining room table, and for a moment, she wanted a mother, a father, and a sister again, but there were no ads for that want, and thank goodness, because if her sister had put something in the paper that read, **It wasn't my fault, please talk to me again**, Edith would start to cry.

At the moment, she couldn't afford to dwell on that. What was important is that there were no halfway appropriate jobs for her that week, and it'd be seven days now before she could look again, and if there were none next week, seven more days after that. She briefly comforted herself with the thought that stretching pennies was one of her two great talents in life. Stanley called her a miracle worker, but there was nothing spiritual about it. She looked at money like how a motorcycle driver looks at asphalt. The more of it you see, the farther you can go, but a single mistake with it can finish you.

She wouldn't make that one mistake now.

"Brendan, I've been noticing something," Edith said to her boss that Friday morning. She couldn't look directly at him, but there was hardly anything else to look at in his small office, just a **Far Side** calendar and a framed picture of him, shirtless in a boat, holding up a rainbow trout. "You know, an awful lot of people are coming here just to eat the pies."

Brendan stroked his chin. "Yeah, that's for sure."

Her hands were already sweaty. "And I'm the only person making them."

"I know," he smiled. "I think that's incredible. That's an incredible job you do."

"I heard you made three hundred and fifty dollars at the door on Tuesday."

He nodded. "Three fifty-four, actually. And I didn't make that money, the nursing home made it. Thanks to you. And actually, that's been our slowest night so far."

She felt all of the blood rushing either into or out of her head, she couldn't tell. Maybe she could just leave the office, leave him to mull it over, and with what she said already, she could expect he'd come to the right conclusion.

Instead, she grabbed the back of a chair. "Well, that's quite the unexpected income."

"Yeah, and we need it, you know, to build a sky-light in the lobby. I want future residents to walk in here, and go, **Wow, this is the place!** Right now it's kind of dim. Don't you think it's dim?"

"I don't remember." Edith never entered through the main lobby anymore since it became full of framed newspaper clippings of her and her pies. This was making her dizzy. To bring this exchange to a swift, satisfactory conclusion, it was clear she had to fire the big guns. "But, as you know, my husband had to retire a while back, and now I'm looking into getting a second job to help make ends meet."

"Oh, wow," Brendan said. "That's a lot for someone your age. Two jobs. Especially when one of them has you on your feet all day."

Right then, she almost said that she could just look for another job altogether, which is what her mother would've done, but she restrained herself. "Oh, it can't be anything too crazy. All I need is a few extra dollars, really."

She could hear the soft creaks of Brendan's wooden chair moving as he shifted.

"Hey!" Brendan said. "You know what? Don't get a second job. How about I just give you an extra fifty cents an hour? I don't know why I didn't think of it before."

Edith exhaled. It wasn't quite as much as she needed, but it was a raise, and that's what she'd set out to do today. She promised herself that morning that she'd walk out of his office making more than $11.50 an hour, and now she actually would be. This had been the most anxious, tenacious, and protracted salary negotiation of her life. Now that it was all over, she was finally able to look at him. "Thank you. And you'll please continue buying the ingredients from the lists I give you."

"Been meaning to talk to you about that," he said, and glanced around like someone waking up on a bus. "That's getting to be kind of a hassle. Like for instance, the store didn't have those Haroldson apples you asked for. Easier and cheaper to just get all McIntosh."

"**Haral**son," Edith said. "It's my fault, I should have made it clear how important they are. Like I said, I go to McBroom Orchards for those."

"You know, that's a forty-minute drive, one way. And I doubt a lot of people would care."

"Well, quality apples make quality pies," Edith said. She felt a little angry, or maybe just frustrated. Wasn't this obvious to him? "If it's such a hassle for you, give me a dollar-fifty raise, and I'll go buy all the apples."

She was so piqued, she hardly even knew what she'd just said. She didn't even know where that $1.50 amount came from, but now it was out there. She'd just asked for three times the raise he'd offered her. She could still take it back before she'd get laughed at. She saw him open his mouth, and tried to speak first.

"I'm sorry—"

He wasn't looking up, and didn't seem to have heard her. "No, I see your point," he interrupted, rubbing his chin again. He seemed like he was about to do the math in his head, but gave up. "Sounds fine to me, I guess."

"Excuse me?"

"A dollar-fifty's fine, if it saves me all that driving."

Yes. He'd said yes.

She was smiling and couldn't even be honest why. She'd made out like a kid left alone in a malt shop. She got a $1.50 an hour raise just to pay for apples. What he didn't know was she'd known the McBroom family for years and they always cut her a deal. Sometimes they'd swap a couple bags for one of her pies—provided it wasn't apple. Sometimes they'd even just give her a bag for free.

"Thank you," was all she could say.

She tried not to smile too much as she held out her hand for him to shake.

Brendan did have a point, though. With these larger crowds, it was certainly possible that some people wouldn't have noticed or cared whether Edith's apple pies had Haralsons. Some of them may not have even grown up with a baker in their family at all, let alone cared about the difference between a Haralson and a McIntosh. Still, that didn't mean that they didn't deserve the best Edith could do. And a lot of people would notice too, not just the newspaper people, but more importantly, other women like her. Edith kept her rabbit ears up, always prepared to defend or explain her choices against ladies from Brainerd and Willmar and St. Cloud who somehow believed that their recipes or methods would be of use to Edith. Edith would just as soon take another woman's husband as another woman's pie recipe, and she had the best husband in the world, so there you go.

Then, one day, Edith had a customer who understood and loved her work completely. Her name was Amy O'Brien. She was maybe in her forties but didn't have a wedding ring, and was tan and pretty, in the slightly intimidating way that some women from fancy suburbs were tan and pretty. However, this woman was instantly warm and enthusiastic. After she introduced herself, she looked Edith in the eyes and said this was the best pie she'd ever had.

That was certainly possible, Edith thought, looking back at this woman, but it was still nice to hear. "Thank you."

"Nice lard and butter mix in the crust," Amy said. "And the rhubarb, what is it, MacDonald?"

"Yes, it is," Edith replied, a little surprised. "But I also sometimes use Victoria and Canada Red." She hadn't been blessed enough to have a conversation about rhubarb varieties with anyone in years. "Of course the MacDonald is my favorite for pies."

"Mine, too. My dad first grew it to try to keep

deer out of the garden. Didn't work. But I fell in love with it. Now, I force my Victoria plants because I can't wait."

"Me, too." This was the first person Edith had ever met, besides herself and her mother, who forced rhubarb plants in the spring.

"My God, I'm sorry, I'm geeking out," Amy said. "Anyway, I love your pie. It's just loaded with fruit."

Well, that's how people like it, Edith thought.

"You know, I'm helping out a bakery down in Nicollet Falls right now, and God, we'd love to have pies like this. I'd love to have you come down, and maybe we can talk some more."

So, this smart, nice, pretty woman, whom she'd just had the best chat with in ages, was a professional baker, and she liked Edith's pies.

A year ago, Edith would have just dismissed this all without a second thought, but a year ago, Stanley had a job, and no doctor visits, tests, or prescriptions. A year ago, Edith wouldn't have even heard the opportunity in Amy's words, because she wouldn't have been listening for it. Even so, her response would still surprise her, because right then, she wasn't thinking of what she and her husband needed, not at all, not yet.

"How's next week?" Edith asked.

"For you, my week is wide open." Amy smiled. "Can you do Monday at ten?"

In that moment, for the first time in decades, Edith felt like she understood Helen. It scared her, because as Edith spoke, she understood how her sister might be happy.

"Yes," Edith heard herself say.

$31.00

Helen, 1959

Helen Calder had her first beer when she was fifteen years old, behind a shed with the Sarrazin boys. Their uncle Moritz and aunt Petunia had come all the way down from Knife River for a visit, and had loaded the fridge with bottles, and Helen figured a few could easily go missing. Once all of the adults were in the front yard, she, Chesley, and Linton made their move.

Just as the refrigerator door closed, Helen's gawky twenty-year-old sister, Edith, popped into the kitchen and clearly saw the conspicuous bulges beneath everyone's shirts.

"There you are," Edith said.

"We're just going out to look at the cows," Helen said, which, as it turns out, was also true. Edith said nothing in reply, and watched Helen run outside with a calm, nonjudgmental expression, as if she were watching a waterfall or a bonfire, a wild entity behaving according to its own laws, immune to her opinion or control.

Helen turned to look back at the house, and there was Edith, watching them from behind the screen door, as if they were on a Ferris wheel that had started without her. Helen almost felt bad, but the problem was, Edith never got in trouble or did anything she perceived as risky. Her idea of fun was putting cake frosting on a bran muffin. Still, Helen had to wonder if maybe this whole time Edith was just waiting for an invitation. She was about to shout her sister's name, when Chesley, the strong and cautious fifteen-year-old son of dairy farmers, grabbed Helen's hand and pulled, not ungently, forward and away.

"Edith better not say anything," he said.

"She won't," Helen said, and she was always right about her sister.

"When she's getting married?" asked the younger one, twelve-year-old Linton, who everyone called Linty. They were intrigued and startled by the wedding, because, until somewhat recently, Edith had been their babysitter.

"Five weeks from today," Helen said, running ahead of them.

"Are you going to be there?" Linty asked. He was confused at how a woman who'd cared for him could somehow prefer a life of her own. "Because I don't think I'm going."

Helen glanced back at the pudgy little kid in overalls, only three years younger but a universe away from his lean, vigorous brother, Chesley. "Of course, she's my sister."

Chesley, now ahead of her again, glanced back at her as they ran. "I heard she's moving away."

"She can do what she wants, I don't care," Helen said, watching Chesley's athletic body pass her as they whisked through the grass together. The truth was, she did care, and she disapproved. Her sister was kind and smart, and if she'd cared to be patient, could've married better than a delivery driver. Stanley Magnusson was a nice guy, sure, but he was just the first boy to ask Edith out two years ago, as if that's all a lifetime with her sister should require.

Chesley led them behind his family's hog pen and stopped in the shade of an old storage shed. The worn-down grass on the east side, where they were, was a testament to the desirability of this location. From where they stood, they faced only a ceaseless, unjudging pasture, and had their backs to their parents, the house, the road, and the whole rest of the tiresome adult world.

"I'm going to leave too, you know," she informed the boys.

"Huh." Chesley grimaced. "Why?"

She looked over at Chesley and his little brother, in their boxy, faded clothes and dirty boots, on a weather-whipped farm of faded buildings, the smell of manure on the hot breeze. She stared out at the Sarrazins' dairy cattle picking apart a field of prairie grass so wide and flat its horizon wobbled in the heat. "You tell me," she said, reaching under her shirt for the beer bottle.

Chesley looked sad as he opened his brother's beer, then hers, then his, and pocketed the caps. "You don't want to stick around and get married instead, like your sister, huh?"

"Well, I want to go to college first," she said, her shoes brushing across her footprints. "But I might come back."

"I bet you will," Chesley said, posing against the shed with his thumbs through his belt loops and his beer bottle at his hip, like he thought he was James Dean, and for the time and place, he was close enough. "Those city boys will chew you up and spit you back out."

Helen was sure that he had no idea what he was saying, and was just repeating something he heard his mom say to someone, but she didn't want to ruin the moment with an argument. As Chesley and Linty leaned their backs against their father's shed and threw back their first swallows, in the imitation of men, Helen stared at the Fitger's label on the wet bottle.

This was beer, the drink that her father craved at the end of a hot day. This is what her mother claimed would make Helen careless with her modesty and desires, and end up like a few local girls who'd been quietly removed from school. This was the stuff that her teetotaling Swedish grandfather claimed that one drop of, just one, would send her to hell. So, like any sensible person, she was intrigued.

She slapped a mosquito on her arm, and then took just a tiny sip, because she believed in hell, and despite what her grandfather said, hoped that one small taste could be forgiven, just in case she hated it. She leaned her sweaty head against the wall of the shed and felt the beer hit her tongue.

Whoa, she thought.

Her body flickered with a fear that had nothing to do with her family's warnings, or Chesley, or anything she'd ever known or imagined. She felt it in her mouth, behind her eyes, in her blood, in places no one had touched. It wasn't just because she was doing something she wasn't supposed to be doing, or suspected it would lead to her finally making out with Chesley. She was scared because it felt good.

It reminded her of what happened at the State Fair, when she was seven, when her family walked past a woman in a black cowboy hat doing tricks with a lasso. She was beautiful and serious and confident in a way that made her seem like a cartoon or a goddess. When the woman asked for a volunteer and smiled at Helen, Helen froze and shook her head, and the woman picked some dumb boy instead. But she kept watching anyway and had probably stood there for several minutes before she realized that her parents and sister had long ago moved on without her. **This is where you ran off to**, her mom had said when they found her, but Helen hadn't run anywhere. She'd found where she wanted to be. **Ride high, darlin'**, the lasso woman said when Helen looked back at her for the last time.

Then one of the boys burped, the other laughed, and she opened her eyes—she didn't even realize they'd been closed—and Chesley asked her, "Hey, what do you think?"

For a moment, her mind couldn't form a single word, but she landed on one that her favorite teacher, Miss McKinley, had once used to describe her ski vacation to Lutsen: **invigorating**. She didn't want to freak the boys out, though, so she just nodded.

Linty hated his beer instantly, but wanting to impress the older kids, kept gamely forcing it into his mouth, his face pinching against each swallow, willing himself to enjoy it. "It's crisp and refresh-ing," he said, squinting.

"Bullcrap, Linty," said Chesley. The way the older boy's face frowned during the exact second the beer hit his lips betrayed that he didn't like the flavor either, but was better at hiding it than his kid brother. "Wow, almost half-done with mine. You gonna finish yours, Helen?"

She held out her empty bottle, mouth pointed down. He took it from her gently, and held it toward the sun, rotating it within his kind but rough hands.

"Huh," was all he said.

"Wow, she really likes beer," Linty said, pouring some of his own on his sun-browned arm, and rub-bing it against his skin. "Look, it's good for mos-quitoes."

"Ha, you're gonna get 'em drunk," Chesley said.

Helen grabbed the bottle from the little boy. "Stop, don't waste it. If you don't want to finish it, I'll have it." The words just came out, before she considered how they sounded. "Or, I'll share it with your brother."

"I'll finish it," Linty said, and, accepting the bottle back, held it against his mouth. As Helen watched the precious beer gather against the little boy's lips and dribble down his chubby face onto his bib overalls, she kept her rage at this waste to herself.

Although she was starting tenth grade in two

months, and figured she'd eventually get invited to weekend parties, she also figured it might be a while before she'd get to have beer again. She knew families who freely shared alcohol with their children on holidays, and she'd heard of teenage boys whose dads offered them a beer after a day of hunting, fishing, or hard work, but she'd never heard of a teenage girl being offered a beer by anyone except a boy trying to get her drunk. No wonder the older girls she knew had such a twisted and cautious relationship with beer; it was often only available to them in moments of social or sexual anxiety.

Chesley could help her out. He always did. After they buried the empty bottles by the row of windbreak pines, she put her hand on his shoulder.

"Let's get another one. Just one more."

"I don't wanna get busted," he said, wiping his dirty hands through the grass.

"Come on." She held his hand and rubbed her thumb over his knuckles. "Let's get one more, right now."

His hand squeezed back, and then he looked her in the face. "Are you really going to go to college?"

"Not if you don't want me to," she said, and maybe it was almost true, just then.

In Helen's mind, the best and worst thing about Chesley Sarrazin was that he grew up knowing he'd inherit a farm, so he'd never once considered another future for himself or any woman he might marry. Chesley was dismissive of other kids who didn't share his singularity of purpose, but Helen had to admit that she envied his certainty.

He nodded and let her hand go as he glanced toward the house. "They might see us," he said, and he walked on ahead of her without looking back, like he was confident she'd follow him.

Helen knew she wouldn't have to go far to find beer again, but she still had to be patient.

Weddings in Minnesota always had beer, and she'd wondered if she could sneak a beer at her sister's. For the purposes of the event, she was invisible any-way. She was too old to be a flower girl—that job fell to Stanley's four-year-old niece—and Edith's four bridesmaids were the other girls who'd been starters on Edith's high school basketball team. Helen would've come late to make a point about how she'd been forgotten, but that was hard to do when her parents were driving her.

Compared to other weddings she'd attended, her sister's was kind of dreary. The only exterior decor on the church was the fake flowers tied to the ban-nisters. The programs were a single piece of folded paper and the food was just glazed ham and salads provided by her mom's friends. Everything seemed so damn affordable. It wasn't the way she imagined her own wedding at all.

"Where's the drink station?" Helen asked her dad.

Her dad pointed to a table in the rear of the church basement covered with a boring white linen tablecloth. "The punch bowl and water jugs aren't out yet. You shoulda drank something before you left the house."

"Is there anything besides punch and water?"

"Why?" her dad asked.

Her mother, who'd vanished for a moment, reappeared and tugged Helen's arm. "Your sister wants to see you."

Good. Edith would know.

Her sister was squirreled away in some office off the side of the entrance, so Stanley wouldn't see her before the ceremony. Edith did look sort of beautiful in her dress. She looked better than usual, anyway. For the second-tallest girl in the school, it probably wasn't easy to find a decent wedding gown, unless the tallest girl had been married already and could loan out hers.

"There you are," Edith said, and leaned forward, holding a white flower. "I want to give you something so that people know you're my family."

"People can figure that out, you know," Helen replied, as Edith pinned the flower on the front of her sister's summer dress. "Oh, and Dad wanted to know if there was going to be beer at this wedding."

Edith groaned. "Now he's sending you to bug me about that. Well, it's certainly too late to have any now."

"Oh, what happened?" Helen asked, trying to sound more bored than curious.

"Stanley's brother and his wife wouldn't attend the wedding if there was alcohol present."

Helen bit her tongue. This had to be a contender for the worst wedding of all time. Not that she could say that, especially to her sister, but she couldn't restrain herself from critiquing this particular detail.

"That's the stupidest thing I've ever heard in my whole entire life," Helen said. "How can you have a wedding with no beer? Just because one person doesn't want it?"

"It's his brother, it's important to have him here." Edith squinted at Helen like a person discovering a stain on a brand-new coat. "Why are you so interested?"

"I'm not interested, I'm asking for Dad."

"You wanted to sneak some again, didn't you?"

"No," Helen said, as convincingly as possible.

Edith's face looked sweet, even compassionate. Then she said, "You're not old enough," and that was that.

The wedding itself was long and stupid. Their mom cried when the vows were exchanged, but everyone's mom does that, and they could hardly even hear the vows anyway. Helen saw the evil brother who put the kibosh on the beer, and he was a hateful-looking man, with his thick glasses and round bald head.

Afterward, the sixty or so people in attendance, who were mostly relatives and mostly old, filed down to the basement, ate their dry spiral-cut ham, and gabbed about the weather and about the people who weren't there. Chesley and Linty were among the absent, so there was no one Helen's age there—the closest were some boys who were eight and ten—and she was given the joyless task of keeping an eye on them. Edith had never looked so happy, and Helen could guess why. She was getting the hell out of this place.

One evening, after the sophomore-year homecoming football game, Helen was walking across the parking lot with Chesley and two of their friends, when a kid in a letter jacket came up to them.

"Hey, man," the kid said to Chesley. "You going to the Dean Travis party?"

Dean Travis, a fearsomely cool jock senior, lived with just his father, a traveling salesman who was known to be out of town that weekend. Dean often had parties under these magical circumstances, and the quantity of beer was reported to be legendary.

"Yes, absolutely," Helen said.

"Gosh, I don't know," Chesley winced at the kid. "It's up to Toby. He's driving."

Toby Chamberlain's father owned the Ford dealership in town, so Toby had a car and always drove, but was usually democratic about their destinations. The problem that night was that they were also with Lucy Koski, whom Toby had a train-size crush on, and Lucy knew this.

Toby was a smart, polite, good-looking guy, and there was nothing that would account for his baffling taste in women. Lucy was like the least-fun parts of Edith jammed into a body half the size and ten times as loud. Because their moms were friends, Helen had known Lucy since they were born. People believed they were best friends just because they were both cute girls who were in the same rooms their whole lives and were often paired together, but theirs was a mutual tolerance forged by involuntary proximity and tradition. What was permanently ending their obligatory alliance nearly sixteen years into their lives together was the fact that Lucy didn't drink, because it was illegal.

"Why don't we go to my place and play hearts," Lucy said, once everyone was in the car.

"Sounds good to me," Toby said, starting the engine.

"Lucy, you can go to the party and not drink. Don't be a pill."

Lucy turned in her seat and glared back at Helen. "That doesn't matter. My mom would kill me if she found out I was even in that house for a minute. And she'd tell your mom too, believe me."

Sure, Dean and his father had a bad reputation among the area's more close-minded parents, but his parties were practically a public service. It wasn't Dean's fault that some drunk kid jumped off the roof last time and broke his legs. "I don't care if I get in trouble," Helen said. "Just say it was my idea."

"Some of us care, OK. It's not just about you, Helen. I bet Toby's dad wouldn't want him to go either."

Toby laughed as he made a turn, away from the lights of town and Dean Travis's house, and toward the darkness of the country. "Nope."

"Toby, then you can just turn around and drop me off at Dean's and I'll find my own way home," Helen said, but Toby didn't even slow down.

"Then, if something happened to you there, it'd be my fault," Toby said.

Helen looked out the back window in the direction of Dean Travis's wondrous house, already over two miles away, as it receded farther and farther from possibility. She glared at Chesley, who sighed. "Some help you are," she whispered at him.

"Toby's the driver," he said, and looked away from her. "I'll try to make it up to you."

"We don't need beer to have fun tonight, do we,

Toby," Lucy said, and then smiled at Helen the way people smile when they've swatted a fly. These kids were her best friends, and they made her feel like the loneliest girl in the universe.

She was attempting to eat breakfast in the company of her parents two days later when her rage about this whole situation overtook her in a way she didn't expect.

"I almost forgot to ask you, Helen," her dad said, folding the newspaper he'd been reading. "What do you want for your birthday?"

"A beer," Helen said.

Her mom, whisking eggs, audibly paused. "I don't believe you're old enough."

"And that's it, I don't want anything else." The words were just coming out. She wasn't even sure why, or where they were coming from. "Just one beer, any beer."

Helen's parents glanced at each other and her mom continued whisking. Her father picked up the paper again.

"If you have any other ideas, just let us know," her mom said.

"I won't," said Helen.

Three days later, Helen came down for breakfast the morning of her sixteenth birthday, and there was her mother, whisking eggs again, and her father, reading the obituary section of the town paper, and a bottle, wrapped in re-used Christmas wrapping paper.

"What?" Helen said.

"Happy birthday," her mom said, and Helen should've known something was up, because her mom was smiling.

Helen tore off the paper. It was a bottle of A&W Root Beer.

"You can have a real beer when you're old enough," her mom said.

Helen had always taken pride in what restraint and forethought she possessed. She wasn't an erratic, emotional lightning storm like some of the girls she knew. Often, she was calm, composed, and maybe even sort of elegant, but in a sturdy way, like a homemade birdhouse, or fur-lined work boots. If she had a major fault, perhaps it's that she wasn't emotional enough, and perhaps, over time, that builds up a little, and perhaps that's how a bottle of root beer gets chucked through a kitchen window.

Helen stared at the unnatural sight of broken glass scattered around the kitchen sink, and felt the crispness in the early autumn morning air, and the smell of diesel exhaust from a passing truck, blowing through the little hole she'd made in her family's home.

"I didn't mean to do that," Helen said, which was true, but it wasn't an accident either.

Her mom reached into the space between the fridge and the wall, and pulled out a broom and dustpan. "You can clean it up," her mom said, just above a whisper. "And then you can go to your room and stay there."

So she did, she stayed there, her whole birthday, lying on top of her bed. She didn't take Chesley's call and she didn't take lunch or dinner and she didn't even come out when her sister and Stanley came over. She just stared at her white ceiling, imagining she was somewhere else, somewhere cool, like Duluth, or St. Paul, living by herself. And doing something cool for work. Maybe even working in a brewery, even just sweeping the floors, but maybe also making the beer. Somebody in Minnesota made beer. Maybe tons of people. No one told her she could be one of those people, but no one ever told her that she couldn't, either. Maybe she could find out something about it in college. From what she'd heard, college sure seemed like the kind of place where she'd learn about beer. She closed her eyes and imagined she'd wake up and magically be eighteen.

———

After the sun went down, she heard footsteps out-side her bedroom door again, her father's; this time, she could tell from the creaks and the slow-ness. He didn't say a word, just slid a yellow note under her door.

THE GARAGE, it read.

The main garage door was closed, as it usually was, but the side door was ajar, and the light from her fa-ther's work lamp cast deep shadows from a corner.

"Dad?" she asked the quiet space. Then she saw it, by the beat-up old gray sofa, a metal pail, with four beers inside, purple bows tied around their necks.

They were beautiful. She held them gently in turn as if they were baby animals. GRAIN BELT, read one. SCHELL'S, another. The last two read COLD SPRING and HAMM'S. At the bottom of the pail was an opener. Her hands were shaking. She picked up the Grain Belt first, and just stared at the simple, handsome red diamond on its label. For a moment, she considered not opening any of them at all, just keeping them under her bed, to take out and look at whenever she wanted.

Then, that moment passed.

She didn't remember falling asleep on the garage sofa. When she woke up, she was stiff and cold and woozy and under a plaid blanket. The pail and bottles were gone, and there was a pitcher of water, a glass, and an aspirin on a napkin.

Helen applied to only one college, Macalester, on her teacher Miss McKinley's recommendation. She was excited about the idea of going to school right in the middle of St. Paul, but once she finally arrived there, it was overwhelming. The only thing she could compare it to was the State Fair, and it was literally that crazy, with people and cars everywhere, making noise, practically all hours of the day and night. There seemed to be nowhere you could even see a horizon line. Macalester seemed like an oasis amid the anarchy, so she decided right away that she wasn't ever going to leave campus unless it was an emergency.

On the day she'd unpacked her suitcases on a bare mattress in Turck Hall, she'd listened to her intimidatingly assertive roommate, Tippi Lindholm from Wayzata—who'd been there for hours and had already exquisitely set up her side of the room in cream, pink, and mint green—blathering about the young men of interest in the boys' dorms across Grand Avenue.

"Kirk has the most interesting men," Tippi said, as if reading it from a glossy magazine. Tippi was the most beautiful person that Helen had ever seen up close, and even from a yard away, Helen could find no evident physical flaws, and she was looking. It was disappointing to Helen that someone as gorgeous as Tippi, who was evidently smart enough to get into Macalester, seemed to view college merely as a dating pool. "That sounds nice. What are you majoring in?"

"I don't know, sociology or something," Tippi said. "It's not like I'm ever going to have to work."

Helen wondered if this mindset was a function of Tippi's upbringing or beauty or both.

Helen was cute, but she knew that she wasn't more than that. She'd once been told that she carried herself like a beautiful person, which she noted wasn't the same as being beautiful. One of her high school teachers said that she walked like a dancer. Her mom just said that Helen had her head in the clouds, which was admittedly more accurate. When someone asked Helen, **What do you do to seem so graceful and happy?**, she said, **I'm just imagining I'm somewhere else**, **talking to someone besides you.** Which is kind of how she felt now.

"That's interesting," Helen replied, sensing, for the first time, that she had a bit of an edge on this girl, in some way, and it made her feel better.

Tippi seemed to sense she was being judged. "Well, maybe when my future children are out of the house, I'll open a cute little bake shop, or something."

"Where? In Wayzata?"

"No, somewhere else. How'd we even get on this dumb topic?" Tippi briefly leaned toward Helen as if she were imparting a secret. "Know what I heard from my friend Stacy? She said that her brother is in Kirk Hall with Pete Lund and Orval Blotz."

"Orval Blotz, huh," Helen said. The name sounded like it belonged to a crop duster pilot.

She continued unpacking, but it was hard for her to ignore that she seemed to have one-fifth as many clothes and shoes as Tippi Lindholm, and they were a fifth as nice. Tippi looked to be about her size, though.

"You never had Blotz Cream Soda?" Tippi asked, staring at her. Maybe her roommate was at least a size larger. "They don't have that out in the boonies?"

"They have it," Helen lied. "I just don't drink a lot of pop," she said, patting her waistline.

"Well, it's just a local brand, but it's something," Tippi said. "It's not like the heir to the Pepsi fortune is going to come to college in Minnesota."

"Yeah, just think of what we're missing by going to college here," Helen said. She wondered if it was a goofy contradiction that her roommate had a Jackie Kennedy hairdo, clearly expensive clothes, and also a neat row of little toy horses on her desk and at least a dozen stuffed animals on her bed.

"His family used to make beer," Tippi said. "My mom would not like that."

Helen dropped her best summer dress on the floor. "Yeah, I don't think mine would either," she said, picking it up and smoothing it out. "So, when was Blotz a brewery?"

"God, who cares. My grandpa used to drink it." Tippi looked at Helen in a way that made Helen feel like she'd been caught shoplifting. "Do you want me to find out if he's single?"

"I've got somebody," Helen said. "Back home." This was true; she and Chesley had been officially going steady since the summer before tenth grade, and technically didn't break up when she left for college.

"No, you don't," Tippi smiled. "You're in college now."

"I'm not interested," Helen said.

"Yeah you are. You should see your face right now. But Pete Lund is cuter anyway."

Helen was done being intimidated by this girl.

"Good for you, go for Pete Lund, then."

"I like 'em cute. If I don't have a cute husband by twenty-five, then I'll date ugly guys. How's that sound?"

"Hey, if I don't murder you in your sleep tonight, I'll light you on fire during finals week," Helen said. "How's that sound?"

"Oh my God," Tippi laughed, like she'd been waiting this whole time to hear those exact words. "I love you."

Helen decided to major in chemistry not just because it was related to brewing, but because she liked it, and wanted to meet genuinely smart people, figuring it was harder for a person to bullshit his way through advanced chemistry courses. Tippi had even tried to convince her that the man of her dreams could be sitting next to her in her first class on her first day. So, of course, there was Orval Blotz, in General Chemistry I, fall semester. Tippi was right; he wasn't cute at all, at least in a typical way. He was pudgy and already balding and his eyes were kind of close together, and he had the S-shaped posture of someone who'd spent too much time at a desk. Honestly, the poor guy lacked any kind of physical allure at all, but he seemed smart, and given his family history, her interest in him was undeterred. When he spoke in class, he was always correct, and always sat near the front but not in the front row, which showed focus, but not a desperate, at-all-costs kind of focus. Helen sat in the front row, so it was hard to invent reasons to turn around and look at him, except for when the people behind her asked a question or replied to one. He had a nice smile, and she tried to smile back at him a few times, but never spoke to him, because she never thought of a single thing to say that didn't make her feel like a trained seal.

Helen was convinced that women must be throwing themselves at Orval Blotz's feet, and since some would be prettier, and most would be richer, she decided she wouldn't just meet him as a woman who merely wanted something from him. She decided that she'd offer him something he needed, once she figured out what that could be.

In the meantime, Helen checked out any book from the library that had anything to do with beer. She learned about the thousands of breweries that once filled the country, coast to coast. She'd read as much as she could find about the history of beer, a history that she had no idea began with a beer goddess and was run by women for centuries. The person who first documented and prescribed the use of hops was a woman, for God's sake. But when the books had photographs, she realized one afternoon, she saw a lot of people who looked like her grandpa, and a lot who looked like Orval Blotz, but no one who looked like her.

That's when the idea that would change Helen's life first occurred to her.

Her first night back home after the end of fall semester, it was a little unsettling to see Chesley again, knocking on the door, cheeks pink, hunting cap on his head. His smell was familiar, but his embrace felt almost like a stranger's, and he looked so scruffy and unpolished compared to the kinds of boys she'd grown accustomed to seeing every day. But he was still so kind. Once inside his dad's old pickup, he revealed a single bottle of Hamm's in his coat pocket.

"I couldn't find flowers," he said.

He knew her. God, he knew her. And once again, he could help her.

"You wanna go?" he asked.

"Actually, let's go back inside for a minute," she said. "I want to show you something."

While Chesley sat at the kitchen table, gamely accepting the pie and tea that her mother forced on him, Helen brought down a couple of books she'd checked out from the college library. Once her mom finally left them alone, she opened one to a diagram of the equipment needed to brew beer at home.

"Ha," Chesley said, wiping the pumpkin pie crumbs from his face. "This is illegal."

"I want to make a beer, and I have a month before I have to be back at school," she said. "Can you help me?"

"Wow, you're serious," he said, scratching his head.

"Very," she said, and felt sorry for him and grateful for him at the same time.

He pulled the book over to him and hunched over it like someone who needed glasses. "Well, OK. Large pot. Strainer. Tubing. Funnel. Thermometer. Water jug. Got all that stuff, no problem."

He was so good at solving concrete, tangible puzzles. He was the sort of guy who'd have endless little projects his entire adult life. But now, all of a sudden, his serious-work face melted into a dumbfounded expression.

"What's the problem, Chesley?"

"The problem is, the ingredients. I don't know where the heck to find hops in December. No clue with that. I don't know where to find the right kind of yeast either. Barley, maybe. I can talk to Ed at the grain elevator."

"Can we do that tomorrow?" she asked, touching him on the shoulder, running her hand down his back.

"I guess so. Dang, this looks like a ton of work. And over Christmas, no less."

"I know," Helen said. "And I can't do it without you."

Ed at the grain elevator was an old family friend of the Sarrazins, and was surprisingly enthusiastic about a couple of local kids attempting to make beer, so much so that he personally offered to help them malt barley, just to show them how. All he asked for in exchange was a few bottles of whatever they were making.

"You don't have time to make a lager, so make an ale," Ed told them, and from his girth and kind openness, she wasn't surprised that he had an opinion on beer.

"Any idea who grows hops around here?"

Ed looked amused that Chesley asked the question. "Why don't you ask your uncle Moritz. I still have some of his beer in my fridge. Good stuff. Kind of strong, though."

Chesley shook his head. "Moritz doesn't make beer. Moritz doesn't do anything."

"Don't tell him I told you." Ed laughed and returned to work. "Especially don't tell Petunia."

Moritz and Petunia lived deep out in the woods, in a falling-apart old house several miles outside of Knife River, north of Duluth. The front yard was a death trap, cluttered with old refrigerators, ankle-scarring rusty tractor parts, and a pair of cannibalized Model T Fords that hadn't seen the road in at least twenty years. They were now full of mice and mice poop, according to Chesley.

Moritz must've heard them coming, because he stood in his doorway, naked to the waist despite the weather, holding a sack of dog food as he watched the pickup trudge down his unshoveled, unpaved driveway. When they got out, he barked at them to come on in and then disappeared inside.

There wasn't a widely understood term yet for the way Moritz and Petunia lived, but it was clear they hadn't thrown anything away in decades. The place smelled like dust, cheese, dirty socks, and musty carpet, depending on which way Helen faced. She followed Chesley into a living room where she was dwarfed by stacks of newspapers, magazines, and old mail. There was just enough space on a balding red sofa for a pale middle-aged woman in a gray bathrobe, Petunia, to sit with an unlabeled brown bottle between her thighs and watch a fuzzy TV that lacked sound. They barely had time to take all this in before they were led through a dining room, where the table and chairs were probably somewhere under piles of clothes, and into a warm, dirty kitchen where two cats twisted themselves between Helen's legs. A couple of disassembled rifles and rifle parts were spread across a sheet covering the dinette table, and Moritz moved a stack of newspapers off a metal folding chair so Helen could sit down.

"Don't touch 'em," he told Helen, when he saw her glancing at the guns. "I'm cleaning those."

He still hadn't put a shirt on yet over his pale, graying chest, and was drinking something from a Hires Root Beer mug that probably wasn't Hires

Root Beer. "So what do you want? You can see I'm busy."

"We heard that you make your own beer," Helen said. Chesley seemed surprised that she spoke first.

"Who told you that? Ed?" Moritz walked into his dining room and came back holding a maroon sweater vest that he put on in front of them. "You can't have any, you're not old enough."

"No," Helen said. "We're making our own beer and we need some ingredients."

"You're making your own?" Moritz laughed. "Sure you are."

"It's for a school project," Chesley said. "Helen's a chemistry major at Macalester."

"Good for you, then." Moritz shook his head and looked her over. "Chemistry major, huh? Well, let's see what you know. Why would a beer smell like cardboard?"

Chesley looked at her nervously. Helen swallowed. She hated being wrong, and felt like it was a trick question. "I don't know yet."

"Because it's been oxidized." Moritz looked annoyed. "What if it smells like burnt matches?"

"I don't know yet." This was total bullshit. She felt her hands balling into fists at her sides.

"Sulfur dioxide. Beer's too young." Moritz rubbed his unshaven jaw. He looked at her and seemed to shrug.

"Look, OK," Helen said as she stood up. "That's not even fair. How would I know any of that?"

"Then better luck next time," he said, and picked up the sack of dog food he'd set by his feet, and disappeared around a corner.

Helen heard a door slam and glanced at Chesley. "I guess that's that," she said.

"I'm sorry," he whispered. "What do you want to do now?"

"Get the hell out of here."

As they walked back the way they came, stepping over a half-eaten sandwich on the floor, a woman's voice said, "Hey."

"Hello?" Helen called out, and turned back into the dingy living room, where Petunia was already staring in her direction, one eye wide, one closed. In the light of the TV, the woman's exposed arms and legs looked mottled and bluish. "Excuse me?"

"I heard what you said in there."

Oh no, Helen thought, as she watched Petunia stand up. What did this scary woman hear? That they wanted to get the hell out of here? I'd offended her in her own home.

"Yeah," Petunia nodded. "I liked that you said 'yet.' That you didn't know anything 'yet.'"

"Thanks," Helen said, trying to guess what this woman wanted from her, and feeling a little afraid to find out. "Well, I guess we better get going."

Petunia had the expression of someone tabulating a restaurant tip in her head. "You strike me as someone who likes to learn things. Do you like to learn things?"

"Yeah," Helen said, frozen in place. What choice did she have? She could hear what sounded like three different dogs barking outside, and then they went quiet.

"Come downstairs then," she said, and smirked at Chesley as she rose. "Him too, I guess."

Compared to the rest of the house, the basement was immaculate. It was completely empty except for a series of spotless stainless steel tanks; pallets of empty, unlabeled brown bottles; a big white Norge fridge nicer than the one upstairs; and an open closet full of cleaning supplies. Even the concrete floor looked new and pristine.

"This equipment, it's all old tanks and stuff from my dad's old dairy," Petunia said. "This is where me and Moritz make our imperial stout."

At that point in her life, Helen had never heard that term spoken aloud before. She glanced at Chesley. "Cool choice," Chesley said.

"What would you know about it?" Petunia laughed, and opened a bottle she retrieved from the fridge.

Helen heard the floor creak above them. She was afraid to say what was on her mind, but spoke anyway. "Is Moritz going to be mad that we're down here?"

Petunia took a sip of her beer and grinned. "If he is, I'll tell him to get lost. I own this house. I can kick him out anytime I want. Want to try some of the stout?"

"No thanks," Chesley said.

"Sure," Helen said, accepting the bottle from Petunia without thinking. She took one sip, and then another. It wasn't like any beer she'd had before—it was oaty and bitter—and she wasn't sure if she enjoyed it. Petunia seemed to perceive this from Helen's expression, and snatched the bottle away.

"I liked it," Helen said. "It was interesting."

"Don't give me that. You two probably want to make a lager."

"No, an ale," Helen said.

Petunia didn't seem happy with that response either. "That figures."

"Well, it's a good place to start," Helen said.

"That's true." Petunia locked eyes with Helen. Petunia's robe was coming undone and was almost hanging open. "I'd like to see more people like us making beer. Provided you don't screw it up."

Helen wasn't sure how to respond; until now, she hadn't considered how, other than sharing a gender, she was like Petunia at all. "I won't," she said, trying not to look at Petunia until she retied her robe, which she finally did.

"Well, I can give you some ale yeast and Cluster hops," Petunia said. "Also some bottles, I guess."

Helen looked at Chesley, who seemed shocked.

It was exactly what they needed, and more than they were expecting. "Wow, thank you," he said.

"Thank you," Helen repeated. "What do we owe you for all this?" She'd brought all of her money in the world—$31—and now realized it might not be enough. She could sell things. Her bicycle. The earrings she got for her eighteenth birthday. Anything.

"How many gallons is your brew pot?"

"Five," Helen said.

"That's about forty-eight bottles, give or take. Give me thirty-five. Plus four more to make up for the four you stole a few years back."

Edith did tell on them, Helen thought, and her eyes burned.

In the moment when that thought entered Helen's head, she'd never been so furious at her sister. She would've taken any punishment at age fifteen—she would've preferred being caught by her mother with her hands on a beer bottle—over this brutally delayed and calamitous justice.

"We maybe wouldn't have noticed just one," Petunia said. "But you kids got greedy. So, thirty-nine, total. That's our payment. And that's if your beer's any good."

Helen bit her lip. Her rash, impotent fury at her sister hadn't yet evaporated, and now spilled toward a new, relevant target. "No," she said. "That's too much."

"I disagree, I think it's the exact right amount."
She shook her head. "Thirty. I can do thirty."

Chesley seemed amazed that someone was arguing with his aunt. He touched Helen's arm, and seemed about to protest, but Petunia trampled over his words.

"Thirty-nine," Petunia repeated. She shook her head at Helen, like she should know better. And maybe she should've. "That's the cost of doing business."

"Thirty-nine's fine, Aunt Petunia," Chesley said, extending his hand.

But Petunia didn't touch it. Didn't even look at Chesley. She only stared at Helen. Even as unsettled as Helen was, it was still something to be the person whose opinion mattered. She shook Petunia's cold, bony hand as briefly as possible.

They told Chesley's dad, Kenny, and after half a day's hesitation, he let them use the milk tank room for their provisional brewery, but only because it was a project for Helen's chemistry class, and provided, of course, that he receive a couple bottles in exchange for his silence and cooperation. By now they had maybe three or four left over for themselves, tops. And that's if the stuff turned out OK, she thought, looking around the compact white room that would be her first brewery.

There, about a hundred feet from where Helen had tasted her first beer on a 90 degree July afternoon, she and Chesley made an ale over Christmas break, in one try. The yield was pretty close to what Petunia predicted, forty-nine bottles and one half-bottle, which Helen poured into a juice glass right there on the floor.

It was beer, and a beautiful, opaque, bronze-colored one. She measured the head at about an inch. It was slightly bitter; much more bitter than she was used to, but it was also a little sweet on the finish. She held the glass under her nose and smelled it like she imagined new parents might smell their newborn baby, incredulous at this gorgeous little alien they made. She made this. And it tasted good.

At least, **she** thought it tasted good. It was a bit high in alcohol for some of the Minnesotans who'd been drinking mild pilsners their entire lives.

"Yeah, I'd say half a bottle of this would be fine," said Kenny.

"Good stuff, but I'm dizzy after one," Ed told them.

"I like it," Petunia told them. "I'll take two more."

After the full bottle they'd shared at the

beginning, and the ones they repaid their benefactors with, they only had a single bottle left.

"Split it tonight?" Chesley whispered to her in the doorway, the night before she had to go back to St. Paul.

"I promised one to my chemistry professor," she said.

"Ha," Chesley said. "I thought that was bullcrap."

"No, that part's true," she told him, but didn't look him in the face.

"Well, let's make it again this summer," he said, holding the pickup door open for her. "I'm just sorry that we don't have any beer for your last night in town."

"Let's go to the lake," she heard herself say. They had plans to meet up with some friends from high school and play cards, so she surprised herself by suggesting that they go to their traditional make-out spot, and by thinking that she didn't want to just make out that night.

"Ha," Chesley said. "But what about Lucy and Toby and everyone? I know you haven't seen them in a while."

"I'll call Lucy and apologize tomorrow," Helen said. She wouldn't, though, because honestly, she never did like that Lucy Koski.

"Well, OK," he said, and as he put the pickup in drive, the suddenly ominous Johnny Cash song "Ring of Fire" came on the radio, and she hoped that he was finally ready for what was about to happen. She hoped that she was, too.

Growing up, Helen had always thought that she wouldn't have sex until she was married, and even when she got over that idea, she thought she wouldn't have sex until she was in love with someone who was in love with her, and after she got over that idea, she decided to have sex just to see what it was like, with a partner she really liked, who'd be kind, respectful, and wild enough to be interesting. But not too eager, either.

But that's not what happened. The first time she had sex, it was cold, and strange, and sad. The first time she had sex, it was to say good-bye.

Back at Macalester, the first day of chemistry class, spring semester, she sat in the same row as Orval Blotz, four seats away. Her beer bottle was waiting under her bed, wrapped up in an old pillowcase, and not even Tippi knew about it.

She glanced at him as he rose at the end of class and almost opened her mouth before she realized it was ridiculous to invite him out for a beer. She was so preoccupied with smuggling the stuff into her dorm room and keeping it hidden that she didn't even consider where they could possibly drink it together. Besides, what was she going to do, just bolt up to him and say, **Hi, I'm Helen, and I made a**

beer I'd love for you try? No way. She'd wait for a situation to present itself, a context into which she could emerge as helpful or useful. The professor had picked the lab pairings based on alphabetical order, and even though Blotz and Calder were close, it wasn't close enough in a class with a Bucher and a Byron. Ground recon indicated that he was already part of a chemistry study group with another freshman boy and a girl named Avis Upchurch, so that scheme was out. Helen wasn't worried about Avis, though, who was reedy, shrill, and going steady with a sophomore.

She'd just have to wait for the right moment.

Weeks passed before she said a word to him.

Finally, one February morning it was sleeting outside, and he came into class soaking wet and out of breath. She could have guessed, but she saw that he wasn't carrying an umbrella.

It was still coming down when class was over, thank God. She saw him leave just ahead of her, hugging his coat around his shoulders and taking a deep breath before stepping outside. As his right foot touched the wet pavement, she silently opened her umbrella over his head.

At least two full seconds passed before he turned around and looked at her.

She frowned at him. "What are you doing without an umbrella?"

"Thanks," he said. "I don't know, I just forgot it." She could tell from his bright, unstressed face and eyes that he was a nice guy, earnest, sweet, and as uncomplicated as a bowl of peas.

"Headed to Kirk?" she asked.

"Yeah, how'd you know that?"

Whoops. "Uh, you look like a Kirk man."

"Not really," he laughed. "All the Kirk guys look like Pete Lund."

That was true, but Helen didn't care. "So, how do you like Macalester?"

"Gosh. Well, except for days like today, it's all right. Only place I even applied."

"Me, too!" She wondered if his story was just like hers. "Why did you only apply here?"

"Oh, my parents met here." Nope, not even close. "Your parents go here, too?"

"No, I'm the first person in my family to go to college."

She almost led them straight into a big puddle on the sidewalk, but followed him as he stepped around it into the wet slush covering the lawn. "Did they make you major in chemistry?"

"No, I picked it."

"That's cool." She was relieved that he didn't add **for a girl**. "You want to be a chemist?"

"I want to make beer," she said. She'd never said that before, to anyone, but it came out of her as if she said it every day, as if people should know this just by looking at her.

"Huh," Orval said, and she was worried that she'd said too much again, so she decided to refocus the conversation on him.

"So, why'd you choose chemistry?"

"You know, I'm starving. Want to go to the Broiler?"

The St. Clair Broiler was not only off-campus, it was the kind of nice diner that visiting parents sprung for. The handful of times she'd conversed with a boy outside of the fishbowl in the lobby of Turck Hall, it was nothing serious, just over coffee on campus at the Grille. Even if the Broiler wasn't anything fancy, it was still a step up, a step out. It was what she'd been waiting for.

"Yes."

"Cool," he said, and smiled, and up close it was sort of a cute smile, if a little toothy.

Of course, she could hardly eat her hamburger and fries, even if he was doing most of the talking, which was a relief. From across a table, he was no more attractive than he was from three rows away. At first, she had a hard time imagining kissing this guy, let alone sleeping with him, but he was candid and sweet, and she told herself to keep an open mind. After they'd mutually discussed what they liked and didn't like about college, and where they were from, they got into what their parents did, and she feigned surprise as he mentioned the cream soda company.

"You know, I've had a lot of girls tell me they love cream soda," he said between bites. "I hate cream soda. When I take over the company, I want to make beer again."

Before she'd even spoken to him, she'd rehearsed this conversation many times in her head, in line at the cafeteria, in the shower, while combing her hair, while on the long car rides to and from campus, and she'd still never dared imagine this, that he shared not only a passion with her, but an ambition, and clearly had the means to make it all possible. She never told anyone, because it wasn't the whole story, but it made him wonderfully, irretrievably attractive.

"Yes, you should," she said, maybe a little too firmly. "So when would you take over the company?"

He made a sad little laugh. "As soon as I present a business plan to my uncle to make Blotz profitable again."

"Blotz Cream Soda isn't profitable?"

"Yeah, everyone's shocked to hear that. But I gotta be honest with people, or they'll be disappointed later."

She nodded at him to go on.

"To be frank, we're totally drowning in debt. I borrowed money to come to school here." He gave her a weak smile. "So now you know. If you don't want to waste your time with me now, I understand."

She was indeed surprised, but not for the reason he'd assumed. "Orval, I don't care. I'd never even heard of Blotz Cream Soda before I came here."

Now he looked disappointed. "Really? Maybe it's even worse than I thought."

It was now up to her to save the suddenly foundering vessel of this otherwise promising conversation. "So, all of the equipment there could make beer again?"

"Yeah, that's what I'm told." He leaned back in the booth, arms in the air, like a man who'd just lost at poker. "But all the guys in my family who knew how to make beer are dead. So that's a problem."

"That's not a problem," she said.

"It is a problem if I want to be a brewer. But that's why I'm taking chemistry."

"I know how," Helen said, leaning toward him, her shadow falling over the table. "I just made some beer a few weeks ago."

She waited to hear him laugh, but to his credit, he was just baffled, not amused. "What? Come on, nobody here knows how to make beer."

"Well, I do. There are books that teach you how to brew beer—I found a few in the library. You want to make beer, you should check them out sometime."

"OK, so maybe you understand the principles,"

he said, shaking his head. "But to really make beer, you need a big factory with a mash tun, and temperature controls, and a bottling line."

"No you don't. You can make it in the tank room of a dairy farm. That's where I made mine."

"You actually made beer?" The fact appeared to be sinking in.

"Yeah, an ale. It was the only kind of yeast I could get. It's kind of strong, but considering the equipment I had, it's pretty decent."

He glanced around as if he was afraid someone would hear. "Do you have any?"

"I'm so glad you asked," she said. "You want to try it?"

"Yeah, I'd love to." He said **love**.

"Let's get it right now," she said, and started to gather her coat and bag.

He laughed. "You've hardly even started eating."

"OK," she said, and settled back into her seat. "Getting a little ahead of myself, I guess."

Still, even if it was rude or weird, she could hardly touch her food. She just watched him eat, and couldn't even smile again until he motioned for the bill.

Right after lunch, she ran up to her room and smuggled her ale back down in a knapsack.

"Forgot my books," she told the unblinking, milky-eyed dorm mother, who hadn't asked.

"It doesn't look to me like there's books in there," the dorm mother replied. "Come here."

Due to her pragmatic parents, Helen learned to instinctually obey when given a direct order, but now, for the first time, there was a stutter in her pace. For the first time, there was too much at stake. "I can't, I'm late," she called out, lifted her umbrella, and bolted out the doors, her worry over her likely punishment vanishing into the cold, wet air.

Orval drove them a long ways off campus, all the way down Grand Avenue to St. Albans Street. She'd never been this deep into St. Paul before, and she nervously counted the blocks. Finally, he turned right, and parked in front of a white house that looked quiet.

"It's warm," he said, when she handed him the clean, brown bottle.

"It's not like I can keep it in the fridge," she said.

"Let's bury it in the snow for a bit," he said, and opened his car door. Watching him outside in a stranger's slushy yard, packing a wet mound around her bottle, reminded her of the Thanksgivings when she was little, when her uncles brought over beer and wine. They'd left the beer outside in a snowdrift, which the men—only the men—retrieved, and this unremarked exclusivity made Helen wild with curiosity, even as a child.

While they waited for the bottle to cool, they swapped stories of their first drinking experiences. Orval's, surprisingly, was even later than Helen's; his father and uncle had been out of the beer business since before he was born, and didn't have it around the house, viewing other people's beer as unpleasant reminders of their own losses. To hear him tell it, they were happy making the fourth-most-popular cream soda in all of southeastern Minnesota and west-central Wisconsin. They'd left generations of beer wisdom behind forever, without another thought.

"I don't have any siblings, and both my cousins are a lot younger," Orval explained. "So there was no one around to even sneak a beer with."

"Didn't you have any friends?" Helen asked him.

"Not really," Orval said, smiling as if pushing against an unpleasant thought. "Well, I do have one friend, Joe Foxworth, but Joe doesn't drink."

"So when did you have your first beer?"

"Actually just this last Thanksgiving, at my grandparents' house. I hardly see them because they live out in Pierre, South Dakota. But they had a bunch of Coors in the fridge that my grandpa drove to Wyoming and back just to get."

"You had Coors? As your first beer?" This may have been the most impressive thing a man had ever said to her. Even in a beer-centric state like Minnesota that was home to several breweries, the scarcity of Coors had made it legendary. Just a few months back, Tippi reported that Pete Lund's even cuter cousin, Travis, had one six-pack of Coors Banquet at his off-campus Christmas party, and according to several accounts, it was all gone in under thirty seconds. Tippi had one sip. She described it as divine, and she was a Catholic, so that word really meant something.

"Let me tell you," he said. "I hate to overuse the word 'magnificent,' because it sounds too fancy. That word should be reserved for wedding cakes and custom paint jobs. But that's exactly what Coors was. I tried more beer since then, over Christmas break. Nothing was as good as Coors. Not even close. All I want to do is make great beer. So when I make beer, I promise you, it's going to be just like Coors. It's going to be the Coors of Minnesota."

This was the most amazing life plan that Helen had ever heard. Now, Helen almost kissed him. She wanted to say yes, and let's get started immediately. She even wanted to say, **Hell, Orval, let's even drop out of college and figure it out on our own, right now.** But in the moment, she was too paralyzed to do anything but smile and nod like a dope. "Let's try yours, first," he said, and left the car again to retrieve the bottle from its slush igloo outside.

———

She took a sip first to make sure it was still OK, after weeks lolling around underneath her dorm room bed. The important things were that the bottle didn't get too hot and wasn't ever in direct sunlight, and perhaps her ale indeed tasted a tiny bit flat, but overall much as she remembered, even if she was pretty sure it was nothing like Coors.

She watched every small movement of Orval's face while he drank her beer.

Orval swished the ale around in his mouth and swallowed. "Different," he said. "Interesting."

She wasn't devastated. She wasn't. But she wasn't going to let him see it, even if she was, a little.

"Well," he said, and gamely took another swallow. "It's just not like any beer I've ever had. It's kinda strong. And, I don't know, sorta spicy and bitter."

"All I could get was ale yeast," she said. "And I suppose I used too much hops."

"It's cool that you actually made beer, though." He passed the bottle back to her. "Can you make something better?"

Something better. Yikes. He hated it. But she could see why. It wasn't anything like the beer he already knew or like any beer he'd been encouraged to admire.

"With the right ingredients and equipment, yeah," she said. "I could make something better than Coors."

This is the point where Chesley would've said, **Ha**. Orval just stared back at her like he was either impressed or scared. "Really?" he asked, earnestly.

She nodded, and then drank as much as she could in one swallow, because she wanted it to be gone, but couldn't throw it away. She leaned her head back and drank, and drank, until the bottle was empty.

When Helen returned home to the farm over Easter weekend, she announced to a room full of people that she had a new boyfriend. This room didn't include Chesley, but she knew word would travel. It was easier on everyone this way, perhaps Helen in particular.

She knew she might never see Chesley again after that day, but by then, she'd seen the Blotz Cream Soda bottling plant down in Point Douglas, and she'd imagined what those giant steel tanks and packaging lines were capable of if given a different life.

All that she and Orval needed was a lot of money.

Helen did her best to talk to her mom that evening while her mom did the supper dishes. She'd have rather spoken with her father, but her mom had made him lie down after dinner because of his high blood pressure.

"Since when did Dad have high blood pressure?"

"Oh, starting around the time you left. His doctor said no more beer."

Helen couldn't imagine. "He must be furious. He loves beer."

"He hardly drinks it."

"Need some help with those?" Helen asked, watching her mom scrub the crusted remnants of scalloped potatoes from a bowl. She'd never noticed how pale and round her mom was until she first came home from college last Christmas, and now, she looked even paler and rounder.

"No, I'll manage. You want to help, you can clean the floor. You're good at that."

"Well, I always liked sweeping the floor," Helen said, as she took the broom and dustpan from their home between the fridge and the wall.

"You're like your uncle Henrik. You're only good at things you want to do," her mom said, which wasn't true. She'd hated geometry and still aced it, not that her mom would care to remember that. Her mom carefully selected her memories to reflect her established opinions, and it turned her mind into a bowl of lettuce she believed was a salad.

The only successful way of dealing with this was to change the topic, and Helen had something on her mind, something she perhaps wouldn't have said to her mother in less-heated circumstances. "How much longer are you and Dad going to work this farm?"

"What do you mean, how much longer?" Her mother laughed. "If you know how much time I have left, don't spoil the surprise."

"You're getting older, you can't farm forever, especially with me and Edith both gone."

"Why is this suddenly a concern of yours?"

"You could sell this land for a lot of money and retire comfortably."

Helen's mother laughed again. "And why would we want to do that?"

"Well, Dad's health, now, for one reason. If you lived in town, wouldn't life be a lot easier?"

"I suppose. But maybe there are more important things to us than life being easy."

"OK, then. But what's going to happen to the farm when you . . . ?" Helen said, rotating her hands in nervous symmetry, unable to complete the sentence.

"I suppose it gets split between you and your sister, fifty-fifty. Unless that seems unfair to you for some reason."

Helen dumped the contents of the dustpan in the trash. "No, that's not unfair."

"You're up to something with that Blotz boy, aren't you?" her mom said with the weary, humorless calm of a preacher disappointed with the Sunday turnout. "What's the story with him? Besides that he's a part of some pop family? Is he nice? Is he good to you?"

"Yes, he's perfect."

"Perfect," her mom snorted. "Well, I thought Chesley Sarrazin was about as upstanding a man as you could ever hope to find. Not that my opinion matters at all."

"Orval's very kind and very hardworking. After we graduate, I hope to help him with his business."

"Getting a little ahead of yourself, aren't you?" her mom said, staring out the kitchen window toward their long dirt driveway. "We haven't even met this perfect fellow yet."

"He can drive us up next weekend," Helen said, and watched her mother's body for signs of shock. "He can spend the night in Edith's old room."

Her mom paused just a moment as she re-wiped the circumference of a glass. Helen lifted a chair to clean under the kitchen table. "Unless you and Dad would rather drive down?"

"It's hard on your father's health to make that drive. But I suppose we better give him a look before you run off with him." Her mom turned off the sink, and stared out the window again as she dried her hands. "Not that what we'll say will make one bit of difference."

Her father wasn't in their bedroom. After a panicked two minutes, she found him in the cluttered garage, futzing with a lawn mower.

"Here you are! You're supposed to be relaxing."

"This is relaxing," he said. "If I lie down, I just end up thinking about all the bullshit I gotta do."

"You feeling good enough to drive down to meet Orval next weekend?"

"Sure. Why wouldn't I be?"

"Mom says that driving is hard on your health."

"Of course it is. It's one of the two things left that I enjoy." He laughed. "You should come up and visit her more often, she misses you."

She knew that was as close as her father would ever get to him telling Helen that he missed her. "Yeah, I know."

"You doing OK down there, grade-wise?"

"All As, so far."

He handed her a socket wrench. "You remember where this goes."

She nodded and walked it over to the biggest of the three Craftsman toolboxes, where she put it in the top shelf. "I'll come back as often as I can."

"I know she'd like that," he said.

A week later, Orval met her parents for the first time, at the St. Clair Broiler, on a Saturday afternoon that was unfortunately too warm and clear to be its own conversation topic for long. When she met Orval in her dorm lobby, she noticed he was wearing a white button-up shirt with a mustard stain on the collar.

"Orval," she said, and licked her thumb as she approached him. "Did you look at a mirror?"

"Yeah," he said. "I know your parents assume I'm from this rich family. I don't want to intimidate them."

She put her hands on his shoulders and kissed him.

"Your family's in the soda pop business?" Helen's dad asked Orval, even though he already knew. Her parents, especially her father, always looked "country" and square in this modern, urban setting, but to their credit, they didn't care. They sat on their side of the booth like it was somehow higher than their daughter's.

"Pretty soon, the beer business," Orval said. "Thanks to your brilliant daughter here."

Helen watched her mom's expression twist upon hearing the words "beer" and "brilliant" in proximity to her youngest child's name. No one, not even Miss McKinley, had told her parents that Helen was **brilliant**. And beer? As far as Helen knew, her parents had never even caught wind of her so-called chemistry assignment last Christmas. Since the drama of her sixteenth birthday, they had no idea of the depths to which their daughter had trawled in search of beer and beer knowledge. When her mother asked, Helen told her parents the whole story, everything she'd done and learned since she was fifteen, except the birthday gift that her dad left her, so as not to get him in trouble.

When Helen finished speaking, Helen saw her mother's lips move into a shape that imitated a smile, and looked at Orval.

"We always knew she'd do something different," Helen's mom said.

"I can't believe it," her father said. "How did Kenny Sarrazin get three bottles of your ale and I didn't get any?"

"I didn't think you'd understand," Helen told him.

He looked down at his empty plate. "I understand free beer."

Afterward, her mother walked Helen outside while the men settled the bill, and told her that Orval seemed much sweeter than she assumed he'd be, but he definitely needed a woman's touch to help make him a tad more presentable.

When her father came out, he took her aside, and stood half a foot away from her, his hands in his pockets, staring into traffic as he spoke. "So, where are you going to get your ingredients?"

"Well, I can order dried hops in the mail, from Washington."

"Kenny Sarrazin has hops growing in his ditch, you know," he stated, as if that were undeniably preferential. "What about the other stuff?"

"I might have some contacts," she said, not that she was eager for a return visit to Petunia's basement. "And Orval's great-uncle Floyd maybe still knows some people," she added, not mentioning that Floyd also had dementia.

"Ah, don't hassle with them," her father said.

She almost laughed. "I don't know if I have a choice," she replied.

He opened the driver's-side door of his car, glanced at his wife waiting inside, and spoke softly as he leaned toward his daughter. "You just let me know what you need."

"How do you think that went?" Orval asked her as she watched her parents' old blue car blend in with all the shiny, newer ones. She watched it disappear into northbound traffic, and then turned her head south.

"We're gonna make beer," she told him.

$15.00

Edith, 2003

E dith had never been to the upper-middle-class Minneapolis suburb of Nicollet Falls before, and she was so anxious, she almost missed the exit, even though she'd been going fifty miles an hour in the eventual exit lane for three miles. She was afraid that once she got there, she'd be honked at, and have to parallel park, but she was even more afraid that Tippi's Café would be difficult to find, and she'd get lost, or be late, or probably both.

Of all the things she feared, there were two things she didn't consider.

First, she loved the place. She didn't know what to expect from Nicollet Falls, but she was pleasantly surprised, like when you walk into a bank and there's a nice plate of cookies. Tippi's Café was nestled on a tree-lined street with a bike lane, in a row of attractive brick storefronts between Klingerhorn Realty and Carolyn's Organic Kitchen. The whole downtown seemed too polished and perfect, like something from a movie or a magazine advertisement. Golden autumn leaves clustered in the storm drains, young women leisurely pushed double-wide strollers, and cars drove slowly and didn't honk their horns. She was an hour early, so she lingered at the window of the real estate office, out of curiosity, and saw that a house the size of her own was more than three times as expensive here. She wondered what these people did to get to live in a place like this, and to stay there.

After walking around the block, she decided she'd just wait out the rest of the time in the café, and she was grateful she did. It was more than the warmth of its light on a cloudy Monday—everything about Tippi's Café was captivating. She'd been in small bakeries and local coffee shops many times, but the commingling of sweet desserts, fresh loaves, women's voices, the scent of coffee, and calming vocal melodies lulled her. The wood-paneled space lined with crafts tables, candle displays, and the staggering assortment of baked goods were designed specifically to make a sucker out of people like her—she knew that—and she was all for it.

The second surprise was that they wanted to hire her. For $15 an hour.

While Amy O'Brien waited for a response, Edith looked across the table at this beautiful middle-aged woman promising an uncertain and compelling future, which was maybe also a future she didn't deserve, but desired, and certainly had earned, and realized that she'd run out of believable and sensible stalling techniques.

Except one. The big one.

"I should really talk to my husband first," she said.

Driving home from Nicollet Falls, Edith gazed past the scrim of dead insects collecting on the windshield, and studied the passing signs and stores for the landmarks of her future turns and exits. The off-ramp is by a Culver's, she noted. Stanley liked their root beer, she remembered, and just then considered buying some, handing it to him right as she walked into the house, and once he was distracted by this momentary pleasure, announce, "Stanley, I've got a job offer."

———

When she opened the front door, a large paper cup of root beer under her left arm, he was asleep in his big green easy chair, three empty Schell's bottles on the end table. On the living room ceiling above the record player, a spider pitched herself nowhere in particular, building an invisible home in the thick air, six feet above the stutter of a Buddy Holly album that had played through its side.

Edith postponed even mentioning the phrase "Tippi's Café" until after dinner, when she was wiping the residue of pork chops and green beans from their plates.

"Oh neat," Stanley said in response, his back to her, as he dropped a scoop of vanilla ice cream in his root beer. His reaction reminded her of their opposite emotional relationships to so many things, like the crabgrass in the lawn. To her it was a depthless scourge, requiring countless hours of vigilance and action. To him, it wasn't their problem as renters, and even added some green to the yard, for free.

When he turned around, though, he looked concerned. Maybe what she said, and what it could mean for their lives, was actually sinking in.

"Wait a second. Do they have an Elks Lodge down there in Nicollet Falls?" he asked.

They did, in fact, she said. She'd made a point of checking.

"How close is it to Colleen and Mark?"

"I think it'd be a much shorter drive." She took

a spoon from the dish rack and scooped a little ice cream for herself. "Forty minutes, maybe."

"Then let's do it," he said, his mouth full. "Screw this town. The video store's closing. The pizza's terrible. The ducks are stupid." He still blamed them for the incident with the fresh loaf of bread, as if they'd personally goaded him into it.

She was alarmed by what her husband seemed to be saying. "You want us to move?"

"How else are you going to work there?"

"I was going to drive," Edith said, and sat down at the dinette table.

"An hour and fifteen minutes each way? And that's without snow or construction."

"We've lived here for almost forty years, we can't just move."

"Why not?" he asked, and in these moments she remembered he was a guy who'd been on the move for a living.

Also, unlike her own parents, his had sold their farm when he was a boy and moved seven times for his dad's work by the time he was eighteen. Like her, he had no family in this town. They had friends and connections and memories here, sure, but on reflection, it was just a place they ended up because of one of Stanley's own jobs, long ago.

"Let me sleep on it," she said, but instead, she was wide awake until midnight, listening to the crickets outside. She did a trick she learned from her grandpa, where she counted the number of chirps she heard in fifteen seconds—twenty-five—and added thirty-seven. Sixty-two. It was 62 degrees outside. She wondered if she'd ever live anywhere again where she'd know the temperature by listening to bugs, and fell asleep.

When word got out that Edith was leaving St. Anthony-Waterside, a miniature rebellion broke out. Clarence Jones blocked the main entrance with a spare wheelchair. Amelia Burch and Lulu Kochendorfer manned the fire exits. Staff and residents of all ages scrambled to Edith as fast as their respective bodies could move and pleaded with her to stay.

"Is it your dream job?" Brendan Fitzgerald asked. "I'd feel better about this if it was."

"I don't know yet," Edith told him. "But I'd like to find out."

It was brutal to say farewell to the residents and her coworkers, and not just because of what they meant to her. Although there was massive turnover in each group over the years, she realized that by unintentionally putting this nursing home on the map as a culinary destination, she'd helped develop a sense of pride in the place for everyone involved. Even if not everyone there knew her well, she was aware that when people asked them, where do you work or live, and they said St. Anthony-Waterside, people would say, **Oh, the place with the pie**, and it made people smile.

Having done that once, she hoped she could do it again.

She also hoped that the kitchen staff would actually use the recipes she left them, and not skimp on ingredients or patience. She hoped that people would still flood the lobby before suppertime and linger with the residents long after dessert. She hoped that the upcoming 26th Annual St. Anthony-Waterside Invitational Double-Elimination Cribbage Tournament would be even bigger than last February's, where there were appearances by KSTP weatherman Dave Dahl and Minnesota Twins prospect Lew Ford. In Edith's honor, two nice young musicians named Tony Norgaard and Korby Lenker even played an instrumental version of the song "American Pie" that lasted all four-and-a-half hours of the tournament. It would be a hard act to follow, but everything should be.

There weren't a lot of rental properties in Nicollet Falls, and few of them were affordable; looking through the real estate listings, she felt like she was asked to buy lunch for four at Red Lobster with a

ten-dollar gift certificate. They did find an apartment building, on the edge of town, maybe not
even technically Nicollet Falls but in the school
district, as if that mattered. It was a brown wood-
and-brick four-story building, and the lawn looked
recently mowed, and it was across the street from a
SuperAmerica, which was nice in case she needed
to buy milk in an emergency.

Their new home would be a one-bedroom, one-
bath unit on the third floor, the kind where you
enter and the kitchen is immediately on your left
and the living room is right in front of you. She'd
guess it was the smallest place she ever lived, but
the rent was only $100 less than an entire house in
New Stockholm. They could see the highway from
the living room window, and she kind of liked it,
because at night they could hear the swish and roar
of vehicles, men and women with the kinds of jobs
like the one Stanley once had, scoring their dreams
with hard, familiar sounds.

"Breaker one nine, this is Charlie Brown, over,"
Stanley said once, in his sleep.

"Hammer down, Charlie Brown," she whispered back.

There didn't appear to be a Welcome Wagon host-
ess or anyone like that in the area, but the neighbors seemed nice and not weird, and one young
bearded man even went out of his way to offer

them use of his internet password for $5 a month. His shirt read R.E.M., which she guessed was either a rock band or an automotive product, so he was either trying to be a cool guy or a useful guy, and time would tell.

"I'm sorry," Edith told him. "The internet's never done me a lot of good."

"Stop by when you change your mind," the man smiled.

Work began immediately. Four thirty in the morning, she had to be there.

They were expected to make twenty-five pies a day, which seemed unbelievable. This being her first day, she just had to prep fruit and pre-make crusts. The kitchen also had a dough sheeter, which they said would save her time. "You'll never have to roll dough out by hand again," someone said, and Edith tried to get excited. She didn't really want to futz with some big machine she'd never used before, but figured she'd have to give it a shot. She liked rolling dough by hand, but twenty-five pies a day was mind-boggling, and there was only one person to help her, plus a third person on other details who could sometimes chip in.

Her new colleagues were younger, more serious, and faster-moving than her kitchen staff in New Stockholm, and in spite of those traits, she liked them all. Amy's solid, bookish-looking daughter,

Maureen, worked the morning crew, along with Edith and three other people, none of whom was Amy. "Mom doesn't do early mornings," said Maureen, who also had another part-time restaurant job and was just helping out her mom as a favor. When Edith first visited, it seemed like Amy owned Tippi's, because she was so knowledgeable and decisive, but it turns out that she was more of a consultant, hired to come in and rescue failing restaurants, and part of that gig was headhunting for appropriate personnel. "She poached you," Maureen said. "I hope you don't mind."

It was a strange thing to hear, but there was nothing that could be done about it now, besides make some pies. "As long as I'm of use," Edith said. "And I want to roll the first pie by hand."

"Awesome. Just don't let the boss see you. She spent thousands on that machine."

That morning, using a mixture of butter and lard, she made the same pie crust she'd made countless times before, and tried to pretend that the countertop of this strange, modern kitchen was the same quiet, broad section of the farmhouse kitchen counter where she'd first re-created the lefse, gingerbread, and risgrynsgröt recipes she'd learned from her grandmother.

The boss was a tall blonde woman named Jackie Lund. Jackie dressed in loose, billowy white outfits all the time, was stingy with praise, and wore makeup that Edith considered to be just a tad excessive. Jackie didn't know how to bake at all, which Edith thought was interesting, but this was only a real problem because she communicated almost exclusively through lists, and sometimes, Jackie's list was impossible or unclear.

"The list says make four apple pies, but there are only enough apples for three," Edith told her one morning. "What should we do? Make three pies or buy more apples?"

"I don't know," Jackie said, glancing up from her cell phone. "Is that an issue you really can't figure out?"

"Yes, so what should we do?"

"What does the list say?"

"Make four apple pies."

"Well, if it's on the list."

"But how should we do that?"

"You know, I don't know, just go by what the list says."

"But you wrote the list."

"And you're the baker," she said, dropping her phone on her desk. "Look, I don't know my way around a kitchen. My mom opened this place, rest her soul, and I'm just trying to keep it going. You're here because Amy O'Brien said you make the best pies in the state. So just make pies however you make them. I don't want to step on any toes here. OK?"

"OK," Edith said, less enlightened than before.

On her way out the door, she noticed the diploma on the wall of Jackie's office. "You went to Macalester," she commented, just because she wanted to end this exchange on a more pleasant note. "I know someone who went there."

"Yeah," Jackie replied, and Edith watched as her boss's impatient demeanor evaporated. She stared at her diploma, smiling like someone who'd just thought of a good pun. "My parents went there, too. They met over a six-pack of Coors. Pretty grim, huh?"

Edith shrugged. "Not if it worked out, I suppose."

"They practically demanded that I go there. They told me my whole life, it's where I'd meet my soulmate."

"Did you?"

Jackie laughed. "Like I wanted to get married right out of college. God, what a disaster that would've been. I was still dating musicians. They're the worst, as you probably know. I had no clue what I was doing with my life back then. Besides excessive drinking."

Edith could only nod. At age twenty, she'd married a man who turned out to be her best friend, but she supposed that her circumstances were more fortunate. "Well, I suppose I'll get back to the kitchen."

"So, did your friend find a soulmate at Macalester?"

"Friend?" Edith replied, taken aback by the word. "Oh no, it was my sister."

"And?"

"Yeah," Edith nodded. "And still married." At least they were, the last she'd heard, many years ago.

"Well, tell 'em congratulations from Jackie Lund, class of '91."

Edith said that she would pass it on.

On Edith's fourth day there, her son, Eugene, showed up. He was dressed how he usually was, in a tucked-in white button-up shirt, red tie, and pleated khakis, an outfit that he called "white-collar office," even though he'd never worked in an office in his life. He walked right behind the counter, grabbed a donut, and took a bite without even asking first.

"It's cool, right?" he asked, after he swallowed.

"I suppose, this time," she said, and let him take another one, just one more.

Once in a while the crumbs of some memory swept into her mind for no good reason, and that morning, watching her grown son eat donuts she'd later have to pay for herself, she thought of the time when he was seven years old and she noticed him filling red tin buckets with the white landscaping rocks that surrounded the house.

"Eugene," she said, opening the kitchen window. "What the heck are you doing?"

"I'm helping the family," he said, not looking up from his work. "I'm selling our rocks to people who need rocks."

She asked him to repeat himself, please.

"To all the houses who don't have any," he said, and held up two silver coins. "See? I made twenty cents. You can have it, Mom. For bills."

She'd closed her eyes to keep from crying.

If there was one thing she'd fiercely wanted to do as a mother, above almost all else, it was to make sure her children got to be children. She didn't want her little boy to know what bills were. She never wanted to explain what she and Stanley sacrificed so that their kids could have what they needed. A lot of parents did, in an inglorious attempt to instill either guilt or responsibility, but she wanted their childhood to be free from her one impregnable worry. And she'd failed.

She watched as Eugene lifted the heavy pails. "Well, I'm off," he said. "Wish me luck."

"Good luck," she whispered.

Now, she couldn't help but smile at him, as he wiped the remains of his free breakfast from his mouth and dropped a quarter in the tip jar. She watched him charm the staff with his smile, thank everyone with the tone of a rock singer thanking a packed arena, and walk out to do what he tried to do all day, which, she figured, must not have been all that different from selling buckets of stones, one stone at a time.

"That's my son," she told Maureen.

"He's kinda cute," Maureen said, and then stared past Edith at the display counter. "Hey, are there any Warren Gs up front?"

"Yeah, but last I checked, it's a Gift of the Magi."

Maureen nodded. Part of what was different about this job was all of the slang for everything, which Maureen in particular used and enforced, having learned it from whoever first trained her in the 1990s. Being included in this world of secret codes made Edith feel like a teenager, in a good way, though they could have made it a little easier on people over sixty.

Maureen O'Brien's Bakery Lingo: A Partial Glossary

Nine donuts: a shutout
Two croissants: a full moon
Three croissants: a ménage à trois
Four bear claws: Full Smokey
Two bear claws: Half Smokey
The last one of any item: the Gift of
    the Magi
A baker's dozen of donut holes: a PG-13
Anything in the unlikely quantity of thirty-
    six, or a lot of something: a Wu-Tang
Blueberry muffin: Chubby Checker

Bran muffin: Warren G (the Regulator)
Any customer who left no tip: a Libertarian
Any customer who only tipped the coins
    from their change: a couch-shaker
Any person who requested a substitution:
    Master and Demander
Any person who requested two substitutions:
    Demander-in-Chief
Any person who requested more than two
    substitutions: the New Executive Chef
And finally, any vegan customer: a Morrissey

"Why do the Morrisseys even come here?" Maureen said, pretending to sob as she cut a vegan, gluten-free sheet cake into the shape of a horse, dramatically pausing just to point at the bags of xanthan gum and xylitol on the shelf. "Look. They've turned my perfectly nice job into a goddamn triple-word score."

Edith picked up the xylitol. KICK THE SUGAR HABIT! AMAZING ALL-NATURAL SUGAR SUBSTITUTE, the bag read, but Edith wasn't amazed. Instead, she wondered how a world came to exist where people who didn't want sugar still wanted sugar. "Why don't you tell them that if they're both vegan and gluten-free, maybe they don't want cake? Maybe they want something else?"

"I've tried, believe me," Maureen shook her head.

"People can change what they do, but not what they love."

Edith watched Maureen—who always dressed simply, usually in a white T-shirt and tan cargo pants—wipe her curly hair from her brow and stare at the vegan, gluten-free cake like it was an injured tarantula.

"I'm going to do my best to help you," Maureen told the cake. "But then I want you out of here."

Thanks in large part to Maureen, Tippi's Café was a nice place to work, in spite of the high expectations, brisk morning clientele, and the uninformed boss. It did smell a lot nicer than a nursing home, and the quality of food overall was markedly better. Also, when Tippi's Café ran out of something like pie or donuts, her coworkers openly recommended local competitors to customers. It seemed like one of those old-fashioned communities where people asked, **What can I do to help?** instead of, **Why is it my problem?** It didn't feel like home yet, but it had the words, the sounds, and the smells of a place that the residents treated like one.

Even before Edith knew the lay of the land, Nicollet Falls became an easy place to live; there were buses in some parts, the roads were smooth, and the people cleaned up after their dogs, so she was never afraid to take shortcuts through the grass. Stanley loved the place right away. Together they'd walk hand-in-hand down to the big park, by the town's little namesake waterfall, and he'd sit on a bench with the calm applause of rushing water in his ears, and ask her what took them so long to live in a place like this.

"I don't know," Edith had to admit. "I guess we just didn't know it existed."

"What's that place there?" Stanley asked, pointing across the falls, where a gorgeous brick building with those huge nineteenth-century windows slept on the riverbank, guarded by old trees. "Maybe I could get a job there."

"Nobody's going to get a job there," Edith said. As far as she knew, it was part of the old paper mill, and it had been closed since the 1980s. "Maybe they should just tear it down and quit teasing people that something's going to come back there."

"Looks like a decent place to work."

"I'm afraid no one's going to be working there, Stanley."

Stanley shook his head like a judge about to deny someone a lenient sentence. "Well, maybe if they knocked on the door and asked for a job instead of just mailing their résumé, they'd get better results."

Sometimes she wasn't sure if he actually knew where he was, or if he even remembered everywhere they'd been by the end of the day, but in the evenings he sat in his big green easy chair with a bowl of ice cream or a bottle of Grain Belt, listened to the voice of John Gordon announce a Twins game on 'CCO, and he didn't have to smile to seem happy.

On Edith and Stanley's anniversary, it was Colleen and Mark's idea to meet up with them in Hudson, Wisconsin, for an authentic German dinner at Winzer Stube. Although Stanley had only been there twice in his whole life, he considered it his favorite restaurant. Stanley's mom was born in Swabia, so he was raised on spaetzle, schnitzel, and blaukraut, and both Colleen and Edith wondered if these childhood tastes would do something, anything, to inspire old memories.

"Just a bowl of spaetzle and gravy?" the waitress asked, confused by Stanley's order.

"Yes, that's all he wants," Colleen said. Since around the time her daughter turned forty, she'd become much more curt. Maybe because she looked like Meg Ryan from **Top Gun**, she seemed approachable and sweet, so she shocked people with her bluntness. "If he wanted something else, he'd say so."

"Spaetzle and gravy," Stanley said again, like it was the title of an important poem.

Edith handed their menus to the waitress. "Bring him a lot of it."

"And a beer," he said.

"Two of the tall ones," Colleen said, and finally smiled at her dad. Colleen was still his favorite, and he was hers. To see them together again, over plates of his childhood food, Edith imagined that her husband must feel more like himself than he had in ages.

After their meals arrived, her husband ate in silence for long enough, that she had to ask, "Stanley, how are you doing?"

He stared back at her, looking as baffled as a newborn.

"This is all I ever wanted, my whole life," he finally said, dipping a soup spoon into a fat bowl of the little gravy-engorged dumplings. He had the brilliant ease of a heavyweight champion on vacation, or a sea bird riding on a boat. "They always made me eat meat and vegetables. Every time, growing up. But I just wanted a bowl of spaetzle and gravy. Just that."

If this were the case, she wondered why he'd never ordered it anywhere before today, the other two times they'd been here, or at any other German-themed place they'd been. Maybe he didn't remember those occasions. And maybe for once in her life she didn't have to vandalize his happiness with an inquiry.

———

Sometimes, if she went home during her break, she'd bring him back with her to the café. He'd sit in a chair in the corner in a fall jacket and brown porkpie hat with a cup of iced tea and watch women in expensive coats and men in ties come in and attempt to make a coffee and muffin order incredibly complicated. For some reason, he kept stats on the people who tipped and presented his findings to Amy O'Brien on the back of a napkin. Amy came back a few times to see how things were going and chat with her daughter, but had the manner of an old friend's ex-wife; her mind seemed somewhere else when her mouth smiled. Stanley still liked her though. Edith could tell because he always remembered her name.

One night, Edith awoke and Stanley wasn't in bed with her, which wasn't unusual because he'd been getting up to use the toilet at least once every night for years, but this time she heard banging, like the back of a wooden chair hitting linoleum, and Stanley's voice shouting, "Get out of here!" and then, "Get up, you damn punk!"

She turned on the light, and there was Stanley in the kitchen, in his thin white T-shirt and underwear, looming over the fallen hat rack that held his blue jacket and little brown hat.

He looked up at her with surprise when she asked what he thought he was doing.

"This studhorse broke in here," he said, pointing to the jacket. "He was coming to get you."

"That's our hat rack," she said, holding his arm. She did suppose that, in the dim light, the jacket and hat on the peach-colored rack looked at a glance like a thin, motionless invader, but not any longer, on the floor, rumpled and silent.

"He was coming to get you," he repeated, looking in her direction, and he sounded like someone telling the truth. He sounded like someone who'd just been of use, in a way that he hadn't been in years.

"Thank you," she finally said, and watched his body relax.

The following weekend when they went down to Hastings to visit Colleen and Mark, Colleen asked if it was becoming too much. Earlier that evening, Stanley had believed that his baked potato was steak—sometimes his misfirings were optimistic like that.

"What are you going to do, Mom?"

"Well, I'm going to buy more potatoes," Edith said, and took the plates into the kitchen.

Colleen didn't laugh. She rinsed her father's beer glass and watched her mom scrape cold bits of asparagus into the overflowing trash can. "You know, Kenny Sarrazin had this same thing. And I heard that Patty just put him in a home last November."

"Yeah, I got the Christmas letter," Edith said. After Helen liquidated the farm, the Sarrazins had become Edith's sole source of lard, but being that the family hadn't rendered any for years now, she hadn't seen them much. Still, thanks to Patty's annual biographical blasts, Edith knew that their son Chesley and his wife, the former Lucy Koski, had sold the dairy farm so they could afford Kenny's care. The land and house where that family had lived for five generations, where Kenny was born and lived his entire life, was now paying for his tiny nursing-home room in Hopkins.

"You're not going to do that to Dad," Colleen said as she lifted the full white garbage bag out of the silver can.

It wouldn't come to that. It couldn't. Edith knew how much even a rural, no-frills place like St. Anthony-Waterside could cost. She could do this. "I'll let you know if it gets to be too hard."

Edith wanted to put it off as long as possible, but knew that one day, one or both of them would move in with Colleen. Colleen was the load-bearing wall in their family, the one who would take care of them. She didn't quite have the money or the space, but had both the ability and the heart.

"We're here to help anytime," Colleen said, and pulled the last garbage bag out of its yellow cardboard box, lined the trash can, and tossed the empty box into the garbage bag.

Even as Stanley's awareness flickered, during every day there wasn't weather, she still walked with him from the falls to the café and back. Even as she sensed him trickling away, his body was there, holding her hand, and could still send her little flashes of her husband. Some days were better than others, and sometimes, out of nowhere, a few moments were beautiful.

One day, they were at the waterfall with a Half Smokey and a PG-13, and he spoke, out of nowhere, looking at the falls, flush with fall storm water. "It's got a mind of its own. It can't ever be the same shape twice," he said in admiration.

Just then, she understood a little bit of where he was, and the difference between a brain and a mind, and whatever his brain was or had become, however the failings of its architecture, his mind was moving, exiled and tireless, and she could feel it already, around her, and hear it in the sounds he loved, in the songs, half-asleep, he sang to himself.

One morning in bed, after Stanley had otherwise gone almost completely quiet, he sang, in a high child's voice, "Toyland, Toyland, little girl and boy land," and she began to sing along, until the line that began, **Once you pass its borders**, when she stopped and let him sing those words alone.

The next day, two years and one month after they moved to Nicollet Falls, his heart gave out when they were walking back from the waterfall, and he didn't crumple in the grass like someone wrestling with death, he lay still like someone waiting to be kissed.

In her last memory of him still alive, he was staring at her, and wasn't trying to speak. Two boys on bicycles about their granddaughter's age, one white, one black, came running over, and when they saw Stanley's face, announced that they would go for help. They looked more scared than he did. That's one thing she'll always remember. He didn't look scared at all. She held his cold hands on the brown spring grass, and told him she'd miss him forever, but if he needed to go now, he could. And then, he was gone.

She hardly wept at first, but when his hearse turned out to be a Cadillac, it all came.

But just that one time.

She was a little proud of that, maybe, and possibly deserved to be, but she didn't know what resilience was just yet. Something else, a little later on, would truly burn her heart to ash, but she didn't want to permit this loss, anticipated for so long, to pull her days into darkness. Her grief was a forest with no trails, and she couldn't guess how long her heart would walk through it, as her body walked other places. For half a century, she had seen or spoken with this man almost every day, so his life didn't end when he died; it found its way into cereal aisles and intersections and post office lines and conversations she didn't intend. When people asked, **How are you?**, sometimes, for a while, she'd say, **Well, I miss him**, and leave it at that.

It reminded her of holding hands on the deck of a swaying boat, when, without warning, the other person lets you go. That moment between when your hand is empty and when you reach the railing can take years.

To a casual observer, she probably didn't appear to grieve at all. Even before the funeral visitation was over, once she realized how much of the deli meat spreads weren't going to get eaten, she wrapped up napkin-loads of sliced ham and offered them to guests as they left. She didn't know what to say to the people like Maureen O'Brien who hugged her and said, **I'm so sorry**. She didn't know what to tell old neighbors like Linty Sarrazin—who was now a successful dentist in St. Paul—when he hugged her and said, **I didn't even know he was sick**. She didn't know how to thank Lucy Koski Sarrazin, who gave her a Crock-Pot full of beef stew. She also didn't know what to think about her sister, who didn't bother to show up.

A lot of people told her, **Let me know if there's**

something I can do to help, which was kind, but clearly said more for them than for her. Sure, she could use help, but she didn't have the emotional steadiness or ability just then to choose and allocate helpful tasks for them. The last thing she wanted to do was call around and be disappointed by what people were unwilling or unable to do. On the days when she lacked the energy or willpower to cook, she just needed dinner to magically appear, and not feel as if she'd been demanding or needy.

They gave her a week off for Stanley's funeral, but she was back at work in two days. There were bills to pay, and it was no use sitting around the house staring into the space where he was. She felt more like herself making pies, and with the frantic pace at Tippi's, it was more difficult to surrender to the sadness that grabbed at her in the quiet times.

As the years passed, many of her coworkers turned over, which didn't surprise her—they were mostly young—but the local customers provided the consistency she missed. She noticed as the news of the real estate economy worsened, some of them began to place orders that were simpler and cheaper than their usual purchases, but knew better than to remark on this. She noticed when a few of them quit coming around altogether, and wished she could've given them a free Chubby Checker to say farewell.

She should've noticed that the fresh juices hadn't been restocked for two months, and certain complex items were removed from the menu, so that when Maureen O'Brien left and wasn't replaced, Edith should have taken it for the warning shot that it was.

One Friday after the morning rush ended, Jackie turned the sign on the door of Tippi's Café to read SORRY COME AGAIN and gathered her employees to the front of house.

"We're closing in three weeks," she said, in a tone more anxious than sad. "Some of you knew my mother, and you knew it was her lifelong dream to open this café. I've tried to keep it running as long as I could. I really did. This is not the fault of anyone in this building except for me. In economic terms, I'm overleveraged, and I need liquidity. It's just that simple."

Edith didn't know those terms and had no idea if it really was that simple—she knew through workplace gossip that Jackie owned several houses, so she obviously had a lot of money—but whatever happened next sure wouldn't be simple for Edith. She was almost seventy years old, and now she'd have to find another job in a town that still felt new to her.

"What about us?" someone asked, and Edith was glad someone did.

Jackie pursed her lips and nodded. "I'm happy to be a reference for anyone who wants one. And if you need to take time off work for interviews, please do."

Edith could tell by Jackie's face that she thought these were kind things to say, and that she believed they would be enough. Edith could hardly pay attention to the piqued questions and curt answers that followed. She was about to be unemployed for the first time in decades.

After about five minutes, Jackie stood up and clapped once, trying to finish off the flurry of inquiry from her aggrieved and confused employees. "Anything else?"

"Yes," Edith said as she raised her hand. "Can someone show me how to make a résumé?"

She wiped her eyes once after she started her car, but as she drove home that afternoon, she decided that losing this job wasn't so bad. Making at least twenty-five pies a day for years like a dang robot had taken a lot of the fun out of it. Maybe it was time for something else, something that didn't even involve baking. She thought about her old job up in New Stockholm and how she'd been sad to leave at the time and now didn't miss it at all. Not that she could go back anyway. Six months ago, she'd heard that St. Anthony-Waterside had been sold and converted to a hospice, which obviously had no need for an experienced baker. Despite that town's many merits, it wasn't the kind of place a person wanted to move to without a decent job lined up.

And anyway, here in Nicollet Falls she lived a lot closer to her kids, had a couple of nice friends in her new building, and there were certainly more job opportunities. She'd work anywhere, she decided that afternoon, as she walked across the hot, smelly asphalt parking lot toward her apartment building. She wasn't too proud for any job.

"Heads up!" a kid's voice bleated, and before she could see who it belonged to, something hit her in the foot. It was a basketball. She hadn't noticed when she parked, but a group of boys in sleeveless shirts and no shirts had set up one of those portable basketball hoops on the edge of the parking lot, maybe sixteen feet from where she stood. Edith picked up the basketball and looked for the voice. A shirtless kid with a tattoo of what looked like a cheeseburger on his left bicep approached her, and held out his hands to receive the ball. She threw it in his direction, as hard as she could—she hadn't touched a basketball since the 1970s—and it sailed away from her, flew over his head, smacking the top of the backboard, and plunked through the net.

"OH SHIT!" the tattooed kid yelled.

His friends looked alternately scandalized or amazed. They barked "Grandma Jordan!" "Air Grandma!" "Mad hops!" "From downtown!" and a bunch of other stuff she didn't understand at all.

The tattooed kid stared at her.

She held his gaze, nodded one time, and walked into the building.

Maybe she could do anything.

On the stairs, she saw Jan Fruechte, a nice woman who lived down the hall. She was in her forties, had a teenage daughter, and it was just the two of them. Edith watched Jan limping up the next flight with five grocery bags for a couple yards before she told Jan to stop and insisted on helping.

"Thank you," Jan said. "But I can take them, seriously. I bought this stuff, I should be able to carry it myself."

"I'm going your direction anyway," Edith said. She couldn't help but glance in the bags as she lifted them. Canned soup, microwave snacks, and frozen desserts. This woman didn't have the time to cook, or didn't know how.

"What was all that shouting about, just now?"

"No idea," Edith said.

She made up her mind just then to make Jan a hot dish that afternoon and bring it over.

———

While she unlocked her front door, the phone was ringing, and she ran to answer it, but had Edith known what she was going to hear, she would've taken her time, and enjoyed the last few seconds before everything changed.

"Mom?" It was Eugene's voice, and he was crying. "Has anyone talked to you yet?"

In that moment, her collapsing heart knew what happened. "About what?"

"Colleen," he said. "Colleen and Mark."

She couldn't move, and the earth went completely still along with her. "No," was all she could say, and her mouth said it again and again.

"There's been an accident," he said. "Mom, they're gone."

Whatever strings from heaven that still held her bones up vanished, right then. There was one word left on her lips, and it took every prayer in her blood to speak it.

"Diana?" she asked.

"Diana's OK," he said.

Edith closed her eyes and thanked God for that one mercy.

That day, and for a long time after, she'd grapple with God's injustice too, but it was also a long time before she learned that God needed an indestructible person for the tasks that lay ahead, and this is how they're forged.

After setting down the phone, she was sobbing, which meant she was evidently still alive. Since that was the case, she stood up, took a deep breath, wiped her face on a tea towel, and picked up the phone. There was work to be done, and people who needed her. She'd lost so many people she loved, and it didn't seem to make any sense that she could withstand it all, but God didn't make mistakes. Whether she accepted it or not, there was a reason.

There had to be. Because Edith Magnusson was still here.

$92.27

Diana, 2007

Diana Winter had three rules. She only stole from middle-class or rich people, never broke or damaged anything, and never took anything that belonged to a child. A teenager, fine; she'd go out of her way to take something from a rich teenager, whether or not they even attended the same school. The house she approached today, a tan split-level with a three-car garage, didn't have a swing set in the back or any other kid stuff visible, which in a house this size meant that the kids were either in their late teens or off on their own already. Ideal.

The side door to the garage was open—she was shocked at how many people left this door unlocked. The vehicles inside were a Cadillac SUV with salt stains around the wheel wells, a black Audi sedan that had a Z-shaped scratch on the passenger-side door, and an empty spot and oil stain probably belonging to another luxury vehicle. Ducking behind the SUV, Diana spotted glass jars full of screws and nails, bolted to the underside of a cupboard by their lids, hanging like light bulbs. A well-used Milwaukee circular saw, its blades flecked with cold sawdust, sat on a cluttered workbench. Diana guessed that in the cupboards and in the cabinets was a buffet of name-brand power tools.

She took a deep breath and went to work.

It used to be that Diana wasn't good at anything. By her junior year of high school, she'd established herself as outlandishly unexceptional at every academic subject, pastime, sport, hobby, game, and parlor trick, from trigonometry to Scrabble to thumb wrestling. She loved books, but not the ones that were assigned; she loved movies, but not the ones that most other people liked; and she liked dudes, but they didn't often seem to like her back. Now, her grades might have been higher if she'd ever done homework, and she may have had better luck with guys if she'd ever spoken more than a few words to them. But in the months after her mom and dad died, she didn't really have much to say to anyone.

The car accident that killed Diana's parents last June revealed a lot to her, especially the fact that every adult and almost every other person her age didn't understand her, no matter what they'd been through. As a new kid in a new town, living with her kind but exhausted grandma Edith, she had to set herself to a frequency that no one could tune in, just to make every day tolerable.

After a while, people confused her quiet, sublimated grief with a Protestant work ethic. "I've had more talkative employees, but she's been great," Diana overheard her boss at the coffee shop tell a customer. "She keeps her head down and does her job."

The only human who seemed to understand her at all came in the unlikely form of Clarissa Johnson. Because Clarissa was Diana's second cousin on her dad's side, Diana had actually known her from before, but not well; just a slightly older girl who she'd seen over the years at weddings and funerals. The remnants of their family assumed they'd be actual friends now that they lived in the same town, and that did indeed happen, but not in the way anyone would hope or expect.

Clarissa was a senior, and claimed to live alone,

and she kind of did. Her parents weren't dead or even divorced, they were just rich, stressed-out, white-collar alcoholics who cheated on each other and mostly ignored their daughter, but Clarissa had the good sense to rarely complain about them in front of Diana. They gave Clarissa the kind of damage that led to more than the usual amount of reckless behavior—she'd shoplifted over three hundred times and only been busted twice, she claimed—but she was also the exact sort of friend that Diana needed. She never once told Diana how to behave or how to react, never once told her to make new friends, or pray to a particular saint, or talk to a particular counselor, or, God forbid, **smile**. She just let her grieve, and even if it was because she was too self-absorbed or fucked up herself, this was something almost no one else was capable of doing. Together they could pass the time like a couple of empty boats tied to a fenced-off pier, and it was beautiful.

Clarissa's friendship made it far easier for Diana to get by in Nicollet Falls, an upscale Minneapolis suburb known for its tree-lined streets, old-fashioned downtown buildings, and fiscal conservatives. Its high school had won countless state sports championships and academic achievements, but her first day there was less awful and frightening than she feared. Her connection with a rich, notorious bad girl acted as a force field around her.

Kids tapped her headphone cord and asked who she was listening to and when she said, **Dessa**, they nodded and said **Cool**, **I've heard of those guys**, which they obviously hadn't. She had Clarissa to thank for their deference.

She had Clarissa to thank for everything, including what she was doing that morning. The night they came up with the idea, they were at a party at Clarissa's then-boyfriend Brody Slager's huge house after a football game. The Nicollet Falls Papermakers had just beaten some other high school by a lot, and this was completely expected, but still, people were in a celebratory mood. Clarissa was elated because there was still beer in the fridge when they'd arrived.

"Thank God," she said, opening a can of Blotz, and throwing one to Diana. "This is why you have to come early to high school parties, before all the good shit's gone."

"Thanks," Diana said, even though she wasn't crazy about beer, this brand in particular. "Do they have any other kinds in there?"

Clarissa didn't seem to hear. She was staring at something behind Diana's head, frowning. "See that over there? That's a five-hundred-dollar chainsaw."

"It is?" Diana asked, glancing back again at the

pristine chainsaw on a workbench. An unfamiliar brand, Husqvarna, was on the blade. "Looks like they've hardly even used it."

"They haven't," Clarissa said. "Brody told me. His dad's a tax attorney, he doesn't know how to use power tools. They bought him a chainsaw for his birthday, and he took a bunch of selfies with it, and now there it is."

Diana shrugged. "Seems like kind of a waste."

"What would you do with five hundred bucks?"

"I don't know," Diana said. The idea of having five hundred bucks seemed ridiculous. At best, it took her over three weeks to make that much at the coffee shop. What wouldn't she do with that kind of money? "God, there's a ton of stuff. Help my grandma with her bills, I guess."

"Sounds like a blast," Clarissa said.

Diana shrugged and sipped her Blotz, which was still as awful as the first time she'd tried it, with her grandpa. She just wondered how long she'd have to nurse it before she left the party. "What would you do?"

"I want to move out of my parents' house, before college. I know you probably don't want to hear it, but it's getting intolerable."

"If you need extra money, I could maybe try to get you some shifts at the coffee shop. It's seven-twenty-five an hour."

"Dude, the woman who runs the Parks department is a friend of my mom's." Clarissa called her "dude" all the time, and she didn't mind. "If I wanted a job, she could pay me eleven-fifty an hour any time I want. But I don't have the time for a job anyway, not with the newspaper and the musical."

"That's true, I forgot." As much as Clarissa cultivated a rebellious image, she was still a serious student and kind of a joiner in after-school activities, and it was hard to tell whether that was to fatten a college application, out of a genuine interest in journalism and theatre, or just an excuse to avoid going home after school. Rehearsing the part of Ado Annie in **Oklahoma!** couldn't have been that time-consuming, but Diana didn't like to argue with her cousin.

Clarissa stared at that orange chainsaw again. "There's so many houses in town, where they wouldn't even miss stuff like this. I can't even tell you. All the parties I go to. All the homes just full of stuff. Basements, garages, filled to the ceiling with crap. It would break your heart, Di." There was an anxiety in Clarissa's voice, as if she was either afraid of what she was saying, or she was afraid to get caught saying it. "No one would ever suspect a girl like you. It's perfect."

"Like me? To do what?"

Then Diana saw the light snap out of Clarissa's eyes as they heard Brody's voice shouting Clarissa's name. "Later," Clarissa murmured. She yelled his name back in response, and Diana's back stiffened as she heard the boys thunder toward them from above. They usually paid no attention to her, which was ideal, considering how the douchey bros like Brody talked to women. Sometimes it's better to be ignorable.

Three months later, Diana had become accustomed to sometimes wearing an orange hard hat and safety vest over her winter clothing on her mile-long walk to high school. Even though it was five thirty in the morning and her grandma was asleep on the hide-a-bed in the living room, Diana always waited to put these things on until she was at least two blocks from home. She figured that everyone assumed that she wore this getup for safety, to be visible in the early-morning darkness, and they were right. She'd learned from Clarissa that in order to enter somewhere you don't belong, she had to be in plain sight. She learned to walk with confidence and boredom, both looking like she knew where she was going and acting like it was the last place she wanted to be. In this outfit, just like she did today, she could trudge up a stranger's driveway, wearily enter through the garage's side door in full sight of the neighbor's kitchen windows, and encounter no apparent alarm.

That morning in January, it was 0 degrees out, and her feet felt numb by the time she reached the brick steps leading to the front door of Clarissa's huge house. Clarissa's mom, Andrea—the hardest-working real estate agent serving Nicollet Falls, according to a bus bench in front of the Arby's—was already in makeup and a power suit, sitting in the kitchen smoking a cigarette and staring at her laptop when Diana knocked.

"You know where she is," Andrea said, not smiling. She was eating egg whites and plain yogurt, a breakfast that Diana had never seen before entering this house, and one that she'd now come to associate with success.

"Thanks," Diana said, closing the door and wiping her feet on the mat.

"How's your grandma doing?" Andrea asked.

"Hanging in there," Diana replied, a little surprised to be having a conversation with this woman. "How's work?"

"We're still killing it," Andrea said. "It's exhausting, but we're killing it."

Everything Diana had heard about the economy and real estate was grim, but what did she know? Andrea might have earned her way onto her daughter's shit list, but she was also obviously confident, attractive, lived in a nice house, and leased a fancy white Mercedes (**Never, ever buy a car**, Andrea warned Diana once), so she must've been doing something right. In spite of the nice stuff, she didn't seem stuck up, and Diana wondered if she grew up poor. Maybe one day Andrea would sense this affinity, and tell Diana, **You're going to be OK. I've been there myself, and I know you'll be fine.**

Clarissa, still wearing the T-shirt and shorts she'd slept in, frowned as she walked into the kitchen.

"What are you talking to her for?" she said to Diana, and turned toward the stairs. "Come on."

Diana followed her to her dark bedroom, where Clarissa kicked a path for them through the clothes on the floor and chucked the backpacks onto her unmade canopy bed.

"So, how'd we do today?" Clarissa asked, unzipping the bags and setting aside the vest and hard hat that Diana had stuffed into the top of one of them. "Makita power drill. Porter-Cable belt sander. Snap-On impact socket set. Snap-On impact wrench. And a Bosch laser level. Damn, dude," Clarissa said. "You killed it this time. Killed it."

Diana smiled. She couldn't help it. "You think there's maybe four hundred here?"

"Yeah, maybe. Did you get everything?" She always asked that.

"Pretty much. Other than this stuff, they just had a Milwaukee circular saw that looked kinda old."

"Dude! That's fifty bucks out of our pockets."

"It was out in the open. This other stuff was all put away in cabinets. It might be a while before he notices this stuff missing. That saw, he'd notice by tonight."

"That's clever thinking," Clarissa said. "But next time, just take it anyway."

Easy for her to say. She wasn't the one who risked being arrested. Even though the whole thing was Clarissa's idea, she was only a crucial part of the operation because Diana didn't have the internet at home. The worst Clarissa could get is possession of stolen property.

"How fast can you sell this stuff?"

"Why, you need another advance?"

Diana nodded. "Yeah, a hundred and thirty bucks."

Clarissa pulled some bills out of a secret hole in the belly of a plush unicorn she had hidden in her closet. "There you go, dude," she whispered.

Diana didn't enjoy being a thief, but come to think of it, she didn't know anyone, except maybe Andrea, who enjoyed their jobs. And unlike any other second job she could've taken, it didn't make her have to cut back on shifts at the coffee shop. It just took an extra half hour in the morning every so often. And, all told, they'd made about twenty-nine hundred bucks total in less than three months. It was the kind of money that could change their lives.

Diana's cheeks were still bright red from the cold when she walked into Mr. Arden's first-period chemistry class. It was like most of her classes in terms of student population and teacher attitude, in that neither expected much of the other. There was one popular varsity hockey player, Trent Amundson, who was righteously maintaining the academic standards for a Division I athletic scholarship, but his ambition was the exception. In this room, Diana's B-average meant she got by with minimal attention from anyone.

Her problem was homework. If she couldn't do an assignment during school hours, during study hall, or another class, she would most likely never get around to it. There were too many other things she had to worry about. For instance, her grandma's car just got towed the day before from the residential street where it broke down. Now it was in an impound lot where they owed eighty bucks for the tow and fifty more a day in storage fees. A few months ago, that amount could've made the car irretrievable. Now, Diana could get it back, and damn it, she would.

It was still two minutes before first bell, and Diana was at her desk trying to complete some proofs for her second-period geometry class, so she didn't hear Mr. Arden call her name until what must've been the third or fourth time.

"Miss Winter," Mr. Arden said, his voice frustrated. "You're wanted in the principal's office."

No one paid much attention; this probably wasn't an uncommon request for a student in Mr. Arden's non-honors classes.

"Did they say what for?" Diana asked.

"You would know more than me," Mr. Arden said, turning away, signaling that he was done with the interaction.

Diana had certainly never stolen anything at school or knowingly robbed a school employee, but she suspected right then that Mr. Arden had guessed what she'd been up to; maybe he'd heard rumors about a spate of garage thefts in Nicollet Park and eyed his classes for persons of interest.

It was a one-minute walk to the main office; not enough time to concoct a foolproof alibi, particularly if someone had followed her to and from Clarissa's. Now, on the day of their biggest take in weeks, it was all over.

"Oh, Miss Winter!" the school principal, Londard Shultz, said as he greeted Diana with a too-firm handshake. He looked like a classic municipal-level authority figure; his bright bald head gleamed beneath the drop ceiling, his gut stressed the lower buttons of his yellow button-up shirt, his tie had a lot of brown, and there was also honest sweetness in his eyes. Every year, some smart-ass boy shaved the crown of his head and went as Londard Shultz for Halloween, and the old principal would laugh about it and even pose for selfies. Diana figured that if she was going to get kicked out of school or turned over to the cops, she couldn't have picked a nicer guy to deliver the judgment.

"It's a cold one out today, huh," Mr. Shultz said. They weren't even in the guy's office, just standing outside of it, where everyone, all the secretaries and office staff, could hear them.

"Yeah," Diana said. The anxious small talk made her want to stab herself in the hand with a number two pencil, but she did her best to appear calm and bored.

Londard Shultz smiled. "Staying out of trouble?"

"So far," Diana said.

Mr. Shultz looked amused. "Well, we hadn't heard back from you, and we were wondering if you received the letter and emails."

"No, what letter?" Diana leaned toward the water machine to let some administrative lady get to the copier.

"Oh wow, then I'll just tell you. You got a perfect score on the PSAT."

"Oh," Diana said.

"You're going to qualify for a National Merit Scholarship." The principal laughed. "It's good news, isn't it?"

She didn't know for sure if it was. Maybe she'd heard of National Merit Scholarships somewhere.

It did seem like a good thing, from the tone of the principal's voice. And was that it? "Is that why I'm here?" she asked.

"No, you're under arrest for grand larceny," he said.

She must've looked as scared as she felt because of how hard he laughed.

"Oh, I'm just joshin' you," he said. "You know, in twenty years, I don't know if I've ever seen a perfect PSAT score."

"Corrina Francis!" one of the secretaries yelled.

"Corrina, of course," Mr. Shultz nodded. "Y'know, I just ran into her dad at Byerlys not too long ago. I guess she's in Prague, on a Fulbright. Not so bad, huh? So, forgive me, you're the second person with a perfect score."

"Oh," Diana said, her body still trembling with adrenaline. She barely remembered even taking the PSAT. If the principal had called her to the office just to convince her that the PSAT did not exist, Diana would've been quicker to believe that.

"How do you feel? You should be excited!" the principal said. There was something in the nice man's smile and open posture now that made Diana think of a salesman, and the worst kind, the kind that tried to sell you things that were completely unnecessary, like chocolate Advent calendars, or lip scrub, or LifeWell brand 8-in-1 cleaner.

"To be honest, I'm relieved," Diana said.

"No doubt, after how hard you must've studied.

And you know, there's also going to be a formal luncheon at the Country Club for you and a guardian. Just for the students who scored in the top three percent. The mayor and some local business owners always come. It's a little tradition I started."

"Yeah, OK," Diana said. This was now one more thing to worry about. "Is there any compensation involved with this award?"

"No, not directly, but it should help you get scholarships."

"What if I'm not planning to go to college?"

The principal gave Diana a look she would've expected to receive if Diana had suggested they tear down the school's hockey rink, and in its place, erect a statue of Lenin.

"Why?" the principal asked, stumbling toward a diplomatic response. "You're planning to enlist in the military?" The armed forces were, of course, the only acceptable alternative to college in the eyes of many people in Nicollet Falls, and to a few, the preferable choice.

"No, I just don't want to go to college."

The principal, who had been leaning forward, took a half-step back. "Well, I'd urge you to start thinking it over," he said, and glanced toward the hallway. "Have you been to see Mrs. Burl in the Career Center across the hall? She's got information on scholarships and grants. Let's set up an appointment for you right now."

Diana was hoping that everyone would be doing lab work or some kind of in-class assignment when she returned. Instead, Mr. Arden was lecturing, saying something about covalent bonds, when Diana entered the room, and rather than continue talking, Mr. Arden went silent and stared at her.

"What kept you?" Mr. Arden asked, in front of everybody. He seemed to live just to make examples of students who were late or called to the principal's office.

"Principal Shultz just had to tell me I'm a National Merit Scholar, or something," Diana said, and off Mr. Arden's confused expression, she offered the letter Shultz had given her.

Mr. Arden accepted the letter with an arched eyebrow. "Let me see that," he mumbled, and read it over. "Huh. Wow. It says you got a perfect score. That's incredible."

"I suppose," Diana said, sitting down. A lot of good it would do her. "Sorry to interrupt the class."

"So, you're a shoo-in to be a Finalist." Mr. Arden walked the letter back to Diana. "You know, some years we don't even have any National Merit Finalists at this school," he said loudly in front of everyone. "You have to be extremely smart to be a Finalist. Extremely smart."

Kids who had never even looked at Diana all year

were now staring at her. As Mr. Arden returned to the lesson, Diana gazed past him at the periodic table at the front of the class, looking at those letters that signified the ingredients of the universe, staring at element 4, beryllium. She realized that she had no clue what it was, and it was the fourth one, so it had to be important, but because she didn't know anything about it, there was no way that she was a genius, and the thought comforted her a little.

At the end of class, Diana caught Trent Amundson's eye, who said, "Hey, congrats." It made her smile.

Mr. Arden called Diana to his desk as Trent and everyone else filed out.

"Are you challenged enough in this class?" Mr. Arden asked.

"Yeah, it's fine," Diana said. "Real challenging."

"You know, I doubt it," Mr. Arden said. "I think I've been severely underestimating your intellectual curiosity. I just want to tell you that I apologize, and please let me know if there's any way I can make this class more interesting for you."

"I don't know how I did so well on that test. I'm actually not that smart," Diana said, and pointed to the periodic table. "I mean, I don't even know what beryllium is."

"Memorizing facts isn't a sign of intelligence," Mr. Arden said. "You know that you don't know things, and want to find out. That's what **smart** is, not a talent for regurgitation."

This exchange was getting worse. She glanced toward the hallway, which was filled with students hustling to their second-period classes.

"I suppose you gotta get going," Mr. Arden said. "Come in early sometime if you want to do some work that's more challenging than what I'm allowed to give you in class."

Diana didn't want school to be more challenging. If this was what being smart was like, it was clearly overrated.

At lunch, Clarissa was already seated at the corner table farthest from the windows, in the darkest area of the cafeteria. Diana's grandma made the strategic decision to make below the monthly gross income limit for the SNAP program, which meant that Diana could receive free school lunches. The cafeteria lunch wasn't cool to eat—most of the cool kids and rich kids ate lunch off campus—but some of their stuff, like the chicken sandwich they had that day, wasn't half bad.

Clarissa had only started eating on campus because the new guy she'd been seeing lately, Ishaq Ahmed, only ever ate in the cafeteria. Ishaq was a notoriously studious kid whose immigrant parents had discouraged him from dating. They'd also explicitly forbidden him from even talking to Clarissa Johnson ever since she and Brody Slager got in the paper for stealing a Zamboni and taking it to the Hardee's drive-thru. Ishaq had told her a month ago that he wasn't allowed to speak to her, that his parents considered her a bad influence. He told her if he did any of the things she did, he'd be shot in the street. Clarissa responded by kissing him.

He was a nice guy, if a little loud.

"Yo, it's the super-genius!" Ishaq shouted when he saw Diana from across the cafeteria.

Word had somehow gotten out. Everyone seemed to be staring at her as she set down her tray next to her cousin.

"No," Diana said, staring at the floor. "I just did well on a test one time." If other people kept acting like she was a genius, and gave her all this new attention, it would cause all sorts of problems.

"No way," Ishaq said. "You don't get perfect by accident. I studied for that thing for eighty hours, and all I got was Commended."

"Only eighty?" Clarissa smirked. "Lazy ass."

"I know, but it was only the PSAT," Ishaq said. "I've been studying for the SAT since my dad was nine."

Clarissa laughed at her new boyfriend's joke, but Diana just smiled. "How'd you do on it last year, Clarissa?"

"Good enough." Clarissa was still waiting to hear

back from the expensive East Coast schools she'd applied to, but didn't seem worried. She'd always done good enough.

"So where you gonna go to college?" Ishaq asked Diana. "You gonna join me at Northwestern? Or follow your cousin to New York or Boston?"

"I hadn't really thought about it," Diana said.

"You got time," he said, and maybe it was kind of him to assume this was the only obstacle.

After school, Diana walked the two miles to the impound lot, which was down a dirt road on the edge of town. A skinny gray dog ran along its side of the fence, gasping at her as she approached a double-wide trailer that read OF ICE on the door, and wondered how long that second "F" had been missing, or if it was torn off as a joke.

Inside the trailer, a large, lone man in a Kurt Busch sweatshirt sat at a desk in front of a wall of numbered hooks. He had the body of a powerful oaf who'd peaked during the early nineties; she was willing to bet that he had boxes of dusty weights in his garage. A stack of business cards on his desk read BRAD BARTT. He looked at Diana the way a high school janitor looks at the senior hallways at the end of the last day of school.

"I'm here about the 1996 Toyota Cressida," Diana said.

Brad Bartt groaned, as if Diana had intentionally

arranged to have Edith's car towed to this place just to annoy him.

"License, registration, proof of insurance."

"The last two things are in the car, in the glove box."

"You have payment with you?"

"Yeah," Diana said, opening her wallet. "So that's towing plus one day of storage?"

The big guy went through some grubby papers on his desk. "Says here we picked it up yesterday at six thirty a.m. So that's two days. Clock started on the second day at six thirty this morning. So that's a hundred and eighty bucks total."

"I have a hundred and forty-six bucks," Diana said.

"Look. I'm tired of you people acting like this is some kind of Arab street market. I don't know what you did to get your car here, but your behavior has a cost. And your cost is a hundred and eighty dollars."

"It's my grandma's car, and she needs it for work—"

"Write all complaints on the check. Local checks only."

Diana wondered if this dude had done something bad, like he'd been dishonorably discharged for firing into a crowd of unarmed civilians, or broken someone's neck on Black Friday over a DVD player, and needed to find a place that wouldn't hold it against him, and found it here, among other people's property.

Brad Bartt looked at his grimy paperwork. "And if it's not your car, you also need a notarized statement from the registered owner. Plus a six-dollar administrative fee."

While walking from the impound yard to her job, Diana knew she would have to wake up early to work another rich person's garage in the morning. She also figured that she should use the computer at work to type up and print the permission statement, get her grandma to sign it, figure out how and where to get it notarized, bring it back to the yard, call a local repair shop to send a tow truck to get it, and also pay for that tow and repair. Who had time for homework? She was passing. She'd graduate.

Either way, it was a relief to be this busy. As she learned since last summer, if she wasn't distracted, she could just start crying, and it was always, always better to be busy than be sad.

That evening, Diana had the closing shift at Gretchen's Café, a mom-and-pop coffee shop in downtown Nicollet Falls. They'd been letting her close recently, by herself, and out of respect for the place, she did very little to take advantage of this. At the end of her shift, Diana would individually wrap up the day's two-day-old unpurchased muffins, bars, and cupcakes, taking care while bagging them so they wouldn't crush each other. When she got home that night, she took an extra five minutes to leave little bags of free pastries at the apartment doors of families that she'd seen around.

That evening, the guy in #212 ran to his door as if he'd been waiting for her, but then the look in his face demonstrated that he wasn't. He was milky-pale and his apartment didn't appear to have a lot of furniture.

"Damn it," he said, hugging his chest as he glanced both ways down the hallway.

"Hi," Diana said, and held open the bag. "Want a bagel?"

"You see a tall guy on the stairs, with a gray jacket?"

"No, I'm sorry."

The pale guy glanced at the bag. "Yeah, maybe I'll take one for later," he said, grabbing a bagel without looking at it and closing his door.

She knew that a few of the adults and older teens in the building were addicts, but she didn't care. It was pretty obvious that there weren't fathers in a lot of the units either, or if there were, often no mothers. She guessed that some of them had left addicted or unemployed partners. Some were the ones left behind. Either way, everyone's gotta eat.

Even when she grazed on the job, Diana was starving when she came home. Her grandma worked part-time at Kohl's, and two or three times a week at the local Arby's, and on those days, she brought back Arby's for dinner, but since her car's transmission shit the bed, she took the bus, and because she lived over a mile from the nearest bus stop, that meant that the food would be cold when she got home.

Diana didn't grow up in a big house, and wasn't jealous of the kids who did, but now, sharing a one-bedroom apartment with her grandma, made her family's little two-bedroom rambler back in Hastings feel like a mansion. Her grandma slept on the couch's hide-a-bed, insisting that Diana have the bedroom, which was incredibly generous, and every time Diana opened that bedroom door she felt like she'd better earn it. After going through the mail last summer and seeing the amounts on her grandma's unpaid and overdue bills, she got that job at the coffee shop.

Of course, the only way Edith would ever accept help with a bill is when Diana just paid it herself. Edith would have never asked Diana to "pull her weight," or "chip in," or anything like that, but it wasn't like Edith to talk about important things. Even when they stumbled across something that had belonged to her mom, and there was this raw, gleaming instant when they could acknowledge this incredible loss they'd suffered together—a loss that created their whole unlikely living situation— Edith would laugh to herself and change the subject. She'd had enough pain in her life, she said, and just wanted things to be pleasant.

Most days, Diana watched her grandma's weary body push open the door after a shift, carrying their groceries or dinner, and agreed that it'd be unkind to remind them both of something so sad.

"How was your day?" her grandma asked, out of breath. There was no elevator in the building and the stairs always took the wind out of her.

"The usual." Diana cut their chicken sandwiches in half so they would heat through quicker in the microwave, and noticed they were still a little warm. "The bus take a shortcut today?"

"No, Betsy Nielsen gave me a ride." Betsy was a service-industry lifer, and the only employee at Arby's close to her grandma in age.

"That's awesome," Diana said, and put the cut sandwiches on LifeWell-brand paper plates with another paper plate on top to trap the heat. There was a ton of LifeWell Home Products around, because her uncle Eugene could never build any kind of downline and ended up with a bunch of shit he couldn't sell to anyone but his mom.

"Did I get what you wanted?" Edith asked. "I know you like chicken."

She'd had virtually the same thing for lunch, she realized, as she smelled the lukewarm mayo and lettuce. "Yeah, thank you," Diana nodded.

Edith picked up the TV remote and turned on the local news.

"I guess something interesting did happen to me today," Diana said, and then hesitated to even mention it, but it was too late now. "I found out that I got a perfect score on the PSAT."

"That sounds neat," Edith said. "What is it?"

"Some academic thing."

"You know, I think you got something in the mail about that a while ago. I was afraid it was one of those scams."

"No, Grandma, it's not a scam," Diana said, taking her sandwich out of the microwave.

"Is there prize money?"

Diana realized in the moment that this was a potential out, if her cash was ever discovered, but decided not to play that card yet. "I'm not sure. I know there's a formal luncheon at the Country Club. And I get to bring someone, if you wanna come."

"Oh, I like luncheons," Edith said, and smiled. "But if I have to work that day, can you go by yourself?"

"Yeah, probably." Diana unfolded a piece of paper from her back pocket and set it on the counter. "Now, can you sign this so I can pick up your car at the impound tomorrow?"

"Oh, I'd feel bad if you spent your hard-earned money on that."

There were many moments, like this one, when she almost told Edith what she'd been doing. She almost told her about the nine hundred bucks she'd saved up, which was just about enough to fix her car with a salvaged or rebuilt transmission—at least according to Brett Victor at Victor Machine Shop. If Edith found out, though, she'd make Diana give back or replace all of the stuff she'd taken, and she knew that the coffee shop would fire her, and that would be the end of everything.

The three times Diana had been caught in someone's garage, she always apologized for startling the homeowner, then asked them where their electric meter was, and immediately left once they replied. The morning after receiving her PSAT score, she freaked out a woman so badly that she fell on the floor.

"Are you OK?" Diana asked, walking around the front of the woman's idling Lexus. She was wearing a fancy-looking white jacket with a fur-lined hood, and her collapse had slapped brown splotches on the back and the sleeves, although she hadn't yet noticed. "I was just looking for your meter."

"Oh my God," the woman said. "Why didn't you knock?"

"I did," Diana said, which is what she always

said when she was caught. "But maybe you didn't hear me over the car."

"No, I didn't hear you knock because you didn't knock," the woman said. Her eyes locked on Diana as she stood up, as if memorizing her face, clothes, and body.

This had to stop as quickly as possible, Diana knew right then.

"The meter's on the other side of the house, under the bedroom window."

"Thank you, ma'am," Diana said, turning her back, moving deliberately to the side door, trying her best to look like a bored, exhausted young woman and not like a savagely frightened girl. "And sorry, once again."

"My jacket!" she heard the woman yelp as the door closed.

She tried the side door again after the homeowner left, and to her surprise, it was still unlocked. Maybe the woman was startled into a negligent stupor, or too distracted by the new stains on her coat. Regardless, all she really had in her garage, besides full ashtrays, bottles of Popov vodka in the cabinets, an empty aquarium, and an old tandem bike with flat tires, was a Craftsman drill with a dead battery, and Diana almost felt bad taking it.

She would only continue to do this, she decided, until she had her grandma's car out of impound and repaired. Clarissa would just have to be fine with that; she already had almost fifteen hundred bucks out of this deal, anyway. With the car emergency over, they could all get back to normal, and maybe everyone would forget that Diana was a genius, and everything could just be the way it was.

The school wanted to take photos of its top three PSAT scorers for some reason, so Diana arrived at the appointed meeting place, the school's trophy case, at eight a.m., an excused absence form in her back pocket. Only one other person was there on time, an honors student she recognized, but didn't know personally, named Paul Jeffrey. You didn't have to know Paul to know of him in Nicollet Park High. He had famously received all As in every class; for years, he was one of just three black students in the junior class; and he was the youngest child of City Councilperson Lisa Jeffrey and her husband, Bert, who owned the local Dairy Queen franchise.

Paul was leaning against the wall, reading a paperback, which made him seem even more intimidatingly intelligent than he already was. She had no idea what she could say to him that wouldn't be dorky or inane. Maybe she wouldn't say anything.

"Hey," he said. "I'm Paul."

"I'm Diana," she said. "Looks like we're the only ones on time, ha."

He smiled.

My God, she hated when she put herself out

there by speaking to someone, and they responded nonverbally. But now that she'd opened her mouth, she couldn't shut herself up, probably just because it now seemed less awkward than not talking at all. "What are you reading?"

He held up **Jesus' Son**, by Denis Johnson.

Nonverbal again. But God, his smile was cute. And he dressed well. Button-up shirt. Shined shoes. Who in public high school wears shoes that need shining? He was trying too hard, maybe, but it actually worked for him.

"Oh, I love Denis Johnson," Diana found herself saying. "His sentences are astounding." Christ, she should really shut up. On top of everything, this was maybe the only time she'd ever talked about "sentences" with someone besides a teacher, and it made her feel like she was jumping off a bridge. He'd clearly read far more than she had, and probably only found her comment amusing, at best.

"Yeah. He's got the voice of a poet." He put the book away in his bag, and she glimpsed two more paperbacks while he organized his stuff, with the names Edward P. Jones and Joan Didion on their spines.

She figured that she should change the subject before her true ignorance was revealed. "So why do they want our picture, anyway?"

"For that wall, by the front door, when you walk in," Paul said. "Where they put up pictures of the top three scorers every year."

"Oh yeah, that wall," Diana said.

"And if you don't like the picture, don't worry. They'll take one again next year if you become a Finalist."

Damn, people who tested well were sure photographed a lot. "So who's the third person?"

"Nate Ryan," he said, frowning.

"Oh." She'd heard of him, but didn't know him. "What's his deal?"

"He paid for both the Kaplan and Princeton classes just to get this. Though I hear that he had the worst score of the three of us."

"That's funny," she said.

"So, did you do Princeton or Kaplan? Or did you do Khan Academy like I did?"

"No, none of them. I don't even remember taking the test to begin with."

"Well, aren't you sharp as a tack!"

Of course he thought she was being too humble. The truth was, she really didn't remember. "Actually, it's probably all a big mistake. I don't even want to go to college, anyway."

"You don't want to go to college?" Paul asked, not scandalized like the principal, but more like someone who just watched a six-year-old choose broccoli over pizza.

Just then, a tall guy with a camera around his neck, and a skinny, bespectacled kid in a white Harvard sweatshirt walked up to them from behind.

"Oh, here you are," Camera Guy said. "You're by the football trophy case. We were waiting for you by the hockey trophy case."

"I knew you guys would get it wrong," Nate Ryan said.

After school, Diana had found a notary, walked there, convinced the notary to stamp the letter, paid his fee, and walked again to the impound lot, pet the skinny guard dog, and this time had to stand in line behind two women who, like Diana the day before, were attempting to locate Brad Bartt's absent good nature.

"You don't understand," one of the women kept saying. She was wearing a pink jacket that was too short for her, and looked Mexican or maybe Salvadoran.

"I **understand** that you owe this company two hundred and eighty dollars," Brad Bartt said. Diana did the math in her head; their car had been impounded for four days. "What **you** don't understand is that you won't get your car back until you pay me. Next! Next!"

The women brushed past Diana and slammed the trailer door behind them, hard enough that it popped open again.

"You mind closing that door?" Brad Bartt asked.

"Sure," Diana said, like a dork, and did what she was told.

"So what about you, you got my money, or what?"

Diana felt bad giving it to this bastard.

Walking to work afterward, it began to snow, and Diana remembered when she'd been thrilled by the sight of the stuff. As a little kid without a lot of toys, snow was versatile, inexhaustible, and dynamic. It was all the toys. Now, it just made her late to work.

She glanced ahead, and counted the remaining blocks to the warmth of the coffee shop. Not including the four minutes she got in the shower each morning, her job was the warmest place in her day, because the owners set the thermostat to 66 degrees, which was way better than the 59 degrees that Edith enforced at home. Her dad would've told her to just put on another layer if she were so dang cold, which she hated hearing at the time. Before leaving school that day, she'd put on the extra sweater she had in her locker, and thinking about it now almost made her smile. She didn't think she'd ever be sentimental about that crap in a million years, but dead parents can do that to you. The most-obeyed parents are probably the dead ones, if they were loved.

She looked around, and as far as she could see in both directions, she saw no other pedestrians, on either side of the road. She wondered how many people in the world, just then, were walking alone somewhere on an unshoveled sidewalk, like her, missing someone.

With the weather keeping the customers at home, Diana looked for something to read to pass the time. One of her favorite parts about this job was that the owners, Ann and Will, had stacked the shelves against the wall opposite the register two-deep with leftovers from their book collection. This was where she'd discovered Alice Munro, Louise Erdrich, Faith Sullivan, and Denis Johnson, just in the last six months. This time, she found a copy of a Joan Didion book, one called **Slouching Towards Bethlehem**.

She had just finished a story about a rich lawyer in California who got away with killing his wife, while his much poorer lover was imprisoned for killing her husband, and wondered if Paul had read that story, when Paul walked through the door.

He shook the snowflakes off his hood, smiling at the shop's ugly seventies-style plywood chairs, the lava lamps, and the vintage turntable, all with the polite wonder of a tourist in an inferior city.

"Nice place," he said, aware that he was the only customer, and Diana the only visible employee. "Cool Eames replicas," he said, pointing to the ugly chairs.

"Thanks," she said, and wrote the name "Eames"

down on the back of a discarded receipt, to remind herself to look it up later.

God, he still looked good.

"Sorry I'm late," he said, smiling. "It's coming down out there."

When, after the photo shoot, Diana mentioned where she worked and he said that he'd come by, she hadn't actually expected him to, especially that day, but now that he was here, she was a bit chastened by her earlier insecurity. Of course Paul was a person of integrity who always did what he said he'd do; no doubt his parents were as well.

"Damn, it's cold in here, though," he said. "Aren't you cold?"

"Not really," she said, glancing around for something that would make her look busy.

"What were you reading?" he asked, and answered his own question by picking up the book. When he saw what it was, he smiled. "Oh, yeah, our teacher assigned this last week. Haven't started it yet. Do you have Pat Tilden for English?"

"No," Diana had to admit. Pat Tilden only taught honors and AP. "I just started it on my own," she said, and then she remembered that she worked there, and she was supposed to sell things, or at least be a good host. "Can I get you something?" she asked.

Paul's eyes searched the chalkboard menu. "Got any Chinese tea?"

"Let's see. We have an oolong."

"That works," he said, putting his hands in his jacket as he ambled over to check out the milk crates of vinyl. "Roberta Flack," he said, holding up the singer's **First Take** album. "My mom **loooooves** this one."

"Yeah, so did mine," Diana said. "My mom used to sing 'The First Time Ever I Saw Your Face' to me when I was little."

"That's cool. She still sing to you?"

"No." She took a deep breath. But she was almost used to saying this now. "My parents died in a car accident last summer."

Paul stood still and looked her in the eyes. "I'm sorry," he said.

"It's OK," Diana replied. Then they said nothing for a few seconds, because how do you end that conversation? Diana still had no idea. "Well, anyway," she said. "My mom had a nice singing voice." She pushed the steaming ceramic mug with its floating tea bag across the counter in his direction. "No charge," she said.

"Thanks." He put a five-dollar bill in the tip jar, which tied for first as the biggest tip she'd ever received.

She walked to the front door and moved the OPEN sign around to read CLOSED. "You can stay until you're done with the tea, I just need to start closing up," she said.

When she turned around, he was facing her.

"Hey, something you said kinda stuck with me. Why does someone with a perfect PSAT score not want to go to college?"

"There's a lot of reasons," she said, slowly wiping up the counter. "I don't need to go into debt, for one."

"I know college is expensive, but most people hardly ever pay the full sticker price. There's going to be some grants you're eligible for."

"Unless they can also help support my grandma, I don't think so. I don't know how much longer she can even work."

"You could get scholarships."

"Probably not with my grades."

Paul was unfazed. "You know, you can go to college, and get a degree, and get a good job, and then you could really help out your family."

It occurred to Diana in this moment that the richest kids in school might as well have been astronauts to her. Most of the time she would let them believe that they really lived in the same world, because it comforted them, and she didn't want people to feel bad or to do something out of charity that would imbalance their relationship.

She began to empty the baked goods display of unwanted cupcakes and muffins, wrapping them individually in cellophane. "I can't afford to wait that long. Do you know what I have to do now, just to help me and my grandma get by?"

"I don't. Would you like to tell me?"

"No, I wouldn't, actually. I don't think you'd understand."

"Why not?"

"I don't want to go into it," she said. On some level, she liked his patient curiosity, but it was also exhausting. "I'm sorry."

"OK," he said, taking a step backward. "I'm sorry, too."

She turned her back to him and turned on the sink full blast, passing the dirty cups and plates under the stream, trying to force her work to calm her down.

"You know, I don't know what I even did to ace that test or even if I could do it again if I tried. But it doesn't change anything. Not for me or my grandma. Not at all."

With the water running, she didn't hear the music begin, but when she turned the spigots off, she heard that Paul had put on Roberta Flack, and cued it up to "The First Time Ever I Saw Your Face."

She looked around the coffee shop just in time to see his hood go up and his body push open the door and vanish into the glimmering snow.

She was a little startled that he'd just left like that. Then again, he had tried to reach out to her, earnestly, and she'd pushed him away. A part of her wanted to run out there and tell him everything, burden him with the sad details of her life, just to see if he could handle it.

Instead, she leaned against the counter and just listened.

Diana had no memory of her mom singing to her. Still, she knew that her mom must've felt happy in that moment, and in her arms, hearing her mom's beautiful voice, she must've felt that no harm would ever come to her.

She hurled a wet sponge across the room at the record player to make it stop.

The next day, outside the cafeteria, Paul came up behind her. She'd been wondering all day when she'd see him again, and when she did, what he'd say, if anything.

"Hey," he said, smiling. "We're going to Chipotle. You want to come with?"

She was too surprised to say anything but the truth. "I'm supposed to have lunch with a friend."

"Oh, who? A dude?"

"No, just a friend, Clarissa."

"Clarissa Johnson?" Paul said, and laughed. "Oh, damn. Well, rain check then, I guess."

Diana sometimes took for granted that Clarissa commanded this kind of respect, but it also meant that someone like Clarissa would rarely have reason to feel abandoned or alone. Diana glanced into the cafeteria, and saw Clarissa and Ishaq seated across from each other in the corner, and Clarissa was laughing. "Ah, she won't mind."

Paul's best friends from his honors classes, Astra and James, who were rumored to be the smartest couple in the whole entire school, were waiting in the parking lot. They saw Paul and Diana approach from a distance, so Diana had a long time to watch Astra's confused expression. Except for her oxblood Docs, Astra was dressed entirely in black.

"This is Diana, who I told you about," Paul said to them.

"Aced the PSAT," Astra said. "Well, look at you."

Diana had seen Astra around in the hallways almost every day, and had never once seen her smile. Even now, around her best friends, her default expression clearly read, **I'm so fucking over this place and you people**. Diana was fascinated and a little scared of her, so in response, Diana just shrugged.

"Astra, be nice," Paul said.

"I **was** being nice," Astra said, taking out her iPhone. Before moving here, Diana had only ever met one teenager who'd had one of those. In Nicollet Falls they were no big deal.

"Hi," James said, and shook her hand. Compared to Astra, he was as intimidating as a puppy. His horn-rimmed glasses sat unevenly across his nose, and under his open North Face jacket she could see a throwback Red Owl T-shirt. "Nice to finally meet you."

Astra was still typing something on her phone. "Sorry, I know I'm being rude."

Paul frowned. "I don't even know if I want a phone," he said, and turned to Diana. "You have one?"

Sure, she had an old red Samsung flip phone, a Christmas gift from her dad, in a drawer at home, waiting until she could afford to connect it to a network again. "Yeah, but I need to get it fixed."

"Everyone's got one." Paul shook his head and started walking.

She let him lead the way through the bustling, noisy student parking lot, a place she'd never been to before, and she felt like she was crashing a party.

Paul had a cool car, a black Audi A4, and although it was kind of beat up—the rear bumper looked like it had endured multiple teenage drivers—the seats were leather and heated. She saw a long scratch in the shape of a Z on the passenger door as she opened it.

"What are you looking at?" Paul asked Diana, then followed her line of vision. "Oh, my brother Tim did that. He can't parallel park to save his ass."

Diana had never been to Chipotle before, and thought it was kind of expensive for what you got. Paul tried to buy her lunch, but she asked him not to, and reminded him that she had a job, and it was the only time they even came close to talking about what dominated their last conversation.

Diana wasn't sure what the smart kids were going to talk about, and was surprised that at first it was just like other school conversations she'd had. They complained about teachers, and were snarky about kids they disapproved of. They asked Diana about the non-honors classes and expressed sympathy like they were some kind of purgatory.

Then, someone brought up the books they were reading, and their hearts came out. These kids loved books, with the same honesty and fervor she did. They had opinions, arguments, counterarguments, and authors they'd pleaded with their teachers to include on reading lists. These kids also loved movies like she did, and everyone was shocked to find out that Diana had also seen virtually every sci-fi film to come out in the last thirty-five years, thanks to her grandpa Stanley. Having this particular common field of knowledge seemed inordinately meaningful to Paul and James, and it felt good to feel a sense of inclusion, to be told, in so many words, **You like the same things we like, Diana, so we like you**.

Only James and Diana finished their burritos. Astra and Paul each ate half of theirs and threw the rest in the trash.

"You weren't going to take it home for later?" Diana asked.

"I know it's wasteful," Paul said. "But I don't want a stinky-ass burrito in my locker for the rest of the day."

When they split up back at the school, Diana slowed her pace when she overheard Astra talking to Paul just behind her.

"Is this going to be like a one-time thing?" Astra asked him, her voice low.

"Only if she wants it to be," Paul said. "She's one of us."

"That's cool," Astra said, which surprised her.

Diana wasn't sure if she was meant to hear that or not, but it put tears in her eyes. Her whole life, she'd had individual friends, but she'd never really been **one of us**. Every time she'd been around a group, she was a hanger-on, an extra member, more tolerated than included. She wasn't quite comfortable with these kids yet, but she was pretty sure she liked them. And they wanted her. They somehow wanted Diana Winter.

Paul called out to Diana, "Same time tomorrow?"

"Sure," she said. She knew better than to ask them if they ate in the cafeteria, because she'd never seen them in there.

"Cool. Do you like Five Guys?"

"Never been."

"Wow." Paul seemed shocked, as if she'd told

him she'd never seen **Star Wars**. "Then you're definitely coming with."

But on the walk home that afternoon, she did the math in her head. She could spend what amounted to half of their monthly gas bill just on lunch, which she usually got for free. Or she could make new friends, smart, rich friends who seemed pretty nice. She could do that instead.

Three days before the awards luncheon, Diana woke up convinced that they'd made a mistake. She was 100 percent positive that the school was going to call her and say that they screwed up the results, and tell her that it was actually some kid in one of the honors classes who aced the PSAT. It didn't sound like such a bad thing, to be mediocre again, with all the wonderful ease and anonymity that went with being thought unspectacular.

Then again, Paul and Astra and James were unlike anyone she'd really hung out with before.

Only once in a while did things get awkward, like when Nate Ryan joined them the previous Friday. The honors social studies class was given the challenge of balancing the U.S. budget and coming to a complete unanimous consensus by Monday—something the school would never assign in a million years in a non-honors class—and he came along for lunch because they were still debating.

Once they crammed into Paul's car, Paul shoved a piece of paper at Nate across the back seat. "Look at how much revenue we could generate by reinstating the estate tax with the exemption set at one million. I did an estimate. Look."

"I'm OK with a death tax set at five million," Nate said. "But then, let's eliminate the SNAP program. Half the people on it are just ripping it off anyway."

"OK, fine," James said. "I'm OK with that if everyone else is."

They glanced at each other, clearly exhausted from arguing with this kid over the last hour, and said fine. Diana was shocked at the complete lack of debate over this. Of course, James would have had no idea that she was on SNAP, but Paul could've guessed she was, and for a second she was a little hurt that he said nothing. He just didn't know, she realized. He was a nice guy, and would've said something if he knew.

"Awesome," Nate said, writing something in a notebook. "Who's even on that program, anyway?"

On another planet, in another time, she'd say, **I am, motherfuckers.** She'd tell them all that only some tiny percentage of SNAP recipients are on the program fraudulently. She'd even say that maybe her family is arguably one of those, and still, they'd be struggling without it. But on this planet, in this time, she said nothing.

———————

She'd thought about inviting Paul over sometime, but after this incident, she decided to wait. Even so, for the first time since her parents died, she'd gone to bed at night thinking about a boy, thinking about Paul's face from the picture on the wall in school, next to hers. It felt good to think about him and imagine doing all kinds of things with him, but feeling that good made her feel guilty. She couldn't just move on to thinking about a boy when she was supposed to still be sad about her parents, and still was. And what kind of relationship could she even handle right now, anyway? And Paul might not even like her the same way. It was probably all pointless. But all this reasonable and unreasonable doubt couldn't stop her from thinking about him any more than she could stop the snow from falling.

The next morning, Diana was standing in the kitchen, eating Budget Value–brand Rice Crisps cereal out of the box, and thinking about Paul, wondering if he ate Rice Crisps for breakfast, or Rice Krispies, or egg whites and yogurt, or if his was the kind of family that bought Rice Crisps but put them in a Rice Krispies box. She put the cereal away in the cupboard, on the same shelf as the salt—just so one shelf had two things on it, which looked better—when she heard a soft tapping at the front door. It was so timid, Diana opened the door without even looking through the eyehole.

It was Jan Fruechte, a neighbor from down the hall who worked as a waitress at Perkins. She was the sort of person who waved at Diana and said hi to her no matter how far she was down the hall or across the parking lot. She was also single mother to a pissy fifteen-year-old girl named Tricia who was famous for both getting banned from Target for shoplifting and for almost drowning in the lake. She was saved when her mom gave her mouth-to-mouth and the whole thing was kind of the big event of the summer, turning Tricia Fruechte from a kind of normal, nondescript girl into "the girl who almost drowned."

"That's the second time I gave her life," Jan was quoted as saying in the paper, and Tricia dressed and carried herself like she'd resented every breath on earth since.

"Oh, hi," Jan said, remaining outside, her back to the morning darkness. She was carrying a plastic bag that had a three-prong power cord sticking out of it. "I'm glad it was you who answered. I just wanted to thank you for all of the muffins and cupcakes you've been bringing over."

"It's no problem," Diana said, because it wasn't. "You want to come in?"

"I have something to ask you," Jan said, holding the bag open. Diana looked into it and saw a black Acer laptop and extension cord. "Do you need a computer for college? I just won a new computer in a drawing at work, and if you didn't have one, I'd like to know if you'd like to buy it for ninety bucks."

"Oh," Diana said. She'd never owned a computer in her life.

"It's practically brand-new, and has the internet and everything. It's the least we could do to thank you, is give you a deal on it."

"I don't know if I can swing ninety bucks," Diana said.

"Seventy, then," she said, and Diana knew then that Jan needed money for some awful reason, and wondered if it was even true about winning the drawing.

Less than a minute later, Diana owned a computer, and it instantly became the most valuable thing that she possessed.

Everyone in the building got the internet from a bearded rando named Rolf Peterson, who changed his Wi-Fi password every month and charged people five bucks for access to it. He was probably pulling in way more than whatever his bill was, but it was still kind of a public service, and one that Diana had pretty much been without, outside of school.

She ran five bucks up to Rolf Peterson's place and it occurred to her as she handed the money over that, if she wanted to continue to do what she'd been doing, she now didn't literally need

Clarissa's help anymore. If she had to keep doing it, she could go into business for herself.

"It's a sign from the Lord," her grandma said, and while lots of things were signs from the Lord to Edith, Diana was frankly relieved that her grandma didn't force her to bring the computer back to Jan. "Maybe this is God's way of saying that you can take online classes if you want to go to college."

Although Diana believed in God, she didn't share Edith's belief in a personal, interventionist God—not that she was about to wedge this argument into a discussion about the merit of online degree programs. "I'm lucky that Jan thought of me," she said.

"You're not lucky," Edith said. "Gamblers are lucky. You're blessed."

The phone rang; it was Brett Victor, the mechanic. He'd been kind enough to keep Edith's car in his lot for free until Diana could afford to pay him for the repairs, but he'd taken forever to get back to her. It took so long for her grandma to get to her jobs in this weather, she'd been late twice, and Diana hated imagining her grandma walking over a mile every day just to get to the bus, crossing iced-over highways on foot during blizzards.

Brett Victor told Diana that the belts and hoses were shot in addition to the transmission and that he had a revised estimate, $1,300.

"You know, it hardly makes sense to put that kind of money into this vehicle," Brett said. "I know a guy who's selling his Eagle Talon for three hundred bucks. It's got some rust on it, and the radio's busted, but it's a runner."

"I'll think about it," Diana said. Edith loved her Toyota, the first car she'd bought herself with her own money, and Diana wanted to restore it, not replace it. Even if it took almost all of the money left from her scheme with Clarissa. After this, she'd have thirty-five bucks left until she got paid next Friday. But this is what all that work was for.

"Who was that?" Edith asked as Diana hung up the phone.

"We're fixing your car, Grandma."

"That's nice," Edith said, and for a moment, she looked relaxed.

Clarissa came up to Diana's locker before the start of school that day, alone.

"Yo, I've hardly seen you lately," she said.

"I know, I've been taking a break from our thing for a while," Diana said.

"That's cool." She nodded. For a moment she was surprised that Clarissa seemed to be taking it well. "Things have been kinda weird, anyway. My parents are finally getting divorced."

"I'm sorry," Diana said, and meant it.

"Don't be, it's years overdue," Clarissa said, and

put on a pair of sunglasses. Was she crying? In school? Diana almost didn't know what to do. She hadn't even comforted anyone since before her parents died. She wasn't sure if she had it in her.

She saw Clarissa take a deep breath.

"Can I hug you?" Diana asked.

"Dude, not here," Clarissa said, and nodded. "But yeah."

They walked for a couple minutes to what everyone called "the dope smokers' fence" on the edge of school property. A couple of sophomore boys were there, smoking dope, but they miraculously let the girls pass by without comment.

"How about here?" Diana asked after they walked another twenty feet down the fence.

"Yeah, please," Clarissa said. She started sobbing, really sobbing, the second that Diana touched her. For a moment, Diana couldn't wrap her head around why—Clarissa hated her parents—but it didn't matter.

Clarissa took off her sunglasses and wiped her face. "What are **you** crying for?" she asked Diana.

"What?" Diana asked. She was crying? She felt her cheeks, and yeah, she was. For the first time in months, she was.

"Oh, duh," Clarissa said, slapping herself on the head. "I can't believe I forgot."

Diana sat on the ground, wiping her face, trying not to sob. "Me neither," she said.

Clarissa glanced over at the boys. "Want me to beat up those kids and steal their drugs?"

Diana laughed a little bit, but then shook her head, and started bawling.

"Dude." Clarissa sat next to Diana. "We gotta do this more often."

On their walk back to the school, long after the first bell, they agreed to quit doing "their garage thing," and Clarissa seemed relieved, which surprised Diana. It turns out that the money Clarissa was supposed to be saving up to move out she'd spent on clothes, and now that her parents were selling the house and she was less than six months from college anyway, there was less of a point, on her end.

"It was your idea," Diana said.

"Yeah, but you're the one who really needs the money."

It was true, especially now that she was paying for a restaurant lunch almost every day, but she felt ashamed to admit that was one of the reasons why. "Well, Edith and I did OK before," Diana said. "If there aren't any emergencies, I think we can scrape by."

"I wasn't even talking about that," Clarissa

said. "I like your new friends. They're a real sharp bunch of nerds. James is gonna be the next Bill Gates, seriously. But they're all gonna be famous after they get outta here. And that Paul Jeffrey's a total hottie."

"Yeah, they're nice," Diana said.

"But two of them live on my street. Or what's about to be my old street. Money ain't nothing to them. I hope they're treating you."

"I don't want them to."

"I get it, believe me," Clarissa said, and held open the heavy school door. "But I thought you were supposed to be smart."

The morning of the luncheon, Diana added up all of her lunch receipts from Chipotle and Five Guys and Culver's and Pizza Ranch. She sentimentally kept them, like other kids did with ticket stubs from concerts. $92.27. This was an incredible amount of money. She knew she still had enough from the garage scheme to help her grandma cover the bills this month, but seeing that number chastened her.

If she were more like Clarissa, she would have instead bought an extremely nice pair of shoes to go with her awards-luncheon outfit; after putting on the best Mossimo dress her mom bought her at Target—which luckily she still fit into—it hit her how old and crappy-looking her pumps were. They were also tight and stupidly uncomfortable to walk in, even more than usual. It had been so long since she needed to wear semiformal shoes that she didn't even think about getting a cheap new pair, and now, an hour before the event, there was no time.

Edith had done what she said she'd do, and left her car keys, but after everything that Diana had done to fix that car, she didn't want to run any unnecessary risks. She'd only driven it twice since she got her license and she'd be damned if she were the one to send it to the shop again. She could've called Paul for a ride but she still wasn't ready for him to see where she lived yet. Besides, the Country Club was only two miles away. She could walk that distance easily. She tossed her pumps in her bag and put on her sneakers.

Even with snow covering parts of the sidewalks, it was a pleasant walk, crossing a highway and a frontage road, following an old state route toward where the larger houses were, past the high school, and into the realm of curvy roads and large yards. As she got closer to where the Country Club was, the sidewalks vanished, and she felt the dirty slush on the roadside swim into her sneakers and grab her toes. The smell of something nice, maybe cedar smoke, floated from one of the homes she passed.

As she walked by a giant brick home on the corner, she watched a short, clean-cut, middle-aged guy with a nice sweater, in the mouth of his open garage, leaping at the handle of a garage door that had stalled out just beyond his reach.

Diana stumbled her way from the roadside, across the man's yard, and onto his clean concrete driveway, past his shiny silver Audi sports car. She noticed that the man was around four inches shorter than her—not terribly unusual, as Diana was five foot ten—and he was extremely tan for this time of year.

"Let me help you," she said, and walked past him, where she saw that, indeed, the man was too short to reach the point where his garage door had stopped. Diana also noticed right away that the garage was full of expensive bicycles and fishing poles. She saw the box for a Bosch laser level on a shelf against the back wall, and a Skil saw below it. Four, maybe five hundred dollars for all this, easy.

She gave the garage door a strong yank, and the door rattled firmly to the ground.

"Hey, thanks," the man said, smiling at Diana, and then Diana remembered that she was wearing nice clothes and her mom's old jewelry, and maybe looked like someone better off than she was, even.

He in no way appeared nervous to have a stranger like her on his property.

"The damn automatic door just quit working," he said, as if she hadn't figured that out already, and extended his hand. "Appreciate the help. I'm Frank Schabert."

"I'm Diana Winter," she said, releasing the handshake first.

"Well, Diana, you just let me know if I can do anything for you," Frank Schabert said, and smiled at her. "Young people like you are a dying breed."

$40,000

Helen, 1965

Thirty minutes after the last final exam of her junior year, Helen was lying on her bed, having decided not to pack until her father came to get her, when she was called to the phone. It was Edith, and she was sobbing. She said that their mother had died that morning of a heart attack, and Stanley was driving down now to pick up Helen and drive her home.

This was impossible. Her mom hadn't even had a cold in over a decade. She didn't have the time for that crap. More than that, she was too self-righteous, pious, and nosy to die. She was going to live as long as she cared to, and probably outlive them all just so she could have the last word. That seemed to be the plan.

When Helen asked about the funeral, Edith replied with what she called an extremely important question.

"Can you please talk about Mom at the service? I don't want to be the only one. I know you two didn't always get along, but it would mean a lot to me."

That was an understatement. They hadn't gotten along since Helen was old enough to form sentences. That seemed to be the breaking point in their relationship. Helen's oldest mental image of anything was of her mom slapping her butt with a wooden spoon, telling her to be quiet when adults were talking.

"I don't know," Helen said. "I'll think about it."

After she hung up, another memory came to mind.

When Helen was nine years old, she set out to make a pie for the first time. The church was having a midsummer fundraiser bake sale, and there were prizes, so it seemed like an ideal competitive venue to test her abilities. She set out alone early one morning, into the marshy forest on the edge of their property that hid the best blackberry bushes from everyone but the deer. She brought home only the ripest ones, and set to work on a pie intended to blow the hats off of people.

She was going to make her own crust, the same way that she'd seen Edith do it countless times already, and was thinking of how to improve on her sister's methods, taking into account the warm summer temperature in the kitchen. She was putting the rolling pin and a mixing bowl in the refrigerator when her mom appeared behind her.

"Go outside and help your father," her mother said.

"I'm making a pie," Helen said, closing the refrigerator door.

"I can see that," her mother nodded. "That's what Edith does. You can do something else."

"Yeah, but I think I can do it even better than Edith."

"I know you could. But then you'll make it into a competition and it won't be fun for her anymore. So get on out of here."

None of this made any sense, so Helen kept working, finding a measuring cup and walking it to the fridge. "But I've already started."

"Sometimes I wish I wasn't blessed with a daughter who's good at everything," her mother said, holding the fridge door shut. "Please, give Edith this one thing." She then touched Helen on the shoulder, which typically only happened when Helen was in trouble. It didn't seem like that, this time. Her mother's tone was milder, but what was happening now was worse than punishment, to Helen.

"She'll still be good at it," Helen said. "It's just one pie."

Her mother walked toward the mudroom door and yanked it open. "Go outside right now," she said, in a tone that made Helen run into the yard just so she wouldn't have to hear it again.

A day later, Edith came home from the church fundraiser with a red ribbon for her blackberry pie, her spirit aloft with fresh praise.

"Well, look at that," their father said to Edith, who smiled. "We got an award-winning baker in the family."

"Don't let it go to your head," their mother said. "The more you blow into your balloon, the easier it's popped."

"Well, I like to see a Calder with a ribbon," their father said to Edith. "Your grandpa Pete used to win ribbons for his hogs."

Helen almost said that she could've won the **blue** ribbon, had she been allowed to enter a pie, but Edith spoke first.

"I couldn't have done it without Helen," Edith said. "She picked the blackberries and did all that work." Edith pulled a pair of scissors out of a drawer in the kitchen and began to cut the ribbon.

This was bizarre, Helen thought. "Edie!" she yelled. "You're ruining it!"

"Here you go," Edith said, handing her sister half of her prize.

As weird and boring as her sister could be, she was so kind and thoughtful. But Helen also knew right then it would've never occurred to her to halve a ribbon she won, were she to win one. Her eyes and hands trembled with shame at being proven so selfish, and then she saw her mother grinning at her.

"What do you think about what your sister just did?"

"I don't know," Helen said, looking at the floor, holding the limp fabric like it was a dead pet.

"You wouldn't have done this if you'd won, would you?" her mother asked.

"No," Helen said, and then lifted her head. "But I can't help it."

"That's why you will stay out of the kitchen." Her mother nodded. "And that's why you shouldn't win."

Helen knew right then that her aspirations would have a mortal enemy, right there under the same roof. She couldn't ever trust her mother with her honest desires again, and would regret it the few times she did.

Now her mother was gone, and she couldn't think of anything to say about her that'd be appropriate for a funeral.

Her mom wasn't a hard person to talk about, if you didn't know her. Outside the family, she was thought of as a sweet, simple Lutheran woman who never drank, never swore, and never wanted more than she had. People who hardly knew her called her a saint, so it seemed by her mother's design that she had few friends and a lot of acquaintances.

At the service, Edith charmed the crowd with cute, saccharine remembrances and a couple of tears. At the time, Helen had no store of either. She gave a short, euphemistic talk about how her mother made her who she is today, and not a word of it was a lie.

Edith had agreed to move back to the farm with her husband, Stanley, and their kids and help out their dad, but within a year, she was quickly overwhelmed by caring for a grieving parent, a husband, and two small children, while helping manage the hired hands and keeping both the house and farm running.

Their mom hadn't ever prepared Edith to work outside on the actual farm she was raised on. Unless it was detasseling season, the fields were just something pretty for Edith to look at while she washed, cooked, and cleaned in the house.

Although Stanley knew his way around an engine OK for a city boy, neither he nor Edith knew their way around a struggling corn, alfalfa, barley, and beef cattle operation, or, more impenetrably, a heartbroken old farmer. Still, Helen would've predicted that faithful, solid Edith would stay with their cranky, disoriented dad until the end.

During Easter weekend of Helen's senior year, she called home, and the usual light conversation with her sister turned unexpectedly meaningful.

"Hellie, I have to tell you something," Edith said, with the hesitation in her voice of a polite child afraid to ask for ice cream. "Stanley has a friend in New Stockholm who just offered him a trucking job."

"Cool," Helen said. It didn't make a lot of sense, though. New Stockholm was at least a two-hour drive from the farm. "What are you gonna do, sell the farm and take Dad with you?" If that's what Edith planned, Helen would be shocked, because that would actually be a good idea.

"What? Oh geez, no. We're never selling the farm. And Dad's never going to leave it, either. Literally, he won't leave it. He won't even go up to Pine City anymore, he says there's too much traffic."

"So, what are you saying then?"

"Well, I'm just saying that Stanley's been offered

a good job in a place with good schools. But Dad's not doing so well, you know. Don't know if it's still that summer cold, or what."

Helen wasn't sure if their dad had something worse than a cold, because he wouldn't let anyone take him to the doctor, but from looking at him, it seemed plausible that something was seriously wrong with him. It was also plausible that if Edith wasn't there, the old man would be eating corned beef out of a can for every supper, maybe do laundry once a year, and go to the bathroom outside just to avoid cleaning the toilet. As hard as her dad worked outdoors, there were many indoor chores in that big house she'd bet he'd never done once.

"You want me to come up for a while?" She actually couldn't, at least until she finished school, but it was expected in her family to offer sacrifices like this.

"Oh no, you can't do that. You got your graduation, and then the wedding and honeymoon, and then you need to get settled. You gotta let me know how I can help you, for your wedding."

"No, Edie, that's fine."

"Oh, hold on just a sec. Let me find the number of the woman who did our flowers."

Helen couldn't remember whether Edith's wedding even had flowers. She just remembered what it didn't have. "OK, sure," Helen said, because her sister would go crazy if she didn't think she was helping with something.

Truthfully, Helen didn't give a shit about the flowers, the band, the photographer, or even the food, but she'd lost sleep over what beer to serve. Orval wanted his favorite, but she said nope, because she had tried Coors by then. She hated to say it, but after all that build-up, she was a tad bit disappointed.

After sampling over two dozen lagers, she decided to brew her own beer, and made it a little on the strong side. At the wedding, it pleasantly distracted everyone, which was ideal, because Helen's dad looked terrible. He gave a sad, rambling dinner speech, fell asleep during the minister's homily, and could hardly finish the father-daughter dance, even to a song by the Andrews Sisters, his favorites.

On the last night of their honeymoon at Lutsen, Helen and Orval were at the lodge, where, over a couple cold glasses of Schmidt, Orval admitted that they still needed another thirty-five grand to get the Blotz Brewery going again. He hated asking her, but did she know anyone? He'd been even more proactive than she'd hoped, securing loans and raising money from relatives nonstop since he had finished the business plan. It was harder than they thought to start a brewery in this competitive market, and it couldn't happen out of their garage.

This wasn't rock 'n' roll, it was beer, and beer was big business.

"Your old neighbors with the dairy farm, maybe?" Orval asked. "Even a few thousand would be something."

"Not them," Helen replied.

She'd known the emergency answer to their money question for a long time, and while she always hoped it wouldn't come to pass, she'd lately come to accept its inevitability. There was one person on earth who'd always helped her, and while it might cost him everything to do so now, he probably still would, if he believed they'd earned it.

"How'd you like to live a lot closer to our ingredients?" she asked her husband.

That September, two months after Helen helped Edith pack for New Stockholm and replaced her as their father's caretaker, Helen sat her dad down in the kitchen of their family's creaky old farmhouse, and poured him a glass of her latest batch of pale lager, a new recipe, made from bottom-fermenting yeast, hops, malted barley, and a little bit of corn.

"This is what we were talking about, Dad," she told him, watching his skinny arm lift the glass to his ashen face. This was a guy who once won $5 in a bale-throwing contest, a guy who used to lift his daughters in the air and ask them if they could see Canada, and they truly believed they could.

"Oh," he said, and took a sip.

"What do you think?"

She honestly had no idea what he'd say. Her father survived a hard enough life without the knowledge that the family farm, which the Calders had owned for over a hundred years, would be sold in his lifetime. He'd expected to die in the only house he'd ever lived in, like his father and grandfather had. It was a house big enough for a dozen people, and in the past, he'd openly wondered if their failure to fill it would one day cause their failure to keep it.

Their family was supposed to be so much larger, like the other farm families they'd known, but Momma's womb was fussy and killed all the boys, half the girls, and a few undecideds. His heirs were two daughters, neither of whom wanted to farm, nor married men who did. And now one of these daughters was asking him to leave it all, every cent, to her. Not out of malice or anger to the other, but just because one had a plan and the other didn't.

Helen planned to call Edith and tell her. It wouldn't be easy for Edith to hear that the farm would be sold and she'd see none of the money from the sale, but it wouldn't be easy for Helen to tell her, either. Helen could certainly pay her back later, the minute she could afford to. She'd make that promise, for sure. It was honestly heartbreaking, but there was just no way they could open their brewery, otherwise. In this farm, there was enough value to sustain the Calder family and keep them among society's producers, but only if it was completely allocated to Helen. She wouldn't have put it in those terms, but that's how her father understood it.

Edith's just going to take her half of this place and fritter it away, her father concluded, a month after Helen and Orval moved in. Helen was going to create and contribute, not just take and spend. That, to him, meant that his legacy and family had not just a chance to survive, but a chance to grow. A chance to develop wealth, which he'd never been able to do. He just had to try the beer they were making, to make sure he liked it, and wanted it the minute it was ready, which was today.

"What the hell?" her dad said, setting the glass down. "This is it?"

Helen took a deep breath.

She'd become used to this new tone; the breakdown of his body had shrunken and bruised his spirit like an unpicked apple. He was often angry now, and she understood why. This man, who'd worked harder than anyone she'd ever met, every day of his life—because "cows don't take vacation days, and beetles, borers, and cutworms don't either"—was not meant to be sitting on his ass all day, and that, much more than anything else in his blood, was killing him. It wasn't personal.

"Yeah, that's it, Dad." She took a breath, but didn't know why she was so nervous. She knew what she was capable of doing. "This is the beer we're going to make the most popular Minnesota-made beer in Minnesota."

"It tastes practically the same as everything else."

"You mean that?" Helen smiled. "Really?"

"Yeah, to me, there's no goddamned difference," he said, and took another sip. "I thought your big plan was to make a better beer."

"We will," she said. "But first, to make our mark, we're making a less expensive beer. Five cents a can cheaper."

"Cheaper? Then people are just going to assume it's lower quality. Beer isn't gasoline." He rose and reached forward just to push the beer glass toward Helen. "Tell Orval that if he wants to make cheap beer, what does he need all that money for?"

"He didn't make it, Dad," she said. "I told you, I did."

"Huh. I always assumed **your** beer would be better. What about the beer you made for your wedding? That was good."

"That was ale, and nobody makes a living selling ale. Nobody in Minnesota, anyway. This is what we have to make to start a brewery."

"I'm not saying it's God-awful." Her dad frowned. "I'm just saying there's nothing special about it."

She noticed the paint peeling on the windowsill. One more thing she wouldn't get to.

"Well, maybe I over-hopped it."

"You should've used Kenny's hops." She had no idea why that was so important to him.

"I'm not using ditch hops, Dad. And I suppose I should also try a different barley."

"What the hell's wrong with my barley?"

"It's two-row Svansota, and I like six-row." Helen loved to see the confused expression on her father's face. "Higher diastatic power, more beta amylase, better for American-style lagers."

He looked at her as if she was a Soviet newspaper. "What does all that mean?"

"It means more food for the yeast to make the alcohol."

"Where did you even learn this?" Now he seemed kind of amused.

"Practice." She looked at his empty glass. "Next time, I'll use different barley, I'll use less hops, I'll make it even better."

He stared out the kitchen window to the west, at his tall grass and dry fields, the sun in his eyes. "I hope so. Just don't get too fancy."

The next day, he drank another glass of her lager, and afterward, without telling her, called their family's lawyer.

Into the following year, Helen and Orval continued feeding, changing, and bathing her father, acclimating to the occasions of his incontinence, putting him to bed, and getting him up. She was there for the most helpless ten months of his life since the first ten, and the whole time he fought against it, like a giant, bony, furious baby. There were moments of peace, like an evening in late April when it was warm enough to drink a beer and watch the sun set from the porch. He wasn't much for saying **I love you**, but that night when he sipped his beer and said, "Thank you, Helen," that's what she heard.

On May 21, 1967, he passed at 2:22 in the afternoon, sitting in his chair in the living room, staring out the leaded glass of the picture window. She was with him the minute he died, but as she gazed upon his uninhabited body, she realized that she'd been grieving his death long before it happened. He left that skin and those bones behind early because he knew what was to come, Helen believed at the time, and from her father's point of view, she'd be proved right.

For starters, had doctors or medicine forced him to live longer, he would've despised what the world around him became, because, among other things, he hated chain stores, pharmaceuticals, and bankers. He claimed to have spent one hour in 1948 trying to think like a banker and he said it was the closest he'd come to suicide. To him, a farm wasn't a thumbtack on a wall map or a spot on a supply chain. Some years, shit just happens, and bankers don't like it when shit happens, but they never cared to understand why it did, and why sometimes it had to. If he had more patience with people who had no patience, he might have died a richer man, but instead he died an uncompromised one, one of the last Helen knew.

So, everything he owned didn't add up to a lot; most of the equipment was leased or not fully paid for, and while most of the vehicles, crops, and livestock more or less paid off debts, they'd receive money from selling the land, and the best offer they got was from a man named Carl Lead, $200 an acre, for two hundred acres. They were lucky that their great-great-grandpa George Jacob Calder, leading his family north, broke his leg at this latitude, the lawyer said. A farm farther up in Pine County the same size had sold earlier that year for half as much.

At the time, Helen felt bad that she couldn't spare even one dime from the farm sale to give to Edith. Starting a brewery was foolishly expensive, and Edith's truck driver husband seemed to be supporting his family just fine—it wasn't like they were starving.

Helen braced herself for her planned conversation with her sister. Helen guessed that Edith would be a bit passive-aggressive for about a week and then get over it and move on and never talk about it again, just as Edith did with everything else that hurt or confused her. Perhaps Edith wouldn't be upset. Perhaps Edith would even approve.

"I really, really want Edith to be happy," she told Orval that night in bed. "But I know we can't do this otherwise."

"She'll understand, won't she?" Orval asked, turning on his side.

"I think so," Helen said, and stared at the popcorn ceiling while Orval began to snore. She stared sleeplessly until he stopped, and until he began to snore again.

The next morning, Helen called Edith's house, and let it ring once before she hung up and decided to write a letter instead. If she'd inherited a ribbon, she told herself, she'd be the one cutting it in half this time without a second thought, but this wasn't a ribbon, this was a key—the sole and crucial key—to the best chance Helen would ever have to achieve her dreams. She explained that it was what their father wanted, and also that, someday, Edith would still see her inheritance, if she could be patient. Helen had chosen a brutal industry to break into, and lean times awaited her. **For quite a while, maybe several years,** Helen wrote, **you're going to be the rich one, Edith.**

When Helen didn't hear a thing back from her sister, she wasn't shocked. But a week became a month, which became six months, which became a year. Somewhere in there, the busiest, most stressful year of Helen's life, Helen realized that Edith had stopped speaking to her. Early on, she wondered if she could pop by with a six-pack of beer, but even back then, it seemed wrong to make the first move. Edith was clearly upset and needed to work through it, Orval said, just give her time.

After a while, it had been so long, the silence became something Helen wasn't inclined to disturb. Forgiveness must be offered, not demanded, and Edith would indeed forgive her, Helen was convinced. For a long time, she believed it would happen any day now, until that belief was shuffled among the dozens of other problems she was powerless to solve alone.

Helen and Orval couldn't have known this, because no one would tell them, but the baby boom generation turned out to be the worst time since Prohibition to start a brewery. Reliable institutions like Fitger's and Hauenstein were now going the way of the aspic salad. Helen and Orval quickly found out they weren't too small themselves to be considered a target in dozens of Mergers & Acquisitions–department meetings. Every year, they were offered money from these chumps, but they didn't devote nearly every resource they could muster into their brewery just to start again from scratch, or worse, work for some snake-faced dweeb who'd rather be golfing.

They knew their scheme to brew a budget-friendly lager during a hypercompetitive era of industry consolidation wasn't going to put them in a mansion overnight. Still, they didn't imagine that they'd have to move into their own brewery. At the very least, their drafty old buildings were located in scenic Point Douglas, at the spot where the sparkling St. Croix River loses its fortune against the merciless bluffs of the Mississippi. Orval liked it because they could see Wisconsin from his office. And now, Wisconsin could see him back, shirtless, brushing his teeth, scratching his crotch in the morning sun.

One morning, they sat in their scarves and hats on the floor, eating another breakfast of Quaker Oats with glasses of watered-down orange juice from concentrate. Those are the details she remembered from those years; the glop of a cylinder of orange paste into a pitcher; the pasty color and mealy smell of plain oats and water.

She couldn't take another bite, and dropped her spoon into the bowl. "That's it," she said.

"That's what?" Orval asked, his mouth full.

"That's it," she repeated. "Today I'm going to try something."

By that year, there were only 110 breweries in the entire country, and falling. Due to the consolidation, competition, and, at the time, no apparent incentives for novelty or innovation, Blotz Brewery's hopes for survival into 1976 and beyond seemed hopelessly grim. With their business probably months from total collapse, she thought back to her father's advice, **Don't get fancy**, and decided to take it one step further.

She made her beer worse.

Although Helen couldn't afford to eat out, she was still attentive to culinary trends, and couldn't ignore that the 1970s were ushering in a new wave of what people called "health food." After her generation had been told they'd live better through chemistry, they were, for now at least, caring about what they put in their bodies.

Of course, a lot of them didn't actually want to change what they'd been putting in their bodies. This was why Helen was intrigued by a new product Miller was marketing called Lite. Almost everyone was sure that it'd be a bust, and no one would swap less flavor and alcohol for fewer calories, because, in her husband's words, the people who drank beer don't give a shit about calories. It didn't help that, so far, the story of "light beer" in America was a tragedy—just ask Meister Brau, Lithia, Old Export, August Wagner, or Rheingold. That's why Miller was alone on that mountain. But the time was right for this risk in a way it hadn't been in the 1960s, and Blotz was in a wonderful position for a brewery: they were about to lose everything anyway.

Helen found out that light adjunct lager is one of the most difficult kinds of beer to make. It's a tightrope of chemistry, skill, and precision where there's a right way to do things and massive opportunity for failure. The sterilization and filtering alone were next-level. She also had no clue what exactly Miller was throwing into Lite, but she assumed she could teach herself a similar workable recipe. The crucial key was probably adding an extra alpha-amylase enzyme, to turn more of those residual carbohydrates into fermentable sugars. Anyone else with a bachelor's in chemistry, a farm-reared work ethic, and working knowledge of brewing properties and practices could have figured this out. This meant that she had to get started immediately.

"Can't you just add water to it?" Orval asked her, after she showed him the recipe she'd devised.

She hoped he was joking. "Come downstairs with me, Orval, and help me save our damn company."

They were up until one in the morning, first mashing the pilsner malt for hours to create the most fermentable, lowest-gravity wort. They hadn't worked together like this in years. They rolled up their sleeves and got dirty together and Orval said that she looked sexy in safety goggles and she told him she'd like to see him in a hard hat and gloves and nothing else.

Throughout her youth, Helen had never thought too highly of what people called love. After all, since puberty, she'd seen people furiously throw their brains, hearts, and other vulnerable organs in and out of love with baseless alacrity. She'd seen her ex-roommate Tippi let the idea of love ruin her diet, grades, and ability to enjoy life. Helen had repeatedly advised Tippi that the quality of every day wasn't to be judged on its potential for massive, consequential, interpersonal romance. Love was just a rationale for boundless drama and error, she'd cynically declared. Still, like most cynics, she wanted to be wrong. And now, here she was, falling madly in love, eight years into her marriage.

Helen hoped that didn't sound mean to say.

Sure, Helen had loved Orval, in many ways, for a long time, but most of all, Helen loved knowing she wasn't alone in this. As strongly as she believed that she could do it all by herself if she had to, no part of her ever wished to. Orval was more than brand equity and real estate and a respected, friendly man who could open doors in the man's world of brewing. He wanted what she wanted, and the moments when he helped enable their shared dreams is when she felt, finally, the kind of love everyone on the radio sang about.

They were up for three more hours after the grind, sweating with blind hope and ecstatic focus, like gamblers at a blackjack table. Orval finally went to bed during the boil, after he threw a tiny smidge of hops extract into the tank. She stayed up to pitch the yeast, cooled the wort to 50 degrees Fahrenheit, crawled into bed naked, woke up her husband, and kept that boy up as long as she wanted.

After twenty-nine total days of fermentation and lagering, and then the most intense filtration she'd ever done, Helen poured Orval a glass of what looked like a healthy person's urine sample but smelled kind of like beer.

Her husband was in his office, gazing at the leaves changing color in Wisconsin as he took his first-ever drink of light beer. "What do you think?" she asked him.

He stared into the glass, eyebrows raised. "It's more like beer than I thought."

"I know, weird, huh?"

He threw back the rest in one gulp. "Well, that was easy," he said. "What's the alcohol by weight?"

"Three point three," she said. "Not the lowest, but down there."

"Christ," Orval said. "Some people will have to drink at least three of these to feel anything."

"You're goddamn right," Helen said.

A short drive from the brewery, there was a restaurant called The Point, a small but quality supper club and bar, beloved by Helen because their taps poured more Blotz Premium Lager than any other establishment on earth. From the bartender's point of view, the beer's sales pitch seemed to be that "it's brewed right down the road, follow the smell." Of the five beers on tap at the time, it was also the cheapest by twenty-five cents, so it had earned a loyal following among the kinds of drunks who tipped the bartenders the difference, when they tipped at all.

In fall 1975, with the economy lurching like a sick carnival pony, multiple women trying to kill the president, and the country whipped by inflation, a lot of people were worried about money. Beer coupons weren't illegal yet in Minnesota, and with that help, Blotz earned a slight uptick in sales. Maybe Blotz would've actually survived that year just based on the improving numbers of the value-priced flagship product alone. The world will never know.

That Sunday, she convened the two other people who comprised their new in-house advertising team. One was their smart, well-dressed, good-looking financial manager, Joe Foxworth, and the other was Orval. They sat in a corner at The Point's dark wooden bar, where the people who knew them left them alone. The Minnesota Vikings were on TV in the background, crushing the Cleveland Browns, and most everyone in the crowded room was in a good mood. Helen was in a good mood because Joe Foxworth had bought her the Surf & Turf. He came from money, like Orval once had, only Joe had the good sense to not spend it all on opening a brewery.

"OK," Joe Foxworth said. "It's a mild beer, right? So how about: 'Blotz, it's the mildest.'"

"No," Helen frowned. "Sounds like a cigarette ad." A buddy of Orval's from high school, Joe was also here not only because he managed the purse strings, but also because he had a little experience in sales and marketing, before he became a CPA. He claimed he loved to write slogans and ad copy, so Helen expected him to deliver.

"Then we'll call attention to some arbitrary detail, like the fact that it's in a can. 'Blotz: It's in the can.'"

"No," Helen said. "That's fine for the regular Blotz, but this new beer actually **is** different."

"I know, it's **light**. So it's a diet beer."

"Been done, failed."

"Then what else does a light beer mean to the average drinker?"

She began to worry that maybe Joe hadn't struggled enough in life to develop any real sense of ingenuity. "It means you can drink a lot of them, and not get hammered."

Orval just appeared to be staring off into space.

"Are we not holding your interest?" Helen asked him.

"'Drink lots,'" Orval said. "'It's Blotz.'"

"What?" she asked.

"'Drink lots, it's Blotz.'"

"Sure," Joe said, before she could speak. "I like it."

As that four-word phrase fell onto Helen's consciousness like a zeppelin landing on a kidney bean, she didn't feel anything, exactly. She **saw** something. She saw it on billboards. TV ads. Magazine spreads. Bus benches. T-shirts. Ballcaps. For years. And years.

"Orval, my fire, my angel," Helen said, grabbing

his head in her hands. "Do you know what this means?"

"What?" Orval said.

"It means that we could be doing this for the rest of our lives."

On November 30, 1975, Blotz put its first commercially viable batch of Blotz Special Light into the world, in what now would be called a "soft release" and back then was just called "pussyfooting." The undefeated Vikings were on the road in Washington, D.C., that afternoon, and down by one point on the last play of regulation, then committed the signature Vikings move, losing the game on a blocked field goal. The chance for a perfect season scuttled, the fans drank more than usual that day, as they always do after a close loss, and something meant to be consumed in quantity was waiting for them, its new slogan goading them on.

Helen and Orval took out a small loan to help buy ad space and produce local spots, and even if it would suck up over half the funds, Orval was convinced they needed a celebrity pitchman. This is where Joe Foxworth proved his value.

"Hey, I know a guy," he told Helen one afternoon, running up to her as she was leaving the bathroom. "My brother's freshman-year roommate at

Augustana was in training camp with the Vikings. His name's Rud Herzog. He says he'd do it."

Helen wasn't really listening, so she was impressed. "You have a friend on the Vikings?"

"Well, he didn't make the team. But he lasted until the final cuts."

"Oh. So he's not actually on the team, then."

"No, but he's a big man. He still looks like a football player."

"But he isn't one. And nobody's heard of him."

"No," he said. "But trust me."

Using his own money, Joe shot a spec commercial with Rud Herzog, which Helen and Orval weren't even aware of until he showed it to them on his home film projector.

"Are you comfortable?" he asked them, which Helen thought was a ludicrous question. By that point, anything nicer than a folding chair and a concrete floor felt to her like a Nordic spa. And Joe had a luxuriously finished basement with a fireplace, burnt-orange shag carpeting, stylish leather furniture, a petrified-wood coffee table, and a wet bar, with cold Harvey Wallbangers for his guests.

Helen winced. "I'm so comfortable, it's annoying."

Joe flicked off the lights, and the image of a giant, bearded man in an unspecific football jersey appeared on a pull-down screen.

"Hi, I'm Rud Herzog," the man said. "You probably don't remember me from my career on the
Minnesota Vikings. It was my lifelong dream to
play for them. Last year, I had my one chance, and
I didn't make it. That was real depressing. We've
all had days like that, I guess. After getting cut, I
felt like drinking a lot of beer. Thank goodness,
my local bar had Blotz Special Light. With its easy-
going flavor and low calories, you can drink a ton
of them. You can drink it all night and you'll feel
all right. Drink lots, it's Blotz."

"It's kind of sad," Helen said. "I don't know."

"I like it," said Orval. "He speaks for a lot of
people right now."

Joe nodded. "I sure hope he does."

Helen held firm in her opposition to the ad, but
was outvoted two-to-one, and with some minor
edits, it hit the local airwaves. It turned out it was
one of the few times she was wrong, but at least she
could admit it.

"You realize that Blotz Special Light didn't even
exist yet when Rud Herzog was cut from the team,"
Helen told the men.

"Nobody cares," Joe said.

Orval put his arm around his wife. "Honey,
you're accentuating the negative again. You should
be happy that we could get Mr. Herzog so cheap."

That was true, anyway. He agreed to be their

spokesman in exchange for the yearly sum of a hundred bucks and twenty cases of beer. His idea. Of course, no one had any clue what was about to happen.

In the months that followed, both Rud Herzog's face and the tagline, "Drink Lots, It's Blotz," appeared on billboards, bus benches, and TV, and not just in Minnesota. A depressed anti-celebrity hawking a strange new beer somehow intrigued people looking for emotional honesty in the wake of Watergate, and soon journalists were reporting on the ad campaign itself as if it were news. After Rud Herzog was invited to **The Tonight Show**, where he was a huge hit, he decided to stay in California. He ended up enjoying a successful career as a film actor, most famously as the incorruptible linebacker Pup Jodorowsky in **The Longest Sunday**. Even so, he continued shilling for Blotz for fifteen years, and never even changed the terms of their contract.

The brilliant thing about an easy-drinking, virtually tasteless beer, in that era, was that few people hated Blotz Special Light so much that they wouldn't have it again. It's fair to say that a lot of drinkers tried it numerous times early on because they'd forgotten what it actually tasted like. Sure, there were always going to be those demanding freaks who wanted to get tipsy after two beers, or thought that beer should have a strong, distinct flavor, but those were eccentric, minority opinions. The tide in beer drinking was still favoring volume drinkers, and Blotz was on the face of its latest wave.

By the end of 1976, Blotz Special Light was the second-bestselling Minnesota-brewed beer in Minnesota. Helen, Orval, and Joe celebrated by going out to eat at Schumacher's, down in New Prague, the first upscale, white-tablecloth dinner they'd had in seven years. It was a stunning, homey, Central European–style hotel and restaurant, in a small town surrounded by ceaseless farmland.

"Let's come back here every year we turn a profit," Orval said, which at the time was a hell of a bold statement.

Five dizzying years later, Blotz Special Light was **the** bestselling beer in Minnesota made by anyone. Helen, Orval, and Joe celebrated that fact one evening in December 1981 by completely renting out Schumacher's for themselves and their employees. "Eat and drink lots," she told them that night, to cheers and applause. "It's on Blotz."

After dinner, after all the bottles of Dom Péri-
gnon were popped, Helen's favorite employee, a
young woman who worked in QC named Agatha
Johnston, took her heels off, stood on a chair, and
shouted for a toast. Agatha was another chemistry major from Macalester who they met in a bar
on the day she graduated, in 1979. The fact that
she'd earned a degree in chemistry as a single mom
with a part-time job told Helen everything she
needed to know about Agatha's work ethic. She
was Ojibwe, which made her only the second Native American employee at Blotz. As someone who
felt demographically outnumbered every day at her
own company, Helen was acutely attuned to this.

"You let me know if you have any friends or relatives who'd want to work here," Helen told Agatha
a few months into her employment.

"When there are openings for good jobs with
real opportunities for promotion," Agatha replied,
"I'll refer some good people."

Agatha was typically pragmatic and serious, so
to see her loud and happy on this day was an occasion in itself.

"Get on up here, Helen," Agatha shouted, cham-
pagne glass raised. "This company wouldn't exist
without her. She's our brain and our soul. Let's let
her know how we feel."

"Hardly," Helen said, as her employees ap-
plauded, but she knew it was true.

———

Looking back on moments like that, Helen wondered if she shouldn't have been more of a public figure. No one on the management level was as charismatic and media-savvy as Joe Foxworth, and whatever publicity and press Joe didn't soak up went to Orval, because he was the putative brewmaster and majority owner of a brewery with his family name. Like all industries, it was male-dominated and certainly sexist, but anyone who tried to send Helen out to fetch coffee she swiftly corrected.

Helen also made a point of hiring women for any damn brewery job they were qualified to do, from production to accounting to driving one of their big red Kenworths, and tried to promote them from within. Maybe if Helen had ended up on a few magazine covers, there'd have been more women in breweries, and more running breweries sooner. Who knows.

After coming home from Schumacher's that night, Helen fell across her white leather sofa, ran her bare toes across her white shag carpet, and watched the moon through the skylight in their ceiling, as Orval poured her a glass of Pétrus. She touched a remote and flicked on the light built into their

awards case; it might be difficult for some to believe, but Blotz Special Light had won several trophies, plaques, and ribbons. The mere idea of an
awards case in a living room would've driven her
mother insane, so looking at it every day, glowing
and irrefutable, made Helen stupidly happy.

Orval set her wine glass down on their petrified-
wood coffee table, and walked to their custom-built
spiral staircase. "I'm going to grab some pretzels."

"Why don't we make pretzels?" she asked, half-
joking, half-not.

"Make pretzels?" He laughed. "What do you
mean?"

"We have to expand and diversify. Joe agrees
with me."

"Well, pretzel manufacturing is a whole other
process. Breweries don't make pretzels."

"Then who makes those pretzels you like? Old
Dutch? Why don't we buy them?"

He laughed again. "No. We'll stick to buying
Old Dutch one bag at a time. Need anything from
the kitchen?"

"No," she said. "I have everything I need."

As her husband vanished upstairs, she lay on the
couch, took a deep breath, and almost believed it.

$5.00

Diana, 2008

Diana had never been to the Nicollet Falls Country Club, or any country club, and didn't expect it would be so surreal. The "clubhouse," where people supposedly hung out after playing outdoor sports, seemed wildly extravagant and clean, with framed art on the walls, flawless navy blue carpeted floors, and recessed lighting. Plus, the bathrooms had cloth towels, not paper ones, and a wicker basket where you threw the towels after just using them once. She'd have to tell her grandma about that. The place made her feel lost, not because she didn't know where she was, but because she didn't know somewhere like this existed, and so close to where she lived.

Adults stationed at various intervals discouraged her from doing any further exploring, and freshly laser-printed signs guided her and the others into a lavish, brightly lit, cream-and-white dining room that looked like it was set up for a wedding. It forced her to think of the last time she even ate somewhere with a white tablecloth. She didn't want that memory to accost her right now, but it did. It was at Vescio's in Dinkytown, the last birthday dinner her mom would ever have, just over a year ago.

The other six qualifying students were there already, including Astra and James, and everyone was there with one of their parents.

"Hey," Paul said. "Beautiful dress."

In his blue jeans, black blazer, and loosened tie, he clearly didn't view this occasion as requiring strict formality, or just wanted to demonstrate to strangers that his mom no longer picked out his outfits. She liked it, though; it was basically what he wore every day at school, plus the half-assed tie.

"You're not so bad yourself," she told him. "The tie adds some intrigue."

"Thanks. I was going for FBI agent, undercover at a poetry workshop."

"Nah. You look like a lawyer who represents drummers."

He laughed, which was polite. "Well, you look amazing," he said.

That was sweet of him to say, but it wasn't true.

She felt sweaty and underdressed and her hair was like a bird's nest compared to expensive salon jobs on all the fancy moms and women here.

Paul smiled at her. "Where's your grandma? I want to meet her."

"She had to work."

"You're here alone?"

She nodded.

He glanced around the room.

"Let's all sit together then, just us," he said, and walked her over to a table near the front, where he removed his jacket and set it across the plush white seats of two chairs. "I'll tell Astra and James."

"They wouldn't rather sit with their parents?"

"Hell no," Paul winced.

It wasn't until she sat down that she realized what Paul had done, masking the absence of her parents, rescuing her from other parents' well-meaning questions and their awkward after-math. If she wasn't obsessed with him yet—and maybe she sort of was—now she was doomed to be, and she was furious. What a dick move on his part, to go and be astoundingly kind like that, and force her further into being into him, when he knew—HE KNEW—she wasn't ready. God, she could strangle him.

Once everyone was seated, she glanced over her shoulder at the other students present, three nice but shy nerdy girls, sitting at tables with their parents. Nate Ryan was there too, at a table with the mayor, Abe Murry, and the school superintendent, Brian Karkoutly, brownnosing his stupid ass off. "All your parents are OK with you sitting here?"

"Please." Astra frowned. "They prefer it."

Paul shot some kind of strange conspiratorial look at Astra, who nodded and rose to her feet. "I should go wash my hands," she said, and slapped James on the shoulder. "James?"

James surveyed his two seated friends. "They're not washing their hands."

"Come on," she said, tugging his striped tie, and he rose to his feet.

"Fine, whatever," James said, and as they left, Paul pulled his chair a little closer to Diana's, and leaned in toward her ear.

"Are you going to prom?" Paul asked her. Hell of a thing for him to ask her now, here.

"I don't know," Diana said. "It seems like kind of a hassle."

"No, it's a lot of fun. What if you had someone to go with?"

He was actually asking her. It made the blood run to her brain, but not enough to drown all logic and reason. This was all too much. She could've stood at least a few more luscious, ignorant weeks of daydreaming about him and picking apart little things he said for hints. And if he was indeed asking, she wanted him to be straight up; no more of this open-ended bullshit. He'd have to lay himself out there.

"Ha, like who?" Diana scoffed. "Who are you going with?"

Paul looked at her and shrugged. "As of this moment, I'm uncommitted."

God, this guy is killing her. "Is there someone you want to go with?"

"I don't know. Is prom something that you'd even be interested in?"

"I don't know, are you asking me? Are you asking me to prom?"

"Yeah, I guess I am."

"Then ask."

"Do you want to go to prom with me?"

She couldn't help it. "OK," she blurted out.

"OK what?" he echoed, wincing.

"Yes," Diana said, and started laughing. Damn it, the words just came out of her. "God, yes. Yes."

Paul nodded and pointed across the room.

James was grinning when he returned to the table. "You're in?" he asked her.

"Yeah," Diana said. She was nervous as hell, all of a sudden, but she was happy, genuinely happy, and it felt unnerving and dumb. But she didn't want it to stop.

"Christ, that took a while," Astra said as she sat down, and she actually smiled.

"Astra, what happened to your face?" Diana had to ask. "Your mouth is curved."

"Shut up," Astra said, now forcing herself to scowl. "Prom actually sucks, you know."

James shrugged. "It'll be way more fun with both you guys."

She and Paul were a "you guys." They hadn't even kissed yet.

"How much is prom, anyway?" Diana asked the table.

The next day, in the late evening, her Uncle Eugene opened the door to the apartment, breathless.

Eugene had met a Moldovan guy named Mihail at a bar in Uptown, and Mihail had offered him $800 for a ride to the Moldovan embassy in D.C., cash on arrival. The only problem was that Eugene's car needed new tires and new brakes—and Edith's car was fresh from the shop.

Edith, of course, let her son do exactly what he wanted, no matter how fiercely Diana protested that Edith's car was for Edith, not for Moldovans with visa problems. As Edith handed over the keys, Diana looked at her tall uncle's wrinkled khakis, Rockports, and tucked-in shirt and wondered if Eugene talked anyone else into giving him anything that day.

"You gotta take opportunities to make easy money when they come up," Eugene smiled as he left the apartment. "Maybe you'll learn that sometime."

In Diana's estimation, Eugene's pursuit of easy money had been expensive for her family. Who amid her uncle's aspirational blast radius could forget his numerous multi-level marketing schemes? Not to mention the short-lived motorcycle detailing company, the supposedly can't-miss pet photography business, and the aborted sober cab gambit, all while borrowing money for maybe half a dozen never-completed degrees and certifications. A two-month stint at a liquor store was the only time he held what most people would consider a regular job.

These costly false starts never once served to remind Edith that her oldest child's dreams were a nut cluster of poor forethought and halfhearted execution. "The law of averages says it's gotta work out for him sooner or later," Edith said.

Indeed, every Eugene needs an Edith—someone who, without judgment, provides the financial safety net and emotional validation that would exhaust a logical, impartial person. Diana sure didn't have it in her.

Twenty-four hours later, Eugene called from Cleveland, saying that "the car had been totaled" and could Diana please wire him money for a bus ticket home.

Diana tried hard not to explode. She thought of the long, cold walks to the salvage yard and the oily smell of strangers' garages, but she didn't say a thing. She couldn't.

"Do you know what I went through to pay for those car repairs?"

"At least you'll get some money from the insurance, right?" Eugene said.

Diana wasn't even sure if that were true. "I don't know."

"Believe me, we didn't want to crash into the back of a semi. Mihail's sandal came off when he pushed the brake. I jammed my wrist and got whiplash."

"And how's Mihail?"

"Oh, he's fine. He met someone who's going to take him the rest of the way."

Sometimes Diana wondered what it would be like to be related to the Mihails of the world and not the Eugenes. Would she be the same person?

After hanging up the phone, Diana called Brett Victor and asked if that Eagle Talon was still for sale for $300.

"You've seen the light, eh?"

"Yeah, the check engine light," Diana said. If only it were that simple. "Do you think the guy would take two hundred?"

"No. Maybe two-seventy-five."

She had only eighteen bucks to her name right now, but her grandma needed a car, and Diana would make sure she had one.

There was something about Frank Schabert that had suggested an early riser, so Diana got up far earlier than usual, and found herself walking toward Frank's house at a quarter to five in the morning. The side door to the garage was locked, and while Diana still planned to exit that way, she'd remembered the alternate way inside.

Lifting the busted garage door just enough to slide her body through, Diana wiggled inside on her back and gently let the door fall and close behind her.

She'd brought two backpacks, and she needed them. Frank Schabert had a Lowrance LCX-16CL sonar fish finder, a Milwaukee lithium ion battery, and an IQv cordless impact wrench, in addition to the stuff like the Skil saw she'd seen before the awards luncheon. The quality of Frank's stuff was staggering. It would be a lifesaver. Diana estimated its total worth at maybe fifteen hundred bucks, and she was out in under ten minutes.

Diana glanced back at Frank Schabert's house once she made it to the main road, and saw a light on in one of the bedroom windows. She hadn't noticed it earlier. But someone was up in the house, or had awoken.

As a precaution, she slunk into the twisting residential streets, making random turns. Two blocks in, she looked over her shoulder and thought she saw a silver Audi on the street behind her.

Home was too far away, so she headed toward Clarissa's. If she only had a working phone so she could text her that she was coming.

She cut through someone's yard to get to Clarissa's house without being seen from the road. It was late enough in the morning that people were up, and although she normally felt invisible in her vest and hard hat, now she felt exposed in a way she never had before, like this, somehow, was the first time she'd ever done anything wrong, the first time she had reason to run and hide.

From a distance, she glimpsed the red Edina Realty FOR SALE standing sign out there in front of Clarissa's, slightly askew in the snow. Diana knocked on the back patio door, hard. A minute passed, and there was still no answer.

Diana pounded the door again, even harder. Nothing.

Diana crouched down, glanced out at the street, threw the bags over her shoulders, and ran to the front door. She rang the doorbell and knocked at the same time.

She didn't even hear any rustling inside or

perceive any presence that someone was awake in there. She didn't see any movement at all until she saw the reflection of a silver Audi in the glass of the door. It turned and pulled up into Clarissa's driveway, and the driver's-side window slunk down as the car came to a stop.

"Come here," Frank Schabert said.

What was she supposed to do? She rang Clarissa's doorbell, again and again.

"Come here or I press charges," Frank said.

Diana felt the breath fall out of her. She hadn't ever been in trouble before in her life, and her body didn't know what to do. She set the backpacks down and took a step toward Frank's car.

"No, bring me my tools." The trunk of Frank's car opened on its own. "Toss them back there, close the trunk, and then get in the car."

Diana did as she was told, and then sat down inside the cleanest car she'd ever seen in her life. The interior vents were all round and silver, and the stereo readouts glowed an alarm-clock red. It was like being in a space capsule, but much more frightening.

Frank pointed at Clarissa's house as he backed out of the driveway. "It looks like your buddy here hung you out to dry," he said, and Diana stared at the silent house, wondering if that was true.

"Are you taking me to jail?" Diana asked. She tried to wipe her eyes as if there was something in them besides tears. Her hands were shaking and she tried to hold them down against her legs to make them stop.

Frank's face and voice weren't unkind. "No. Back to my place, to put my stuff back. You're lucky I caught you. If you'd gone into that house, I would've just gone to your principal and pulled you out of school, Diana Winter."

Diana exhaled. That would've been the end of everything.

As far as she knew, Clarissa still had at least one of Bert Jeffrey's tools, so if Paul and his smart friends didn't abandon her simply because she was a thief, Paul might never speak to her again forever because she'd been his family's thief. Money allows people to survive their mistakes, she knew from having observed that phenomenon from a distance, and people like her were fucked. No one would want anything to do with her after this. Everything from the last few months would disappear, except the receipts.

"I thought you were a good kid," Frank said. "What, last week you were on your way to an awards banquet? I read about you in the damned newspaper. And you helped me with my garage door? And now you're robbing me? I just had to know why. Was I an asshole to you or something?"

"No, you were pretty nice actually."

"Then what the hell were you doing, stealing my tools?"

Diana took a deep breath. "There's a lot of reasons."

Frank stopped the car at a stop sign and used the opportunity to glare at Diana. He seemed to enjoy that Diana couldn't bring herself to look back at him. "Name one. Go ahead."

The tips of her fingers were just below the door handle. She could reach up right now, pull it, and dash into the street. She imagined some gutsier version of herself bolting away, dodging between houses. "For a while, it was so my grandma could get her car fixed. Before that, it also helped pay the rent, electric, gas bill, phone bill, car payment, car insurance."

"How were you and your grandma paying for all these things before?"

"Sometimes we weren't."

"Don't you have a job? You're more than old enough."

"Yeah. At Gretchen's Café."

"How's that? Are Will and Ann nice to you?"

"Yeah. They pay me under the table. That helps."

"Why? So you can still qualify for assistance? Your family gaming the system?"

"No." Diana had always hated when people said this about her family. The bosses who made her dad list a payroll company as his employer, **they** gamed the system. The assholes who convinced her parents to take out both a second mortgage and a HELOC in 2006 gamed the system. The employers who would never give Edith enough hours for benefits gamed the system. But ask a lot of people, and they'd tell you it's people like her grandma who game the system. They'd tell you that an old woman who's worked hard every day of her life and still struggles to get by is a malignant vacuum for their personal tax dollars, and a blight on their lives as free Americans. "We're just trying to live."

"So you need to steal to do that."

"To pay rent and bills and eat three times a day, yeah. Yeah, I do. But my grandma doesn't know I do it."

"That's good, I guess. You live with just your grandma then? No parents?"

Diana shook her head.

"You said that she works, though."

"Yeah, at Arby's and Kohl's."

"Two jobs. That's a decent living, isn't it?"

They passed a sign for the golf course, getting closer to Frank's street. "I can see how it would comfort you to believe that."

"You know, I've never met someone who stole from me before. And from the sound of it, you think you're some kind of Robin Hood vigilante."

"I don't. I'm not proud of it. If there's something else I could've done, I would've."

"Well, the vast majority of people don't steal to

get ahead. A lot of people work their way up from nothing without stealing."

"I don't think a lot of people work their way up from nothing, ever. People like you want to believe it happens all the time. But it really doesn't."

Frank stopped the car in his driveway. "Well," he said. "For now, you can put my things back the way they were. You know how to get in."

"So you're not going to press charges?"

"You watch too much TV," Frank frowned. "I can't press charges because I'm not a prosecutor. What I could do is file a police report, and from there, you'd probably get arrested and arraigned. But I don't know juvenile law in this state. You're not eighteen, right? And no priors?"

"Are you a lawyer or something?"

"No, just married to one. I run a brewery. Heartlander Brewing. You've heard of us?"

She'd had maybe three different kinds of beer in her life. And this wasn't one of them. Frank frowned. "Sixth-oldest continuously running brewery in Minnesota?"

Diana shook her head.

Frank looked disgusted. "Just put my stuff back."

Walking to school from Frank Schabert's house, her mind spun around one thought, one phrase, again and again. Frank had almost pulled her from school. If Clarissa had let her in the house, it would've happened. Her life would have been over. But she still wished that Clarissa had opened that goddamn door.

Half a mile from school, Diana walked by the Pizza Ranch, where she'd recently eaten lunch—it was dark, and hours away from opening—and threw her hard hat and orange safety vest into the trash around back.

Diana wasn't surprised to see Clarissa waiting by her locker, but that didn't mean that Diana could look her in the face, or that she wanted to.

"Dude!" Clarissa said, like nothing was wrong.

Diana's jittery body burned with anger. She was focusing so hard on opening her locker, she actually screwed up the combination. "Where the hell were you this morning?"

"Everything's so fucked."

"You should talk." Diana still couldn't look at her. "Why didn't you answer your door?"

"What? Dude, my dad locked me and my mom out yesterday. He literally changed all the locks on the doors."

"Oh," Diana said. "Where were you then?"

"We got a room last night at the Embassy Suites in St. Paul."

The Embassy Suites did sound like a fancy place to crash, though, and all this still wasn't close to almost getting thrown in jail. "Could be worse," Diana said.

Clarissa was just staring off into nothing. Her body and face seemed radioactive. "He wouldn't even let me in to get my shit, just because my mom was with me."

"Yeah, that sucks."

"Thanks for your concern." Clarissa shook her head. "So what the hell are you so pissed about?"

"I got busted."

"Busted?" Clarissa almost laughed. "Busted doing what?"

"I got caught. With tools."

"What?"

Diana nodded.

"Dude, I thought you weren't gonna do that anymore."

"I know," Diana whispered. "It was just gonna be one last time."

"Whose place?"

"I don't know. Does it matter?"

"And you weren't gonna tell me?"

"Yeah I was. I came to your house this morning, but you weren't there."

"Sorry." Clarissa laughed a little to herself. "Well, I hope you woke my dad up."

"I don't know, it didn't seem like he was there."

"Hmm, interesting," Clarissa said. "When they caught you, did they press charges?"

"Duh, only a prosecutor can press charges."

"Dude, I don't know, I don't watch TV." Clarissa glanced down the hallway. "What's going to happen to you?"

"I don't know. He said something about a police report."

Clarissa sighed. "Dude. You're a minor, don't even sweat it. Did you say anything about me, though?"

"Of course not." Diana took a deep breath. Of course she'd ask this. Then again, Diana probably would've, too. "I never would."

Clarissa leaned against the locker next to Diana's. "I just want this all to be over. I want to wake up tomorrow and be twenty-five and have total control of my life." She paused and glared as she waited for a preppy girl who she hated to pass by, and then turned back to Diana. "What are you doing for lunch today?"

"I hadn't thought that far ahead."

"Let's meet up in the cafeteria then. I gotta catch you up on some shit."

She wondered what she'd tell Paul, but hoped he'd understand. "Fine. I'm short on funds anyway."

"Wow. Just because you're short on funds, huh?"

That wasn't how she meant it, but just then, Diana didn't have the energy to apologize. "I gotta go to class now," she muttered, and merged into the crowds that had begun to thicken in the hallway.

Clarissa was in a far better mood at lunch. As Diana approached them from behind, it looked like she and Ishaq were laughing their asses off.

"What's funny?" Diana asked, setting her tray down, and saw that it was just Clarissa cracking up, and Ishaq looked a little annoyed.

"Nothing," Clarissa said, wiping her eyes. "Hey, what are you doing over prom weekend? You wanna come with us to Mystic Lake?"

Sometimes Diana forgot that Clarissa was old enough to get into casinos. Diana was mortified by those joints. The idea of putting a dollar into a machine and just losing it forever gave her a heart attack.

"You're not going to prom?"

"Hell no. Prom sucks, dude. Come play slot machines with us."

Diana gazed down at her flat, jaundiced square of school lunch pizza, and tried to think of a composed, diplomatic response. She didn't want to be all judgy about her cousin's idea of a good time just because gambling scared the crap out of her. "I'm not old enough to get into Mystic Lake, anyway."

"Yeah you are. Use one of my fakes."

"I don't look like you."

"I don't look like any of my fakes either. No one's gonna care." She elbowed Ishaq, who was busy eating. "She should join us, right?"

"I don't like to gamble," he said, dabbing the top of his pizza with a paper napkin, soaking up the bright grease. "I gotta save up for college like a normal person."

"God! Nobody's any fun anymore."

"Hey." Diana tried to get her cousin to make eye contact. "I thought you needed to talk to me about something serious."

"This is serious," Clarissa said, and then started laughing, and that's when Diana finally figured out that Clarissa was totally high.

"Let's talk later," Diana said, and picked up her tray. She didn't know where else she was going to sit yet, but didn't want to be here. Diana wasn't in the mood that day to get real with someone who was actively trying to avoid reality.

"Dude! Where you going?" Clarissa called out to her.

Diana hoped it didn't make her a bad person that she couldn't handle Clarissa when Clarissa was totally baked. But it just made her feel alone, and if she was going to feel lonely, she might as well be by herself.

Coming home that night after her shift at the coffee shop, she wanted to go straight to bed and smother this day under a blanket. In the lobby by the mailboxes, she saw the oldest man in her building, Marvin Roen, who everyone called Marvin

Gardens because of all the plants on his deck, and tried to ignore him. He was pretending to be helpful, mopping up the snow that people tracked in, even though it wasn't his job. The guy was also an infamous conversational vortex, and Diana was relieved to successfully dash past him without meeting his eye.

"Hey, Diana," Marvin called out. "Some man came asking about you today."

Diana stopped. "What? What did he look like?"

"Looked like an FBI detective. Don't worry. I told him you were a good kid. I told him whatever it was, you didn't do it."

An hour later, while Diana was watching a can of LifeWell Iowa-style chili excrete its contents into a saucepan, there was a noise at the door. Three loud bangs. Someone serious. The person banged again, three times, slightly louder.

Diana turned off the burner, and took a deep breath before she turned the doorknob.

"May I come in?" Frank asked. He was wearing a white button-up shirt, a nickel-colored blazer, pressed slacks, and shiny leather shoes. Marvin Gardens's idea of an "FBI detective," apparently. It's true, men who looked and dressed like Frank Schabert were typically a bad omen in buildings like Diana's. It seemed as scary as letting a bear inside.

"So this is where your family lives," Frank said, looking around. "You and your grandma?" Diana wondered what he thought of the couch made up like a bed, or the stains on the carpeting, or the cold saucepan of smelly, uncooked chili. She wondered if he even perceived these things.

"I've talked with my wife about it," he said. "She wants to make an example of you. Just so you know." He stopped on the edge of the carpet. "Shoes off?" he asked.

"You can leave them on," Diana said.

"Nice laptop," Frank said, pointing to the computer on the kitchen counter. "That's the kind I just bought at work. To replace the Macs that were stolen."

"I just bought it for seventy bucks."

"Wow. You practically stole it. Unless you did steal it."

"I know I stole from you, sure," Diana said. "But I haven't once lied to you."

Frank nodded. "I suppose you haven't."

"Can I get you anything?" Diana asked, to be polite, suddenly afraid that he was going to ask for something like whiskey and be mad that they didn't have any.

"No thanks," Frank said. "One question. You have one job, right? At a coffee shop that doesn't pay you much?"

"Yeah. They've been good to me, though."

"I know. I talked to the owners. They think you're the best high school employee they've ever had." Frank laughed. "You know, I spent all day asking around about you, and everyone I met who knows you says that you're the nicest, smartest, most considerate kid they know. In my head, I was thinking, **That thieving little piece of shit?**, but not one person had anything bad to say. Even the old fella with all the plants."

"You talked to Marvin?"

"Yeah, for like forty minutes. Fascinating guy. You know he was an Army medic in World War Two? He was in the Battle of Kasserine Pass. It's amazing he's still alive."

Diana didn't know any of that. But then again, she never asked; no one did.

"I apologize for what I did," Diana said at last. "What can I do to make it up to you?"

"OK. Well, I'll tell you what you can do, Diana," Frank said. "My wife thinks I'm crazy. But you're going to work it off. We need a janitor at our new space. And we also need a security guard for a few days, until I get a better system installed."

That sounded like the dumbest idea Diana had ever heard. For a few seconds, all she could do was just stare back at this guy and ask him why.

"Well, you need to make right what you did wrong. And I need someone to clean up and guard my brewery. If you're not incompetent, we'll talk further. That's my offer to you. It's on the condition that you never rob anybody again."

Diana's mind went blank. Her disbelief seemed to lift the bones out of her body. She had to lean against the kitchen counter just to stay upright. Only the acrid, farty smell of the cold chili in the pan to her back shocked her into the present. When she was able to speak again, all she could say was that she didn't even know how to be a security guard.

"Can't be that hard. But you won't just be standing around, you'll be cleaning kegs the whole time. If you do OK, after two weeks, I'll give you nine-fifty an hour."

"What about my job at the coffee shop?" Diana said.

"That's up to you. Talk to them and work something out, if you want."

"I don't know," Diana said. She earned $7.25 an hour at the coffee shop, but there were tips, and they paid her in cash. Maybe she could do both.

"Are you saying you deserve better?" Frank said. "After what you did?"

Maybe it wouldn't have sounded appealing to most people, but Diana knew even then that this job offer, and what it meant, was like a bus that came around maybe every ten years, and here it was, pulling up to the sidewalk in front of her face, idling.

Frank Schabert's Heartlander Brewery was not what she expected a brewery to look like. It was in an office park on the outskirts of town, next to a document shredding service and across from an auto upholsterer. It was almost impossible to find unless you were looking. There were only four full-time employees: Frank; his wife, Anna, a serious-faced lawyer who also handled operations and finances; the hip master brewer, Mo Akbar; and the quiet, tattooed, gruff-looking Matt Duncan, who did the graphic design, social media, and the website in addition to doing physical grunt work with Mo.

It was around nine in the evening on Diana's third day on the job; she'd just arrived at the brewery after a shift at the coffee shop, and only Mo was still around, unwrapping pallets of bottles, his black hair hanging in his face. The cavernous room was cluttered with boxes and kegs, and a giant industrial Koh-i-Noor refrigerator hummed against the far wall. Mo seemed like the mayor of this unglamorous space, even off the clock. He'd stay late, put on some music—today it was something that Diana had never heard of, a gorgeous, melancholy record called **The Coctails**—and did whatever needed to be done.

Diana saw the lights of a strange car stop outside,

and Mo turned down the music. They weren't expecting anyone. "Wonder if this is our burglar," Mo said.

Diana recognized Clarissa's outline before she opened the frosted door. She had a heavy-looking black bag with her, and was limping, maybe from the weight of the bag.

"Wow, it's real," Clarissa said. "You're actually working here."

"Yeah, for now," Diana said, glancing back at Mo, to see if he was within earshot.

"What do they have ya doing?"

"Random stuff. Cleanup in the day, security guard at night."

"That's kinda ironic, huh?"

"I suppose," Diana said, stepping outside, and closing the door behind her. "What do you got in there?"

Clarissa dropped the bag. "It's all the shit I couldn't sell. I got it out before my dad found it. Just thought maybe you wanted it."

"You brought it to my new job?"

"Where else? School? Your grandma's?" A gust of cold wind pulled Clarissa's long hair across her face. "Your grandma finds it, she'd probably die."

Clarissa kind of had a point. "Why didn't you just get rid of it?"

"Seems like kind of a waste," Clarissa said. "But OK, I'll chuck it in the trash, then."

Diana watched as Clarissa lifted the bag to the

edge of the dumpster in the parking lot and emptied it inside. She didn't mean to call Clarissa's bluff, but now there it was, all gone.

"Well, that's an end of an era, I guess," Clarissa said, and stood there in the parking lot as if she wasn't done with the conversation, but didn't know what else to say, or maybe just couldn't say it.

"How are you doing?" Diana asked. They'd only spoken once in the days since that lunch, and they'd each apologized, and pretty much smoothed it over. Still, it didn't alter the fact that they'd changed, like how something that's been burnt can't be unburnt, and they were each going to keep changing, because they wanted to.

"I'm going to Oberlin," Clarissa said, leaning against the back of her mom's car.

"Oh. Cool." Oberlin wasn't close, but it was, by far, the closest of all the places that Clarissa applied, and by that standard alone, the choice was a surprise.

Clarissa pushed her windswept hair out of her face again. "I'm gonna miss you though. Kinda miss you already."

"Yeah," and Diana almost said she'd miss her too, but for now, she just wanted that little imbalance to hang over them, as the one being left behind, as the one who couldn't stand missing one more person.

"By the way. Your boss still hiring?"

"No," Diana had to say, because it was the truth, as far as she knew.

"Thought I'd ask. Seems like a cool place to work," Clarissa said. "Imagine you and me, working at a brewery? Oh my God."

"It's just a job," Diana said, and walked toward the doorway. "I guess I should get back to it."

"Hey." Clarissa took a deep breath. "Ishaq dumped me."

"Oh my God." Diana felt it was polite to act surprised. "I'm sorry. What happened?"

Clarissa looked annoyed. "He thinks I smoke up too much. What a fucking joke. I know people who smoke waaaaay more than I do."

Diana nodded. Clarissa probably did know such people.

"Anyway," Clarissa said. "You should get back to work. Don't wanna get you fired."

"Are you OK, though?" Diana asked.

"Yeah, fine. Holler at ya later."

"OK."

"Hey," Clarissa said, holding a joint. "Mind if I light up out here? My mom doesn't want her car smelling like weed."

I can't imagine why, Diana wanted to say, but it seemed rude to not extend this tiny favor. "OK. Just be subtle about it."

"Later," Clarissa said, already flicking her lighter, cupping an ungloved hand around the delicate flame.

The following Monday, Diana brought Paul's dad's impact wrench, the one item from that particular garage that Clarissa hadn't sold, and handed it to Paul before school.

"I found this by the trash behind the brewery. I saw the name 'Jeffrey' on the box and I wondered if it was your dad's."

"Damn," Paul laughed. "No, it's my brother Doug's. He left all his tools here when he moved to Zurich. He's the carpenter of the family."

"Not your dad?"

Paul laughed. "My dad doesn't know one side of a drill from the other. He tried to use the saw last year and almost hurt himself."

"That's funny."

Paul chucked the tool in his locker. "I bet he didn't even know this thing was missing. I wonder how the hell it ended up out there?"

"Who knows," Diana said.

Several days a week now, Diana traversed the four miles to work and back on a mountain bike that Mo Akbar lent her. Frank Schabert had given her the important-sounding job title "cellar master," but she was mostly still a glorified janitor, lugging around kegs, pushing mops and brooms, and lifting fat white bags of malt all day. Frank didn't talk to her much, and neither did his humorless wife, Anna, but the two young dudes, Mo and Matt, were nice and did the grunt work right alongside her most of the time, instead of just ordering her to do everything. Now, much more often, she came home exhausted, but it was a ripe, enlivening physical exhaustion, hatched from productive effort. And even better, she was making money.

By the afternoon of prom, as she buckled her seat belt in the front passenger seat of Paul's car, she sensed him staring at her body, and today it felt different. Her makeup, nails, and hair were nicer than normal, sure, but not anything special. She'd borrowed a white sleeveless dress from Clarissa; it was the least low-cut one she had that fit her.

"Damn," he said. "You're beautiful."

"Thanks," she said, but he kissed her before she could compliment him back.

As he relinquished the kiss, he was still staring at her body. "Sorry, you're just so damn hot in that dress."

Was it too revealing? Maybe she shouldn't be wearing this in public. Now she wished she'd brought a scarf, or light jacket, or anything. "Thanks, it's Clarissa's."

"Gonna have to send her a thank-you note," he said, and drove them out of the parking lot and toward the school.

Clarissa turned out to have been right; junior prom was totally overhyped. Diana had forgotten that she had nothing in common with most of her fellow students, and seeing them all overdressed sure didn't add anything to her life. It was kinda nice to see Ishaq there, looking happy, dancing with one of the shy nerdy girls Diana recognized from the Country Club luncheon, but overall it was just a louder, bizarro version of high school, and she couldn't wait to leave. The memorable part of the whole evening was afterward, when she and Paul and Astra and James all convened in Astra's basement, and it was just them again.

Astra's parents were gone for the weekend; she wasn't even sure where. Although Paul didn't drink, and no one did drugs, they felt they should do something, and while Astra dug around upstairs trying to find her parents' liquor, James had a bolder idea.

"Hey Diana," he said, putting his shoes back on. "Let's go get some beer from your job."

The thought had never even occurred to her before. But Diana knew she could. She had the keys. "No," Diana said.

"Well, don't they have like a warehouse full of bottles? They'd hardly even know."

After Paul, James was the smartest person that Diana had ever met. Clarissa was right, there was no doubt he'd be a famous tech-nerd millionaire someday. Everyone would say they knew him when. It was something to be friends with people like this. And he'd accepted her. He'd been so kind. Maybe she owed him. It'd be the least she could do.

"No," Diana said, closing her eyes. "Absolutely not."

"Please! They obviously trust you."

She wasn't even sure if they did. Even after a few months, Diana was just settling into this job. It had only been two weeks since Anna had last given her the stink-eye. And if there was anything she couldn't do without permanently ruining her reputation and maybe her life, it was steal twice from Frank.

"We don't need it anyway. Astra's already getting stuff from upstairs."

"Her parents hardly drink. They probably don't have anything. Please."

These people had been friends for such a long time before she met them. They'd been through some shit together. They'd been in a car accident that totaled Astra's car. They took James to the hospital when his appendix burst. Paul said that he and James once saw an old man die in the park by the waterfall. They'd bonded. And still, they let her in. She was one of them.

"James, no. No."

"Don't be such a loser. Come on."

Paul, thankfully, had heard enough, too. "Dude, you better listen to her."

"God," James said. "What good is it having a friend who works at a brewery?"

Diana shrugged. "I've never even tried it."

Even Paul was surprised. "You work at a brewery, and you've never tried the beer?"

"It's not part of my job."

"What the hell!" James blurted. "Even by accident?"

She shook her head.

"That sucks," James said, now taking his black wingtips off again, defeated. "Well, that's the stupidest brewery job of all time. You could be working a shit job anywhere."

Before Diana could respond, Astra appeared at the foot of the staircase, holding a nearly full bottle of green liquid and three wine glasses. "I'm sorry. My parents aren't really drinkers. This was the only thing I could find."

"Finally, someone comes through!" James shouted.

"What is it?" Diana asked.

"I don't know, never heard of it," Astra said, reading the label. "Midori."

"Midori!" James repeated. "We are gonna remember this night!"

Hours later, as James and Astra coated an upstairs bathroom in a flume of hot green vomit, a sober Paul and a somewhat tipsy Diana had sex for the first time. It happened on a brown couch in Astra's basement, while a toilet repeatedly flushed upstairs, and Radiohead played from the speakers of Astra's laptop. They had come close before—he'd even taken the condoms from his wallet twice—but they'd never done it, because she'd told Paul she was waiting. **For what?**, he'd asked her at the time, and she wasn't sure yet, but she didn't owe him an explanation, besides that she was.

That night, she finally felt like a different person, one who wouldn't do something stupid no matter who suggested it, one who could trust herself. That was the version of herself that she'd been waiting for, the one that was ready for this.

Diana was a little bummed to go back to school for her senior year after being able to work full-time at the brewery all summer. While Paul's family went on a two-week vacation to California in July to look at colleges, she worked even more, but as the shape of her boyfriend's inevitably distant and spectacular destiny emerged, it was difficult to keep her mind on work.

"Do you have any advice for me about my future?" Diana asked Frank Schabert one fall evening while they locked up.

"Write thank-you notes," Frank said. "Thank-you notes are the grease on society's bearings."

Diana had never even bought thank-you notes before. She hoped that, when the time came, a postcard would suffice. They had free retro-looking postcards at the Minnesota Welcome Center over by the Wisconsin border. "OK, thanks," Diana said.

"Oh, and one more thing," Frank said. "Let me know if you're going to college."

Paul wanted to apply early action to Stanford and wanted Diana to join him. By this time, the months she'd spent with him and the other smart kids had normalized the concept of higher education. Even after everything she'd once said and believed, it still didn't feel all that strange to hear her voice now say the words, "I'll do it." It was possible. Her grades weren't the greatest, but she continued to test well—her near-perfect SAT score was the best in the school. Everyone thought she'd get numerous scholarships and grants, and now she had people to help her access them. Ironically, her GPA was too low to make her a National Merit Finalist, which sucked, especially because Paul was named a Finalist, but everyone said that Semifinalist was still impressive. She figured she'd continue working, wherever she went, and send money home to Grandma Edith. She'd do something.

Paul's father, Bert Jeffrey, helped her with the FAFSA, and Paul and Diana submitted their early action applications on the same day, October 28. They ran off to Dunn Brothers to celebrate and they each had their own iced mochas. Paul insisted. Not having to fight Paul for her 50 percent, she sipped her sweet, cold reward with unhurried delight.

Diana didn't even know what she'd major in. She thought about it while staring up at the white ceiling fan in Paul's bedroom. She thought about it while cleaning kegs. Mo Akbar finally suggested chemistry, biology, or electrical engineering. "And then come straight back to Minnesota," he said. "We need you. Way more than they do out on the coasts."

Diana sent Bert a thank-you postcard for helping with the FAFSA. The front featured a map of the state and a walleye. Bert Jeffrey put it on his family's refrigerator and now Diana saw it every time she was over.

Ever since Diana took the PSAT, people who talked to her about success had always conflated it with getting out of Nicollet Falls. She'd actually miss the hard, wet, smelly work at the brewery. She'd miss Mo, Frank, Matt, and sure, even Frank's wife, Anna, even if Anna still didn't like her.

Mo and Frank had nicknames for each other—Mo's was "Cool Pants," Frank's was "TV's Frank"—and no one else was allowed to use them. One time, Frank hired a mime to follow Mo around for an hour and imitate everything he did. Another time, Mo commissioned a college kid to do an oil painting of Frank's high school graduation photo. He also had Matt set up a convincing but fake website with a fake review from Pete "Flavor Dave" Michaels, the most controversial and hard-to-please beer critic, giving Frank's newest beer a 0 out of 100. Frank apparently really lost his shit over that one.

Neither man ever complimented the other, and definitely never complimented each other's brewing. Diana wasn't involved in any of this. No nicknames, no practical jokes. Over seven months in, and they'd also never let her touch the beer or the equipment that created it, except to clean it, which Diana did all the time.

"Heard from the coastal elite yet?" Frank would ask while Diana cleaned the mash tun.

Paul's answer arrived first. There's no experience on earth like being near someone when he's about to open the decision email from his dream school.

When her eyes fell on the phrase "great pleasure," Diana knew he'd got in. She leapt into his arms and spun around in his bedroom. He was going to a prestigious university far away. He was going. He was gone.

Diana received her message the next day. She was alone, in bed. She didn't see the phrase "great pleasure," or anything else either great or pleasurable. She read it again and again anyway, scanning its impersonal regret for something positive.

On her way out to work, she saw Marvin Gardens outside with a watering can. "Gonna fill it with snow," Marvin said, even though Diana didn't ask. "Gonna fill it with snow and feed my plants a hundred percent natural meltwater."

Sometimes she looked at people like Marvin and wished she never wanted anything besides what was freely given. But she hadn't been lying in bed that morning hoping for something easy. She wanted something beyond her control, and now, she was stuck. If she'd learned one thing about college in the last year, it was that it was one of the few places on earth where it was permissible to change drastically. She didn't know yet what she wanted to change into, but that's what she felt she needed, more than the education, more than anything.

———

Edith did her best to be supportive. "There's something wrong with them if they don't want you," she said, buttering a fat slice of homemade bread.

"There's nothing wrong with them," Diana said. "I don't have the grades." She looked out the living room window at the freeway, grayed and scumbled by the dirty glass. "I never had a chance."

She dog-paddled through the rest of the day. Everywhere she went, everything in Nicollet Falls looked ruined and broken. It was as if fifty streetlights went out and a dozen square miles of pavement and concrete all cracked and faded at once.

She told Paul about Stanford that night over onion rings at Culver's. Until that point in the day, she'd lied to him and everyone else that she hadn't heard yet.

He seemed far more upset about her rejection than she'd been. She didn't even think she was going to cry about it until she saw the tears in his eyes.

He wiped his face and cleared his throat. "You didn't get deferred to Regular Decision?" he asked her.

Diana shook her head. Stanford was one school where that kind of deferral wasn't automatic if an applicant was denied early action.

Paul's grades had been far better, and for longer.

He'd also gone overboard on after-school activities. He was going to be an American Studies major and had spent last summer doing PA work on commercial shoots and volunteering at the Minnesota Historical Society. He'd also lettered on the soccer team. Diana had none of these things. She had been a janitor, security guard, and gofer at a brewery. She didn't even bother to write about her brewery experience in her essays, much less the circumstances around it. She didn't want to get into college on a pity vote.

Good old Principal Shultz reminded Diana that it still wasn't too late to try for a few more schools if she wanted to, and that she still had three unused application fee waivers. But Stanford was the only place she'd wanted to apply. It was where Paul would be.

"I'll work at the brewery, save more money, and apply again next year," she told Paul. They'd get at least three years at Stanford together. In the meantime, she'd try to figure out how she could beef up her application. There was a lot about it she couldn't change in a year, but there were a few things she could. "I need to do something impressive," she said. "But I have no idea what that would be."

"Why don't you ask Frank?" Paul said. "Maybe he can help."

"Ask him what?" she replied. And then she knew.

———

"I need to make a beer," Diana told Frank the next day.

"That's the most ignorant thing you've ever said," Frank said. He was stocking the fridge in the office and didn't even look up. "Why would you need to make a beer?"

At this point Diana explained to her boss that she didn't get into Stanford and it was mostly to impress them on the next go-around. So she and Paul could be together.

"OK. How does any of this benefit me? Why should I let you use my hops and malt and yeast and equipment to make something that a dog wouldn't pee on?"

"Because I'm going to make a pretty decent beer, I think." That kind of statement passed for arrogance in this workplace. She couldn't even believe that she said it.

"Cool Pants!" Frank shouted, and Mo scrambled upstairs. "The kid here says she can make a decent beer using our ingredients and our equipment."

"So, you want to be a brewer now and not a janitor," Mo said, removing his gloves and tossing them at Diana.

Diana tried to appear confident, and stood up straight, remembering she was taller than both men. "Yeah," she said.

"Well, hate to break your heart, but they're the same thing. The only difference is a brewer also makes beer once in a while."

Frank frowned. "What kind of beer do you want to make? Impress me."

"A kind that I would drink myself," Diana said, pleased with that answer.

"That's not enough. You don't know jack shit about beer."

"OK, then. So how do I learn?"

"Wow," Mo grinned. "I envy you."

When Diana arrived at work the next day, Frank had left a paper bag outside the office with DIANA EDUCATION written across it in black marker. The bag contained just three bottles and a can.

The bottle of Pliny the Elder was labeled TODAY, the bottle of Bell's Hopslam was labeled TOMORROW, the bright silver can of The Alchemist's Heady Topper was labeled THE DAY AFTER THAT, and the bottle of Dogfish Head's 90 Minute IPA was labeled FIGURE IT OUT YOU DINGUS.

The four examples of IPAs were meant to break Diana's brain open about the possibilities of what an IPA can do, but these beers were too far beyond her comprehension.

Her first, second, and third impression of each IPA steamrolled her ignorant palate; drinking them was like losing a boxing match to become a better boxer. It's unfair, she thought, that whatever the hell she'd make would be called beer, on a planet where these beers existed. They made her feel terminally bewildered.

"Now you know just a small taste of what's possible," Frank said.

"You said your grandma's sister works for Blotz," Mo said. "What do you think of that stuff?"

Even before her grandpa first exposed her to the stuff at age twelve, Diana was made to understand by her parents, with no small amount of venom, that Blotz Premium Lager, Blotz Special Light, Blotz Ice, Blotz Draft, Blotz Dark, Blotz Ultra Dark, and Blotz Urban Malt were the worst varieties of alcohol ever conceived by man. In high school, though, its cheapness and availability made it the most likely variety of alcohol a teenager was likely to encounter, and friends of hers, like James, even wore Blotz T-shirts to school and claimed they weren't being ironic.

It was only when she hung out with Clarissa that Diana came to associate Blotz with the true misery it wrought: fights in parking lots, roadside vomit, riveting public breakups, highly preventable swimming pool accidents, nonconsensual groping, and crude, percussive hangovers. In the summer before senior year alone, she'd understood that Blotz beer was a scourge, the anchor of a lifetime's most haunting regrets, a signifier of an ignorant tastelessness, and a bitter trial for drinkers of little experience or cash.

"To be honest, I'm not that crazy about it," Diana said.

"Good. Give us a couple days, and we'll re-educate you about our homeland."

The following week, Frank let her sample another range of beer, this time 100 percent from Midwest breweries, and no IPAs. For the first time, she tried New Glarus, Surly, Three Floyds, and Founders.

"I thought I didn't like beer," she admitted later.

"So there's hope for you yet," Frank told her.

For her final lesson, Frank let her go home with two six-packs, with at least one bottle each of everything Heartlander currently had in production or storage: Akbar American Ale, 213 Pale Ale, Shore Leave Porter, Honey Badger Hefeweizen, Minneapolis Woman Blonde Ale, and Frank's Mistake Triple IPA. She'd only ever had beer at the brewery before, and she was particularly nervous about what her grandma would say.

Edith was standing at the kitchen counter, squirting a packet of Horsey Sauce onto an Arby's turkey wrap. The first thing she saw when Diana walked in was the beer.

"Ho boy," she said.

"It's homework," Diana said as she hung her winter jacket in the closet. "They want me to learn their product."

"Oh, it's from where you work?" The exhaustion

in her grandma's face was always evident, but now it was dabbed with relief. "I don't understand why they want you to drink if you're just the janitor."

"Well, I'm brewing beer there now," she said.

"They can't make you do that. You're seventeen." Edith leaned her body against the kitchen counter like she'd fall over otherwise. "They can't make you do that!"

"They're not making me, Grandma. I want to. I'm trying to brew my own beer, to invent a new one."

"Oh." Edith seemed to think about this for a moment. "Well, then I guess that's nice of them."

"Thanks," Diana said.

"Just don't let them push you around just because you're young and you're a girl. They better let you make whatever beer you want."

She thought she knew what her grandma would say, but it wasn't this. Before Stanley died, Edith always struck Diana as one of the most accepting people she'd ever met, and although the losses her grandma had suffered had faded some of this radiant generosity, that brightness was still there, at unexpected times.

"You should come visit us," Diana added, putting the beer in a fridge where she hadn't seen beer since her grandpa was alive.

She realized that today, just now, was the first time she'd said "us" when referring to Heartlander, and it felt a little scary.

Frank ordered Diana to come to the brewery first thing Saturday morning. It was just the two of them. Diana knew all the equipment already, but Frank walked her through all of it again, stopping in particular at a little fifteen-gallon Blichmann BoilerMaker.

"This is what I started on," Frank said. "You're going to start with this pilot system."

According to Frank, the first time that a new brewer makes a beer, it should be immediately dumped down the drain.

The second beer that they make could be poured into a pint glass and smelled and maybe tasted once. Then it should be tossed, just like the first batch.

Same with the third beer. The fourth, maybe the unlucky person who made it should drink a glass of it. But by no means should it be shared with anyone they like.

Frank Schabert said that a brewer should make a beer thirteen times before they think about putting it in a bottle or can or glass for a stranger. Mo Akbar said that Frank was a little extreme, considering the weeks required to make a beer, from grain to bottle. Frank used to say fifteen, but he's getting old and running out of time.

Frank starts all his apprentice brewers on IPAs.

The hops drown out the obvious mistakes, he says. A beginner's IPA is like a heavy metal riff. Obvious, inelegant, indulgent. The right IPA is like a Miles Davis trumpet solo. Consistent, yet surprising. Both obeying and breaking the rules. A mixture of simple things. Air. Water. Time. Heat. Add either trumpet or malt, hops, and yeast.

By the time Paul left for California, Diana had made a beer that she called CoMa IPA eleven times. Each time she poured it into the great wide hole in the floor. She was growing tired of this routine. Attempt #11 tasted pretty damn good to her. Floral notes on the nose, as sweet as the typical Midwestern IPA, but with a sustaining bitterness in the finish. People were selling worse, and seemed proud of it.

Frank didn't even want to look at beer #11. Neither did Mo. Matt Duncan, who'd worked there for three years and had never made a beer, at least smelled it.

"You might be on to something," Matt said. He was probably just jealous that he'd been working there longer and she got to make a beer before he did.

Diana was only applying regular admission to Stanford this go-around, so she had a few more months both to brew that magical IPA #13 and get it into the world somehow. In a brewery that wasn't run by Frank Schabert, it would be more than enough time.

They wrote in marker on the fermentation tanks whatever was brewing, and one day Frank asked Diana why she gave her beer that stupid name, CoMa. "I hope to God you didn't use cobalt sulfate for head retention. I'd kill you myself right now."

She had no idea what he was referring to. "No, it's for my parents, Colleen and Mark."

"Oh," he said. "That's so cute, I want to vomit. You really want to honor them by making a beer you're going to dump out over a dozen times?"

"If that's what I have to do," she said, and got back to work.

Paul texted or emailed her every day. His family was well-off for Nicollet Falls but Stanford was another planet. His first week, he met students with their own Porsches and students with famous surnames. It was also crazy diverse, by comparison. There were kids from Malaysia, Japan, Kenya, China, and Spain in his dorm. He also had his first ever classroom experience where the majority of the students were black. Coming from Nicollet Falls, that must've been mind-blowing.

But what was new with her?

Still just trying to make a decent beer, she said.

IPA #12 was a step back. It was excessively sweet in the finish, and the apricot and peach notes from the Citra hops were overpowering. She wanted the Citra hops to whisper a suggestion, not derail the conversation. Mo said that in every great multi-hop IPA, the various hops are like childhood friends who complete each other's sentences. No one hop should have both the greeting and the last word. She was trying to repeat this to Paul one night on the phone when she realized that she'd been going on for almost ten minutes straight.

"Do I talk about beer too much?" she asked him.

"It's what you're doing," he said. "It's what you're doing so we can be together out here. I'd be sad if you didn't talk about it."

He was right, it was what she did. It was all that she did.

"So, you ready to make the best beer of your life so far?" Mo asked her after she dumped #12 down the drain and began cleaning the equipment.

IPA #13 would be the first one she would pour for Frank. It would be the one she'd send out to bars and stores so she could tell Stanford that she had a beer in the world before January 3. With any luck, it would be the beer that would introduce her name to the world as a brewer.

She poured a glass for Frank at the end of a day in mid-November. The head retention was decent, mostly thanks to the percentage of crystal malt, she figured. In any case, it was a handsome pour.

"Not a terrible aroma," Frank said. "Reminds me of a tangerine in the bottom of a Christmas stocking. You wasted four kinds of hops in this, didn't you? Citra, Columbus, Simcoe, and Centennial, right?" He smelled it again. "But it's your malt bill that concerns me. How much crystal? Five percent?"

"Six," Diana said.

"Well, this'll finish like a Midwestern IPA then," he said.

Diana watched as Frank brought the glass to his lips and held it in his mouth. Frank swallowed, took a deep breath, and set the beer down.

Diana watched Frank's face for an answer.

"It's not ready," Frank said, and stood up. "You can do better."

But this was the best she could do. This was the best she'd ever done. And she didn't have time to do better. "I disagree," Diana said. "This is the best beer I can make."

"I believe you," Frank said. "But it's not the best beer you **could** make. When I taste this beer, I can taste the thought that went into this. I don't want that. I'll show you what I want to taste."

Frank grabbed the beer glass, turned its mouth in the direction of Diana's face, and flicked his forearm, tossing the contents of the glass all over Diana's clothes.

Diana screamed. She stood there, drenched in her own beer. "Asshole!" she yelled.

"There!" Frank said. "That instinct. That's what I want in here. Do that."

Frank made Diana leave his office, and she just sat on the floor by the fat gray mash tun, soaking wet on a November Monday, figuring that if she started now, she'd maybe be able to complete one more beer by Christmas. Maybe. Right then, however, she didn't want to start a new beer.

But she did.

Diana tried something completely different for IPA #14. She added a fourth grain, hoping for a firmer malt backbone, dropped the crystal percentage to 4 percent to make the beer less sweet, and switched it up to just three hops—Citra, Simcoe, and Columbus.

It was almost ready by the time Paul came home for Christmas break. She borrowed Edith's Eagle Talon to pick him up at the airport.

They kissed for what felt like several minutes. At

a certain point it occurred to them that the airport cop was just watching them and waiting for them to be done before forcing them to pull away from the white curb.

"Where do you wanna go?" Diana asked him. Paul had grown out his facial hair, and his body was slightly strange to her touch, but he was smiling.

"I don't even care," he said. "How about Arby's?"

She hadn't told Paul until the fall of senior year that her grandma worked at the Arby's in town, and even though they'd never been there together before, Paul began to insist on going there when Edith was working. He'd be in line and yell, **"Hi Edith!"** like a superfan in the front row shouting to his favorite singer. He seemed to love Diana, and said that he did, but it was in moments like that when she realized that she loved him, too.

Number 14 was ready two days later. She was surprised when Paul told her he wanted to try it, just because she'd never seen him drink. She brought him to the brewery after hours and poured him a sample out of the pigtail.

"Let me know what you think," she said, smelling the grapefruit, pine, hibiscus, forest floor, and apricot on the nose. Paul brought it to his lips.

"Oh, my God," Paul said. "You made this?"

She nodded.

"Don't tell my parents, but I had a lot of beer this last semester. And this, this is amazing."

"You like it," she said, not quite believing him yet.

"Diana, it's incredible."

She had to kiss him right then, and they almost even had sex right there except for the fact that it was super cold in that part of the brewery.

Everyone else at Heartlander got to experience this one. Mo loved it. Jealous Matt loved it. Maybe he wasn't jealous. Even Anna claimed to like it. Frank said he'd try it over lunch. Then after lunch. Then after he was off the phone.

Frank finally made time to try Diana's IPA #14 at 3:39 that afternoon. Diana set a glass on her boss's desk, and Frank held it to the light, smelled it, and finally took a sip.

"You're closer," he said. "Now make this one thirteen times."

It felt like Diana's heart shot through her ribs and splashed onto the iced-over Mississippi River. She stared back at Frank's unmoving, unmoved face. "But it's good now, isn't it?"

"Yeah, it's good. But is this B-plus beer the best you can do?"

"Maybe," Diana said. "I don't know."

"You don't know? Then why would you bottle

this stuff?" Frank pushed the mostly full glass of IPA #14 toward Diana. "Dump this out and get back to work."

Diana paced around as Mo sat at his desk and unboxed little spools of beer bottle labels.

"I have to bottle this beer," Diana said. "I'm out of time. I have to."

"It's December 19," Mo said. "You'll hardly have time to do that, much less get it in stores, much less get strangers to actually drink it. And certainly no one like Flavor Dave is going to review it that quickly."

"It doesn't matter, I think I just need to be able to say it exists. It exists in the world and people can buy it and I made it."

"Do you want to go to college or do you want to be a brewer? Because you are almost a decent brewer."

"I don't know," Diana said, because she'd never asked that question herself.

"Well, what did you want to be before you started working here?"

"It didn't matter," she said. "I was just trying to survive."

That night, Diana told Paul that she couldn't apply to Stanford this year, because there was no way she could get her beer out in time to mean anything.

"In six months," she said, "I'll master this recipe, get it out there, and then have the next six months where people will buy it and drink it, and maybe review it, and write about it. That's what I need. What do you think?"

Paul lay flat on his bed, and stared at his ceiling. "Do you know what I think? I think you're cheap labor to them and they just want to keep you around."

Diana sat up, facing Paul's **City of God** poster, an image Diana had seen shimmering from all angles, and now just looked stark and flat and glossy. "I don't think that's true, I think they're trying to make me better."

"Then go in and ask for a raise and see what they say. You can't let them use you."

"OK," Diana said, already scared of what would happen.

Frank Schabert had a completely different perspective on Diana's employment.

"I've let you use I don't know how many dollars' worth of malt, hops, yeast, and water. I've let you use equipment that I should be using myself to make beer that I'll actually sell to people. You get all of this free and unlimited and indefinite. Who's using who, you idiot?"

"I see your point," Diana said.

"But about the raise. You show slight progress as an employee and a human being, and you still haven't stolen anything that I've noticed. I'll bump you up to eleven an hour starting in January. How's that? It'll go up again if you ever make anything worth selling. Unless you run off to college and abandon us."

"I'm not applying to Stanford this month," Diana said. "I'm going to wait another year."

Frank nodded. "Then get back to work."

Diana wasn't sure if she could get better. Avoiding the simple mistakes, like not using dirty equipment, was easy enough. She doubted that she had much to learn from simply repeating the process, but somehow, she was wrong. IPA #15 was an incremental step up from #14, #16 and #17 were no worse, and #18 was perhaps a full flight of stairs up from #17. It was early April and perhaps it was the fact that it was the first day the sun had come out in more than a week, but #18 was the first time Diana actually felt the work had become mindless. The work, the measurements, and the timing were all becoming automatic to her. She was no longer just moving water, malt, hops, and yeast from one place to another. It felt like they were moving on their own.

"A-minus," Frank said. "I know some places who would even bottle this. But I don't want to bottle A-minus beer and neither should you."

Even Mo seemed impressed. "Hey," he told their boss. "I think we're going to need to design a CoMa IPA label." This was something they had to do months in advance, because of the government approval process.

"Only if Matt Duncan has run out of actual useful things to do," Frank said. "And only if you're absolutely sure about that name."

It was Memorial Day and Diana had just tasted IPA #20 for the first time when she and Mo went to Burnsville to check out a used Volkswagen Golf hatchback that would end up becoming the first car Diana ever owned.

"The hatchback will be great," Mo said as he drove. "There's a surprising amount of storage capability in those little cars."

Diana's phone chimed. She was still used to thinking that every time a phone made a noise, it was someone else's.

It was Paul. They hadn't communicated in a while, maybe three days.

"What's up, babe?" Diana answered.

"Hi," he said. His voice seemed serious. "Is now a good time for you to talk?"

"Yeah, I guess," she said, glancing at Mo, who was lowering the stereo volume.

"I've got something to tell you," he said.

Diana supposed it was just fine that Mo overheard her reaction to Paul breaking up with her. With the rest of her friends off at various colleges, he'd pretty much become Diana's best buddy anyway. This didn't mean that Diana wanted to start crying or anything in front of Mo, even though she felt like it. No, Diana pretty much managed to keep it together just then, in as much as someone can when the first man she ever loved tells her that he's staying in California for the summer and maybe it's best that they take a break for a while.

It wasn't until she'd hung up that she realized that she didn't feel like taking a break, and for Paul to do this to her after all these years of her working to be with him felt like he'd driven a forklift through her heart.

Mo had wise, decent advice. "Write him an email tonight," he said. "Then wait three days. And if you still want to send it, send it. But tonight, write something down, get it out."

"I want to call him back right now," Diana said.

Mo grabbed Diana's arm. "No. I'll throw your phone out the window. Leave him alone."

The world outside felt sideways. Everything they passed looked too bright, and stuttered along like she was drunk, but with no giddiness or pleasure. She was momentarily furious at a billboard for a local dentist, and the giant fake smiles of a fake white-toothed family. No one was ever that happy because of dentistry. She wanted to climb up there and choke them, the whole lot of them. Well, maybe not the kids.

"My wife works with some cute interns," Mo said. "When you're ready."

Diana couldn't even look at him. "No. Not even close."

"OK. But you know that old saying about how to get over someone?"

"No, how?"

"Buy a used Volkswagen Golf."

By the time they got to the guy selling the used VW, Diana didn't really feel like negotiating. The guy hadn't mowed his lawn in weeks from the looks of it and his backyard was filled with cars in various states of disrepair. This would be the most she'd ever spent on anything at once. But her goal was to buy a car that was in decent shape that she could afford outright.

Diana wondered if the guy could tell that Diana had just lost the first love of her life on the drive over. Maybe he just saw a simple business trans-action, a young woman who knew nothing about cars, or nothing at all.

"Want a beer?" he asked, after he handed her the keys.

"What do you have?" she replied. She didn't want one, but she had to know.

"I got something for everybody," he said, and opened a fridge filled with Blotz, Miller Lite, PBR, and Corona.

Diana was now a person who judged people by what kind of beer they had in their fridge. She felt like an idiot giving this guy almost three thousand bucks, if this was how he spent it.

"I'm not old enough," Diana said. "I was just curious."

Three blocks from the guy's house, she pulled over. She couldn't see the road with Paul's face and words blossoming in her brain. She'd finally bought a car of her own, completely hers, with her own honest money, and now she couldn't even drive it. She could only sit in it and cry.

Without the dream of someday attending Stanford with Paul, returning to the brewery the next day felt like surrender.

"Hey, Diana," Mo said, and threw her a navy blue bundle wrapped in plastic. "Here's a free jacket. You're a medium, right?"

Diana could always use free clothes, especially

a jacket. Of course, this one had the Heartlander logo stitched on the front and the back. She already smelled her work on her clothes and wiped it off the bottoms of her shoes and saw it in the back of her car. Whatever she used to be, they'd colonized.

The last time dumping all of her beer out, it got to her. The name in honor of her parents was losing its meaning. She'd save it for when she was better at this. She told Mo she was going to re-title this beer "Brutal Chaos IPA."

"Oh, cheer up," Mo said. "But I do kinda like it."

"What's the point of what Frank is doing?" Diana asked Mo.

"What's the point?" Mo replied. "I don't think he's trying to make a point, I think he's trying to make the best beer in the goddamned world. Dude, he's been at it for twenty-five years. He was making craft IPAs before the term even existed."

"No, I mean with me. Did he put you through this?"

"Shit yeah," Mo said. "When Kristin and I moved here, I came from a distillery. I'd cellar mastered at breweries, I'd made all kinds of beer at home, and he still made me re-do a bunch of crap. You came in, you'd hardly even drank beer before. Now look at you."

"I just don't know how much longer I can do this."

"Yeah, you do."

Brutal Chaos IPA #20, as Diana could have predicted, was not good enough for Frank, even with the less sentimental sobriquet. Nor was #21, or #22, or #23. IPA #24 was finishing just as the trees began dumping their leaves and Mo quit wearing shorts to work. As far as Diana knew, she'd done nothing differently. Maybe there was half a pinch less of one thing and half a pinch more of another thing, but to Diana it was the same damn beer, and she doubted her ability to be any more articulate with these ingredients and equipment at her skill level. The only thing she could say for sure was that she'd come a hell of a long way. This beer was her blood, heart, and mind, and for that hour, that day, almost perfect.

"It's pretty good," Frank said. "I can probably sell it."

Diana was certain she misheard her boss, and asked him to repeat himself.

"I said, you're done. Now thank me, before I change my mind."

"Thank you," Diana said. She had tears in her eyes. Her heart was exploding from inside. Her first thought was that she wished she could tell Paul. Maybe she would, in an email. But this was it. She'd have a beer out in the world, even if it would just be in southeastern Minnesota. Brutal Chaos IPA would exist, among all the other beers on the planet.

Frank frowned. "But I'm just one guy with an

opinion. The people you really have to worry about are sitting on a barstool right now, ordering something that they've heard about already. But yeah, let's try to put this stuff in front of them."

"I can't believe it," Diana said.

"I can't either, but this is a beer that you couldn't have made eight months ago. There's a little bit of life in this one, somehow. Not a lot, but enough."

Frank intended for Diana to do a dry run one time on the big equipment before making the batch they'd sell, but Diana nailed it in one. They'd now be bottling her beer in the middle of football season. Perfect IPA weather.

It was a tradition at Heartlander that every brewer had to label and package his or her own beer themselves, and to rally volunteers to help, the brewer would provide free food and drinks, and they'd make a little party out of it.

The people who showed up for the bottling, labeling, and packaging were Grandma Edith; Mo Akbar; Matt Duncan; good old Principal Shultz; Ann and Will from the coffee shop; a couple of the dudes from the document shredding place next door; plus Uncle Eugene, who initially protested against working for free but changed his mind at the promise of complimentary beer; and Clarissa, who drove all the way from Ohio just to be there. They hadn't seen a lot of each other since Clarissa left, and for a while Diana assumed they'd just grown apart. Still, she felt herself smile, involuntarily, when she saw her old bestie walk through the door.

Clarissa loved Oberlin, and that place had changed her in ways that made Diana wish she'd witnessed the transformation. She now had pink hair and a wrist tattoo that read VIRGINIA DARE, the name of her all-female college dance-punk band.

"Dude!" She play-punched Diana in the arm. "So what kind of beer do ya got for us? Any of that Two Thirteen Pale Ale?"

God, it was good to see her. "Anything you want, babe," Diana said.

Even with a gut full of free beer, Clarissa busted her ass for Diana that night. Everyone did, even Eugene. Though it obviously made the work a lot easier, Diana couldn't relax, because all she could think about was the next beer she wanted to brew, and all the things she'd do differently next time.

The next morning, Frank asked the rep from the distributor if Diana could tag along when he brought Diana's beer to bar and restaurant managers. Over the next few days, Diana rode along as a handsome young dude named Andy Nakagawa visited places during their quiet, early hours with his blue Volkswagen Golf full of boxes, cases, and POS promotional materials. Andy had cut himself shaving, wore a blazer that was maybe a size too large, had cute hair, and listened to audiobooks as he drove.

"It's awesome to have a brewer along," Andy said. Diana couldn't tell if he meant it.

"I've got the exact same car as you," she said, a brightness in her voice.

"Oh, cool," Andy said. "It's got a lot of storage for a little car, doesn't it."

"Yeah, looks like you need it," she said, like a dork. Why is she pointing out the obvious? He knows that. It's why he owns the damn car.

"Yeah." He looked behind himself at his cargo-loaded vehicle and sighed. "This is my life, driving a carload of alcohol around. Who'd have thought? Eleven years of violin lessons, all for shit." She laughed, but wanted to change the subject. She noticed a plastic bottle in his cup holder that wasn't in English. "What's this?"

"Just some tea."

"Where'd you get it?"

"United Noodles," he said, like it was obvious.

"Where's that?"

He seemed halfway between scandalized and amused. "You've never been to United Noodles?"

"No," she said. "Where is it, Minneapolis?"

"Yeah. Wish it was closer."

She figured; that's why she'd never heard of it. "I don't make it down there too much." Like, just once in the last year, but she wasn't about to admit that.

"It's awesome. My grandma loves it. It's where she can get Japanese ingredients."

"Your grandma's from Japan?"

"Yeah, she's American, but she was born in Kyoto," he said.

"That's cool," she said, and meant it. She hadn't met many people of Japanese descent in Minnesota. "Maybe I should check it out."

He glanced at her and pursed his lips. "On second thought, I don't know. You white Minnesotans sure like things bland. I like the ramen there the way it is now. You start eating there, it's gonna mess things up."

"That's probably true," Diana said. "But I like spicy things."

He seemed mildly impressed. "Oh yeah? What's your favorite spice?"

"Butter," she said.

He laughed hard enough, he almost drove them into traffic. "Dude!" he shouted.

She liked that he called her dude without thinking. Not that he'd understand why. "Actually, it's not butter. It's a tie between Citra and Willamette."

"Don't tell me, I know what those are," Andy said, smiling. "OK, tell me."

"Hops."

"Of course," he nodded, and then made a face like he'd just thought of an answer to a difficult question. "Hey, did you use those hops in your beer?"

"No," she replied...
"Just looking for a...

She wasn't sure what he'd ...
soon became evident that A... that, but it
wasn't easy. She answered direct... of work
her beer, but otherwise remained qu...s about
all the ways bar managers delivered ...rbing
ment. "We already have three IPA ta...pint-
doesn't move in this bar." "We only sell ...PA
from [insert multinational corporation] as pa...
our deal with them." "We don't know that kin...
we want the other kind our customers like." It sure
wasn't enough just to have an amazing new IPA
from a known craft brewer.

After a stop in Nicollet Falls, they drove past
the last Elks Lodge where Diana's grandpa used to
hang out.

"I'd love to have my beer sold there," Diana said.

"You won't," Andy said. "That's not the craft
IPA crowd so much."

"Have you ever tried?"

"Maybe the day I get the Blotz account."

After yet another place turned down Brutal Chaos
IPA, Andy admitted that maybe they were doing
this all wrong.

"I can't believe we didn't do this earlier," Andy

28 per name alone obviously

said. "But th
isn't selling
your story
bet it's ir

) let's try something. What's
t's the full story of this beer? I

"We
"D
we'r

it started when—"

me now," Andy said. "Wait until
I can tell it's a good one."

n minutes after they walked in the door of a
in Woodbury, Diana was finished telling the
ory of Brutal Chaos #24.

"Wait a sec," the bar manager was shaking his head. "You've already made this beer twenty-four times? And you're nineteen years old?"

Andy banged his head on the bar. "Oh my God. Well it's a good thing we only show up before places are open. I thought you were older than me. I thought you were at least twenty-five."

Diana took it as a compliment. "I turn twenty in two months."

"Well, let's quit dicking around!" the bar manager said. "Pour me a glass."

Over the next two days, they got Diana's beer in every place she told the story, which ended up being nine bars, two restaurants, and a family-owned liquor store. It was like she was waving a magic wand. People were intrigued by some facet of the tale, whether it was Frank catching a kid stealing from his garage and turning her into a brewer, a nineteen-year-old girl creating an extremely good Midwest IPA, and/or the amount of work it took Diana to create it while helping support her grandma.

"Hearts and minds," Andy said, and then glanced behind himself at a cardboard box that read EXXXTASY NEW YORK CINNAMON VODKA. "Hey, can we take just half a day and lie to people, and say that you also made this? I can't move one bottle of this shit."

Diana pointed as they passed the Elks Lodge. "Please can we stop there?"

"No. Don't waste your time. You could give it to them for free and they won't sell it."

"Just give me a six-pack. That's all I ask. Please."

Andy shook his head. "You're going in by yourself," he said, and instantly dipped his eyeline toward his phone, as if he'd just switched her off.

Twenty-five minutes later, she came back empty-handed.

"I'm not even going to ask," he said, not looking up from his phone.

"Pop the trunk," Diana said. "They want two cases."

Andy stared up at her like she'd come back from the dead.

"Oh. And your business card."

Later that day, they had an early dinner at a restaurant in St. Paul called The Barbary Fig, which he paid for, and even though she was impressed by the food—it was her first time ever having "tagine of chicken"—he hardly seemed attentive to the meal. He still couldn't get over the Elks Lodge stop, even on their way out the door.

"You're a miracle worker," he said, for maybe the third time. "I'm taking you everywhere."

Although she sure wouldn't mind spending more time with him—in addition to being good-looking, he'd proven to be smart, funny, and a little cynical—she was about to remind him again that the Elks Lodge thing was just a family connection. But before she could speak, he ran ahead of her, to open the front door for a mother carrying what looked like a brand-new baby.

"Thank you," the woman said, smiling.

"Ope," Diana said, staring at the tiny baby, but forgetting to get out of its mother's way.

As they walked toward the sidewalk, he glanced behind himself. "God, I want one of those some-day," he said.

Who the hell was this guy?

She'd never told anybody, but she wanted a family. And for the dumbest, most obvious reason, too. To replace the one that was gone.

She didn't want one now, by God, or even soon, but there was no question that she did. Thinking about it now, in public, with this guy, made her feel like her fantasies were fluttering around her in the air like bits of paper.

"Where did I park?" he asked, glancing around. When he looked her in the eyes just then, he seemed to perceive he'd triggered something in her, or at least that's what she wanted to believe.

"I could go for some coffee," she said.

"Coffee," he repeated. "I know a place."

He turned his body left, and she walked alongside him.

A day later, as Diana was hosing out a keg, Frank came down from the office and sat on a folding chair and stared at her.

"How the shit did you get your IPA in an Elks Lodge?"

Diana walked over to the spigot, turned it off, and nodded as she coiled the hose. "I just told them about you, and how we met, and how hard you made me work, and how many times I made this beer, and how many years I worked on it. Just that, basically."

Frank looked Diana in the face and smiled. "That's why I did it, you know."

"Did what?"

"Oh, your beer was ready over a year ago. We could've bottled #14 and sold it, easily."

There weren't a lot of times in Diana's life so far where anger came quickly to her. This time, what she heard Frank say ignited too much fury for her to contain. Her fainting head hit the concrete floor so hard, it made a sound that probably hurt the teeth of everyone who heard it.

When Diana came to, her body was on the black leather couch in the office and her brain felt split open. She saw Mo standing over her. Someone handed her an ice pack.

"Hey, Elkhorn," Mo said. "You're a badass."

Diana had to close her eyes against the light. "Elkhorn?"

"That's your new official brewery nickname. Elkhorn. Hunter and tamer of Elks Lodge bottle lists everywhere."

Diana's skull hurt too much for her to appreciate this. "Where's Frank?"

"He's here," Mo said, and stepped away.

"Sorry about that," Frank said. "Maybe I should've told you to sit down first."

Diana held the ice pack against her temple and closed her eyes. "Why?" she asked aloud. She was pretty sure. "Why did you do that?"

"It worked, didn't it?"

"What do you mean it worked?"

"Your story. The craft IPA market is becoming oversaturated. You saw that your first day out with Andy. He likes you, by the way."

"Oh," Diana said.

"Asserting a new brand is all about forming one-on-one relationships with vendors, and they can share your story with their customers. And now you have a hell of a story. I would've kept you going, but I wanted to get you out there before you turned twenty. People love the whole teenage brewmaster thing. You know, both the St. Paul and Minneapolis papers want to do stories on you. This is great exposure for the brand."

Diana sat up, one hand against a throbbing eye. She took a deep breath. "You used me."

Frank seemed to be smiling. "Jesus, you and your persecution complex. Who used who, kid? You have a life now. You have a career. I wanted you to earn it and you did. I've only told two people in my whole life that I loved them, and that's my wife and my mom, but you'd be number three if I could say it."

Diana stared up at an orange stain in the drop ceiling. "So you made me work my ass off for your goddamned brand."

"You got better at it, didn't you? You could make that beer in the dark now. When you had to reproportion the recipe for the larger equipment, you got it in one. I didn't do that. And I didn't make you get better. I didn't make you keep going. And I'm not out there telling your story, getting your craft IPA into bars where no craft IPA has ever set foot before. That's all you, kid. Now it's up to you to appreciate it or not. But I hope you do. Because you're nineteen years old and you're damn near great at something. That's like less than one percent of the population. So why don't you find out what it's like to get even better."

"OK," Diana said.

"But take tomorrow off," Frank said. "You look like shit."

One week later, Andy Nakagawa finally built up the nerve to ask Diana out on an actual date. He'd picked a restaurant down near Hastings called The Point, because he knew that they served Diana's beer. She might have kissed him for that reason alone. It was the first time she'd seen the phrase "Brutal Chaos IPA" in print on a menu. They were charging five bucks a bottle for it.

Andy ordered one. He looked good, in his black button-up shirt, and when he looked at her, she noticed he was always smiling, like he couldn't help it.

The waitress came over and set Diana's water

down first, and then set a chilled, empty pint glass in front of Andy, and opened the bottle of beer.

"Here's the Brutal Chaos," she said, pouring it deliberately against the side of Andy's glass. "I love this IPA. Have you had it before?"

"No," Andy lied, and smiled at Diana. "First time."

"It's got quite a story," the waitress said.

$18.95

Edith, 2016

It seemed like a strange thing to admit, but Edith didn't expect to live to seventy-seven. No one in her family would've, if they were being sensible. Between her parents, grandparents, and great-grandparents, only one of them, her grandma Doris, even made it to seventy. As a child, it was strange and a little sad to hear stories from schoolmates of doting grandparents and visits from great-grandmas, when the old people in her family were as common as cherries in a can of store-brand fruit cocktail. Still, she'd done her best to accept her heritage of stunted mortality, and it helped a little to put a cheerful spin on things. **God must like**

our family, she used to tell people, **because He sure can't wait for us to join Him**.

Edith had no reason to believe she'd have a different fate, which is one way of saying that she didn't plan for the future, besides the vague expectation of Social Security and Medicare. Nowhere she ever worked had a pension plan anyway, and no one she ever worked alongside could afford to save for retirement, and they certainly didn't have the poor manners to talk about it if they did. So here Edith was in 2016, on her seventy-seventh birthday, and she wasn't only alive, she was still working, every day they would let her.

She supposed that her parents and grandparents would've been proud of her. None of them would have ever retired, had they lived that long. Maybe, like in her father's case, they slowed down later in life due to illness, but her father had never said, "I just want to quit and do nothing," and never would've, as far as she knew.

Admittedly, her work was much different from theirs. Her parents and grandparents had corn-fields, manure, the metallic tang of country water; she had employee discounts, customer complaints, and the dim lighting over Seasonal Clearance. Her parents never grew weary of their work in the way she had, not that she was complaining about Arby's or Kohl's.

Then, a month before Diana and Andy's wedding, Kohl's let her go. They were nice about it, and reassured her that it wasn't anything she did. More of that business was just moving onto the internet, someone said. People didn't need to try on a jacket or a pair of slacks before they bought them anymore. It was nothing personal.

They'd miss her, though. She was sure of that. Edith was the best in the whole store at spotting expired coupons, even if she often let them slide when her boss wasn't around. She'd also become a real ninja at dealing with customers who tried to return things they'd bought at another store, or attempted to return with an incorrect or phony receipt. Edith was amazed at the amount of effort and dignity that someone would expend just to relieve Kohl's of $18.95, but she was never unsympathetic. There were plenty of times in her own life when an extra $18.95 would've made a difference.

Like now, maybe. When she'd be out hunting for a job. Again. As a seventy-seven-year-old woman.

"Don't worry about it," Diana's kind fiancé, Andy, told Edith over dinner that night. "Maybe it's time for you to kick back and relax. Take some time for yourself."

Even after five years of dating her granddaughter, coming over for dinner at least once a week, he still didn't truly know her. She'd been supporting one person or another almost her entire life. Relaxation was never part of the schedule. It'd really only been in the last year with Diana moved out, and her son, Eugene, relatively stable, that no one depended on her full-time. She'd had more time to herself than ever before, and found it both anxious and boring.

The only reward she'd imagined she'd receive was that people would finally recognize her effort when it was gone. She wouldn't dare admit it to anyone, but she may have occasionally comforted herself with her daydream of people sobbing over her casket, and saying, **She worked so hard just to make a better life for others, and no one ever appreciated her**.

"We appreciate everything you do for us, so much," said Andy. "I think it's our turn to help you out. So don't worry about getting another job. Just take it easy."

Diana put a sealed white envelope on the table. Edith knew it contained money, from the careful way Diana handled it. "You took care of me for so many years."

This was foolish. Even if Diana was sharing a place with Andy out of wedlock, they couldn't be saving enough money to just be giving it away. Edith did the smart thing with the envelope, which was to not acknowledge it. "You know what you haven't told me?" Edith asked them. "What kind of cake you want at your wedding."

Diana frowned. "We told you, we don't want cake, we want pie."

Oh, and on top of it all, they wanted her pies to be served instead of wedding cake, which was kind of them, but ridiculous.

"Don't be silly," Edith said. "People like wedding cake."

"We don't care what other people like. We want your pie."

That was nice to hear, but again, they were completely wrong. She was shocked at still having to keep arguing in favor of cake, being that she vastly preferred pie herself, but instead she did the polite thing and just changed the subject.

"Is the wedding indoors or outdoors?"

"Both. The ceremony's outdoors and the reception's indoors."

That's right—it was at some park on the river, down between Rosemount and Hastings. She'll have to remind people to bring bug spray. "What kind of band are you having?"

"We're not having a band. We're going to use a playlist on Andy's phone."

"Well, that sounds affordable," Edith said. She admired the frugality, certainly, but this seemed a little extreme. "But isn't your cousin Clarissa in a band?"

"You wouldn't like Clarissa's band, Grandma. Believe me. And anyway, they broke up when she went to grad school."

Edith had tried to envision this whole shebang and she couldn't. The ceremony wasn't even going to be in a church, and a person who wasn't even a real minister was going to be the officiant. But they didn't ask for her money or wisdom, so they didn't deserve more of her complaints. Even if the cake thing was a travesty.

"At least you have your drinks situation figured out."

"Yeah, Sarah Allison is gonna be our bartender," Diana said.

Edith had met this Sarah Allison girl a few times; when Heartlander converted part of its space to a taproom a few years ago, that was who Frank and Anna hired to run it. She had a few too many tattoos for Edith's taste, but was otherwise pleasant enough.

"Well, that's nice that friends from the brewery are helping out."

"Yeah, the hard part is deciding on which two beers. Frank will only give us two kinds for free."

"Besides the ones you made?"

"Including them. I don't own those beers. Frank owns them."

Right then, for the first time in a long time, she

felt worried about her granddaughter's future. She was worried about what Frank was getting away with, what other behavior he was masking behind slightly generous favors. Then again, maybe behind-the-scenes Frank was actually as charitable as he seemed. She didn't know. She just wanted people to be happy, so she kept all of this to herself.

Edith wasn't usually one for crowds, but wedding crowds were an exception, because in that case it was all people you knew and people you ought to know. It was one of the few happy occasions when a person could see extended family and distant cousins all in one place, so it puzzled her that Diana and Andy only invited about forty people—and mostly friends at that—and only let six of them witness the actual vows. At least she made the cut there. And they also let her bring someone, so she invited Lucy Koski Sarrazin, although it was awkward that Lucy couldn't attend the ceremony.

"Oh, I don't mind," Lucy said, when she arrived early anyway. Long ago, she'd been one of those pretty girls, and was actually friends with Helen until sometime in high school. She was petite back then, and wasn't anymore, but her power was that she'd always acted like she had the exact body she was supposed to have, at every age, like most men did. She also had the air of someone who had a complete handle on things. Right away, Sarah

Allison came up to Lucy and asked her where to set up the bar inside.

"Anywhere not in direct sunlight," Lucy said, without hesitation, peering into the oblong, modern-looking wood building that would host the reception.

"Thanks," Sarah said. The young woman was wearing something sleeveless that showed off all the tattoos on both of her arms. Edith looked over at Lucy, her lips pursed.

Lucy sighed and shook her head as she watched the girl walk away. "So where am I supposed to be during this private ceremony?"

"I'm afraid they want you to wait in there," Edith said. "I'm so sorry."

"Ah, you can't tell these kids nothing," Lucy said. "Do you know how I handle my grandkids? I do what I want anyway, and if they get mad, I pretend that my memory's going."

"Yeah, that's pretty much what I did today," Edith said, which wasn't true, but was agreeable, which is often more important. "They only wanted pies for their wedding, and I did that, I made pies. But I also made a cake."

"That'll show them," Lucy said. "No wonder you look so tired. What kind of cake?"

"Red velvet, with white frosting."

"Oh, I like those," Lucy nodded. "That's the kind Julia Roberts had in that one movie."

"**Steel Magnolias**," Edith said. It was one of

the reasons she chose that kind; she remembered Diana and Stanley watching that movie, a couple of times, and how much Diana loved it.

Waking up this morning, she'd felt the absence of the people missing from this day, Stanley's most of all. When she looked at her granddaughter, walking through the grass in her shiny white dress, she could almost see him tugging at Diana's hand, leading her forward toward the altar, wanting this "boring part" to be over with, so they could hurry up and have some dang beer together.

For her part, Edith considered the wedding a success. All of the cake was gone in minutes—someone called it "magnificent," but they'd probably just never had that kind before—and there was only one piece of pie left. Clarissa Johnson and another one of the younger folks, that Astra girl from Diana's high school, drank too much and embarrassed themselves, whether they realized it or not. Then Frank Schabert gave a rambling speech where he not only mentioned supplying the beer, but also claimed that he arranged the venue, which Edith found a tad prideful. Maybe it didn't matter. The couple was happy, and Andy's family, the Nakagawas, were extremely kind and sweet, except for his ninety-year-old grandma Chiyo. Edith figured Chiyo might be trouble when she instantly got along with Lucy. Together, they made some comments about other people's clothes and eating habits that were accurate but that Edith found too unkind to repeat.

"How come the bride's not drinking?" Chiyo asked at one point. "She made the beer."

"Maybe she wants to give everyone else a chance to drink it first," Edith said. That'd be polite, which Diana certainly was.

"Maybe she poisoned it," Chiyo said, and looked in her glass. "We're all gonna die."

"Maybe she's pregnant," Lucy shrugged.

Edith bolted up straight in her chair as if she were a puppet animated by God's own hand. Of course. It was right under her nose this whole time, all of those recent Sunday dinners at her place when Andy drank beer and Diana didn't, and Edith had never thought to ask, or even wonder.

Before the dancing started, Edith pulled her granddaughter aside and asked her, as directly as she was able.

"Yeah," Diana said. She looked more nervous than happy. "I haven't told anyone yet. I've already miscarried twice. I just don't even want to talk about it, if you don't mind."

So she'd been trying. And she was cursed with her great-grandma's genes.

"It'll happen this time," Edith said, and she hoped she was right.

———

Edith first heard about Autumn Pines, whose brochure claimed they offered ASSISTED LIVING FOR MATURE ADULTS SINCE 1983, from Marvin Gardens, right after coming home from Diana and Andy's wedding. Edith had somehow got roped into drinking some celebratory lilac wine at Marvin's apartment, and she accidentally put her glass on a shiny lavender brochure instead of a coaster.

"Whoops," she said, catching her mistake.

"That's OK, ruin 'em," Marvin said, hovering his trembling wrist over the array of pamphlets and brochures on his shiny maple-wood coffee table. "That's where my daughter wants to put me."

One glance and Edith knew what was up. The names on the glossy, full-color handouts were things like CHERRY ORCHARD MEADOWS and THE RESIDENCE AT AUGSBURG CIRCLE with pictures of well-groomed seniors laughing like teenage models in a Dr Pepper commercial. The properties themselves looked uncomfortably flawless—like golf courses with fancy motels in the middle—and none of them showed anyone doing anything useful.

That's why the brochure on the bottom of Marvin's pile caught Edith's attention. It was a single, two-sided card with no photos of enforced gaiety, just plain, peach-colored paper stock with dark blue lettering reading AUTUMN PINES: THE PLACE OF YOUR LIFE.

"That's the real cheap one," Marvin said, waving

at the brochure as if it was a fly over his mayonnaise. "What does that even mean, 'The Place of Your Life'?"

"I don't know," Edith said. "But there's something I kind of like about it."

It said in the fine print that Autumn Pines was a chain with facilities throughout the Midwest. There was even one just a fifteen-minute drive away.

Marvin started futzing with the remote. "Oh, **Jeopardy!**'s on," he said. "You know my granddaughter can say the answers before Alex Trebek is even done with the question."

Edith, transfixed by the brochure, just nodded. "Do you imagine they serve halfway decent desserts at a place like Autumn Pines?"

"I don't even want to think about it," Marvin said, and then yelled the name "James Buchanan" at the TV.

"Was it James Buchanan?" Edith asked, looking up a few seconds later.

Marvin shook his head. "One of these times it's gonna be."

"Can I have this one?" Edith asked, already putting the Autumn Pines brochure in her purse, certain of the reply.

As it turned out, Autumn Pines was better than she'd imagined. It was out on the calm, scrubby outskirts of town, between a baseball diamond and a closed-down carpet wholesaler; there wasn't a pine in sight. But in Edith's opinion, unless they were used for a windbreak, pine trees were over-rated. Maybe there had been pine trees once, and they had to cut them down to build Autumn Pines, in which case it was for the better.

The building itself was well-enough maintained. At the covered entrance to Autumn Pines—a very nice touch—there was an old woman in a pink bathrobe sitting in a wheelchair parked directly in front of the sliding doors, no one hovering over her or bossing her around. Edith liked the idea of a place that let a person be completely in the way, hassle-free, whenever one felt like it.

There was no one at the security desk. The fact that they were evidently understaffed got her excited. She signed her name in the guest registry, and stepped confidently into one of the hallways.

For a place that appeared to be no-frills, it had everything, or it had once. A chapel. A library. A beauty salon, which looked closed, but maybe it wasn't permanent. Ha! Stanley would've liked that one.

As she hunted around for the main office, a tired young woman with a big black cross tattooed on her forearm appeared around a corner, pushing an empty wheelchair, and nonchalantly stared past her.

"Excuse me, please. Who do I see about getting a job here?" Edith asked.

"What?" The woman laughed a little. "You want to work **here**? Wow."

"Yes, I have forty years of nursing home kitchen experience. At St. Anthony-Waterside, up in New Stockholm." She thought she'd be specific, just in case. It was in all those newspapers, after all.

"Oh," the woman said. Nope, no hint of recognition. "Well, Peg's office is down there, at the end of the hall. Good luck to ya, I suppose."

Peg, the administrator of Autumn Pines, didn't smile much and wore a lot of makeup, but was refreshingly to the point. She claimed they weren't presently hiring, not in the kitchen or anywhere else, so Edith offered to volunteer a few days a week to get in the building and be first in the know when something opened up. Peg said fine, some people needed extra help getting to and from the dining room at mealtimes, and encouraged Edith to take a brief tour of the common areas.

With each minute Edith spent roaming around, and each face she looked into, she felt she just had to work there. Sure, maybe most people wouldn't consider it the nicest place in the world, but there was no doubt that Autumn Pines needed a lot of help, and figured it could use her kind of help in particular.

The next day at Arby's, during one of their breaks hanging outside by the dumpsters, Betsy Nielsen—her favorite coworker and the only other one over sixty-five—asked Edith if she wanted to go on a "girls' trip" to Door County with her and her friend Linda.

"I'd love to," Edith said, moving her head to dodge Betsy's cigarette smoke. "But who can afford that?"

"Oh, live a little for once. There's a ton of cheap motels," Betsy said. "One room split three ways will be like twenty bucks. Anyway, didn't you just get that new job?"

"It's a volunteer job. At least until a paid one opens up."

Betsy almost spit her cigarette onto the asphalt. "You're working for free?"

"I like the work," she said, because she was pretty sure she would.

That evening, Edith had Diana and Andy over for dinner, because it was the night before they left for their honeymoon in the Black Hills, and she insisted on seeing them off. Being that Edith was cooking for someone who was expecting—she hadn't heard any different since the wedding, and had been praying that she wouldn't—she made a four-cheese lasagna, steamed some broccoli, and poured Diana an extra-tall glass of milk. Pregnant women need a lot of real dairy, no matter what those vegan Morrisseys try to tell you.

They were most of the way through dinner when it came out that Edith would be volunteering at Autumn Pines.

"What? No!" Diana shouted, and dropped her fork.

Andy had the expression of a mildly concerned parent. "That old place, north of town there, by the baseball field?"

"Grandma, that place sucks!"

Edith was baffled to hear this from a girl who'd grown up visiting a nursing home, and had been raised by a mother who had as well. "Well, that's not the fault of the people who live there."

"Well, I don't think you're going to march in there with a pie and fix anything, is what I'm saying." The phone in her dirty tote bag buzzed, and she frowned. "Sorry, I better see who it is."

"Diana," Andy frowned. "We're having dinner."

Diana was already standing up with her little red phone. Even if she let it interrupt everything, at least she didn't waste money on one of those fancy new smartphones, and stuck with the one her dad gave her, which still worked perfectly well. "It's work," she said, and walked into the hallway in an attempt to be more discreet.

Edith refilled Diana's glass of milk as she turned

to Andy. "Do you know someone who lives at Autumn Pines?"

Andy shook his head. "No, we just know someone who used to work there. She said it was a total shitshow." He touched his mouth. "Sorry about the language."

Edith waved it off. When she found out that, as a small child, he'd lost a parent—his father died in a horrible accident when he was four—and that he had no siblings, Edith's heart went out to him. She'd also since learned in their rare private conversations that he wanted to be a father, maybe even more eagerly than Diana wanted to be a mother. He was equally frustrated at the tragedy of their childlessness, and perhaps for that reason, he cursed now more than he used to. So what? She was never going to mind it, coming from him.

Edith could hear Diana in the hallway, shouting at someone, but the words "what" and "when" were the only ones she could make out.

"Is everything OK?" Edith called out.

Diana walked out to the kitchen, one hand over her mouth.

Andy spoke his wife's name as if it were a soap bubble on his fingertips.

She stared at them, her eyes full of tears. "It's Frank."

While Andy drove them all to the hospital, Diana told them that Anna and Mo had found Frank bleeding at the foot of the stairs, and he was unresponsive but still alive. Diana found out from the doctor that night that Frank had had a stroke, a pretty bad one. He couldn't move the entire right side of his body, and he couldn't speak or respond to people who were speaking. They didn't know if any of that would ever come back, or if it did, how long it would take.

"Andy will take you home, Grandma," Diana said. "Get some rest before your new job tomorrow."

"And you," Edith replied. "Get some rest before your honeymoon."

"We'll see."

"That brewery's not going anywhere," Edith said, and even though she knew nothing about that business, she was positive of that.

Edith arrived at Autumn Pines the next morning, thirty minutes before breakfast, and walking across the small visitors' parking lot, she heard a man's voice yelling hello. Before she could locate the voice's owner, a husky man in coveralls and a Vietnam Veterans ballcap ambled toward her, wrapping a garden hose.

"I'm Bernie Berglund," he said, extending a hand for her to shake. "I'm the maintenance guy and groundskeeper around these parts."

She liked him right away; maybe it was the ballcap—she had an inherent trust of old men who wore those veterans' caps—maybe it was the mild, familiar Swedish accent, and maybe it was his attitude, which reminded her of a reluctant sheriff in an Old West pioneer town.

She shook his hand briefly, and introduced herself.

"Well, let's get you inside, and we'll get some friends of mine to breakfast."

He took her straight to room 206, where he knocked on a door with a handmade sign that read WELCOME BACK, SHOTTY!

"Shotty, your ride's here!" Bernie called out, and opened the door himself when he heard it unlock. In the doorway of the small, dim apartment was a pale little man in a wheelchair, wearing a Minnesota Twins T-shirt.

"Shotty Vecchio, this is Edith. What's your last name, Edith?"

"Magnusson."

Bernie arched an eyebrow. "Swedish?"

It was her married name, but she wanted to stay in his favor, so she just politely nodded to Shotty. "Nice to meet you."

Shotty squinted up at Bernie. "She's even older than I am."

Bernie laughed. "Beggars can't be choosers, Shotty."

Shotty wheeled himself backward, as if retreating. Edith had dealt with old men like this innumerable times, and figured if he was going to make a stink, she could just let him have his little tantrum and wait it out. Instead, he picked up something from the floor and eked his way forward, holding out a bright orange vase.

"Want to buy a vase? Ten bucks. Bargain of the century."

"Come on, this ain't **Antiques Roadshow**," Bernie said, and took the vase away. "You want breakfast or not?"

"I suppose," Shotty said, deflated. "It'll pass the time."

In the dining room, Edith met the other people who helped bring residents to the dining room; they were mostly younger women CNAs who were courteous to her, but nothing more. Edith suspected that they wouldn't bother to get to know her until she'd put some time in, which was understandable.

Unfortunately, Diana had been correct about a certain prediction.

"Our contract doesn't allow for outside food to

be served in the dining room," Peg replied, when Edith asked her if she could bring in a few pies. "Our staff can't serve them, or even touch them, for liability reasons. If you want to just give them to a resident in their unit, that's different."

Edith didn't want to toot her own horn here and mention that her pies had been a big hit years ago, and written up in all of those papers, and she still wouldn't. The pies ought to speak for themselves. "But I want to share them with everyone," Edith said.

"Then try your luck door to door, if you want," Peg said, already walking away. "We can't stop you."

But Peg had indeed stopped her, which was a shame. She was waiting for a situation like this to inspire her to get baking again. For now, she just put it out of her mind.

After lunch, Edith was curious if Diana and Andy had indeed left for their honeymoon to the Black Hills. She didn't want to call them because then she'd be accused of being nosy when really she was just concerned. Instead, Edith cleverly called Heartlander's main office line.

Anna Schabert answered, which was both a surprise and a relief.

"Is Diana there?" Edith asked.

"No," Anna said. "She's out on vacation. May I ask who's calling?"

"Oh, nobody important," Edith said, smiled, and hung up.

When she had them over for dinner after they returned two weeks later, she expected Diana and Andy to be happy, or at least relaxed. Instead, they came in the front door after half a month of relaxation, looking like God had broken their hearts.

"How was the trip?" Edith asked, taking in their expressions. "Something happen? Is the car OK?" That's what Stanley would've asked.

"We lost it," Diana said.

"Lost what?" Edith asked, but then she saw Diana's face, and knew.

The next morning, Edith was sitting on a nice floral-patterned wingback chair in the Autumn Pines lobby while Bernie Berglund was kneeling about a foot away, fixing the water fountain.

"I don't know," Bernie was saying. "I don't believe in fate, but I do believe that some people are just stuck a certain way. Like, they're born left-handed, and no matter how much they try to be right-handed, they're still left-handed."

"I pray for them every night," Edith said.

"Maybe that's a bad example. I'm left-handed, and I like being left-handed. Ever go to a left-handed store? I don't think they make 'em anymore."

"Because of the internet," Edith said.

"Anyhow," Bernie said, and groaned as he leaned back toward his toolbox. "I don't know why bad people like your sister get whatever they want and good people like Diana don't. But that's why I get out of bed in the morning. To help the good people."

"Me, too," Edith said. "And I didn't say my sister was bad. It'd be too easy of me to think that. I know she's still good inside." She hoped that was true, anyway.

"You're right, you didn't say that," Bernie nodded. "Forgive me if I was out of line."

"She's just doing what she thinks is best, and I don't agree with it."

"People change."

"I don't know." Edith suddenly stood up. "Anyway, thanks for listening."

Bernie glanced at her as she walked away. "Where are you headed?"

"I just had an idea," she said. "I'm going to do something I haven't done in a little while."

When Edith was feeling low like this, baking a pie had never failed to make her happy. Like how some people talk about yoga or mountain climbing or music, it was how she lost herself and touched something else. It was her church away from church. It wouldn't solve any problems, but it might make her and a few other people forget them for a while, and that was something.

She stocked up on ingredients at Cub Foods. She took out the last of the canned rhubarb from Lucy, and used the fancy lard from Block's Provisions, that expensive and tiny store on Hennepin. She felt the dry flour between her fingers, and thought about being a great-grandmother. She thought about it like how a tree in winter thinks about its leaves. She rolled this thought over the dough, and pressed it into its edges. The sun fell outside, and she didn't reach for the lights. The pie baked in the dark, and she sat in her quiet kitchen and waited. She was good at that. She was seventy-seven years old, and she had all the time in the world.

$100,000

Diana, 2017

One year to the day after their wedding, Diana told Andy that she was pregnant again. She'd known for a while, but waited for this day not only because of its personal significance but also because it was one more day their baby was still inside her. One more day that she was still a mother-to-be, and not something else, not just another woman in her twenties.

When they told Edith, her grandmother claimed it was because of a damn pie, but that was bullshit. For starters, that specific pie was made almost a year ago and this child was conceived three months ago. Still, it pleased Edith to think that she was of some consequence in this matter, so Diana let her believe it.

"Are you doing anything different this time?" Edith asked her over dinner.

"Yes," Diana said, which was true. Unlike the last three times, when she freaked out about her diet and sleep and exercise and vitamins, this time she just lived her life, ate what she normally did, and worked up to six long days a week at the brewery. It had become a much weirder and busier place without Frank around. He was still alive, but he hadn't recovered either, and in the intervening year, Anna Schabert ran the place with no new hires and all of the passion and generosity of an absentee landlord. The extra work and stress sometimes even made Diana forget she was pregnant for up to several minutes at a time. It was unsustainable, she knew that. But that's also what made the phone call she received at dinner that night less of a surprise.

"It's Anna," Mo said.

"Is she dead?" Diana asked.

"No," Mo said. "She just sold the brewery."

This news wasn't a shock at all, but it hit her like one. Diana's fingers tingled. She felt ill. All that work, she thought. My whole life.

"You there?"

"Yeah," was all she could say.

"She's calling a meeting tomorrow, nine in the morning."

"OK," she said, and hung up.

Diana thought that being down the hallway, she was well out of hearing range, but Edith had rabbit ears for certain words and phrases. "Who died?" Edith asked her, when she returned to the table.

"Heartlander," Diana said.

"How are you feeling?" Andy asked her on the drive home. It was hard to ignore how the last few years had put some flecks of gray in his hair and bags under his eyes. He was still the same sweet guy, but his repeatedly crushed dream of fatherhood was wearing him out, like a shirt put through the wash again and again, but never worn.

"I don't know," she said, which was honest. "We don't even know who bought it or what's going to happen. So I guess it's not worth worrying about yet." Still, deep down, she felt incredibly doomed, but she didn't want to release that hopelessness into her blood, not now.

"How is everything?" That was as close as he could get to asking about the baby. That was a word they'd long ago quit saying, in any context.

"No difference," Diana said. "I think it's just riding it out."

"Keep riding," he whispered, and touched her belly.

The next morning, Diana sat on a cool metal stool at the taproom bar, between Mo Akbar and Sarah Allison, tired and motionless. Whether they'd all lose their jobs at the end of the week, or next month, or just be working for a different boss, no one knew for sure yet. They were waiting for Anna to get off the damn phone, and while everyone else sat still, Sarah was rubbing against a stain on the bar's varnish with a white rag.

"Stop that, there's no point," Mo told Sarah.

Sarah kept rubbing, a little harder.

"Stop that," Mo said again, and Diana was a little worried that he was going to yell, until the door from the brewery office gasped open above them, and the clicking of Anna's heels accompanied her down the stairs.

Anna's formal clothes and demeanor usually made the rest of the defiantly casual brewery staff seem like children, and today that seemed to be the point. Anna didn't begin with any pleasant, buttery, **I know you've all worked so hard** crap that would've wasted everyone's time. She straight up told them that she had indeed sold the brewery, to a private equity firm called Tennessine Partners. They only wanted Heartlander's recipes and trademarks. They weren't interested in retaining the employees, or even the brewery and its equipment. All of the beer that Diana had developed, perfected, and brewed at Heartlander she could never make legally again. It felt terrifying and cruel, but it wasn't unfair. The beer she made in this building never belonged to her. It belonged to Frank. And his wife could now sell it, so she did.

At this point, Mo yelled out that this was all total bullshit.

"How?" Anna said. "I don't want to keep running a brewery. It was Frank's dream, and I helped him for thirty years. Now I need the money to take care of Frank, and, honestly, it's my turn to do what I want for once."

"What about us?" Sarah asked. She'd been as still as a green sky, and was about to burst; you could feel it sitting next to her. She was a single mom of a kid with health problems, and for her, this wasn't just like getting kicked out of a family, but a family that paid her a living wage with the lifeline of full benefits. Not a lot of breweries were still on their first taproom manager after so many years. Frank had always done what he could to keep good people around.

"I was about to get to that," Anna said. "Once the sale is final, you're each getting a severance of one hundred grand." She paused after she said this and looked them over, as if she were expecting a round of applause.

For this group of young men and women, though, this kind of statement couldn't be processed that quickly. None of them ever had six figures in their bank accounts, Diana was pretty certain. This amount of money all at once was just plain abstract, and overwhelming enough to dislodge them from further pointed inquiry. That too was probably intentional on Anna's part.

"If you have no other questions, you'll get the severance checks by the end of the month, and your final paychecks, through today, next week," Anna said to their startled faces, as she made two steps toward the stairs. "If you want to take some time here to say good-bye, it's OK with me. Just leave your keys in the tip jar before you go." She looked everyone over again. "I know Frank loved working with each of you. You were like his kids to him, and I wish you all well."

Mo raised his hand, parallel to his face, lowering it as Anna glanced at him. He nodded in the direction of the brewery. "How much is all of that equipment worth?"

Anna didn't quite smile. "More than a hundred grand."

"I supposed it would be," he nodded, and everyone watched Anna walk up the stairs and close the office door behind her.

Diana looked at her coworkers, the same four full-time employees who'd worked there together for years, and everyone looked back at her like they didn't know whether to group hug or trash the building on their way out. She couldn't do either, because her body wouldn't move. The fact of it finally hammered her in the stomach. Heartlander Brewery was gone.

This place wasn't just a job to her, it was a forge, and it had bent her into a shape that had one function, and done it so aggressively that she'd never even conceived of working anywhere else. This place was who she was now. She'd somehow found that in the same beautiful, infinite way that her grandpa Stanley had driven a truck for the same company for more than thirty years, and loved it. How someone could just take that away and sell it was everything that was wrong with this country.

She watched her friends start to hug each other, the kinds of hugs people give when they don't expect to see each other for a while.

"Hey," Diana called out. "Maybe if we all pool our money. Four hundred thousand dollars. That'd probably be enough to buy everything."

They all looked back at her, and their eyes brightened for a moment.

"It does sound nice in theory," Mo shrugged.

Diana couldn't believe it. "You just wanted to do it, Mo. We could all keep our jobs."

"Actually, we couldn't," Mo said. "Even if we did all chip in. We'd have to get all-new permits, and licenses, and trademarks, and insurance, and everything, before we even could sell one bottle of beer."

"I know that. So?"

"You don't know how long that takes, but I do. At best, it'd be several months, at least, with no income, so we'd all have to get new jobs anyway."

"I don't know," Matt Duncan said. "It just occurred to me that I could pay off my student loans. I seriously thought I'd never be able to do that."

"I can't not have health insurance," Sarah said. Her son was born with a heart defect and she had eight years' worth of expensive medical bills. "And I can finally pay off some credit cards."

Mo nodded. "Kristin and I always wanted to buy a house."

"I can't believe it," Diana said.

"Well, I can," said Matt. "We can all either get a hundred grand, or gamble it away. Seems like an easy choice to me."

"Then wipe those fucking tears off your cheeks," Diana said.

Mo reached out to grab her hand as she passed by him, and said her name, but she shook him off and bolted toward the stairs. She couldn't even look back at them, because she didn't want to see on their faces again how quick they'd been to move on.

Anna looked surprised, but not angry, when she saw Diana burst into the office. The little room had gone to shit since Frank was gone. Clothes, files, and boxes were piled up on the couch, every surface cluttered with notes, flyers, unopened mail, and empty diet pop cans, and the trash can was overflowing with takeout boxes. A white jacket and a pair of women's sneakers were on the floor, and Diana almost tripped over a shoe as she plowed her way toward Anna.

"How much are you selling the equipment for?" Diana asked, her face hot, her sweaty hands on the front edge of Anna's cluttered desk. "Who are you selling it to?"

Anna groaned as she sat down, like an old man. "I don't know, to be honest. With all the new breweries around, I could probably sell everything in a week. But that's not the question you should be asking. You're taking this all too personally."

Diana thought she was about to swipe her arm across the top of the desk and send the coffee mug, laptop, pens, and all the rest of that crap flying at the wall, but somehow her brain went into critical override and canceled the order.

"How am I supposed to take it?"

"What do you want?" Anna asked. Diana noticed a tiny hole in the right elbow of Anna's white blouse as she leaned back in her chair.

"Well, how much is the equipment?" Diana asked. She hadn't thought about it until now, because she had no reason to, but yes, come to think of it, she wanted that mash tun and those old tanks and kettles more than anything else in the world.

"You really want it?" Anna actually seemed happy to hear this, but in that anxious, menacing way that Anna was when she was happy. "I know Frank always intended to pass it on to you in particular. You were his favorite. He just never wrote it down, so I have no legal obligation to give anything to you."

Damn. So that's how it all ends.

For a second, Diana felt like a scared girl caught in a stranger's garage, but she was able to compose herself, as she used to, back then. "Fine. I'll start my own brewery, somewhere else," she said, and stepped toward the door, reaching for the knob.

"I was hoping you'd say that." Diana could tell Anna wasn't joking, even with her back turned. "But don't you want to use Frank's equipment and do it here?"

Diana stared back at Anna, who she guessed had never really liked her, and who, to be honest, she never liked much herself. "You just said you don't want to give it to me."

"That's true, I don't. But I'll sell it to you, for half your severance. It'd save us both a hassle."

"What?" Diana asked, as if repetition would make the statement less baffling.

"I said I'll sell it to you. And just you."

When Diana didn't reply, Anna kept talking. "I was just trying to scare you off earlier. It'd be a pain in the ass to sell. If I'm a new brewer, I'd buy new equipment that works for my space. All our crap is old, and customized for this building."

"OK," Diana said. She was still dizzy from this blast of new information. It was probably true about the equipment. That was something her mind could grasp on to. But there was a lot more than just that. "What about the building?"

"Oh, that'll be the easy part. I'll get you in touch with my commercial realtor, Susan Fishback. Best one in town. She'll get you excellent terms. You probably won't even have to make a payment until you're up and running. Which is good, because the permits and licenses can take a while. You'll need your own, of course."

Diana sat down again. "Why me, and why not Mo? He's been here way longer. He knows everything."

"You showed some initiative," Anna said. "You didn't come to my office thinking you deserved the equipment. Look, right now, you were ready to blast out of here and go do it all yourself. Mo's sitting downstairs moping, and you came up here."

"But he deserves it."

"He deserves nothing. None of those people downstairs do. They're all going to waddle on home now, happy that they got some money, and in a month or two, they're all going to be doing the same dumb job somewhere else."

Diana almost agreed, but didn't want to give

Anna that satisfaction. She was about to say something about the years they'd all put in, but Anna spoke again first.

"Frank would be happy for you. He always wanted to prove you wrong, you know."

"About what?" She had no clue what Anna was talking about.

"When you told him that people can't start from nothing, work hard, and become successful."

"No," Diana said. "He actually proved me right. It wasn't just that I worked hard."

"You did, though," Anna said. She seemed almost angry. "You still have that same pathological work ethic that Frank had when I met him. You know, he almost died his first year trying to do everything himself. Don't make the same mistake."

Diana nodded, thought of her friends downstairs, and about whether they'd be pissed off. Although she was mad at them, she didn't want them to be mad; she still loved them, and couldn't imagine working in this building without them. Then again, they wouldn't help her right now. They made it clear that they couldn't sit on their hands and wait for her to open her own brewery. Her own brewery. Good Lord, her own brewery.

Anna had barely moved. "So what do you say?"

"Tell me what I need to do," Diana replied.

Andy was thrilled for her. His career wasn't advancing nearly as quickly—he was probably still a couple years away from being promoted to territory manager—but he wasn't competitive with Diana over things like that.

"You're very lucky," Andy told her that night in bed. "Most of the breweries I know, either one of the founders came from money, or there were angel investors. But you've just earned your way into one. That's so rare."

She loved that he knew her well enough not to say she'd just been handed a brewery, as some people may certainly claim. He knew what she'd done and was capable of doing.

"Thanks," she said. "God, I wish you could quit your job and come help me. But someone needs to be making money, I guess."

He looked like he wanted to ask her, **Do you think you can handle this while pregnant?**, but he wisely didn't. Still, she replied anyway.

"I don't have a choice."

"I was going to say, I'm proud of you," he said, and kissed her.

Before she could pour a glass of her own beer, or even order a bag of malt, there was a long, shallow puddle of bureaucracy she had to wade through. Among other things, she needed to submit a brewer's notice application to the Tax and Trade Bureau and get a TTB number, before she even applied for state or city liquor licenses. She needed to get business and liquor liability coverage. She needed to set up a business account and trademark a name. And, as Anna unsubtly reminded her, she needed to find cheap, dependable staff. She had one old friend in mind already.

As Anna predicted, all of her old colleagues from Heartlander were working at other breweries within a month. Matt took a job all the way up in Duluth, so they wouldn't be seeing much of him anymore. Mo was the nearest; he'd scored a brewmaster job at Alter Ego, a new brewery right across the border in River Falls, Wisconsin. After just a few months, he'd already put them on the map, brewing them a habanero-infused triple IPA called The Runny Nose Warrior.

Frank never would've let Mo or anyone make a 12.9 percent ABV beer that was brazenly painful to finish, and would knock you on your ass even if you did, but those Wisconsin college kids loved it, and Diana had to drive over there one afternoon and congratulate Mo personally.

Alter Ego's brewery space was tyrannically contemporary—reclaimed wood, squirrel-cage bulbs, high ceilings with exposed pipes—and all of that crap looked great with Mo right in the middle of it all. It seemed like he'd been working there for years; he was wearing a company shirt that had already faded, was calling people nicknames, and humblebragging to Diana how his first batch of cask ale had room for improvement. Frank never would've let them make an unpasteurized beer like that, either. Now, Mo had the freedom to do whatever he wanted, and had the attitude of a kid determined to eat all of his Easter candy in one sitting. He'd have a dozen new beers out by the end of the year, he said, and while it was nice to see him smiling again—it really was, honestly—she regretted visiting him, now. Maybe if she'd waited until her brewery was open and had brought beers of her own to trade, she wouldn't want to strangle the joy off his face, or start crying in front of him.

In the four months since she'd last seen Mo, Diana hadn't done a damn thing, as far as the outside world of beer consumers were concerned. Sure, she'd opened a business account, taken out a loan, secured the lease agreement, and trademarked an unoriginal name, Artemis Brewery, not that she felt like a goddess. She was really starting to show, and the whole experience of pregnancy was becoming unrelentingly gross and miserable. She'd never made it to five months before, and even though she and Andy were nervously thrilled, every day also seemed to introduce some grim new humiliation. The worst part was, she couldn't even talk about all this honestly with people looking at her like she was batshit.

"But you're beautiful," Sarah Allison insisted, over lunch at Pizza Hut one afternoon. "You're glowing."

"Yeah, it's the acne," Diana replied. "I haven't broken out like this since I was fifteen. I can't sleep, I vomit all the time, I'm constipated, and I literally peed my pants at work the other day, for no reason at all."

"I liked being pregnant," Sarah said. She wasn't nearly as dark or cynical as her dyed hair and tattoos would have a person believe. That's what Diana needed right now. It was a damn shame that Astra was in Chicago and Clarissa was now in New York. It wasn't that she wasn't grateful—she was possibly the most grateful pregnant woman on earth just then—still, Diana believed that you could be both grateful and miserable, but no one seemed to agree with her.

"I'll like it when it's over," Diana said, watching their pizza arrive, suddenly wanting it all for herself.

Their waitress, who was younger than them, and had the careless vibe of someone merely working for extra spending money, somehow couldn't help herself. "You're not supposed to say that," she said. "Pregnancy is a miracle."

"This pizza's a miracle," Diana said. "Pregnancy can suck it."

Even as she became more anxiously, ruthlessly pregnant every day, Diana still went to the brewery every morning at seven o'clock. She hadn't meant to guilt Sarah into helping her, but Sarah claimed that she'd never helped brew beer before and was curious. Diana had already riffled through the malt, yeast, and hops in storage, and found some saison yeast that Frank had never used. Around lunch, Sarah came over, left her son in the taproom with an iPad, and they got to work.

It wouldn't be ready before the end of summer, which was usually when the saisons came out, but what the hell, it was just for them anyway.

For the first time in what felt like forever, brewing beer was a blast. It was such a riot watching that saison yeast go to town like a mother on that mash, they literally started laughing. They actually laughed out loud at yeast. Truly, saison yeast is something everyone should experience at least once. It's a lot cheaper than a trip to Paris, and probably more entertaining.

"I want to lay it down for a month after we keg it," Diana said, at the end of the day, exhausted and smelly. It felt like a miracle to make beer again, and with another woman, even if that woman wasn't a brewer. At least not yet.

"Cool," Sarah nodded. "You'll have to mail me some, then."

Diana laughed. "Why? You should just come over. Then we can start another batch."

"I'm moving to Columbus to take care of my mom," she said. "Next week."

"What?" My God, she didn't just say that. "Columbus, Ohio?"

"Yeah." Sarah nodded again. "She's stage three, and I got nothing keeping me here now."

Diana felt like crying. "Yeah, you do. When I open up next year, I want you to run my taproom. And be an apprentice brewmaster. Wouldn't that be awesome?"

"Yeah, sounds nice," Sarah said, and Diana knew right then that Sarah wasn't ever going to come back, that this was good-bye.

Two months later, she let her husband and his friends drink all the saison, so long as they all gave her honest tasting notes. She also now had spent grain for the first time in a while, so she brought it home and made all kinds of hipster crap out of it—waffles, biscuits, pizza dough, cookies, and pretzels—mostly just to be efficient and save money. She'd learned from Sarah Allison years ago that it was expensive to have a baby, and adulthood was expensive enough already.

"You should sell these at the taproom," Andy said one evening, eating the pretzels while watching a Minnesota Wild game. That was actually a great idea.

In Heartlander's day, they only ever had two snack choices. One was Frank's (a plastic tub of peanut butter pretzel nuggets from Costco), and the other was Anna's (a box of N. W. Gratz's Vegan GMO-Free Gluten-Free 72% Cacao Bars). This was even better; convenient and cheap like Frank's option, with the foodie cred of Anna's.

Diana knew in her heart already, but still, she didn't want to be told her baby's gender yet. Then, after her last ultrasound, someone said it in passing. **There she is. She's looking good**. It was for real. Diana and Andy were having a daughter.

She'd known the due date, January 14, for a long time, but suddenly it wasn't just some abstract number anymore, and she realized right away, this is why she didn't want to know. Although she lived every minute with the relentless trials this tiny being forced on her through its willingness to exist, and love, she'd become accustomed to them, even as she became more afraid. She was so sure she'd get it wrong somehow, and screw this person up, papering them over the holes in her own perforated life. This child within her was somehow a survivor, like the others hadn't been, but if it had any idea what it was getting itself into, it'd stay where it was, sleeping on the pillow of her mom's bladder, yawning in the bloat, forever retesting a kickable horizon.

She felt again like she had at twenty-four weeks—which she'd read was the earliest point you could deliver a healthy child with modern medicine—that she'd crossed a line, and this was happening. She'd wanted a baby so much, for so long, and now that she'd be bringing her daughter into her anxious, uncertain life, she felt so scared.

Stay where you are, baby, if you want to be happy. Stay right where you fucking are.

In the car, as Andy drove her home, smiling, weeping at the news of a daughter, she just stared out the windshield at the yellowing leaves outside, her hand on her stomach, in restraint and unease, imagining something impossible.

"What are you thinking about?" he asked her.

She didn't want to tell him that, yet. "Can we go on a vacation this weekend?" she asked him instead. "To Gooseberry Falls, before it gets too cold?"

"What?" he asked, distracted by his own, doubtlessly more positive thoughts. "I'm sorry, I'm just a little out of it right now," he said, wiping his eyes, glancing at her belly. "It just hit me today. It's real."

"Yeah," she nodded, and rubbed her belly. "Sucks to be her, huh?"

To her surprise, he laughed. "Little twerp had better like spent grain."

Diana loved being in the brewery by herself in the morning, but Anna was right, there was no way she could do this alone for much longer. Especially now, feeling her extra weight as she dragged hoses and pushed mops, her head and body burning up in the frigid, humming room, peeing so often that she just dragged a bucket to the middle of the brewery floor for convenience. Staring at the chasm of her quiet brewery, the only sound a stream of urine hitting against thick orange plastic, she knew it was beyond time to get some damn help in here.

Mo had been nice to her and stayed in touch over email—he probably didn't even notice that she'd unfollowed him on every social media platform—and when she mentioned that she was looking for cheap help, he immediately offered to come in when he could, and he actually did. She tried to pay him for his time, but he wouldn't take anything; he even brought his own lunch.

She wanted to make something simple for the soft launch in early January, a 100 percent Citra IPA, and to have someone as knowledgeable as him give her an assist was huge. She hoped to get a few contract brewers leasing her equipment in the meantime, so she could be making a little money by the time she gave birth, and save the big opening party for when she was ready to return, probably in February.

She knew that her old high school friends James, Astra, and Paul would be wonderful help if they were available, which they weren't. Astra was still living with her grandma in Chicago, hustling as a freelance journalist, and was too buried in student loan debt to move for a job that wouldn't earn her a lot more. James was programming video games in Venice Beach and had fallen in with the Burning Man crowd. Paul and his wife were starting a nonprofit to help the schoolchildren of Detroit. They were all supportive of Diana, but none of them were going to return to Minnesota to do underpaid grunt work at a brewery, and as the sole owner of the equipment and the only name on all of the paperwork, she was too paranoid to bring in a stranger, at least until there were no other options. And there was one more to try.

Diana wasn't much for phone conversations, but she'd always made an exception for Clarissa, even if they only talked a couple times a year now. Still, Diana couldn't recall the last time she'd been this nervous to ask her a question.

"Yo, dude!" Clarissa yelled.

Hearing that rude, braying voice was like coming up for air. Clarissa had Diana laughing, crying, and laughing again in under twenty minutes. Still, it was almost a half hour before Diana brought up the reason for the call.

"Dude, I'd love to," Clarissa said. "But I just got an unbelievably cheap sublet in Red Hook. It's got its own bathroom, and a real kitchen, like with a stove. It's a total jackpot. I can't leave."

Diana, who had never in her life been east of Eau Claire, Wisconsin, tried to envision a realm in which this living situation constituted a "jackpot," but knew that she couldn't counter with the relative merits of the Midwest's rental housing. Clarissa had just completed her MFA out there, and wanted to stay in New York to work on her book. Plus, Clarissa claimed that her day job, doing social media and community outreach for a local coffee company, allowed her a ton of free time to write. But just because all of this made sense didn't mean that Diana wasn't heartbroken.

A month later, Diana and Andy were at Edith's for the traditional Christmas Eve dinner of spiral-cut ham, potatoes au gratin, boiled carrot medallions, and green-and-red Jell-O salad. This was never Diana's favorite of Edith's meals, but this year she went to town on the entire spread. She figured it was because she was close to the end. Her due date still wasn't for three weeks, but she felt like she could, at any moment, blast amniotic fluid all over the smiling reindeer on the festive holiday table runner.

Halfway through a glass of Noble Star Starkeller Peach—Andy was the one person drinking—he was still trying to explain to Edith why, even though he worked for the alcohol distributor with the best craft beer reps, he couldn't help Diana's new brewery get distribution.

"I'm just saying, it's a bad idea right now," he said. "At this point, she'd be paying us, and have very little leverage."

"Can't you at least put in a good word?" Edith asked. "Doesn't it matter that she was the nineteen-year-old with the new beer everyone was talking about?"

"It matters a little, yeah," Andy said. "But that was almost a decade ago. No bartender is going to just hand her a tap. I mean, yes, my company would take her beer at this point, for sure, but only if she paid us. Because we'd be doing all the work of building her new brand's equity in the market-place."

Diana, who knew this already, didn't want to hear it again. "I'm going to go to the bathroom. Please change the topic by the time I get back."

———

At the end of the night, Diana asked Andy to bring their presents from Edith—a child-size quilt, an embroidered bib, a car seat, and a weird, bright orange vase—down to the car, and said she'd catch up with him in the parking lot.

"Grandma," Diana said. "My first beer's almost ready. And I might need you to come help me for a little while."

She'd thought about it for weeks, and hated to ask, but Diana was literally out of options when it came to people she knew and trusted.

Edith passively stared back at her granddaughter, as if Diana hadn't even spoken yet.

"Grandma?" Diana asked.

"I heard you," Edith said, and plopped down on her sofa. "What kind of help?"

"Almost everything. I think."

"You mean making beer?" Edith laughed to herself. "Oh boy. But I don't even like beer."

"You might have liked that Berliner Weisse that Andy was drinking. It was flavored with peaches."

Edith seemed confused. "What does the work entail?"

"It's actually mostly cleaning and paperwork. And I'll do the paperwork."

"Don't you have Mo helping you out already?"

"He's got a full-time brewmaster job somewhere else. And they pay him more than I ever could. He can only come twice a month, tops. Seriously, Grandma, you'd be a huge help. You're in great shape, especially for someone your age. I mean, you go out and volunteer at that nursing home almost every day already."

"Well, I enjoy doing that," Edith said. "And I have the job at Arby's, too."

"I know," Diana said. "And this would be a job, too. I'd pay you. Not a ton, but eventually a lot more than Arby's."

"But I have friends at Arby's. I can't just abandon them."

As far as Diana knew, Edith only had one friend there, named Betsy. Not "friends," plural, but this seemed like a mean thing to point out on Christmas.

"Well, think it over, Grandma."

"I already thought it over," Edith said.

"Just think it over some more," Diana said, and hugged her grandma good-night.

"Christ," Diana muttered to herself, making her way through the dim lobby of the building she used to call home. She couldn't help but notice that it looked kind of cluttered and grimy; whoever was supposed to clean it up didn't do it in time for the holiday.

"Now it's really official," she told Andy after she crammed her body into his little car. "Nobody I know wants to work with me."

"Then why open the brewery now?" he asked. It

was a reasonable question. "Why don't you wait a few months, after the baby?"

She was already exhausted and frustrated, and didn't want to remind him that the lease payments were scheduled to begin in January. Nor did she want to remind him that she'd already spent money to buy the ingredients to make half a dozen varieties of beer, started four of them with Mo's help, and one of them was already a week from being ready to pour.

"It's too late," she just said.

"Well, maybe it's for the best that you won't be working with people you know," he said, switching off the hazard lights. "I think the right people are still out there somewhere."

It was the first week of January, two days before the scheduled soft open, and she'd just finished hooking up a keg to the freshly cleaned lines when the taproom door opened.

In the doorway was a middle-aged woman with a herd of four young children, and they stood there for a moment, silently sussing the whole place out. She hadn't expected customers, let alone children, and was playing a mix of Lizzo songs on the taproom's speakers that she didn't find inappropriate, but she would bet some Minnesota parents might. Either way, she couldn't very well run up to the office and turn it down now.

Diana waved. "Can I help you?"

"I just read about this place in the paper," the woman said. "Are you open yet?"

If she'd read the whole article in the **Nicollet Falls Viking**, this woman would know that she wasn't. But there was now beer on tap, and Diana literally hadn't made any money in eight months, so what the hell. "Sure, come on in."

She'd seen other brew halls, like Surly's, do a good job of being family-friendly, and even though she didn't have a hell of a lot for kids to do in the brewpub yet, she'd made a point of declaring that kids were welcome. The headline of the recent article was, after all, LOCAL BREWER OPENS "FAMILY-FRIENDLY" BREWERY. And now, here they were, seemingly all at once, as her first customers.

The children were around six or seven years old, and were happy and excitable but seemingly obedient.

"Wow," the woman said, trying not to stare at Diana's belly. "When's your due date?"

"About a week and a half," Diana said.

"You must be so excited," the woman said. "Is it your first?"

Diana nodded and saw a little boy in a purple Vikings jacket just unabashedly staring at her, in the intense, unnerving way that kids get away with.

"Congratulations," the woman said, and turned to the boy. "Winston, can you go sit nicely with your friends?"

"She's knocked up," Winston said.

"Winston, that's not polite."

"It's a true fact," Winston said, and sauntered off.

"What a day," the woman groaned, and shot Diana a look that said, **Other people's kids, am I right?** "A Blue Moon for me and four small root beers for the kids," the woman said.

There were multiple issues with that request, so she started with the easy one. "We don't have root beer on tap," Diana said, holding up a bottle of local Tree Fort root beer. Thank God that order just arrived yesterday. "But we have these."

"Can you split two bottles into four equal glasses?"

"No problem," Diana said. "And I'm sorry, we don't carry Blue Moon. We make our own beer here. Right now we have a hundred percent Citra IPA. Would you like to try it?"

"Oh, I don't like those," the woman said.

"Well, they're not the hop-bombs that a lot of people make. This IPA is a single hop, with citrus notes, less bitter."

This didn't seem to register. "Do you have anything like Blue Moon?"

Diana didn't, and probably never would. If it was wheat beer or Belgian whites this woman liked, at best she might like the 50 percent wheat gose that Diana planned to brew. She just had to get out of the taproom and back into the brewery and start making it. "I'll have a gose ready, in a month or two. In the meantime, do you want a root beer for yourself?"

"No. It's been a crazy-ass day and I just want a drink. Do you have anything, **anything**, that's not an IPA?"

There was one Shore Leave Porter in the office fridge, just one. It was the last one that would ever be made. She'd been saving it the way responsible children saved their Halloween candy, but now there were more important things than memories. "Do you like porter? I have one bottle left."

"Just so long as it's not an IPA, I'll try it," the woman said.

"So you know, it's nothing like a Belgian white. It's dark, with chocolate and coffee notes."

The woman nodded and pointed at the big glass jar of homemade spent-grain pretzel sticks, sitting on a wooden keg in the corner. "Are the pretzels free?"

"You bet, help yourself," Diana said. "I'll be right back with the porter."

She sat down on her old Eames replica chair in the office for a moment, staring at the last bottle of Shore Leave Porter, the first porter she'd ever tried in her life, and still her favorite. She remembered when they kegged it, just a small batch that used up the rest of the black malt. Frank would've been brewing more right now, if he were here. Frank would've been furious if his brewery didn't have porter on tap in the winter.

She wasn't sure if she could part with it, and it wasn't just the contents. The label was beautiful. Matt Duncan had done his most gorgeous work with this one. This ship that curled around the circumference of the bottle was the **Edmund Fitzgerald**, and Sarah Allison used to give a free sample shot of porter to whoever guessed that correctly.

Now, this was it, this one bottle, the end of an era.

It occurred to Diana just then that death doesn't happen all at once. The public death is just the beginning, and the rest takes as long as it has to, in private bits and pieces, without any warning, schedule, or validation. A pen they once held, now out of ink. A bag of their favorite chips, past its expiration date. A crack in a personalized coffee mug. She wondered who else in her life had, put away somewhere, a dry pen, expired chips, a broken mug, an aging bottle of beer. She wondered who had the courage to let them go, without ceremony or reflection.

"Here's your porter," she told the woman, popping the cap, which bounced off the bar and clattered out of sight. It was just then that she noticed the pretzel jar had been toppled, and the entire contents scattered across the floor.

"Sorry about that," the woman said.

Just then, a Lizzo lyric that loudly proclaimed the phrase "that bitch" landed right in the pocket of silence, like a commentary. The woman winced, and glanced back at the kids, but didn't speak.

"No problem, I'll sweep it up in a sec," Diana said. It was her only batch of pretzels, crushed by kid feet into the concrete, gone, all gone. It was a miracle that the jar only cracked and didn't break. She reminded herself to keep a cheerful attitude, because the day's tip jar was obviously empty, and this woman now truly owed her a big one.

One of the kids now started begging for an artisanal chocolate bar. Diana had forgotten that they were still out on display. Anna ordered those damn things last February. Was organic chocolate still good after eleven months? Too late to Google it now.

"And one of these," the woman said, holding up the chocolate bar. "Can you please cut it into four pieces and bring it to our table? Just try to make sure that each piece of chocolate is exactly the same size."

"I'll be happy to go the extra mile for you today," Diana said.

"Thanks," the woman said as she set down her credit card. "And yeah, it would be great if the chocolate was in four equal pieces." As if she hadn't heard her the first time.

"You're a good parent," she said, laying it on thick.

"Ha! That could be, but none of these kids are mine. I'm just their nanny."

Just as good. Didn't they get reimbursed? "Well, you're doing great."

Diana noticed that she drew a line through the tip area on the receipt. Nor did she put any cash in the jar. Maybe she'd tip when Diana brought the chocolate out.

The woman left her almost-full porter at the bar. "You didn't like it?"

The woman shook her head. "It's not like Blue Moon."

Diana stepped across the field of pretzel crumbs, and set the carefully proportioned quarters of chocolate, on their own napkins, in front of each child.

"Anything else I can get you?"

"Thank you, and I think we're good," she said, and turned her attention to the kids. Winston was bragging that he got the biggest piece, although he did not.

Diana didn't move. She just stared at the woman, patiently, calmly.

The woman finally looked up at Diana and opened her mouth in surprise. "Oh, a tip! Of course. I'm sorry. I'm totally out of cash. Can I get you next time?"

Looking back, sure, Diana could've handled this

better. It wasn't even the woman's response that set Diana off; she seemed genuinely apologetic. No, it could've been because, by now, Diana had a throbbing headache. It could've been because she'd been holding her urine for ten minutes. It could've been because she hated front-of-house work, and had still tried so hard to give exemplary customer service and earn a tip, not just expect one, and she'd failed. It could've been the wanton disrespect and destruction wrought by these demanding little brats, and the burgeoning fear that her taproom would in time become a filthy, helpless playpen. But she certainly never expected to say "fuck you" to her first customers.

After they stormed out, she put a CLOSED sign in the window and locked up the tasting room. She was done with customers for the day. Done. After drinking half of the porter, she called Mo to see when he could come over to help her start the gose.

The day wasn't a net loss, though; sweeping under the table where those kids were, she found a Vikings beanie, probably belonging to that asshole Winston.

She put on the calmest music she owned, the **Suspended** soundtrack by Lucinda Chua, and put it on repeat. It made her feel like she was moving through sheets of honey.

Thirty minutes later, after sweeping up the pretzels and the rest of the mess those kids had left in their wake, Diana received the kind of phone call she was expecting, but it still surprised her.

"Excuse me," a man's serious voice said. "I'm calling on behalf of my nanny, Olivia Ying. You had her as a customer today."

"Yes, I remember," Diana said. "I've apologized and refunded her money. I apologize further to you and your family."

This apparently wasn't good enough. The man had mentally prepared a screed and he was going to deliver it, whether Diana was contrite or not.

"We're telling everyone that your brewery is not appropriate for kids," the man said. "The language you use! In front of children! And the inappropriate music! We're all leaving one-star reviews on Yelp."

The front doorbell buzzed. Mo, who'd turned in his keys, must be here already.

"Hey, hold that thought, sir," she said, the phone crammed between her neck and her shoulder, as she moved toward the front door as quickly as she could.

The toes on her right foot hit something hard. A bag of malt. What was that doing there, she thought, and then felt herself completely in the air for just one long, terrible moment, before her right knee took the full, fierce weight of her fall, and after just a second, an incredible, indescribable pain exploded through her leg, into her brain, and burst out of her mouth at a volume that rattled the glass fifty feet away.

She felt moisture around her legs, she remembered that. Her arms were around her stomach, instinctually, she remembered that, too.

The black cordless phone was on its side, ten feet away, and she could hear a man's voice saying, "Hello?" and "Are you OK?"

"Stay where you are, baby," she whispered. "Stay where you are."

$200

Helen, 2001

Vacations made Helen sad. Especially the five-hour trips up north to their beautiful lake cabin. She'd come to especially fear the last hour of the drive, through the smattering of small towns and lush wild forest and the cleanest-smelling air she'd ever known.

She used to revel in these things, every Fourth of July and Labor Day weekend, since they bought their cabin in the late seventies. Until 1999, when Orval sold the boat—"a hole in the water you throw your money into," according to him—they boated, but she didn't miss being on the lake as much as she missed the pure joy in the getting there. It wasn't anticipation; the trip was a delight in itself.

By summer 2001, that drive had become a disheartening trek through the eroding small towns of what had once been Blotz territory. In 1983, she'd counted thirty-one Blotz signs between their home in Marine on St. Croix and the lake cabin. Because she'd noticed that, now she couldn't ignore how every summer their telltale orange-and-white logo was in fewer and fewer bar and bait shop/liquor store windows—only six, by last count. When she found out that July that the closest bar to their cabin quit carrying Blotz, Helen drove back to the lake and just sat in her car for half an hour, staring at the calm evening water from the driver's seat like a tourist.

"There you are," Orval shouted, walking up from the dock with a fishing pole, and no fish. "Well, it looks like we're having the steak tonight. It's tougher without a boat."

"Thank you for trying," she said.

Right then, she knew that weekend would be the last time she'd be there.

It wasn't that they hadn't perceived the warning signs. Unless you were at the very top, or an emerging "craft" brewer, the early-twenty-first century was a tough time for a brewery that only made lagers. Helen and Orval had done their best to stay afloat, selling their struggling Galesburg plant, laying off the newest hires, and shuttering product lines. They also experimented with new slogans, from the practical ("Blotz: The Best Beer For Your Buck") to the cheeky ("Blotz: Good Enough For Who It's For") but neither had moved the needle like their most famous slogan once had.

A decade before, as the other major Midwestern breweries within a two-state range all seemed to be rapidly expanding or contributing to another's expansion, it was Orval and Joe's idea to put their money to use, eat instead of be eaten, and grow Blotz's brand portfolio. By the end of the nineties, they'd heavily leveraged themselves, purchasing six regional breweries, including the locally famous Kramlinger's Brewing Co. out of Spring Green, Wisconsin; Pond & Beyer Brewery of Perry, Iowa; and Chamberlain's Gold Cup Lager of Petoskey, Michigan. Outbidding larger Midwest giants Pabst and Stroh's for each one was a leap of faith that every brewer in the Blotz family would continue to thrive. For the first time since the early seventies, they were in debt. Now, they'd begun leasing out their equipment to contract brewers to help bring in cash, but Helen knew that to stay alive, they also needed to evolve. Last time they were looking at this kind of balance sheet, they'd scraped out of it by doing something few others were doing. Helen hoped she had the stomach to do that again, and the wisdom to know that opportunity when it emerged.

One of the contract brewers who leased Blotz's equipment in summer 2001 was making an obscure beer variety called an IPA. A brutish, simple, palate-searing ale, to hear Orval describe it. He looked around the room at Helen, Joe, and the newest member of the inner circle, the fast-rising Agatha Johnston, in turn. "Who's up for an adventure?"

As Orval passed bottles of this IPA around his office, Helen decided to lighten things up before they got started. Joe was wearing a black suit and tie, which was unusual for him, and she knew he could take a joke.

"Joe, are you moonlighting as a limo driver for extra cash?" Helen smiled. "I could use a ride to the airport next week."

He grinned, briefly and gamely, before he spoke. "I had a funeral this morning. My cousin Carole."

"Oh," Helen said. Now she felt awful. "I'm so sorry."

As everyone else in the room offered condolences, Helen felt like she still hadn't said enough to cover for her wretched comment. "She was older, right? You were expecting it?"

Joe shook his head. "No, she was forty-one. Slipped on her basement stairs and hit her head. Just landed wrong."

Nobody, not even Helen, said anything for several moments.

Joe clapped his hands softly. "Well, let's talk about beer."

"Yes, please," Orval said, as he finished handing out the bottles to everyone but Joe. "What we're looking at today is this new India Pale Ale beer. So, is this just a trend, or a tiny subculture, or is this the next Blue Moon?" he asked. "Should we sell something off and make an offer?"

Everyone took a sip at the same time and stared at each other afterward. They'd been far too late to the Belgian white market—their copy of Blue Moon, Pale Sun, was not a success—and now, everyone was afraid to be wrong again, either way.

"Huh," Helen said, and tried it again. There was something familiar about it.

"Well, personally, I don't get it," Orval said, setting his bottle down like a gavel. "I can't imagine drinking this at a ball game or a picnic."

"I don't mind it," Agatha said.

"So what's the current market for it?" Joe asked her.

"Beer snobs," Agatha said. At forty-seven, she was the youngest person in the room; she would know. As the director of quality, she'd also know if what they were sampling was tainted or compromised, and knew this variety well enough to say, "And it's supposed to taste like this. This is how they like it."

"I can't even believe there's such a thing as beer snobs," Orval said. "There's not supposed to be hierarchies among beer drinkers. Either you like it or you don't!"

Helen looked worried. "Are Miller or Budweiser getting in on this?"

Agatha shook her head. "Well, there's no Miller or Budweiser IPA in the works, no. Anheuser-Busch owns a part of Redhook, though. I think that's going to be a continuing trend, the big conglomerates either buying ale breweries, or buying a piece of them, and letting them still do their thing, but with wider distribution. Sort of like what Miller did with Leinie's."

"What about Schell's?" Schell's out of New Ulm, one of the oldest family-run breweries in the country, had been making craft beers for a while, and had also been a contract brewer for both Three Floyds and the popular Pete's Brewing Company.

"It doesn't look like Schell's is making their own IPA."

"Let's leave Schell's alone," Orval announced. "They always respected Blotz territory and my grandpa always respected theirs."

"Orval, it's not 1915 anymore," Helen frowned. "Good Lord, we have a German name, we should be brewing bocks, like they do."

"That's their thing, Helen." Orval turned to the group. "But let's say we wanted to make an IPA. How could we package it?"

Joe smiled the eager way he always did when he thought he had something useful to contribute. "We could do what Coors does with its Killian's Red."

Orval looked surprised. "Coors owns them?"

Agatha nodded. "Yeah, and we could buy an existing name like that, or even just make up a new name, and no one would have to know it was us."

Helen tasted the beer again, and again it jogged an unpleasant, insecure feeling. "I don't want to sell a beer I won't drink."

"It's not just about your personal preferences," Orval said. "Joe here has never had a drop of beer in his life, and he's been with us more than thirty years."

"Joe doesn't brew it," she said.

Agatha closed her notebook. "I guess that's that."

As Joe left the office, Helen told him again that she was sorry. "I used to have a sense of humor, long ago," she said. "I guess that's gone."

"If I owned a big brewery now, I'd have lost my sense of humor, too," Joe said, not looking back, as he turned down the hall.

Helen may not have thought of this entire conversation again, for a long time, if at all, if something frightening hadn't nearly happened the next day.

The following morning, in the shower, reaching

for the shampoo, her feet slipped in her claw-foot tub and she tumbled, grabbing onto the white cotton shower curtain, somehow tearing it from the wall, support beam and all, and falling onto the bathroom tile, her wet body tangled in the curtain.

She blinked. Her forehead throbbed. Her right arm and her right hip hurt, but she could move. Nothing felt broken. Orval burst open the door and saw his wife, naked, soaking wet, splayed on the floor, as the unmuffled shower roared and steamed.

"Oh my God," he said, as he took in the whole scene, and then fell to his knees.

Somehow, she was fine, miraculously. But it wasn't until that fact sank in that she truly felt afraid.

They went to Helen's doctor anyway that morning, who confirmed that she was just a little banged up, and lucky to be so. When Dr. Dille asked what, if anything, might have caused the fall, Helen didn't say it was a message from God, or a punishment—that's something her mother or Edith would've said aloud—but she still thought that.

"I think I just need one of those stupid rubber mats," she said.

By the time they arrived at the brewery later that day, everyone else was already there. In all this time, they'd never been late for work together, so they'd never experienced Blotz Brewery quite like this before, this immediate sense of the place running without them.

Helen stopped at one office before she even went to her own.

"Agatha," Helen said, opening the younger woman's door without knocking. "Do you have a minute?"

Agatha was on the phone, but quickly told the person on the other end that she'd call them back, and then invited her boss to come in.

Helen sat down in one of the expensive ergonomic chairs she'd ordered ten years ago, for everyone in the entire office except her. The surprising comfort distracted her momentarily; her body was accustomed to the old leather executive chair she'd bought in 1976.

"Orval and I were talking on the way in today," Helen said. "We want you to take over the company when we retire. Or if something happens to us."

Agatha winced. "You're not much older than I am. You're what, fifty-six?"

"Something like that," Agatha was one of three employees who knew Helen's age.

"And you're not going to retire. You're the one person I know who doesn't like travel or vacations.

You don't have kids or grandkids. You hate golf. The only thing you love besides your husband is making beer. You'd get bored out of your mind."

Helen loved that Agatha was no bullshitter; it confirmed their decision. "If something happens, I need to know that Blotz will go to someone I trust."

"Well, I'm honored," Agatha said, and seemed to be. "But why not Joe Foxworth?"

"Joe's our age. And he's probably going to retire well before Orval and I do. Plus, he doesn't even drink beer. You know it inside and out. You know the business and the production. Blotz is going to you. You have no say in the matter."

"Are you OK, Helen?" Agatha asked.

"Yes," Helen said, rising from the chair. "I'm just scared."

She looked at the framed picture of a South Dakota Badlands sunset on Agatha's wall, a beautiful, lonely orange-and-blue landscape that would've looked the same a million years ago and would look the same a million years from now.

Agatha nodded. "I know."

That evening, as Orval drove them north toward home through the dim, gently rolling farmland, he turned down the radio, and suddenly spoke.

"What about Edith?" he asked.

"What about her?"

"What about leaving the brewery to her?"

"No," Helen said, without thinking.

"I know she's older than we are. She has kids and a grandkid, though. Maybe them."

Helen was unusually nervous about the road. For more than thirty years, they'd traveled this narrow road among big trucks and impatient commuters without a second thought. Tonight, each approaching pair of headlights seemed ripe with potential doom. "No," Helen said again. "What would Edith even do with it? The point is to keep the brewery going, not give it to someone who will either drive it into the ground or liquidate it."

Orval shrugged. "We do kind of owe her something."

The bruises on her right arm from that morning nagged her as she leaned against the car door. "What do we owe her exactly? It was my dad's decision."

"We wanted it. We planned for it."

"Sure we did, and we earned it by taking care of him."

"But what kind of family gives everything to one sibling and not the other?"

Now he has a moral dilemma over this? "I'll tell ya. Ours does."

"Have you heard from her lately?"

"Of course I haven't."

"You know what you could do." **You could just write her a check now**, Orval had suggested once, long ago. **We have the money.**

"I have a plan for Edith," Helen said. She didn't though, at least not yet.

She'd never been able to wrap her head around just handing anything over to a sister who hadn't spoken to her in over three decades. With each passing year, it somehow became ten times harder to do, and the excuses she made for never making good on her promise about the farm sale seemed ten times more reasonable. It was Edith who declared and enforced the silence between them, not Helen. And in the meantime, Edith had raised two generations of descendants who surely hated Helen without ever knowing her. Edith was probably so mad by then, if she received something now, she'd give it away out of spite.

"Well, I'd love to hear it," Orval said. "All this time, you've only ever done what's good for Helen."

"I had to." The nerve of him, pretending that he's been a good angel on her shoulder this whole time. "It's worked out for you too, hasn't it?"

"I'm saying, you've never thought about your sister once. You could at least give her what you promised her."

She thought about Edith all the time. She just didn't know what to do. And whose side was he on? "I can't just give her money," Helen said. "It'll take more than that now, anyway."

"If you do have a plan, do it now, while you're both still alive."

"Well, she won't get the brewery, and that's final."

He seemed a little sad. "You don't want to keep it in the family?"

She was a little sad too, to be honest. "I want to keep it going. While we still can."

"OK then," Orval replied.

Fifteen years passed, and in that time, Blotz went from being one of eight breweries in Minnesota to one of over a hundred. By then, however, they were barely still even one of the eight largest; Blotz had sold off every acquisition in its portfolio, stripped its staff to just its most essential employees, and was down to just a single plant, its home base in Point Douglas. They blamed it on something they'd judged and dismissed, on a summer morning back in 2001.

"The horror," Joe moaned during a meeting, his bleached teeth and silver hair gleaming beneath the lights. "It's death by a thousand hops."

She didn't need to hear it. Their most recent plan for salvation was to repackage the same old beer with nostalgic throwback cans and bottles. It wasn't enough.

"We still have loyal customers," Helen reminded him.

"Yeah, and more and more of them are dying every year. And these kids today, they want hops. Hops up the wazoo. The other day I saw an IPA with five kinds of hops. Five. All listed on the bottle, by name."

"Sounds cool to me," Agatha said.

"Helen, what kind of hops do we use?" Joe asked. "Maybe we can start putting it on the label."

She shook her head. "It's a proprietary extract."

Orval looked at his wife, even after all these years, the way a small child looks at the presents under a Christmas tree. "I bet you can make the best IPA in the world," he said to her, smiling.

What could she say to that? "Well, I suppose I can try."

"Blotz can't put out a craft IPA now," Agatha said. "Maybe you could've back in 2000, under some other name. Now, everyone would know it was us right away, and it'd be a disaster. Our customers won't buy it and the craft beer crowd won't touch it either. We have to buy one that already has credibility in the marketplace."

Helen supposed Agatha was right. There was still no such thing as a Budweiser IPA or a Coors IPA, but now, those brewers did have a ton of craft brands in their portfolios.

"Is that the only way we can survive?" Helen asked the room.

No one said anything. Things had been getting worse for a long time, but the idea of Blotz Brewery going out of business seemed ridiculous. They were a Minnesota institution.

"I think so," Agatha said.

"Sure we can buy a damned craft brewery," Joe said. "But with what money?"

"Let me figure that out," Helen said.

The following morning, Orval was in the kitchen peeling an orange with a $200 Japanese santoku knife, probably just because the peeler was still in the dishwasher. "I just had a good idea," he said.

She watched the blade making its slow spiral, and his long, pale fingers a bottle cap's width away. "No, you didn't. Put that down."

She was a second too late. As she reached to take the knife, his blood slapped across her open palm, and for a moment, it was all she could see.

As she drove him to the ER, his wounded finger provisionally bandaged up and elevated, he tapped her shoulder with his good hand. "Do you still want to hear my good idea?" he asked.

She glanced over at him. He had blood spots on his clothes, clear up to his collar. That was a nice shirt he had on too, one of the tailored ones from Heimie's Haberdashery, and it reminded her of a time when they had money, more money than they knew what to do with.

"I suppose," she said.

"Well, we know we can't afford to acquire a popular or successful craft brewery," he said. "So, let's find one on the way up or on the way down, and help them out."

"Sure, whatever," Helen said. She was trying to make a left turn at an intersection where there was no left turn signal, and was in no mood for a conversation on this topic. "Just keep your hand up. We're almost there."

Orval was in a pretty good mood that day for someone who needed three stitches on his middle finger. He apologized for flipping off the doctor, and the doctor politely laughed as if he'd never heard that one before.

On the drive home after buying gauze and bandages at the drugstore, he pointed at a passing sign. "Hey. Let's stop and get some Dairy Queen."

"Not before lunch," Helen said, but then thought about it, and turned the car into the parking lot.

He ordered a large Heath Blizzard. She just had a few bites of his. They sat at one of the outdoor tables, under a red umbrella, and he commented on passing cars, if they were cars he'd owned, or ones he wouldn't mind owning.

He didn't bring up the brewery again, except to say, as he was buckling his seat belt, that everything was going to be OK.

That afternoon being a Saturday, he took a long nap, and after they had Chinese takeout for dinner, they watched a movie together, one they'd never seen called **Lost in Translation**. He seemed to like it; he was laughing throughout the scene where Bill Murray shoots the whiskey commercial, but he zonked out on their worn-out leather couch before it was over. She decided to let him sleep for a bit longer, and the next morning when she got up, he was still there, and he wasn't breathing.

Helen always had a way of explaining everything, to other people, and especially to herself. But she had no words for this.

He was literally just at the hospital, she told the EMTs. A doctor checked him out, and everything was fine. **Brain aneurysm**, one of the EMTs guessed, and she ended up being right. There was nothing anyone could've known, and nothing anyone could've done. In an invisible burst, her life as she knew it flickered away, leaving only the sets and the props and the extras.

The first time she was alone in the house, she just sat on the floor of the kitchen for two hours, not even crying, just sitting, trying to wrap her head around what happened. They'd done nothing to prepare for this. That conversation they had after her shower accident in 2001 was the only time they'd even admitted silently to each other that they were possibly mortal beings.

It was hard to make sensible decisions before the shock had worn off, everything was so lurid and meaningful. It took an hour to do things like unload the dishwasher when she realized that Orval's last plates, bowls, forks, and spoons were in there. She requested an open casket, and when the mortician said he'd remove the bandage on Orval's middle finger, she said absolutely not, because it reminded her of their last day together.

Edith wasn't at the funeral. Not that Helen expected her to be. In the front row next to Helen sat Agatha, Joe, and a couple of Orval's cousins. She wouldn't have minded seeing Edith there, though, just so she could walk up to her and say, **I know what you've been through**.

Before this, she never had any true idea of what exactly her sister must've felt; Helen heard she had also lost an adult child in addition to a husband. But at least Edith wasn't alone, she thought. Edith still had a son, a granddaughter. Helen had Helen.

A day after the burial, Helen was alone in her kitchen with Agatha, who'd brought a pork loin over. The poor woman had barely taken her jacket off when Helen accidentally blurted out, "You're the only person I have left."

"That's not true," Agatha said, not looking up, as she seated herself at the kitchen island. "A lot of people want to be here for you. You just have to let them."

"A lot of people want my money," Helen said, opening a 1990 Château Latour from the cellar. No damn time like the present. "You want some of this?"

Agatha shook her head. "I think you should relax for a while and take some time off."

"That's impossible," Helen said, thinking back to her father, after her mother died. That's what he would've said. "The best thing for me is to come back tomorrow."

"Are you sure?" Agatha asked. Why did she look so upset?

"You know what I want? You know what would really help?"

"Tell me," Agatha said, and leaned forward, like whatever it was, she'd jump off the kitchen stool and do it just then.

"I want you to help me find a craft brewery. One too small to be on anyone's radar yet. A cheap one, on the way up."

Agatha looked like she was about to say something, and then closed her mouth. "OK," she finally said, resting her elbows on the kitchen counter. "But give me some time."

Eventually, Agatha would indeed find a good one, and both the brewery and the circumstances would surprise Helen, but no one in need of a rescue gets the savior of her choice. They usually just get whoever's closest, and someday, there would be one far closer than all the rest, ready for her, reaching out.

$57.00

Edith, 2018

Edith arrived at the hospital twenty minutes after Frances Colleen Nakagawa came into the world, at five pounds, nine ounces. There she was, a great-grandchild, breathtaking and real, as unimaginable and perfect as heaven.

Diana was holding the little baby against her chest and quietly crying.

"Is everything OK with the baby?" Edith whispered to Andy, who'd clearly been crying himself.

"Yeah," Andy said. "She's fine. We've just been through a lot."

The short, serious-looking nurse glanced toward Edith. "You should let them rest. They've both had a tough day. You can come back tomorrow."

"Is she getting knee surgery?" Edith asked.

"I don't know the answer to that," the nurse said. "If so, I wouldn't imagine it'd be soon."

Mo had been kind enough to drive Edith there. With how shaken she was by the news of Diana's accident, she definitely couldn't have driven herself. As they walked to his rusty red pickup in the cold, smoky parking ramp, he was the one who brought up what she'd been thinking.

"Well, her brewery's sure not going to open in two days," he said, unlocking and opening her door. "Maybe not for quite a while, now."

Edith wondered if this meant that Diana's new brewery wasn't supposed to happen, if this was God's way of saying, **Stop making beer, Diana**. Then she wondered why God would even say such a thing.

This was evidently what Diana was meant to do, because it brought her such strength and purpose. Edith may not have always loved the idea of her granddaughter making beer, but she loved how its discipline had transformed that quiet, sad girl into this bullheaded and remarkable young woman, who now, somehow, had opened her own brewery. No one, immortal or otherwise, ought to stop that joy and passion from existing in the world.

Edith climbed up into the cab of Mo's truck and stared straight ahead. There was no getting around what she was about to say. "Just take me there."

"Where?" he asked, turning the key in the ignition, looking confused.

"The brewery," she said. "I suppose I'll do it."

He was looking behind himself as he backed out of the space. "You suppose you'll do what?"

"If she needs someone to run the brewery, I guess I'll run a brewery."

Mo stopped the truck right there in the middle of the parking lot, and stared at her. He seemed like he was about to laugh. "What?"

"Well, who else is going to do it?" she asked him, and stared at him, until he quit smiling. "But someone's going to have to show me how."

Before that night, Edith had only been to Heartlander twice in her entire life. Now, when she walked through the quiet taproom onto the brewery floor, she saw an immense, cold, intimidating zoo of metal robot monsters. She saw impossibly heavy stacks of white bags and dry-erase boards with words and numbers she didn't understand. She saw pallets of unlabeled brown bottles, wrapped in heavy plastic. She imagined being alone in here, with all of these things.

"You don't have to do this, you know," Mo said.

"Someone does," Edith replied. "So, where's the actual beer, in all of this?"

"Well, there's a single-hop Citra IPA that's in the taproom already, and there's different ones in a couple of the fermentation tanks," Mo said, and led her to one that had the word "Vulcan" written on the side. "At the time she was hurt, she was about to brew a gose. That's eventually going to go here in Vulcan. Alderaan down there has a Kölsch that's fifteen days along. Oh, and Arrakis over there has another IPA, using one hundred percent local Cascade hops, which we can tap by this weekend. Have you ever had an IPA before?"

Edith shook her head. "Absolutely not."

"We can remedy that," Mo said, and led her to the giant Koh-i-Noor refrigerator, where he pulled out a bottle of beer that read ALTER EGO BREWING CO. and THREE AMOKAS IPA, and popped it open with his keychain. "Try this one out. It's one of mine."

She held the bottle to her lips and tilted, slightly. It tasted like how she'd imagine dirt would taste if someone burned it on the grill. "Nope," she said, and handed it back.

"You don't like it," Mo said, frowning. "**The Growler** just named it the best new IPA of the year."

"It's not for me," Edith said.

"I have to be honest," Mo said, wiping the lip of

the bottle with his shirt and taking a drink. "I'm not sure if you're the person for this job."

"Why not? I don't have to drink it to make it. I used to make twenty-five pies a day, five days a week, and I never ate one slice of any of them." Edith looked around the room, and started to notice that all this intimidating equipment might just be larger and stranger versions of what she'd been working with most of her life. "From what I can tell, this is just a big kitchen, and beer is just a big recipe."

"That's a bit oversimplified," Mo sighed. "And I'm guessing that you know what good pie tastes like. And I don't mean to be rude, but I don't think you know what a good IPA is supposed to taste like."

"I know people who do, if you're not around to help with that part. I sure don't plan to do all this by myself." She glanced back in the direction of the fermentation tanks. "And it's not like we're expected to brew a beer from scratch, or something crazy."

"No, like I said, the hard part's done on that Kölsch and the IPA. When they're ready to be kegged, at the very least either Diana or I can talk you through it on the phone. Which reminds me . . . ," Mo said, leading her back into the dark taproom, where he flicked on some lights and led her behind the long wooden bar. "This is where she really needs help right now. Until she starts self-distributing, this is the only place where money will be coming in."

"Oh, I suppose," Edith said, looking at the empty picnic-style tables, and wondered how terribly different a beer hall would be from Arby's, a nursing home dining room, or even Tippi's Café.

"You'll want to have at least two people here in the taproom every day during business hours, and maybe more on weekends," Mo said, and circled two different dates on the wall calendar behind the bar. "When that Kölsch and IPA are ready, on these days, call me. You'll just have those three beers to serve, until Diana can come back and make more."

Edith was relieved that all this wouldn't be harder. Here she was afraid she'd be up to her knees in a vat of beer every day—which she was prepared to do, of course, if she had to—but now it looked like she'd mostly just have to be a bartender until her granddaughter was better. "Did Diana plan to serve food?"

"She had some pretzels around here somewhere. They're supposed to be out on that keg over there. They're probably in the office upstairs. Also she still has these chocolates," he said, pointing to a box of small, tan-wrapped squares that read N. W. GRATZ'S VEGAN GMO-FREE GLUTEN-FREE 72% CACAO. "They're not bad, but probably kind of old. Anna was into them."

"We can do better than that. Where's the kitchen?"

"It's a packaging brewery. She can't prepare food for sale onsite by law."

"That's a little disappointing." Edith had to remind herself that wasn't why she was here.

"You can get food delivered, or get food trucks in the parking lot if you want, but let's not get ahead of ourselves," Mo said. "The most important thing is to keep everything clean. As I told Diana when she started, you're pretty much just a janitor who very rarely makes beer."

"That's a relief." This was sounding better and better. "How early can you meet me here tomorrow morning?"

"Frank would've liked your attitude," Mo said, and looked a little sad. "How's seven? If that's not too early. I just have to be at my real job by ten."

"No time is too early." Who was he kidding? She watched Mo begin to turn out the lights. "I appreciate the help."

"Well, I wish I could do more," he said. She knew that he had a full-time job and a young family, and she was lucky he took the time to be here at all. "I hope I can call you, when I have questions."

"Sure, but you should probably call Diana first." He stared at the taproom's front door, as if he expected it to suddenly open. "Believe me, she'll be coming through that door as soon as she can."

Edith looked around the cold, quiet, cavernous space. She felt like an astronaut on a distant moon. "You weren't mad that she took this building over?"

"I can't be mad," he laughed, ruefully, as he led the way out the door. "I mean, I would've taken it if it was handed to me, but I guess that's just a way of saying I didn't want it enough."

She watched him lock the door as she built up the nerve to ask him an extremely important question. "Can I bring some friends tomorrow?"

"Yeah, of course," Mo said, handing her a stainless steel key ring the circumference of a donut, weighed down with half a dozen color-coded keys. "Red one gets you in. And yeah, bring whoever you want. Can't be any weirder than some of the people we've had in here over the years."

"We'll see about that," Edith said, and followed him outside into the parking lot, where she practiced locking the doors, and gave the knob a pull, just to make sure.

Before Edith even stepped out of that building, she had people in mind. She was pretty sure they wouldn't all say yes, especially considering that the job required a lot of cleaning and probably low or deferred pay. She'd just hope that they had the time to spare, and would be willing to come to the aid of a young mother with a newborn for a few weeks.

Edith had a reliable inner circle of fellow grandmas after so many years in Nicollet Falls, and three of them said they would help, right away. She had her best friend at Arby's, Betsy Nielsen, who moved to Nicollet Falls way back in 1971, had worked thirteen different restaurant and hospitality jobs since that time, and by now had probably fed or cleaned up after almost everyone in town. Betsy's best friend was a retired nurse named Linda Arquillos, who Edith also knew from the Wednesday morning quilting group at church. Finally, there was Lucy Koski Sarrazin, who now lived a short drive away in Hopkins. Edith had seen her regularly, ever since she had to return Lucy's Crock-Pot after Stanley's funeral.

True, only one of them, Betsy, even claimed she liked beer. But when Mo Akbar met them there on Thursday morning to show them how to operate everything, walk them step-by-step through the brewing process, and tape explanatory Post-it notes next to some of the more unfamiliar machines and gauges, Edith believed that any of them could do what Diana required of them, if they were paying attention.

"This won't be impossible," said Lucy, who'd lived on a dairy farm most of her adult life, and was used to an environment of stainless steel tanks, long hours, cold work, hot work, and high cleanliness standards.

Linda Arquillos claimed that it all looked fun. As the organizer of the church quilting group, member of the Nicollet Falls Memorial Day Parade

Committee, and founder of two book clubs, she was also the most outgoing of the bunch, and was excited to work behind the bar and meet people.

Finally, Betsy Nielsen was not only a sincere beer lover, she was the best cook of the group, which is saying something, because added up, these four women had nearly two-hundred-fifty years of home and professional cooking experience. They not only believed Edith when she told them that beer is just another recipe, it was part of the draw. But Edith had Betsy at the word "brewery."

"I can't believe I get to do this," she said, approaching one of the fermentation tanks with the awe and apprehension of a small child meeting a beloved cartoon character.

"Diana would appreciate the enthusiasm," Mo told them. "Frankly, she's still blown away that you all agreed to help her."

That was one thing that a lot of folks didn't understand—why they all would do this. But why wouldn't they? They were all between sixty-seven (Betsy) and seventy-nine (Edith), so they weren't **that** old, and they were all in decent health with at least fifteen to twenty years ahead of them, maybe more. And, most importantly, this is where they chose to be. What else, after all, were they supposed to be doing?

"Edith, I raise a practical question," Betsy said. Like Edith, she was still working at Arby's, and had to juggle that schedule to be here, but it was clear right away that she would. She was as nervy and excitable as a girl about to win a spelling bee, and in her uncoordinated work and safety gear, looked like someone no one would hire if she weren't in the building already. "How many beers can we make of our own?"

"Pump the brakes, there," Lucy said, crossing her arms. "I didn't hear anything about that. I think we should leave everything how it is."

"But she said we could make our own beer, though, right?" Betsy asked.

Edith tried to remember exactly what Diana did say, and how best to explain it now. One of her friends was explicitly here because she loved beer and always wanted to make her own, and another of her friends here would probably bolt back home the minute things got complicated.

"She said, only do whatever you're comfortable with," Edith announced.

Edith, for one, sure wasn't comfortable with the idea of brewing beer from scratch. She was completely on Lucy's side in this debate. But it was Diana's brewery, not hers.

A few hours later that day, at the hospital, Edith tried to broach the subject of brewing new beers to a granddaughter who was exhausted and may have been floating in and out of lucidity.

"Diana," Edith said, trying to hold eye contact. "Some of us have noticed that you have beer ingredients and recipes that you haven't used yet."

"Oh yeah," Diana said. "There's lots of beer I wanna make. I wanna make a gose. I gotta get outta here and get started on that."

Edith leaned in closer to her granddaughter's ear. "I suppose, what I'm saying is, maybe with Mo's help, some of us could brew it for you."

"Really? Oh, wow." Diana seemed loopy and delighted, neither of which was like her.

"Would it help you if we made more beer?"

"Yeah, wow," Diana smiled, and fell asleep.

"That sounds like a yes to me," Betsy said the next morning.

Oh boy, here we go, Edith thought.

"Well, first things first," she said, walking to the dry-erase board in the office, where she wrote CHORE BOARD. "The taproom opens this evening, and before then we have to divide up some duties."

They were all seasoned pros at allocating and accepting responsibilities, and unlike some of the younger people they'd all worked with over the years, happy to do any job. At one point Edith had to mediate a small disagreement over who got to be the martyr who cleaned the bathroom.

"What about the brewing part?" Linda asked. "That sounds kind of fun. I figure, as long as Diana said it's OK."

Betsy must've gotten to her. Now two of Edith's friends wanted to brew beer. At least Diana did indeed imply that it was OK. She seemed to indicate that it would be a big help, even.

"We'll get to that part last," Edith told everyone.

In the end, each woman was assigned responsibility over a beer currently on the production schedule—the two IPAs, the Kölsch, and the gose—and to be fair, she also gave everyone the option to brew her own beer, if she chose.

Edith was not only surprised that everyone did indeed choose to make a beer, but what they selected:

1. Linda Arquillos elected to make a chocolate stout. It was the only kind of beer she liked, because it went well with a donut.
2. Lucy Koski Sarrazin, who initially didn't want to make a beer at all, changed her mind and said that she decided to make a "light beer." Can't be that hard, she told everyone.

3. Betsy Nielsen, the lone honest beer
   enthusiast at this point, narrowed it down
   to either making an ale brewed with
   strawberry and rhubarb—"like a pie in a
   bottle," she said—or a plum saison, and
   ultimately decided to save the saison for
   summer, and start instead with the heavier
   ale, being that she had a ton of frozen and
   preserved strawberries at home.
4. Edith liked Betsy's pie-in-a-bottle idea
   but now didn't want to steal it, because
   that would be rude. She'd heard from
   somewhere, a while back, that a brewer
   could put fruit into beer. It made the
   whole shebang a heck of a lot more
   interesting. Just like she always did when
   she and a friend went out for a nice lunch
   to Panera, she would decide last, so she
   had more time to make up her mind.

She'd need it. Beer definitely wasn't anything
she'd imagine making for herself one day. It was
just something unappealing that men seemed to
enjoy, and they could have it.

Growing up, her sister, Helen, was the only girl
she knew who had any interest in it at all. She remembered catching Helen and the Sarrazin boys
stealing beer from the Sarrazins' fridge one summer
when Helen must've been about fifteen. Edith's instinct, of course, was to run to the adults. She used

to love getting her braver, smarter, prettier sister in trouble. But that day, Edith did nothing. She just stared out the screen door at Helen running out to have a fun time with the boys, and even though Edith was older, and was trusted like a parent, she was not a parent. She was still one of the kids, or at least in that moment, wanted to be.

She did nothing, even when that Petunia woman opened the fridge ten minutes later, and asked out loud who took her damn beer.

Because of what she'd seen that day, Edith wasn't surprised when her mom called her that fall and told her what Helen wanted for her birthday.

"The nerve of her to even ask for that," her mother said. "Can you believe it?"

Edith, by now, certainly could, but instead appeased her mom by calling the request "ridiculous."

"Scandalous is more like it," her mom said. "Imagine what they'd say about us if we bought beer for our sixteen-year-old daughter."

"Then don't do it," Edith replied.

Edith and Stanley visited the farm on Helen's birthday for dinner, cake, and to spend the night, but Helen refused to come out of her room.

"She can stay there all week, for all I care," their mother said. "Her birthday present is that I won't make her pay for a new window."

After dinner, Edith told her parents that she was

going to walk around outside alone for a while, because she said she missed the farm, and she did indeed do this, but at the end of the walk, she retrieved a metal pail she'd hid in the trunk and ran it out to the garage. That afternoon, she had set out to buy beer, but not knowing what was good, or what kind her sister liked, she ended up buying one bottle each of four different kinds. It was the first time she'd bought alcohol at all since she'd turned twenty-one, and the whole thing made her nervous, but now here she was, setting a pail of beer down by the old sofa, hidden by the dimness of the evening.

"Dad?" Edith asked, handing him a folded yellow note. "Can you run this up to Helen's room and slide it under her door?"

He seemed pleased by the request. "Sure, maybe it'll get her out of there."

Once everyone had gone to bed, Edith stayed up and waited for the sound of Helen's footsteps on the staircase. It was Stanley's idea to wake up early and set out the aspirin and water.

A week later, Helen told Edith that her father had done all of those things, and Edith let her think that.

"Dad understands me," Helen said, pleased. "He can't tell Mom, he can't even tell me, but he understands me."

At the time, Edith wanted her sister to believe that, because it made Helen happier and more confident at a time when she needed it. From that point on, Helen also trusted her father in a way she hadn't before, and it changed their relationship, because in response, he began to trust her more, too.

Years later, she even helped her sister a second time. Kenny Sarrazin called Edith one winter day out of the blue and asked if Helen really was supposed to make beer for a college class—like Edith would even know—and she lied to him, and said yes. She even added that at Macalester only the smartest chemistry students earned that assignment, and this satisfied him.

She just wanted to see what Helen could do. Everybody did, especially Mother.

But only Edith had figured out, that whole time, what Helen really wanted. She wasn't a goofy party girl trying to score booze to get drunk with her friends. She'd been lucky enough to find what she loved at a young age, and bold enough to think she could make a life out of doing it.

Now, for the first time since they were children, they would be competitors. Helen always won, and had been winning at beer for decades, but if some circumstance pitted them against each other, this time their mother wasn't around to help make things fair.

———

Edith wondered what her mother would think now, if she were alive that snowy evening to see her oldest daughter opening the door to a brewery taproom, flipping a sign around to read OPEN, and announcing "OK, we got beer, I guess!"

About a dozen bundled figures huddled outside, mostly young men, and they seemed a little surprised to look across the room and see Betsy and Linda, two kind-looking grandmas, pouring beer.

"Where's the brewmaster?" asked a big guy with a graying, patchy beard.

"She just had a baby," Edith said, figuring that she'd leave out the part about the knee injury, but still added, "I'm her grandma," because she couldn't help it.

"Oh, nice!" the big guy said, as she took his coat and hung it on a brass hook by the doorway. "Well, congratulations there."

He turned to his buddy, an even larger guy, and they crossed the room toward the beer with the feverish faces of kids dragging their sleds up a virgin hill. Even the soft launch of a small brewery evidently brought out the zealous fringe.

Edith joined Linda and Betsy behind the taproom's bar—Lucy still wanted no part of customer service—and helped pour Diana's 100 percent Citra IPA to Artemis Brewery's first paying customers. A lot of them were men who seemed to know way more about IPAs and Citra hops than they did, and were extremely willing to share this knowledge. A few of them were even interesting, briefly.

Despite the exposure in the **Nicollet Falls Viking**, and plenty of word of mouth at the nursing home, Arby's, and Linda's Bible study group, not a lot of people came that first night, but maybe because of the weather. They made $316, Lucy calculated, from pouring sixty-one beers at a couple different price points, but only made an extra $55 in tips, and mostly because the big guy tipped them a ten.

He waved at them as he put on his coat. "Tell the brewmaster congratulations, from Jake and Eric at the Nicollet Falls Elks Lodge."

It couldn't have been the influence of painkillers, because they wouldn't let her take anything stronger than aspirin, but Diana seemed amused by the grandmas' beer plans. Maybe she was happy that the brewery was still open, and didn't care how. Maybe for her, motherhood swept away smaller concerns. Maybe she was in love with the world, or just really tired.

"Just don't mess with the IPAs or the Kölsch," she told Edith, as her newborn daughter slept beside her, a diaper up to her armpits, a little yellow stocking cap on her head. "And how are you paying for these extra ingredients?"

"We're pooling resources. And got a little help

from Lou, Linda's husband," Edith said. Lou was a retired fire chief with a nice pension, and seemed happy to loan them some money. "We're doing fine, so far," Edith said. "It was Lucy's idea just to make small amounts of everything first, to see what sells."

"Limited release," Diana said, her head on her pillow, eyes closed, like she was receiving unearthly messages. "Call it a limited release. And that stout and that ale you can also call a seasonal release. What was the other one?"

"Lucy wants to make a light beer."

Diana's eyes snapped open. "Please don't let her do that. She's out of luck anyway, because I don't have any lager yeast, unless you order it, and please don't, because I'll never use it. Tell her to use the Wyeast 1968 and make a session ale. That's as close as I'll go. And tell her to call it a session ale, not a light beer. Please."

"Got it," Edith said, writing this down on a pad of yellow sticky notes in the shape of a duckling, which were her favorite ones, and not that easy to find. "Anything else?"

"Yeah," Diana replied, a defeated but relaxed expression on her face. "I need to get labels made, and send them out to the TTB for approval. That can take a while. It'd be a huge help if you can help me find a new designer, preferably a woman." Here was one more detail Edith never would've thought of. How one person could keep all of this stuff straight and run a successful brewery, she had no idea.

"Just let me know if I can help with anything else," Edith said, and she would, even though there was so much she still didn't know about everything.

It turned out that gose was a pretty interesting kind of beer! Edith had never imagined that a tart, cloudy, partially wheat beer with added coriander and salt even existed. It was also low in alcohol, not bitter, and it tasted pretty decent when fruit was added both during the boil and during secondary fermentation. Mo brought one over that his brewery made, and everyone seemed to like it, except Lucy.

When they all picked an existing beer of Diana's to see through to completion, Edith did find it curious that Betsy, who chose first, picked the beer that hadn't even been started yet. Her reasoning was simple. "You told us that Diana said not to make any changes to the IPAs or the Kölsch," Betsy said. "So I knew I didn't want to pick one of those." Betsy also let Edith pursue the strawberry-rhubarb ale idea, mostly because she used all her own strawberries on the gose.

That's how Betsy's beer was finished first, weeks before even the most ambitious gardener would have rhubarb for sale that Edith could use in her beer. Since Linda's chocolate stout wasn't ready yet either and Lucy was having problems making her session ale, it turned out that the first time the grandmas brewed a beer, it was the creation of a woman who, until now, had worked all her life as a hotel maid, aircraft cabin cleaner, dishwasher, fry cook, line cook, and fast-food franchise shift manager.

Mo had brewed gose "seven or eight times," and had strong opinions on how he thought it should taste. So, everyone was surprised that he seemed unhappy, because he'd guided Betsy through every step.

"It's a bit on the sweet side," he said, after one sip. "You didn't put in the lacto, did you?"

Edith knew by now that "lacto" was some kind of bacteria that she wasn't ever going to futz with. Edith sure didn't want any bacteria in her beer. Betsy apparently agreed.

"Well, I don't want it that sour, I want it sweeter," Betsy said.

"Then you should've made something besides a gose. You're going to have a lot of annoyed customers."

"Didn't you tell us that there's no good beer or bad beer? People just like what they like?"

"I would've never said that." Mo shook his head. "There's a whole ocean of bad beer out there, trust me."

"Well, somebody said it," Betsy replied. "Maybe I'll say it."

Diana was not all that enthusiastic about what her grandma's friend did to her gose.

"Who the hell would make a strawberry gose as their first beer?" she asked, in a tone that made it clear she'd be shouting if there weren't a baby in the room.

Andy was sitting on the floor with their daughter, next to the couch that Diana was lying on, and fortunately he laughed, taking some of the tension out of the room. He never went out with his friends anymore; he was home now, every chance he could be.

"I'll tell you who," Andy replied. "Someone who has a freezer full of frozen strawberries in their basement. And access to all of the ingredients. And commercial brewing equipment. You unleash a grandma into a brewery, this is what you get."

Edith nodded. "If any one of us can do it, it's Betsy."

"Well, the reason I didn't even mention it was because I was sure no one would touch it," Diana said. "What the hell is Betsy's deal, anyway? Like, is she into BASE jumping, or microdosing?"

Edith had never heard of those things. "I know she likes **Storage Wars**."

Andy laughed. "It's actually not a bad idea for a new brewery to lead with something that no one else is doing. Isn't that why you were doing a gose?"

"True," Diana said. "I just hope she didn't put the wheat on the bottom where it would gum up the works."

"Mo was there to help her," Edith said. "He said that she didn't use the lacto, whatever that is."

Diana sighed. "Lactobacillus. It means that her gose isn't going to be tart, like a gose is supposed to be."

"Oh, no one's gonna mind," Edith said.

Andy laughed again. Diana looked disgusted.

"Grandma, the people who like gose are absolutely going to mind. It's like having rhubarb pie on the menu but serving blueberry pie instead. Do you get it?"

Edith didn't know it was that serious. Now she felt a little bad. The official grand opening was in four days, and it'd be there, on a tap right alongside all of Diana's beers. "Well, I guess we'll find out. But I don't want you to worry about being there on Friday if you're not up for it."

"I'd crawl there on my elbows," Diana said.

Diana, in a wheelchair, her baby slung over her chest, was at the brewery with Andy that Friday morning at nine. She supervised Edith and Betsy while they cleaned the brite tank, and chatted with Linda and Lucy as they swept and opened the taproom. The rest of the time, she was passing the baby around and delegating a galaxy of minor party tasks. For this landmark event, Diana had emailed press releases, sent invites, ordered more bottled pop for the kids, and had Andy make more spent-grain snacks. For hot food, she bought a couple six-packs of frozen Heggies pizzas, which Linda heated up in her oven at home and brought over one by one as the next one was baking. That ended up being the most expensive part of the whole shebang.

Some people had told Diana that she should go bigger, you only get one grand opening, and she should have a live band, hire food trucks, print up special T-shirts, and give away free beer and gift cards as door prizes. Diana dismissed all of these ideas out of hand, just because they'd put her over budget. Edith and the other ladies all approved of the frugality.

In fact, as relatively cheap as the party was already, Edith wondered why the whole dang thing couldn't just be a potluck. The grandmas were already contributing some homemade salads, bars, and dips. There were even two different seven-layer taco dips, because not everybody likes olives.

Edith wasn't sure if the crowds would really be much bigger than the soft launch, even with all the hoopla, but seeing the first customers come through the door that evening made her less nervous. They were three men and a woman, probably in their early thirties, each in a jacket, sweatshirt, and jeans, and they seemed neither snobby nor demanding.

Diana certainly wasn't crazy about Betsy's strawberry gose, but Edith figured you never know about these things. Even though it was probably a little unsettling to these customers when everyone in the brewery dashed into the taproom, no one could pretend to ignore that one of their own beers, the first grandma beer, was about to be judged.

The woman and three men each asked for an IPA, but Linda was already pouring gose into sample glasses. "Would you first like to try our new strawberry gose?" she asked, setting them across the bar.

"No thanks," one of the men, a beefy blond guy in a camouflage jacket, said. "Gonna stick with the IPA."

"It's a limited release," Linda said.

"Seasonal release," said Lucy.

"Seasonal limited," Betsy said, from across the room.

Linda nodded. "Limited seasonal release."

The other three customers all at least sipped theirs. "Too sweet," said the woman. Only one of them finished their sample, the tallest and biggest of the men. He asked the other two if they were going to finish theirs, and when they said no, he drank the rest of the two-ounce pours on the bar in about eight seconds.

"What did you think?" Linda asked.

"Not bad," the big man said.

"He liked it," Betsy whispered, and looked at Diana. "He liked it."

"One person," Diana told her. "Out of four."

"Well, that's something," Edith said. "Better than zero."

They almost had two grandma beers ready that day. Earlier that afternoon, Diana had sampled Lucy's session ale. But the way Diana's face twisted when she smelled the beer, Edith knew right then it wouldn't make the cut. That was the first time it really hit Edith that no matter what they thought they knew, or how easily they could learn, brewing would be harder than they thought.

"What's the problem?" Lucy asked, her hands on her hips.

"Creamed corn," Diana said, pulling the glass away from her nose, and holding the beer out for Edith and Lucy. "Smell it."

"That can't be," Lucy said. "I didn't use any corn."

"It's dimethyl sulfide," Diana said. "That's not good. How quickly did you cool your wort down after the boil?"

"I had to go pick up my daughter from work at Rocky Rococo, and run some errands," she said. "I figured it would just cool down on its own."

"So how long?"

"Maybe three or four hours. But I got it to seventy right away when I came back."

"Well, that probably explains it," Diana said, rubbing her forehead. "We'll have to dump it out."

Lucy's back straightened and arms crossed like a woman ready to argue. "Yeah, why?"

"Don't feel bad," Diana almost laughed. "If Frank were here, he wouldn't have even acknowledged this beer, let alone smelled it. He dumped out so many beers of mine over the years, you have no idea."

Edith took the beer and smelled it again. "Can you do anything to fix it?"

"I can't, but Lucy can," Diana said, taking the glass from Edith and pouring it into the drain in the floor. "The next time she makes it."

Linda also struggled with her chocolate stout. Even with Mo's help at the beginning, and Diana's advice throughout, she still went a little overboard with the cacao nibs and ended up with a beer that was way too harsh for her taste, or probably anybody's. This time, with Diana's hands-on guidance, Linda soaked the nibs in vanilla vodka for a week before adding them during secondary fermentation, and used half as many.

"Last time you also poured too early," Diana told her. "This isn't a race. You do this right, we should lay it down for a little while, and not touch it until May at the earliest."

"That's no fun. I want it now," Linda said. "I don't know how much time I've got left on this rock."

"All the more reason to get it right," Diana said.

Diana did seem impressed at how serious all of the grandmas were and how willing they were to learn from their mistakes. Like Edith, they all had other obligations, but even with Diana back in the building every day, none of them showed up less often or took on fewer duties.

For someone who claimed that she didn't like beer, Lucy Koski Sarrazin worked incredibly hard at improving as a brewer. In early March, after the failure of her first attempt to make a session ale, she got permission from Diana and the others to brew two more attempts nearly simultaneously. That week, she stayed late and cleaned alone, with just Mr. T, her Pomeranian, to keep her company. By early April, she was the second most effective, after Diana, at lautering (separating the sweet wort from the spent grain) and sparging (gradually adding hot water to the wort after lautering).

"I haven't busted my ass like this in a long time,"

Lucy told Edith one night while they were mopping, pushing everything toward a drain in the center of the floor. "It feels kinda good."

Edith nodded. "I wouldn't want to work like this every night, though."

"No way in hell," Lucy said. "Done enough of that."

"You ever miss the farm?"

Lucy stopped mopping and stood there as if she was looking at Mount Rushmore and trying to remember the names of the two guys in the middle. "Cows and hogs don't care it's your birthday," she said, and started mopping again.

May 11 was the first day when Artemis Brewery had three grandma beers on tap—Linda's new, less bitter stout, Betsy's gose, and Lucy's "light ale" (the name was a compromise with Diana). Diana had sold out of her two single-hopped IPAs by then, and had replaced them with a high-alcohol imperial brown ale and a hazy New England IPA to give the menu a little variety. Lucy then came up with a pretty decent way to introduce them to customers.

"For a dollar, we give customers a one-ounce pour of each of them," Lucy said, placing a stack of little home-printed slips of paper on the counter. "And on here, they can vote for the one they like the best, and explain why, if they want."

The women glanced at each other. "I didn't

think I was entering my beer in a popularity contest," Betsy said.

"It's not," Lucy said. "If we want to make money at this, we need to know what people are responding to, so we can make more of it."

No one had a problem with that idea. Betsy did admit that on days when she worked the taproom she'd still push her gose on people, though, just because it was an unusual variety and it needed pushing.

None of the grandmas got to push anything on a particular customer who came in alone around lunchtime. He was a big guy, wearing a sweatshirt that had some NASCAR driver on the front, and his clothes had the kinds of stains that made Edith guess that he was a mechanic or worked in an auto junkyard.

Diana saw this man, told Betsy, "I know this guy," and grabbed her crutches and hopped up to greet him as he approached the bar. This alone was strange, because Diana had declared that she'd never work front-of-house as long as the grandmas were there, and until now, never had.

"We can take care of him," Edith said to Diana's back. Why was she in such a hurry? "The floor's wet out there!" Edith yelled, and even if it wasn't anymore, it could be again, real easy. Diana waved her grandma off.

"What kinda beer do ya got in this place?" the man asked.

"Did you park in the lot?" Diana asked. "Right out front here?"

"Yeah," the guy grunted.

"That's an eight-dollar parking charge. Plus a two-dollar venue convenience fee."

The guy glanced around. "I didn't see no sign."

"Those are the rules. Come on, this isn't an Arab street market. Ten dollars."

That phrase sure didn't sound like something Diana would say. Glancing at her friends, it was clear to Edith that everyone wondered what the heck was happening—besides, they'd never charged for parking before, not even during the grand opening, nor did any of their neighbors.

"Shit," the guy said, and put a ten-dollar bill on the counter. "OK, what now, the beer is free?"

"Would you like to try the imperial brown? It's got the highest alcohol content."

"I don't know, I'm here on my lunch break."

"It's free if you can finish it in eight seconds."

All of the grandmas in the tasting room glanced at each other again. No one had any idea where this was all going. Diana seemed obsessed with provoking this guy, and all anyone else could do was just stand back and watch.

The guy tried his best to chug that beer, and maybe he got close, but his glass was still against his mouth when Diana said, "Time."

"I finished it," he said.

"So close. Just missed by a second," Diana said. "That'll be twenty-four dollars, plus a two-dollar glass-cleaning fee."

"Twenty-six dollars for a beer?"

"Those are the rules," Diana said, and pointed to a mounted camera. "You're on video as consenting to the contest. Now, if you can drink two more in sixteen seconds, you get them all free, and I refund your parking charges."

"Shit," the guy said, and shook his head.

"A man like you can't do it? You were so close just now. Come on."

The man shook his head.

"Don't be a little coward."

"OK," the guy said, taking a deep breath. "Whatever, fuck it."

By now, everyone who was at work that day was rapt. The big guy, taking in his attentive audience, finished the first beer in about eight seconds again, but these were twenty-four-ounce pours of heavy imperial ales, and the second one, well, he wasn't close, and seeming to know this, finished the beer anyway.

"All right. That's fifty-seven dollars."

"Bullshit," he said, and turned to leave. "You know, fuck this place."

"Sir, that's theft, and I will press charges," she said. "I have you on tape, Brad."

The man jolted at the sound of his name, came

back, slapped three twenties down, kicked the bar, and stormed out of the place, swinging the door open wide as he left.

"Betsy," Diana said. "Run out there, get his make, model, and license plate, and call the police to report a drunk driver. I don't want him hurting anybody."

None of them had seen Diana so serious and focused. Betsy did as she was told, and as she dashed outside, a jittery chill seemed to fall over the room.

"What was all that about?" Edith asked.

"He and I go back," Diana said, and put his money in her pocket, not in the register. "Remember when your Toyota Cressida was towed?"

"Vaguely," Edith said, though she really didn't.

"Well, I do."

Whatever Diana's reasons, for Edith it was upsetting to witness her granddaughter behaving like this to another human being, even a rude one who may have had it coming. Diana seemed to believe that not every wrong against you is forgivable and not everyone should be forgiven. It frightened Edith that Diana would come to this conclusion, and Edith wondered who in Diana's life might have influenced that conviction.

Later that afternoon, they finally received approval from TTB for their beer labels. Edith was pleased that they had kept them extremely simple. Other than all of the stuff the government required, each label just had the Artemis logo and the name of the beer. Along with the beers that Diana had brewed, the Artemis lineup now included Grandma Betsy's Strawberry Gose, Grandma Linda's Chocolate Stout, and Grandma Lucy's Light Ale. This is what Diana had been waiting for. At last, they would distribute their beer well beyond just the kegs in their taproom and the friendlier bars of Nicollet Falls. Their beer would be out there in towns Edith had never visited, looking for strangers to give it a chance.

Even though Edith hadn't even bought her rhubarb yet, much less brewed the ale, they'd also made a label for Grandma Edith's Rhubarb-Pie-In-A-Bottle Ale. She never thought that she would look at a bottle of beer and see her name. But here it was, and it made her smile.

For the first time, she just realized, she was making something for herself, and she hadn't even given one dang thought as to who else might like it. She would never tell anyone, but that felt wonderful.

She put a label on an empty bottle and brought it to Autumn Pines over the dinner shift that night to show her friends there. Bernie Berglund was the most impressed. "Geez, pie in a bottle," he said. "They're actually going to make this."

"**I'm** going to make it," she said, taking the bottle

back and wrapping it in a tea towel before returning it to her bag. "No idea how it's going to turn out, though. So don't get excited."

"I'm not that excited, I'm a Grain Belt guy," he said. "But I never known anyone that made a beer before. At least one you can buy in a store."

"It's going to take a lot of work before then," Edith said, almost to remind herself.

"Oh, sure," he nodded. "You won't get too busy on us, then?"

Edith knew what Bernie meant by that question. Autumn Pines had been laying off full-timers and replacing them with part-timers for a while, and including Bernie, there were now only six full-time staff employees left. There had also been so much turnover with the part-timers, Edith couldn't keep their names straight. By now she'd been volunteering at Autumn Pines longer than a lot of people had been working there. Still, Bernie had nothing to worry about. She couldn't leave these residents she'd been getting to know, now that she was a consistent presence in their world.

"Oh, it's the lager queen, again," Shotty Vecchio liked to say, ever since he'd been informed of her new job. Even though she'd never made a lager and didn't intend to, she'd never corrected him. "Come on, dinner waits for no man. Let's try to not be the last ones there this time."

She knew she wasn't the fastest at getting people around, but he didn't have to constantly remind her. "Be polite, Shotty, and maybe I'll bring you some beer one of these days."

"Why'd you have to go and say that?" Shotty asked. "Now I might look forward to seeing you."

At the time she just thought it was a clever comeback from a clever old man, but on her drive home, she heard the sadness in it, the sadness of a world where the people who cared for him were swapped out like baseball cards, the peril of attachment in a world of dependence, and the fatigue of anticipation, anywhere.

As Diana had warned them, the evening of the first bottling and packaging was truly a call-everyone-you-know kind of situation for a fledgling brewery.

Luckily for them, more than thirty people came—old friends like Linty Sarrazin; Diana's high school principal, Londard Shultz; Linda's retired fire chief husband, Lou; some new faces like Bernie Berglund and Lucy's smart, youngest daughter, Tarah; and even, surprisingly, Edith's old coworker Maureen O'Brien, who brought some fancy desserts made by her new boss, who was some famous chef somewhere.

Edith's son, Eugene, who'd agreeably come by several times already when they needed some literal heavy lifting, was the first to arrive. Eugene had rarely been the first to show up for anything that involved labor, let alone volunteer work, and to see him come prepared with boots and gloves was kind of touching. More shockingly, he didn't ask for money, and didn't take a single beer with him when he left, even when Diana let everyone know they could. "It's been one month and eight days, now," he told Edith.

"Here," Edith told him, trying to slip him a twenty.

"You've done enough, Mom," he said, and looked at the cash once before walking away, his hands in his jacket pockets.

A half hour after the packaging party was over, Edith found Diana back inside trying to work. She was still not completely recovered physically, but was up off the ground at the edge of the giant brew kettle, supervising an IPA boil with Betsy, reminding her about when to put in the hops. "If you want more bitterness, put 'em in ten to fifteen minutes before you're done," she was saying. "If you want aromatics, put 'em in almost at the very end." She turned and nodded at Edith when she noticed her grandma standing there. "Grandma, you can go home, we got this."

Edith watched the boil for a few moments, because she'd be doing this herself before long. Since the boil acted as a sterilizer, this was a stage where she learned that she could add fresh fruit, juices, or any fruit puree that wasn't already pasteurized. This wouldn't be difficult at all. The only thing about it that made it seem strange was that no one who looked like her and her friends, to her knowledge, had ever made beer on this level before. The beer books she'd leafed through at the library didn't have any pictures of old women in work boots, goggles, and coveralls standing next to giant stainless tanks. Maybe someday someone would come in and take a picture of Betsy up there, standing over the boil like a master chef about to make soup for a thousand children.

"Grandma," Diana said again. "What is it?"

"I know there's been talk about bringing a few more people aboard soon."

"Yes," Diana said. "And?"

"Well, I think that when we have it in our budget to hire someone in shipping and receiving, we should hire Eugene."

"Oh, why's that?" Diana never did care too much for her uncle.

It was hard to blame her. Maybe Edith, as a mother, did forgive him too easily and too often, and with all the money her forgiveness cost their family, she could understand the resentment. But could any mother of a son, a son with nowhere else to cushion his falls, do any differently? She wouldn't want to know.

"Because I tried to give him money tonight and he said no," she said.

"OK, then," Diana said. "We'll see."

Without telling Edith, Diana hired him three days later. That morning, he was just there, in a T-shirt and blue jeans, slicing open a pallet of bottles with a box cutter, and when he saw his mom, he just nodded and went back to work.

The following Monday, Edith had a bad day at Arby's. Rude customers, lots of spills, and bathroom detail. She could be wrong, but it seemed like a lot more of the days at Arby's were bad days since she started at the brewery. She didn't know yet if Diana could pay her more, or give her more hours, but either way, Edith wanted to make it work. She would have to make it work.

"I'm sorry, but I'm afraid I would like to quit," she told her manager, who now happened to be Betsy. "I'm going to ask for more hours at the brewery."

Betsy looked puzzled at first, and then grinned.

"Well, me too, damn it," she said, and took off her nametag and visor as if they were on fire.

Edith had been to a bar maybe once since she moved to Nicollet Falls, by accident, when she got lost looking for the flower shop. She certainly

never imagined that there'd be a weekday afternoon when she'd personally visit five bars and liquor stores, talk about beer at each one, and know
what she was talking about. It was what they called
"self-distribution."

The first place she, Diana, and Linda visited was
one of those windowless saloons right off the highway, on the scrubby outer edge of the metro area.
Edith wasn't that nuts about these kinds of places
and let Diana know.

"Oh please, Grandma," Diana said. "This bar
sold my first beer. The owner's a friend."

Even though it was before noon, the place wasn't
completely empty, which Edith thought was a little disquieting. The interior smelled like cigarette
smoke and wet carpeting, and the young man
behind the bar was bald and didn't look friendly.
Edith was about to suggest that she just wait in the
car when a middle-aged woman in workout clothes
appeared from nowhere and hugged Diana.

"Hey!" the woman said. "Haven't seen you in a
minute."

"Yeah, I've been a little busy," Diana said, and
introduced the woman—"Shasta, like the pop,"
she said—to Linda and Edith.

"Nice to meet you both," Shasta said. "So, you
girls just tagging along today?"

"No, they are not," Diana said, and nodded

toward the young dude behind the bar. "Who's the new guy?"

Shasta glanced back at the bartender. "Oh, that's Fuzzy. He's my new resident beer snob. He's here to keep us relevant. Want to try some beer, Fuzzy? This is my favorite local brewmaster."

"I guess," Fuzzy shrugged.

They laid all of the bottles across the bar, both the grandma beers and Diana's IPAs and Kölsch. Shasta picked up one of the grandma beers first. "Grandma Linda's Chocolate Stout?"

"I was gonna tell you to pick that one up first," Linda said.

"You're the Grandma Linda?" Shasta asked, staring at the label. "You made this?"

"Well, I didn't get it in one, this was my second try."

"So it's not just a name." Shasta looked over the bottles. "Grandmas actually made these beers."

"Yes, we did," Linda said.

Diana nodded. "They've come a long way in a short time."

"Naw, no way," Shasta said, still looking at Diana. "You made 'em and you're just using these grandmas to market them. Which is good, I'll give you that."

Edith glanced over at Linda. "Why don't you tell them how you made it?"

"Sure, Edith," Linda said, clearing her throat. "Well, here's my grain bill. Eighty percent two-row barley malt. Six-and-a-half percent American roasted chocolate malt. Three-and-a-half percent crystal malt—"

"Damn," Fuzzy interrupted. "You're serious."

"Young man," Edith said, and spoke up so that not just the bartender and Shasta, but the other customers, could hear her. "This is the best stout I've ever had in my life." Edith didn't add that it was the first and only stout she'd ever had in her life, but she felt that this was how sales were done.

"When you're ready, I'll continue," Linda said, not smiling.

Diana's old Volkswagen left the parking lot quite a bit lighter, and Edith had to admit that this all seemed easier than she was told to expect.

"I have a history with that place, and they're sympathetic," Diana said, turning the car back onto the highway.

"Betsy's gonna be bummed," Linda said. "Shasta didn't order the strawberry gose."

"That bar doesn't cater to the fruity beer crowd, so much. But we'll try it at some brunch places."

"Well, I hope so," Edith said. "I would feel bad for Betsy if we didn't sell her beer."

Driving through at least two counties in the five-county metro area, moving through numerous neighborhoods and suburbs, they must've passed dozens and dozens of little bars, grim strip-mall liquor stores, and colorful restaurants advertising drink specials. Until now, when she had a hand in creating and selling alcoholic beverages, it had never really registered to Edith before just how many places within twenty miles of where she lived sold alcohol, and now, how many of these places would be dismissed out of hand by her granddaughter, their guide and expert.

"Not that one," Diana said, when Edith pointed at a nice-looking hotel. "Only works with the major brand houses."

"Nope," Diana replied, when Edith asked about a liquor store attached to a supermarket. "Can't muscle in on that shelf space. Staff isn't knowledgeable either, and won't hand-sell for us."

"That looks like a cool place," Linda said, pointing at a sports bar with a Minnesota Wild banner in the window.

Diana shook her head. "They used to sell my IPA, but we pulled it all when we found out that they only clean their lines once a month."

Edith hadn't even heard of a tap line before all this. But she imagined drinking beer from a plastic cup that had been used every day and hadn't been washed in weeks, and wondered if it was something like that. "Well, I guess we won't stop there, then."

Diana gave the place a lingering look as she drove by. "I just heard that they have Heartlander on tap again, as of yesterday."

"I guess the new owners don't even care," Linda said. "What do you think about that?"

Diana just kept driving.

Once they'd had their beers in the world for about a month, had their name out there, and had a sense of what was selling, Diana suggested they try an infamous beer bar in St. Paul called The Happy Pig. It was one of those places with more than forty tap handles, and a chalkboard over the bar listing all of them. There was also another small chalkboard at eye level listing the date they last had their lines cleaned, and it was yesterday.

A couple of bored-looking bearded guys were behind the bar, and one of them, the one with a little gray, and wrinkles around his eyes, smiled when he saw Diana and said to meet him at the big table. Diana told them that his name was Gus Jimenez, and he'd managed this place for twenty years.

Unlike a lot of the people they'd met so far, Gus was unfazed by the fact that the grandmas had made two-thirds of the beer that Diana had brought to him. Maybe she'd told him and it had sunk in already. He was far more surprised by something else.

"None of you grandmas made a pale ale or an

IPA," he said, after sampling everyone's beer without comment.

Edith pointed up at the tap list, where there were
at least a dozen listed. "Seems like you have a lot
already."

"We could always use another good one."

"Well, I guess most of us are making a beer we'd
actually like to drink ourselves."

"Betsy's making a New England–style IPA,"
Linda said. She seemed equally irritated and proud,
like when a guest loves your dessert but obviously
hated the meal. "But Betsy's probably going to
make everything."

The man picked up one of Betsy's bottles. "This
so-called gose was the one grandma beer I liked.
This the same Betsy?"

Diana and Linda each blinked and gently
twitched in reaction to Gus's admission that he
didn't like any of the grandma beers but one. But
Edith didn't move.

Gus, meanwhile, continued talking, oblivious to
the women in front of him who were restraining
their honest emotional reactions. "Look, Diana,
it's impressive what you've done. You've taken complete outsiders and taught them how to make com-
petent beer in a couple of months. They don't seem
to know exactly what they're doing yet, but they're
so into it. I love that. You'll sell beer based on that
alone. But come back in six months, or a year, or

a couple years, or however long it takes them to make beer that's actually really, really good."

Edith had been waiting for this. At the bars and liquor stores they'd visited over the last few weeks, people had been surprised, people had gushed, people had even been patronizing and condescending the same minute they bought cases of beer, but no one, Edith felt, had been honest.

"We're happy to do that," Edith said.

Linda, though, wasn't having it. "I hate to break it to you, Gus, but that strawberry gose was the first beer any of us made."

"You know, it's a complete failure as a gose, but I love it," Gus said. "It's so off, I can actually work with it."

"Yeah, most people find it too sweet," Diana said. "You're actually only our second taker on it."

"Sure," Gus said. "But I don't have anything else on my list that fits that flavor profile. I know it's not cool to like sweet. But I'm a human being, and I like sweet sometimes, and this is actually how I like it. However much you have left, I'll take all of it."

"Wow," Linda said. "We didn't make a lot. We're down to our last three corny kegs."

He nodded. "You know, I'm going to have to call it something else to sell it here, though. The people who want a real gose will hate it. So how about 'Grandma Betsy's Strawberry Ale'?"

Everyone looked at Diana.

"Perfect," Diana said. "Let me know how it does."

They were back in Nicollet Falls by suppertime, and went straight to the brewery to drop off the unsold stock. Afterward, Linda and Diana went home to their families, but Edith, not feeling like being alone, went back inside. Betsy was in the tasting room, talking with a middle-aged woman who looked familiar. Her clothes and shoes looked brand-new and expensive.

"This is Agatha," Betsy said. "I just poured everything for her and she told me exactly what was in all of it without me even saying."

"You're off to a pretty good start." Agatha lifted her glass. "But you have a ways to go."

"We know," Edith said. "I don't suppose you have any useful advice."

"As a matter of fact, she does," Betsy said.

Edith sat down and looked this woman in the eyes. She seemed educated, intelligent, confident, and despite her fancy clothes and curt language, not unkind. "Have you worked in the beer business before?"

Betsy smiled. "You are not going to believe where."

It was so early in the morning, the light in the sky was just a dab of orange, and by the time Edith arrived at the brewery, the automated exterior lights were still lit and humming. As she turned off the engine, papery bugs rested on her windshield, and she watched the same insects convening in the beams of every light throughout the office park, spinning in woozy swirls, clustering on the bulbs.

Eugene had beat her to work, and she was glad he had, because he and the rest of the crew had a lot of work to do loading up the vans for their trip to the Upper Mississippi Beer Festival that morning. It was their first festival, and even if they only got in because some other Midwestern brewery had to drop out at the last second, it gave everyone a sense of accomplishment, of progress. Of course, she'd heard by now that festivals didn't mean much in terms of reaching customers, many of whom would already be tipsy on other people's beer, but they'd help put Artemis on the map with other brewers in the community, and they seemed like fun. They had two more regional beer festivals coming up on the calendar, but no one wanted to pace themselves. All of the grandmas were coming to this one.

"Mayflies," her son said, as if she didn't know, and watched him disappear into a shiny white van with the Artemis logo on the side, one of the many things Agatha Johnston helped provide.

Edith had to admit that she was one of the two votes against bringing Agatha on board, the other being good old reliable Lucy, but Diana reminded everyone that Artemis Brewery was not a democracy. She alone made all the major decisions, and her decision was to accept Agatha's offer to volunteer the skills she'd developed over thirty years of working for a major brewery. It didn't matter at all to Diana that the brewery was Blotz.

Yes, Edith had publicly opposed Agatha, but as time passed, she'd admit to anyone that she was wrong. Agatha not only improved quality control and operations immediately and immeasurably, she lent Artemis Brewery a lot of money, so much that Edith didn't really want to say. Even though Diana said they were already working toward being able to pay everyone a competitive salary and hire more workers and improve the interior decor, Agatha's money enabled them to do all of those things right away. They hired Eugene full-time, and when Autumn Pines laid off Bernie Berglund and replaced him with a part-time contractor, the brewery snapped him up to handle facilities and maintenance. The same week, on Londard Shultz's recommendation, Diana hired a pair of high school seniors named Sammy and

Mia, to be cellar masters and help Eugene with the physical labor. Edith heard they were each poor kids who had academic potential but also some scrapes with the law.

"These kids deserve it more than I did," Diana said when she hired them, which Edith thought was an exaggeration. Edith never asked what they'd done to get themselves in trouble, but after seeing them work, she never again thought about it.

Only four weeks later, Edith happened to be cleaning the office when Diana called them in. Sammy and Mia didn't know why their boss wanted to see them, so it was heartbreaking to see them enter the room as grim and anxious as soldiers surrendering to an invading force. They stood there, Sammy with his pimply cheeks and crisp jeans, and Mia with her dyed hair and clunky glasses, each with rigid faces acclimated to bad news.

"Once you graduate high school, let me know if you want to apprentice under me to be a brewmaster," she told them.

The kids glanced at each other like they weren't sure what they'd just heard.

"No pressure," Diana told them, smiling at their surprised relief. "It's OK if you want to keep working here either way, and don't want to be a brewmaster. Because if you do, I'll be working you a lot harder."

"OK," Mia said.

"OK, what? You want to be my apprentice?"

Mia nodded. "I want to make a sour."

"Yeah, me too," Sammy said. "And a double IPA."

"Wow. Well, both of you are in for it," Diana said, trying to sound stern, but she seemed amused by their beer choices. She glanced over at the office fridge. "If it's OK with your parents, I'm giving you both some homework. And I gotta know if you can help at the festival."

They both said yes, enthusiastically, even if it meant that they had to ride along in a van with Eugene and listen to his music.

The Upper Mississippi Beer Festival had outgrown its original site in a small island city in Iowa called Sabula, and moved up to a big riverside park in southeastern Minnesota, conveniently, just this year. If the festival were still in Iowa, they would have had to leave yesterday morning at the latest, and wouldn't be sleeping in their own beds. If they were ever lucky enough to get into Great Taste of the Midwest in Wisconsin, it'd be that kind of ordeal.

The pilot batch of Grandma Edith's Rhubarb-Pie-In-A-Bottle Ale had just been kegged and bottled three days before, and another batch was in one of the fermenters. It was a tricky ale to pull off, it turned out, and Agatha had been a giant help. She was a vital troubleshooter all up and down the production line, with her incredible knowledge of enzymes, off-flavors, phenols, and esters. She knew when a beer wasn't working and how to make the exact correction required, far more precisely than Diana, even.

When the first kegs of beer with Agatha's fingerprints on them were brought to Gus at The Happy Pig, he was startled at how quickly and substantially the beer had improved.

"What did you do?" Gus asked them. "Please be honest with me. You've gone from hitting .250 in the minor leagues to batting .400 in the World Series. No one evolves like this. Please tell me what happened."

"Well, Diana's back at the brewery every day now," Edith said.

Diana shook her head. "It's not just me."

"Agatha," Linda blurted out, like a child telling on her sister.

"We brought in a quality expert," Diana said, trying not to skip a beat. "Agatha Johnston, formerly of Blotz."

"Well, she came to us," Linda added. "Just walked in one day and asked, how can I help?"

Gus leaned back in his chair. "Wow. Someone

got up and left a six-figure job at a corporate swill factory. All to come make peanuts with you guys."

"For free," Linda said. "She's not accepting a salary."

Gus shook his head. "This is what insurance adjusters call an Act of God."

"Well, she loves beer," Edith said.

"She must, if she left Blotz. Still strikes me as weird."

"And the irony is, she's a grandma, too," said Linda. "Has a little one-year-old grandson."

"That's not irony," Diana said. "That's coincidence. It'd be irony if we were specifically not hiring grandmas."

Linda frowned. "Well, excuse me."

"Whatever you want to call it, it worked," Gus said. "And anything you have in a keg, I'll put on tap. And do you have any more of that strawberry stuff coming up? I want it for summer."

"What did you say?" Diana asked.

"Whatever you have," Gus said. "I'll take all of it."

Since the explosion of exposure at The Happy Pig, and after the taproom was refurbished and modernized, the brewery became a heck of a lot busier. Their reputation spread, and by late June, they'd had visitors from as far away as Santa Cruz and

Tampa. They'd even had a couple from Klagen-
furt, Austria, who were passing through Minnesota when they'd seen a magazine article with a
picture of Edith, Diana, and Francie. They said
they just had to check out a brewery run by "three
generations of women and a team of grandmas."

It was eight in the morning by the time they hit
the road. Eugene and Bernie drove the vans full
of beer while the grandmas and Diana went sepa-
rately in Diana's car. Edith sat in the middle of
the back seat between Lucy and Linda, which she
didn't mind, because she was nervous, and it felt
good. It felt good to care about something enough
to feel nervous. If she participated in any conversations on the way, she couldn't recall them later.
She only remembered a few more bugs hitting the
windshield, and Linda saying, "Mayflies," and
Lucy saying, "Good," and nobody else saying anything about that.

Edith hadn't even attended a festival of any kind
in decades. An hour before the gates opened, she
felt like too many people were there already. Men
outnumbered women by maybe three to one. Most
everyone was friendly, but there was hardly anyone her age, and virtually no other women who

looked like her besides the group she came with. She decided early on she would just stay at the booth the entire time.

"Don't you want to walk around and sample other people's beer?" Betsy asked.

"Why would I do that?" Edith asked. "I like ours."

Once they let in the attendees, Edith hardly got to sit down. Everybody—men, women, old people, young people—wanted to come meet the grandmas who made beer. Someone gave her a Sharpie, and she signed bottles until her hand got sore. Dozens and dozens of people asked for selfies with them. Sammy and Mia were on full-time camera duty for what seemed like hours. A few people commented that the Artemis grandma beers weren't their favorite, or that it was "a funny gimmick," or that "they made OK beer, for a bunch of old ladies." Not everyone's going to like it, and a few people are going to hate it, Edith reminded herself, also reminding herself that there was no way in hell even six months ago she'd have predicted that one day, she'd be at a beer festival, pouring beer that she'd brewed. She was almost eighty, and look at all this. Her name was on a giant canvas banner behind her.

Andy arrived with Francie around lunch. Wow, never underestimate the power of a baby as a promotional magnet. People saw a young family selling beer together and practically ran across the grass to hand their money over. Francie wasn't the only baby or little kid there, but something about seeing her among all the grandmas gave their tent the feel of a family reunion picnic, in a good way.

After two hours, Francie grew sullen and tired from the sun, the heat, and the ceaseless doting strangers, and finally melted down, with a full-on, red-eye-flight wail.

"She hung in there," Betsy said, with respect.

"It was a good run," Linda agreed.

"I'll try to bring her back," Andy said, as he lifted his screaming infant into his arms. "A little later."

Edith watched them until they vanished into the crowd.

Around four in the afternoon, Agatha showed up. It seemed strange to Edith for a moment, that this new woman would show up anyway, after they'd told her to take the day off, but Diana hugged her, and no one acted like it was unusual or unwelcome, so Edith didn't either.

"I know you didn't ask me to work the booth, but I couldn't miss this," Agatha said to everyone, and in under a minute, she was pouring samples for customers.

Linda and Betsy were having a blast visiting the other booths. They came back with a couple of imperial stouts from Central Waters Brewing out of Wisconsin, and were raving about them like teenagers, until Diana finally told them to either help her out or get out of the way and let the customers through.

"Beer is so good!" Betsy said.

"All beer, or that stout in particular?" Edith asked.

"Beer!" Betsy said, and sat down on a cooler. "I need a break."

When the sun went down, the gates closed, the attendees were ushered out, and Eugene drove the young cellar masters home. Some of the booths stayed open and swapped beer with their fellow brewers under generator-powered lights and solar-charged lanterns. The mayflies were much worse down south than they were up in Nicollet Falls, clustering under the mounted lights in a swaying copper veil, their bodies piling up in small brown drifts around the generators. It didn't bother Edith at all, or Lucy, both of whom grew up on farms and dealt with stuff that was a lot more disgusting, but Diana was urging everyone to pack it all up and get back to the brewery, as the wispy, harmless brown bugs hit her in the face and crawled over her hair.

Edith, Agatha, and Betsy sat on coolers and watched other people work, as Lucy and Linda passed out the rest of their beer. Betsy was nursing the last bottle of Linda's chocolate stout, when she said something kind of amazing.

"I want to die doing this," she said, staring straight ahead at the tents coming down.

"Me too," Linda said. "I want to be found in a pool of my own beer."

Agatha was smiling. "I've never thought of it before," she said. "But me, too."

"Definitely a stout, though," Linda said. "Guess I'll have to make some more."

Betsy laughed. "I'd like to drown in a triple IPA."

"I hate to say it," Agatha said. "But I want to die in a pool of lager."

"You are all crazy," Lucy said. "I like you guys and everything, but I want to die at home, in bed, surrounded by my children and grandchildren."

"Loser," Betsy said.

"That sounds kind of dumb," Linda said.

"Well," Lucy said. "I'm not cleaning up your dead bodies."

On the drive home in Diana's car, as they approached a bridge over the river, the mayflies clustered in a pulsing brown blizzard, flickering in sheets beneath the streetlights, their wispy corpses piling in foot-high drifts at the base of the poles. Edith stared out at the slow-approaching cars pushing through a whipped fog of insect death, windshields spackled with mayfly corpses.

"I like this," Betsy said.

"What's there to like about it?" Diana asked. "You wanna drive, be my guest."

"It means the river's healthy. It means everything is working the way it should."

A snowplow drove past, pushing the soft drifts of dead and dying bugs into the invisible water below, clearing the bridge into a smooth, glistening path of guts and wings.

When she was a child, Edith had heard about a version of heaven where the recently deceased, upon meeting St. Peter, is presented with an option of reliving her or his favorite day for eternity. Of all the versions of heaven she'd been told about, this one appealed to her the most, even though she didn't have a particular day in mind yet. She knew she'd have one eventually, and figured that she'd know it when she was there, even if some obvious candidates along the way had to be discounted. The distant cousins who'd snuck in a flask and started a fight with Stanley's brother marred her wedding. The births of her children were miraculous, but there was no way she'd want to relive the hours of labor leading up to those deliveries again and again. Sometimes she looked back fondly at her time in New Stockholm, working at St. Anthony-Waterside, but that time of her life was also sometimes anxious, unpleasant, and stressful, especially after her pies became famous.

If she could choose one day, it'd be August 26, 2018, the day that a couple of her friends might remember, if they do at all, as the day her second batch of Rhubarb-Pie-In-A-Bottle Ale completely sold out at the Minnesota State Fair. The third batch was in a conditioning tank already, and would be ready before Labor Day, meaning that she could get more to the State Fair before it ended, but for now, on this day, there was none left in the world.

Other than that, it was both a typical and pleasant day. Around lunch, there were people outside, waiting for the taproom to open, and a few of them said hi to Edith by name.

At Autumn Pines that evening, it was Shotty Vecchio's birthday, and after dinner, he asked Edith to wheel him outside to watch the baseball game between the Nicollet Falls Nicks and the Miesville Mudhens up close. He used to coach the Nicks, long ago, he said. She didn't know if that were true or not, because Shotty's mind was a little unreliable, but it was his birthday, so she didn't question him.

They lost track of time watching those young

men swing their bats, sprint across the dirt, and whisk through the grass. Then, as the team filed off the diamond, one of the players dashed over to Shotty and placed something in his hands. It was a ball that everyone on the team had signed.

For dinner that night at the brewery, Andy brought pizzas over, and he brought Francie over, too. At eight months old, she already looked around the place and smiled as if it was built for her.

"Someday, this will all be yours," Andy said, stroking his daughter's wispy hair.

"Well, if she wants it," Edith said.

Andy laughed to himself. "Yeah, I suppose that's up to her, isn't it, when she inherits it."

Edith supposed that it was nice that her family finally had something worth inheriting again, maybe. It was a lot of work for everyone involved, and there was certainly no promise that it would continue to be successful, but she could've said the same things about the farm.

"Let me get a picture of just the two of you," Andy said, taking out his phone. "Great-grandma and great-granddaughter. I don't have one yet."

"I don't think anyone's taken one yet," Edith said, which was hard to believe. Although Edith was dirty and disheveled after a day of work, and her hair looked like a squirrel's nest, she said OK. Of course, then, this was the picture that eventually ended up in the newspaper. It also evidently made it onto the internet, which Edith didn't care for, no matter how many "likes" it got.

Other than these small events and circumstances, there was nothing apparently special about this day. It was simply one more cradle of hours when everyone who she cared about and loved in her life was taken care of, either directly at the brewery or as a result of it. She was a great-grandmother, and she could look around herself and know that things were holding steady, for the time being. If it all got worse again, at least there'd be good days to look back upon, and it was rare to recognize them as they were happening.

One morning, the week after Labor Day, that Clarissa Johnson girl walked in the door fifteen minutes before they were open. She was carrying a backpack with her and had the glow and grime of someone who'd been traveling for days.

"Oh, hello," Edith said. "Back visiting your folks?"

She'd heard that Clarissa had chosen to stay in New York just because she'd found an apartment with a kitchen, and had refused to come out and help her pregnant best friend build a new family business. Not that anyone asked Edith, but someone in Diana's life had dropped almost everything to help her and someone else hadn't.

"Nope," Clarissa said, and then looked up toward the office upstairs, and Edith heard a door open.

"Clarissa!" Diana shouted from above, and limped down the stairs and hugged her friend. Clarissa shouted "dude" repeatedly, like a weirdo on dope.

"What the hell are you doing here?" Diana asked.

"I lost that sublet," Clarissa said. "But I figure I can write anywhere. So, I'm moving back."

"REALLY?" Edith hadn't seen her granddaughter this excited in a long time. Edith supposed it was nice to see. "For how long?"

"I don't know. Can you get me a job?"

The next day, Diana introduced Clarissa Johnson to the rest of the staff as Artemis Brewery's director of social media and community outreach. Edith wanted everyone to know that she clapped and smiled at the announcement just as much as everyone else did. She was sure grateful that there were people in the world for those bizarre jobs that she didn't want to do.

About five months later, on a gray, unremarkable winter morning, Edith got to work early with Lucy and Agatha, to clean up from the night before and fill a few kegs with Linda's new oatmeal stout. Agatha wanted to sample it first, and if she wasn't also willing and able with the assorted janitorial tasks, Edith would've been a little frustrated at how Agatha liked to pour almost a full glass from a zwickel, take one sip, and dump the rest by the drain on the floor, but never perfectly into the drain.

"I'll mop it up," Edith offered, because it was easier work than sweeping beneath all those tables around in the taproom. "Where's Diana?"

"She just texted me," Agatha said. "She's on her way in. She's bringing someone."

"Well, that's fine," Edith said, wandering over to the utility closet. "We could use the help. Lord knows Clarissa doesn't do much physical labor."

"I don't know if it's help," Agatha said.

"Is someone going to buy us?" Lucy asked. This made Edith nervous, because Lucy's gut instincts were usually right. "I don't want anyone to buy us."

"We can't worry about that," Agatha said. "Let's go sweep up."

"That's what happened, isn't it!" Lucy shouted as she followed Agatha out of the room.

Edith stood there for a moment, alone again, staring at the mop like it was a shy man who'd asked her to dance. Even if Lucy was right, the floor still needed to be cleaned. Edith reached for the mop, as she had her whole life, but for the first time since she'd been in that building, the trickle of fear in her heart made it feel like work.

$1,020,000

Helen, 2018

Sometimes, during her lunch break, or after she left work at Blotz, Helen went to a bar, ordered a club soda with one slice of lemon and one slice of lime, and waited.

Perhaps now, because she was in her midseventies, it had never been easier for her to get what she wanted. Most men in the kinds of establishments she visited hadn't looked in her direction for many years now, which was perfect. Instead, she could watch those men, as they glanced at her, sat down, and ordered their beer, and the more they ignored her, the more powerful she became.

As she got older, Helen spent more and more time in dark, unwelcoming, windowless roadside bars.

She'd come to like their unpretentious tap lists, faint country music, and old smoke that clung to the walls like a memorial to her generation of dead and dying customers. Now, she hadn't always preferred these places, of course, at least any more than she'd liked any other public setting, but one thing was still true about many of them that was less and less true of everywhere else in the world with tap handles—they were still hers. Here, it would take no more than fifteen minutes for a man to come in and order a beer that Helen invented.

Tonight, that man looked like the old Brawny paper towel guy, the sexy one with the moustache, but with greasy hat hair, an extra forty pounds, a dirty Carhartt jacket wet from the rain outside, and a right hand missing half of a thumbnail. If she could draw a picture of her key demographic, it'd be something like him—a big, filthy man who has enjoyed life, and Helen was there to help him. In her white collared blouse and single-pleat slacks, she couldn't look less like these guys, but because she knew that they were from the same people, she was never uncomfortable in their company.

A young bald bartender in a sleeveless skeleton T-shirt changed the channel on a muted TV, until the bright images of a baseball game flickered across the bottles. "How's it goin'?" he asked the customer, without looking at him.

"Not too bad," the man replied. "And you?"

"Oh, not too bad."

"Blotz Light," the man said.

For decades now, Helen had watched as people chugged, spat, spilled, laughed, and wet themselves. She watched gallons of beer come out of thousands of noses. If you've drunk beer in a dark bar in southeastern Minnesota or western Wisconsin in the last fifty years, she'd probably watched you.

Whenever they introduced a new product line, she'd observe the reactions, and whenever they tweaked the recipe for her signature lager, she'd see if people could perceive the subtle change. Only one person ever did, back in 1979, and it was Agatha Johnston, whom they hired on the spot that day. Had anyone in this room been given those talents and the willingness to use them correctly, Helen might still do the same, but in the meantime, she remained quiet, and just took it all in.

The bartender, still a boy both in his eyes and his wasted movements, had heard his customer, but didn't fulfill the order.

"Local beer is two bucks today," he said, turning toward and pointing at an LED menu board. "We got Bent Paddle, Lift Bridge, Steel Toe, Summit, and Artemis."

Artemis. Helen didn't know much about them

yet, but they'd only been around a few months and were already in a bar she'd have considered a tough spot for craft beer. She'd have to send someone over to their taproom to check them out. Helen was also shocked that a joint like this even bothered with a craft list. She could tell from its dusty museum of disused liqueurs that this dive hadn't chased a trend since the days of the Harvey Wallbanger.

The customer took his time processing this new, unsolicited information, long enough for Helen to hear half the chorus of the song "Gone Country" playing from the kitchen.

A bony, delicate-looking woman at the bar, younger than Helen, but not young, spoke up in the crumpled voice of a veteran smoker. "Well, Blotz is local. It's from over by Hastings."

The bartender almost laughed. "No, I mean **good** local beer."

Helen took a deep breath. She'd tried beer from the other breweries the bartender had mentioned, and he was right, they each had far better flavor, a more appealing aroma, a more complex mouthfeel, a longer finish, and more hop character than Blotz. If that's what a person calls "better," then fine. But that wasn't the point. There was a lot more to beer besides objective standards of quality.

"I tried all those other ones for ya, Bob," the woman said, and then reached for the bartender's arm. "Get him a Blotz, Fuzzy." Helen wasn't surprised that the two other customers at the bar knew each other, but if they'd greeted each other, she'd missed it.

Bob nodded back at the woman. "What Louise said."

Fuzzy threw up his hands. "I'm just pointing out that the local stuff's on sale, is all."

"Blotz is more local than those other beers," Louise announced, which was at best a questionable claim, but Helen appreciated the spirit. "Y'know an interesting fact? The lady that runs it? Grew up two miles from my dad's place."

That fact didn't appear to be remotely interesting at all to anyone at the bar, except Helen, who couldn't say a damn thing. Helen didn't recognize this Louise, but it had been so long since Helen had been up in that area, there was no use sorting through the bits and pieces in her head to recall this face when she couldn't even remember what year the Sarrazins sold their dairy farm.

"Oh, sure," the bartender said. "And you know how she got the money to reopen that brewery? She ripped off her sister."

Helen fought her face muscles into imitating a bland expression. It was now nearly impossible for Helen not to correct this guy, but if people started to recognize her, she believed she'd get ceaselessly hassled in public, and one of the last things in life she still enjoyed would be gone. She'd kept away from photographers for thirty years for a few reasons, and this was now the main one.

"She invented Blotz Special Light," Louise said, staring straight ahead toward her reflection in the mirror across the bar. "In fact, all those Blotz beers, is what I heard."

"That part's true," Helen murmured. It just came out; she couldn't help it. Her mother used to lecture them about not blowing into their own balloon, and it turns out she was mostly right, but there had to be exceptions.

"No way," the bartender said, facing Helen now, all eyes on him, and therefore her. "Blotz was around forever. My grandpa used to drink it. All those beer recipes came from the actual Blotz family."

"They did not," Helen said, quietly. "They were hers."

Bob glanced at the bartender. The poor guy just wanted a beer, not a dispute over its origin. He'd taken out his keychain, and trickled the keys between his fingers while he waited.

"Nope," the bartender said. "She married into that family and took them over, that's what happened. She didn't make anything herself."

"You're wrong," Helen said, at full volume. "Completely wrong."

She hadn't even identified herself yet, but her full voice, a voice that had commanded production lines and truck fleets, was enough to elicit his surrender. She watched him step back, until his elbow clanked against a half-empty bottle of bar chardonnay.

"OK, then," the bartender said, crossing his arms, preemptively defensive of his expertise. "What, were you Helen Blotz's college roommate or something?"

"Not even close," Helen said.

"Well this oughta be good," Louise said, pivoting in her stool.

"Who the hell are you, then?" the bartender asked, with the flushed, toxic ardor of a man who'd been embarrassed.

Yes, she shouldn't have challenged a bartender in his own bar, even if he deserved it, because now a simple disagreement had foolishly escalated. For the first time in years, everyone in a bar, everyone, was looking at her. But if a professional bartender, especially one in a bar like this, couldn't believe that a farm girl could come from nothing and create the most popular beer in Minnesota—at least for a few years in the late seventies and early eighties—then a part of her couldn't live another minute without throttling the facts into him, whatever the cost.

Instead, Helen put a ten-dollar bill on the bar, stared at the bartender, and said just one more thing as she rose from her stool.

"Just someone passing through," she said. "Get that man his Blotz."

Walking through the rain to her car, with the fat cold drops pummeling her hair and clothes, she felt relieved. As much as she knew she'd long deserved personal recognition, she also recognized any desire for it for the vanity it was. For fifty years she'd been brewing beer, and she'd do it for fifty more if God allowed her. At no point along the way had widespread personal validation been required for its understanding or enjoyment.

Yes, there were many times, like now, when she'd almost stood up and told strangers what she'd done, but she wouldn't leave the legacy she desired simply through prideful public displays, like some men did. There were advantages to a low profile. It was like a man to scratch his name on the banister of history, but Helen had come to believe that it was better to be the stairs.

The next day, Agatha went to Artemis Brewery, and was there for three hours. She seemed energetically beguiled by the place, like a widow who'd just had her first promising date in years.

"It's almost all women," was the first thing Agatha said when she returned to Blotz. "The brewmaster is Diana Winter."

"From Heartlander?" Helen knew the name. Got the credit for a popular IPA a few years back, when she was still a teenager. Helen had sent her a nice congratulatory email, but never heard back. That can happen when people get success too young; it goes to their head, and they think they can quit listening to people.

"You'll never guess who's working there," Agatha said. "Your sister."

Agatha was right. Helen never would've guessed that. "Doing what?"

Four months and two days after nearly revealing herself in that roadside bar, Helen came home from work early, parked her car in the garage, and walked down her cracked driveway to retrieve her mail from the black box out at the curb.

Out of any living relative she could recall, there was one name that she never expected to see on the cover of the respected industry trade publication **Independent Brewer**, which Helen had subscribed to long ago just to scout for potential breweries to purchase. But there it was, in bold print on the cover's lower-right-hand corner: FLAVOR DAVE REVIEWS "GRANDMA EDITH'S 'RHUBARB-PIE-IN-A-BOTTLE'!"

Helen knew it couldn't be any other Grandma Edith in the world.

Review: Grandma Edith's
Rhubarb-Pie-In-A-Bottle Ale,
Artemis Brewery

By: Pete "Flavor Dave" Michaels

Let's all take a step back from the ledge, people.

Let's remember that most of us who are old enough to drink in America were born in a country where the vast majority of beer was piss-poor lager made by a tiny handful of companies. If you claim you love any of that watery effluence now, it's either because you've tethered it to some insidious nostalgic sentiment or it's because you're too cheap to drink anything better. Either way, when your liver kills you out of spite, it's your own damn fault, and I hope your city coroner has the brains to call your death a suicide.

Since every other product in the world is rapidly becoming what beer was in 1975, and for the same reasons, let's pause at this moment. It's a glorious time, perhaps never to be seen again, and even as I write this, my fridge rattles twenty feet away, crowded with thirteen varieties of beer from twenty-one different brewers, all of which I can personally visit in under an hour's drive. I already weep for the inevitable demise of this era, and most of all, its ability to surprise me.

As you know, I buy most of my beer at Cragg's Wine & Spirits in Dinkytown, half of it special-ordered by KT, the smartest and therefore angriest woman in customer service. Last night, KT immediately handed me a six-pack of something called GRANDMA EDITH'S RHUBARB-PIE-IN-A-BOTTLE, and told me to go home, drink this crap, and shut up. She helpfully added that if I didn't like it then something must be wrong with me, because every white hipster who she had the tolerance to remember had come in either to buy it or ask about it.

The hipster crowd does love an unlikely origin story, and this is a memorable one. The brewer, Artemis, is operating out of the old Heartlander facility in Nicollet Falls, Minnesota, and the brewmaster, Diana Winter, is apparently the same ex-Heartlander employee who brewed her first IPA there at age nineteen. She's hanging her own shingle now, but before we confuse it for some bootstrapped operation, the reader should bear in mind that she has (earned?) professional facilities and relationships far beyond the reach of most first-time brewmasters. With these home-field advantages, she needs to be up to something different to be respected, and indeed, there's some superfreaky shit happening there, starting with the girls on her payroll.

Ms. Winter's entire production team is a cadre of women over sixty-five, all of whom happen to be grandmothers, and one of whom apparently is this selfsame Edith. I had my doubts, but it's the real thing; for better or worse, an actual damn Grandma Edith made this damn beer. That's not even my favorite thing about it. My favorite thing about it is that it's just OK.

And before I explain why that's my favorite thing in the world, you should hunt this shit down and drink as much of it as possible, because this beer represents something nearly extinct from every shelf in every store in America.

This beer doesn't make any sense. It didn't fill any obvious market niche, meet a known customer demand, or pursue any recognizable trend. This beer is merely the ultimate expression of its brewer, a seventy-nine-year-old woman named Edith Magnusson, who has next to no internet footprint, and about one-millionth the social media presence of my neighbor's two-year-old. What little exists about Edith online indicates that she may have worked at a nursing home in New Stockholm, where her pies were enough of a foodie fetish to turn the joint into a brutal Friday-night dinner reservation, but there was nothing to indicate any access to or even interest in brewing. Until, of course, this pie in a bottle, which seems like a smoking gun of a correlation. The actual pie was almost certainly better.

The beer has a fluffy pink two-finger head and smells like malty rhubarb, so it's certainly not out to fool anybody. No flavor notes I can write, however, are sufficient, and in many ways, they're beside the point. Even as the primal forces that created the beer of the 1970s from the beer of the 1870s recast their shadows, hope remains in this specific bottle, because all of the chemists, focus groups, AI, and boardrooms in

the world will never create a beer like Grandma Edith's. This beer is flawed, wonderful, and strange in a way only a certain kind of individual could devise, and it renders every other beer on the shelf a faceless SKU. Grandma Edith was just making a beer that she wanted to drink, because it didn't exist yet, and the result is not a beer in the sense you know it. It is the heart and guts and ignorance and beauty and dreams of Edith Magnusson, and that is all.

God bless it, and God bless America.

Rating: 100 out of 100.

Editor's note: Flavor Dave is now on an infinite sabbatical.

Helen Blotz sat down in her driveway and reread Flavor Dave's final beer review again and again. The rest of the day's mail was on the pavement, fifty feet away, scattering itself in the breeze.

Of course, she'd heard by then, from Agatha, that Edith had brewed and bottled a beer. Helen certainly didn't expect it to be popular and critically celebrated. Not like this. Her sister, who she'd never seen drink more than a sip of alcohol in her life, received the only 100 out of 100 score Flavor Dave ever conferred.

Helen crawled to the grass, and sat in the cool shadow of her new, small ranch-style home. Her new neighbors could see her, but so what? Her fingers shook over her smartphone as she pressed a name.

"Agatha," Helen said. "Are you busy?"

Agatha arrived thirty minutes later, serious and unperturbed. Helen poured her a glass of sparkling water and made small talk for about fifteen seconds before Helen showed her guest the review.

"Yeah, we just heard," Agatha said, glancing at the magazine. Helen flinched at the "we," but that's the way things were now.

"God, I shouldn't have waited," Helen said, shielding her eyes from the setting sun outside the kitchen windows, and moving out of its sharp harassment. "You're the one who told me to wait. Now, they might be out of my price range. That Diana seems too clever. She knows what something like this is worth."

"That's all true, and I'm sorry," Agatha said, and stood up to point at Helen's skirt. "Oh, and you have some grass on your butt."

"I know." Helen ran her hand briskly down her backside, and she bent at the waist to collect the blades that drifted to the kitchen floor. "So, you still prefer it over there? They can't be paying you half as well."

"I never said I prefer it. And I'm still retired. I don't draw a paycheck. I come and go as I please."

"That's ridiculous. You should be the highest-paid person at that brewery."

Agatha shrugged. "I made my money. Now I want to do something for fun. Helping out at Artemis is fun."

"You don't want to lose money either," Helen said, which was hard to forget, looking around this little humdrum home. At least Orval didn't have to live to see her sell the house in Marine on St. Croix. "You don't want to sink aboard the SS **Helen Blotz**."

Helen didn't want to remind Agatha again about how she was supposed to take over the brewery when Helen was gone, because she still could, while the company still existed. She and Agatha remained close, Helen explained to people, because she perfectly understood the move. Blotz had been in a terrifying death dive for years, and almost nothing creative or dynamic was happening, not like at Artemis. It was absolutely impossible to begrudge someone from making such a wise choice. Absolutely impossible. But it still hurt, so much.

Agatha nodded. "Do you know how much I look up to you? I don't know where I'd be without you."

Helen tried, but couldn't return the eye contact. "I know," she said.

"And I had to look at you every day for years as your company failed, and what it did to you. I couldn't do that anymore."

"I suppose those women at Artemis have more

to be happy about," Helen said. "Can any of those grandmas actually brew beer worth a damn?"

"Yeah. One of them is actually a really promising brewer."

"Not Edith."

"No, not Edith. Edith will get better though. She has the right instincts. It's a woman named Betsy Nielsen."

"Never heard of her. She ever work at a brewery before, on any level?"

"No, I think she was mostly a hotel maid. And until I showed up, she was still working at an Arby's."

"Yikes." Helen shook her head. "By the way, did you buy them those vans, with their logo on the side? I saw one the other day."

Agatha nodded.

"You spent your own money on that?"

Agatha looked like she was going to laugh. "Now you're telling me how I should handle my money? If you have advice, I'd love to hear it. Seriously."

This was sure the wrong river to cross. Agatha was actually incredible with money. She owned two homes and several commercial real estate properties. She'd started scholarship funds for both Native American students and single mothers. Her own daughter had become an accountant, for God's sake. Agatha had made a lot, and turned it into more than she believed she could use in a lifetime. Helen remembered what that felt like.

"What were they doing for distribution then, before you showed up?"

"Diana drove around in her Volkswagen. For the bigger jobs, they were borrowing Bernie's truck."

"Bernie?"

"He's this groundskeeper from a nursing home who works at the brewery now."

"Jesus," Helen said. "It's the Island of Misfit Toys."

"Maybe that's why I love it."

Helen shuffled out of the kitchen. "Just a minute. I thought I heard a truck. It's probably the art movers."

Agatha followed her. "Art movers? What art are you moving?"

"Just selling some pieces I don't have space for anymore," Helen said, as she reached for her front door.

"Why are you selling them now?"

"I told you."

Helen opened the front door and saw nothing in the driveway, no truck, no art movers. She only noticed that her neighbors across the street and one house down were sitting in folding chairs in their open garage, facing out at the road, drinking beer. Even with her glasses on, she couldn't identify the brand from this far away, but she tried to. They saw her staring at them and waved, so she did the polite thing and waved back.

"No," Agatha said. Helen had forgotten for a moment that her friend was still there, hovering behind her in the doorway.

"No to what, Agatha?"

"I won't let you do it. No matter how much stuff you sell, or how many people you lay off, or what investor partners you wrangle. You can't buy them."

"I can. What you're telling me is that I shouldn't."

"Fine then, that's what I'm telling you."

"You know, somebody's going to buy them, someday." Helen leaned against her door frame. "I guarantee you. Better me than some private equity group. And from the looks of it, my window is closing, thank you very much."

"You're not listening to me. I don't think they'll sell to you or anyone, at any price."

"I know, that's something they have to say," Helen sighed. "And I get it. Nobody likes the idea of being bought. But it's not even being bought. It's being replenished. More money is never a bad thing."

Agatha walked toward the driveway and turned to face Edith from the grass.

"These women," Agatha said. "They feel a sense of pride and identity in their work. For the first time."

"You think I'm going to ruin that? I mean, whatever's working, I'm not going to mess with it. I'm just going to make them a little richer."

"You don't get it. They don't want that. They've been working for money their whole lives. This is something different."

"I know, and that's one reason why I want to have it."

"You don't seem to understand that you buying this brewery is going to fundamentally destroy what it is."

"You're right, I don't understand that, because it isn't."

"Pick another brewery. There are literally thousands."

"This is the only one I want."

"But it's your family."

"Yes." Helen nodded. "Yes, it is."

"I'm gonna go," Agatha said, and turned toward what looked like a brand-new pickup, a shiny black Ram 2500.

"But I'd be helping them."

"There are other ways to do that, you know." She opened her driver's-side door and glared back at Helen. "Why are you doing this?"

Helen didn't know how to put it in words. "Because I have to."

"If this is the only way Blotz can survive, maybe Blotz shouldn't survive."

When she watched Agatha slam the door of her truck and speed off down the street, Helen felt a tense coldness she'd felt once before. So Helen again did the only thing she could do. Nothing.

She'd worked with Agatha for thirty-seven years. Other people, all other people except for Agatha and Orval, were a wrinkle in Helen's life she could never completely smooth. Since college, new people seemed to come into her life only for a specific purpose and were usually enjoyed or tolerated only to the extent they filled that purpose. She assumed that was just part of what it meant to be a boss. How could she have many friends when there were so few people like her? How could she consider a building and an industry full of people who wanted something from her as ideal places to make meaningful emotional connections? She'd lost count of the amount of times she walked into a room only to hear the abashed mumbles and see the flushed faces of a topic being abruptly changed. These are the people she was supposed to personally confide in?

And every year, the fresh college grads and vo-tech kids who came in for interviews were a little less convincing. Blotz was their favorite beer, then their father's favorite beer, then their grandfather's. It was their dream to work at Blotz; then it was their dream to work at a place like Blotz; then it was their dream to work at a brewery; then, finally, it was a job, close to home, and do the benefits include vision and dental?

The men at or near her level across the industry were often exhausting. Very early she'd been spiritually and emotionally corroded by the roomfuls of them at various industry gatherings, men who talked over her, explained to her, asked her to fetch them lunch or coffee, planted and reaped her self-doubt. In the underpopulated women's restrooms at brewers' conventions, she'd sometimes heard of industry women experiencing far worse, but Helen quit attending these caustic functions before she personally experienced anything horrifying.

But this also meant that she never stuck around to one day meet women like Kim Jordan from New Belgium or Deb Carey from New Glarus Brewery, never got to attend a Pink Boots Society meeting as an aspirant, and besides Agatha, never even worked long-term with a woman in the industry she considered a true equal. How she wished she were starting now, from scratch, anonymous and unmasked, an eager kid in a field with tens of thousands of them.

"Hey!" a woman's voice yelled out of nowhere. Helen looked around and saw that her neighbors in their lawn chairs across the street were waving at her again.

As she approached them, she saw that the couple was younger than they seemed from a distance, somewhere between fifty and sixty-five. The woman radiated an old warmth; her politeness seemed involuntary. The man had the rigid calm of a retired cop not yet acclimated to retirement.

By the time she'd reached the foot of their driveway they'd set up another folding chair for her, between theirs.

She had tried not to stare at what was in their Twins beer koozies as she approached, but even from twenty feet away, she knew the tops of those cans. Blotz Special Light. She felt her muscles ease and her heart slow. It was just two cans out there in the world, but they seemed to tell her she could relax, that she was safe for the moment, and the world wasn't all bad.

"I'm Rosa, and that's Edgar," the woman said, extending her hand. Helen introduced herself, but just her first name as well, as she'd much preferred to do anyway. She'd been in this new place for two weeks, and these were the first neighbors she'd met, but she'd hardly been home.

They'd been living here for a while, judging by the clutter she could see behind the scratched-up minivan in the garage—a faded dartboard; a yellowed refrigerator; a United States Marine Corps flag; a cracked, plastic, football-shaped toy box now full of rakes and shovels; rows of old wooden Northland hockey sticks mounted on the walls; and several framed pictures of three young men, two in Marine Corps uniforms. Over half the photos were of one boy in particular, so she guessed that he might be dead.

"How's it going over there?" Rosa asked. "Are you still settling in?"

Oh, pretty good and **Yes, just perfectly**, she wanted to say, and those would've been the right things to say to a couple of strangers, especially ones who she'd be living across the street from for the foreseeable future. It would have been the right way to start off a friendly acquaintanceship. Today, though, she couldn't do it.

"I've had better days, to be honest," Helen said. It came out sounding more sad than she intended.

Edgar and Rosa glanced at each other. "Sounds like you could use a beer," Rosa said, and she rose from her chair, pivoting toward the fridge.

Across the street, Helen saw a van park in her driveway, and watched the art movers exit and knock on her door, and she decided to stay seated, as Rosa asked her what kind of beer would she like, they had a couple different kinds.

Three months later, the Friday before Christmas, Helen was in her basement. She moved the box that read TROPHIES AND RIBBONS out of the way, and knelt before one that read, in permanent black marker, SASSICAIA 1998. She and Orval had splurged on a case of it, way back in 2001, for special occasions, and they'd only made two such special occasions before he died.

Now, Rosa and Edgar across the street were having a Christmas party, with their boys back home for the holidays, and the whole street was invited.

Helen knew it was a bit ridiculous to bring such an expensive bottle of wine to a neighborhood Christmas party, but Edgar and Rosa loved the stuff when she'd brought one over for Thanksgiving. She'd go over early to make sure the wine was decanted properly this time. They might like it even more.

She felt the chill in her nose and teeth as she closed her front door behind her. Her driveway glimmered in the garage light, and she could see the streaks and clumps of winter across the road. She held the wine bottle firmly in one hand, the decanter in the other, making slow, soft steps across the ice.

"Helen!" Rosa shouted when Helen entered. Her mother had told her once that the nicest thing you can do for someone is be happy to see them, and Helen thought about that now, as she felt herself smile, involuntarily. Still, there were a lot of people in that living room who she didn't know; the Thanksgiving crowd had been much smaller.

"Everyone," Rosa announced. "For those of you who haven't met her yet, this is our new neighbor, Helen Calder. She brings the most delicious wine."

As people greeted her en masse, one of the older men in the room grinned. He had the body, clothes, and facial hair of someone who would've worked on her production line, and it occurred to her right then, she'd miss those guys. Looking at someone who even reminded her of them almost made her start to cry.

"More of a beer guy myself," he said.

Helen nodded. "Honestly, me too."

Three weeks later, Helen was in her most expensive suit, watching all the lawyers rise from her conference room's long wood table and file to the door.

"Where's there to eat around here?" one of the lawyers from California asked.

Helen was about to say The Point, but it had been closed for years now. She still wasn't used to that. Strawberry Fields and The Steamboat Inn over in Prescott were long gone as well. "Try The Onion Grille," she said. "Down in Hastings." They didn't serve Blotz, but now it didn't matter to her who would.

The people she was meeting with today were from Oganesson Brands, a company founded in Yorba Linda, California. A year ago, they were fifteenth in the world in total alcohol sales, and by the end of this year they estimated they'd move up at least one spot, with the help of the year's acquisitions, the latest of which was Blotz Brewery of Point Douglas, Minnesota.

Their chairman, the grandson of the immigrant

who'd founded the company in the 1950s to import specialty alcohol from Asia, had made a point of coming out to Minnesota to oversee this transaction. He said that being fifteenth in the world, which meant billions in sales, wasn't good enough for him. Even though Helen didn't ask, he'd still told her that Oganesson's goal was to be in the top ten by 2025, and top five by 2035.

It's a shame, but Helen doesn't have a good memory of him anymore. Even a day later, she felt like a child trying to describe something she'd imagined under the bed. He was vivid at the time, but now she only remembered that he was a lean, swarthy white man who wore a gray Italian-cut suit. "Call me old-fashioned," he said. "If I spend twelve bucks, I don't need to know the vendor. If I spend twelve million, I like to meet them and shake their hand."

How lovely of him, Helen thought. Hearing the amount again reminded her that she could leave the humble little suburban neighborhood she'd been in, and move back to Marine on St. Croix, if she wanted. The thought passed as the man extended his hand. His grip, like hers, was firm, but brief.

"Where's Joe Foxworth?" he asked, smiling. "I was looking forward to meeting him in person."

"He left." Joe's longtime partner, Blake, was a principal at a new student loan servicing firm, and

Joe departed last spring to help him out. "He's out of the industry. He's helping kids consolidate their college loans."

"Student debt. That's a growth industry, from what I hear," the man said. "What about Agatha Johnston?"

"She's working for a smaller competitor." They hadn't been in touch since their argument last September, but Helen planned to patch that up, now that this part of her life was over.

"So it's been just you, for a while."

"For a while." She stared out the window at the trees across the river in Wisconsin, one floor below where Orval used to stare every morning before he began work. Helen still couldn't look back at this man. She just kept gazing out at the St. Croix River valley. It was January, and whatever wasn't beneath snow was a shade of rust. "And to think, in the nineties, I could've sold this company for two hundred million dollars. To a fellow brewer."

"Well, a lot has changed," the Oganesson man said. "'Drink lots, it's Blotz' sounded great in the seventies. But 'Drink responsibly, it's Blotz' doesn't quite have the same ring to it."

"I guess not," she said.

"And you don't have the most diverse brand portfolio. In fact, you don't have any brand portfolio, pardon me. You've sold everything, and no acquisitions in the last ten years. If it wasn't for your loyal Blotz Special Light customers, I wouldn't be here."

She didn't care to be reminded. She knew she was kind of lucky to get much of anything for the Blotz name, let alone $12,000,000. Maybe that was a good price, maybe it wasn't, but she wasn't about to ask around the industry. She didn't want to have those conversations, and suffer the questions, and hear the defeat in her own voice.

"Orval and I just wanted there to be good beer in the world. I can't help it if the world has changed its mind about what good beer is."

"Which, by the way, what happened with the craft brewery you were rumored to be interested in?" he asked, leaning toward her. "That would've made you more attractive."

"Something changed."

"Who were they, again?" The man took out a slender silver pen. "Maybe we can pay them a visit."

Helen finally looked the man in the eyes, and released a deep breath.

"Mountain Central Brewery, out of Fort Pierre, South Dakota," she said. "The owners are Mike Rother and Page Thorvald. Their flagship beer is called Prairie Page IPA."

What she'd just said was the extent of what she knew about Mountain Central Brewery, all recited from an advertisement that shared a page with a certain review in **Independent Brewer**. She hadn't ever visited the place, or even tried their beer once.

"They are now on our radar," the man replied. "Thanks for the tip."

"Don't mention it," Helen said, rising from her chair at the head of the table, for the last time, looking around at the scuffs on the chairs that will never be repaired, the dead bulb in the chandelier overhead that won't ever be changed.

"So, out of curiosity, what are you going to do now?"

"Honestly?" Helen was surprised he gave a shit. "Go up to my office and try not to cry."

"No," the man laughed politely, like he couldn't tell if she were kidding. "With your life?"

Hasn't he asked for and received enough? she wondered.

"You'll be the last to know," she said.

"Keep us posted if it's a brewery," he smiled, and left her alone in the long, quiet room. She'd just put a price on her entire life, and even if she begged right now for the exchange to be reversed, they'd never do it. There was absolutely no confusion over who got the more valued asset. There never was, and that's without Helen being sentimental, because she wasn't. She had to sell while the place still had value to someone else, while her husband's last name was still worth buying.

For Helen Calder Blotz, that was the end of Blotz Brewery. Like Schmidt, Old Style, Shaefer, Schlitz, Hamm's, Rainier, Olympia, and Stroh's, among many others, the label would persist, applied to a light adjunct lager made somewhere else, untouched by the people who created it, who'd made it into something that sustained lives and families. The name on that label was now just a nostalgic reminder of the real thing, and for years to come, increasingly old men and women would sit in little bars off the highway and order it either way. If hearing themselves say the word "Blotz" makes them feel young, or beautiful, or invincible again, maybe it's OK that it survives. Maybe, for many years now, Blotz was already better as a story than as a beer.

Helen decided that Saturday to visit someone she'd never once spoken to.

Before leaving the house, she called Agatha for the first time in months, and was surprised when she picked up.

"I heard about Blotz," Agatha said. "How've you been?"

"I'm OK," Helen said, but didn't want to go any further into all that, right then. "I need to do something for somebody," she said. "Can you help me?"

"Straight to the point, as always," Agatha laughed. "You first want to tell me who?"

Agatha told her exactly when Diana would be home alone, and gave Helen an address that was surprisingly close, so the drive was short. It didn't give her enough time to prepare an explanatory statement, so she decided that she wouldn't deliver one. She'd confirm the correct location, strike quickly, and vanish.

The bag of $1,020,000 was fairly heavy—maybe half the weight of a bushel of barley—and she couldn't wait to set it down. Walking up the driveway, she saw a baby's car seat in the screened-in porch, and braced herself for the possibility that she was right about this. Even though it was overcast, it was bright, and she had debated whether to wear big sunglasses and was now glad that she did. She took a deep breath and knocked three times on the screen door.

A young woman answered the door. She was wearing a plain black sweater and blue jeans. She was tall, and pretty, but had a look on her face that said, **Look, I've heard it all, so this better be good, whoever you are**.

"Can I help you?" she asked, trying her best not to sound too unfriendly.

A little curly-headed girl was on the carpet behind her in a green onesie, yelping, staring at the strange new person in the doorway.

"Diana Winter?" Helen asked.

"Yes?" the woman replied. The little girl waddled behind her mom's leg and curled behind one of her calves.

Looking behind them into the living room,

Helen could see a framed painting of a farmhouse. She'd seen it before, long ago. The house had its lights on and a different family member was visible in every window. She'd always hated that painting. She'd assumed that no one in that family could stand to be in the same room together anymore.

Helen was about to introduce herself, but then closed her mouth.

"This is for you," Helen said, and set a tote bag on the ground near her own feet. She then turned her back and walked briskly down the snowy drive-way to her car, which was parked across the street.

She could hear Diana gasp. "Wait!" Diana said.

Helen could hear the young woman running be-hind her. "Wait," Diana said again, as Helen got in her car and closed the door. Helen saw Diana's face, and past her, the face of the little girl in the bottom panel of the screen door, gaping at them both, and couldn't find the car keys in her bag, as Diana knocked on the driver's-side window, again and again.

The two women sat at an old dinette table, sipped cups of anxiously brewed tea, and ate these inter-esting spent-grain crackers from a chipped white bowl. She remembered living as a young brewer on a budget and how long it had been before she and Orval replaced their own chipped dishes. An empty plastic pitcher with a built-in plunger was on top of the fridge, and a giveaway 2019 calendar was tacked onto the wall, scrawled with a family's coded messages to themselves.

Helen glanced down at the money at her feet. She knew Diana would've been confused by the strange amount, but when the news got back to Edith, and it would, she'd understand its significance. It was $20,000, Edith's half of the farm sale, times fifty-one, for each year since.

Helen had answered Diana's frenzied queries about who she was and where the money came from and where she'd been, before Diana asked a question that Helen felt unprepared to answer.

"I don't know if I can handle this right now," Diana stammered, as if she were on the verge of tears, or fury, or both. "Why the hell would you just drop a bag of money on my doorstep and take off?"

She looked at this young woman, this cluttered, simple house, the empty hook by the door for a working husband's coat.

"Because I wanted to help you out," Helen said. "And we don't have any kind of relationship. It just seemed like the best way to do it."

Diana stared at the cash on her kitchen floor like it was about to disappear. "I just can't even tell you how much even a fraction of this, at any point, would've changed my life. And Edith's life, too. I'm not trying to be ungrateful, but do you know what we did to get by? You have no idea."

"I can guess," Helen said, glancing around the little kitchen, touching the chipped bowl, noticing the peeling wallpaper.

"No, you can't," Diana said. "It's just a little hard for me to wrap my head around. That you would do this."

"You probably heard a lot of horrible things about me growing up."

"Not from Edith. Just from my parents."

How interesting, Helen thought. "I didn't even know your parents."

"Agatha told me that you were going to try to buy my brewery. We're not for sale."

"I know. But someone else is going to come for you, someday soon," Helen said. "Someone way bigger."

"Let them try."

"It's going to be harder to say no next time. Much harder." Helen glanced at the baby, who was sitting on the floor, her expression tethered to a TV show's balmy narrative, having long since moved through her brief trepidation and fascination with the strange guest.

"Are you going to try to give any money to Edith?"

"No, because I know she won't accept it."

"You're right, she wouldn't." Diana almost laughed. Whatever defensiveness she'd once held onto seemed to be vanishing. "Did you give anything to your employees?"

"Yes, and that arrangement's between me and them."

"OK." Diana stared at the bag. "So, then. What would you do with this, if you were me?"

"That's up to you," Helen said, and rose to her feet. "It's freely given. There are no conditions."

Helen thought she had sensible, practical reasons for giving this money to Diana and not Edith, and while there weren't conditions, there were expectations. This young woman could expand her business and Helen would always know that she'd had a hand in that. She could stand at a great distance and look on in pride at the family she helped.

But she was wrong, and she saw that now. This money ceased being hers the second she handed that bag over to Diana. Whatever choices this young woman would make with it, Helen would have nothing to do with them. Maybe they wouldn't be the right choices, or the smart choices. Maybe that never matters.

She reached out to shake Diana's hand, and for the first time she felt Edith's honest fear and hope in that young woman. "I should go."

"Francie?" Diana called, failing to break the grasp of the television. She said it again, louder, and finally the little girl turned her head. "Let's get your coat on."

"You're heading out, too?"

"Yeah, to work. And I want you to come with me. In my car."

"Is she there?"

Diana nodded.

Helen sat down again at the dinette table. "I can't do it," she said, and then looked up to see Diana standing in front of her.

For a while, neither woman moved.

Helen stared through the windshield as Diana drove them for miles, to a desolate, stunted office park on the edge of Nicollet Falls, past a bright green sign jammed into the snow that read ARTEMIS BREWERY & TAPROOM and through an icy, sparse parking lot. Diana stopped her car at the windowless gray side of a large building, and turned off the engine.

"Go on in," Diana said, as she unbuckled herself and glanced back at her daughter.

For a few moments, Helen watched Diana unbuckle the baby from the car seat, and thought she'd wait, and they'd all go in together.

But then she looked at the building. Edith was in there, somewhere.

Helen turned a cold stainless steel doorknob, and felt the heat and light hit her from inside.

Lucy and Agatha were in the middle of the long taproom, cleaning up between the picnic-style tables, and when Helen walked in, neither of them said a word. Lucy recognized her, Helen could tell, from the way Lucy pursed her lips and gripped her broom handle like it was the top of a flagpole. Helen never did like that Lucy Koski. Agatha nodded once as Helen passed.

Through the glass wall that separated the brewery from the brewpub, Helen saw her. Edith had her back to the door and was mopping something that looked like a puddle of oatmeal stout. She halted in the doorway between those rooms, her blood full of sparks.

It was evident that Edith had suffered. She would be almost eighty now, and her body honestly told the tale of those years. Her tall shoulders had stooped like willow branches, and her hips had widened, but by the way she worked, Helen could tell it was still Edith. In her sister's thick arms and bowed back, Helen saw her mother bent over the sink, and her beloved father, leaning over an engine, both still alive. There was her family, with a gray head and stained shoes, still working.

Edith lifted her head and turned.

Helen couldn't move. She looked into those eyes and guessed at the losses, the joys, the hard years that forged this woman into a shape that could endure until now.

Helen had had fifty-one years to consider this moment, and think about what she would say, but on the short ride over, anything she'd ever premeditated seemed foolish. Considering the circumstances that led to this day, there was no reason that her sister should even tolerate her presence. Edith would tell her to go away, and she wouldn't be wrong. She would guess that Helen was here only because she'd lost everyone else, which made Helen cold with shame. She searched her heart for something to say. But nothing Helen could tell Edith would be enough to be loved by her again, as she once had been, when they knew each other, when they were sisters.

"There you are," Edith said.

Helen closed her eyes at the sound of that voice.

"Hi," she managed to whisper.

"I was wondering when you'd come," Edith said. She was as calm as a small town on Christmas morning. "I always knew if I walked into this brewery, so would you, one day."

Helen gazed at Edith's wrinkled face.

She knew one thing about her sister, and only one thing, for sure. "You could use a break," she said, and reached for the mop.

Helen mopped the floor, and because she felt her sister staring at her, she worked as slowly as she could. Edith just stood there and watched, as if she was just waiting to see what happened next.

As Helen finished, Edith glanced around the

cold, gray room. "There's a lot more that needs to be done."

"I know," Helen said, and stood next to her sister. "You want me to say it, I'll say it. I'm all alone, Edith. I've got no one else left in the world. Just tell me what I can do."

"Don't leave me," Edith said.

Helen remembered a summer afternoon, sprinting from a farmhouse, a cold beer bottle tucked into a waistband, looking back at her sister standing in a doorway.

In this version of the memory, she calls her sister's name. A screen door squeals open, and she watches her lanky sister step onto the lawn. Helen feels a mosquito on her neck as she waits. She feels the sun shine on the entire state of Minnesota. Edith is running now, toward her. Helen sees her sister racing through the tall grass. And she sees her own arms, right now, reaching out.

ACKNOWLEDGMENTS

This book wouldn't exist without these people: Brooke Delaney, Pamela Dorman, George Ducker, Ryan Harbage, Meg Howrey, Julia Ingalls, Lou Mathews, Jeffrey Stradal.

Immense gratitude to these writers and editors, who read versions and sections of this book over the years, and whose guidance was irreplaceable: Angela Barton, Cecil Castellucci, Melissa Chadburn, Seth Fischer, Spencer E. Foxworth, Sacha Howells, Sarah LaBrie, Ashley Perez, Erin Pinheiro, Daniel J. Safarik, Susan Straight, Chris L. Terry, and Rachael Warecki. Extra special thanks to Christopher Hermelin, for truly going above and beyond.

Giant thanks to these beer industry professionals, scholars, and enthusiasts whose knowledge and generosity guided this book: Amy Fox, Jen Fox, Nick Fox, Luke McGuire, and Claire Sandahl at Spiral Brewery, Hastings, MN; Molly Butler at Three Weavers Brewing Co., Inglewood, CA; Ted Marti at August Schell Brewing Co., New Ulm, MN; Will Glass at The Brewing Projekt, Eau Claire, WI; Mike Mallozzi at Borderlands Brewing Co., Tucson, AZ; Mark Jilg at Craftsman Brewing Co., Pasadena, CA; Leoš Frank at Lazy Monk Brewing, Eau Claire, WI; Derek Fernholz at Fernson Brewing Co., Sioux Falls, SD; Dr. Jennifer A. Jordan at the University of Wisconsin-Milwaukee; Jason Davenport and Tyler Jepperson at Remedy Brewing Co., Sioux Falls, SD; Eric Geier at Bad Habit Brewing Co., St. Joseph, MN; Brian and Amanda Trimble at Bill of Rights Brewery, Pierre, SD; Erik Amaya at Marcus of Queensbury Brewery, Los Angeles, CA; Matt Kivel, Amy and Jay Kovacs, Diana Kowalsky, Peigi Malec, Steve Marseille, Jeremy Schmidt, Mark and Sara Finnerty Turgeon, and certainly not least, Ryan and Katie Vincent. Whatever I've gotten wrong about beer in this book is my fault, not theirs.

Also, thank you to the people who helped me troubleshoot various other details over my years writing this book: MJ Adams, Anne Bramley, Patricia Clark, Christopher T. Davis, Beth Dooley, Becca Doten, Daniel Gill, Trent and Amy Hanson, Patrick Hicks, Brent Hopkins, Carolyn Carr Hutton, Susan Klein, Mildred Larson, Doug Latch, Alea McKinley, Dana Menard, Louise Miller, Doug Moore, Eric Ottens, Stuart Sandler, Jason Sexton, Liz Silver, and Allison Valencia. You took time out of your day to help a writer, or found someone who could, and even if the relevant information didn't always make it to the final draft, this meant a lot to me.

Thank you to these people and organizations who provided crucial tangible and intangible support: 826LA; Doris Biel; Summer Block; Stefan Bucher; Ellen Byron; Carlynn Chironna; Tricia Conley; Kathryn Court; Brian Dille; Carmen Dyar; Janet Fitch; Brendan and Gigi Fitzgerald; Susie Fleet; Ann Friedman; Joan Funk; Rico Gagliano; Kate Gibson; Taylor Grant; Nathan W. Gratz; Anthony Grazioso; Amelia Gray; Anna Grosmanová; Monica Howe; Sophie Howlett; Peter Hsu; Cindy and DJ; Ciara Johnson; Amanda Karkoutly; Matt Kay; Anne-Marie and Abe Kinney; Beth Kochendorfer; Corrina Lesser; Gabriel Levinson; Brad Listi; Michael Loomis; Erin Merlo; Anthony

Miller; Amy Murry; Ken Nicholas; Patrick Nolan; Tony Norgaard; Jeramie Orton; PEN America; Gretchen and Mike Perbix of Sweetland Orchard, Webster, MN; Lindsay Prevette; Jason Ramirez; Frances and Erick Roen; Scott Rubenstein; Kim Samek; Andrea Schulz; Roseanne Serra; Elina Shatkin; Joshua Wolf Shenk; Marisa Siegel; Connie Simonson; Jen Sincero; Pete and Ashley Slapnicher; Jill and Aaron Solomon; Kate Stark; Cindy Stevens of Carina Cellars; Eric J. Stolze; Mary Stone; Roger Stradal; Jacob Strunk; Brian Tart; Alison Turner; Shannon Twomey; Claire Vaccaro; Jennifer Widman (thanks for letting me write part of chapter six in your car); Rich Widman; the Stradal, Johnson, and Biel families; all the amazing salespeople at Penguin Random House who've helped introduce my books to the best readers in the world; and Tim Kelly, who found the notebook I'd left behind in a rental car, looked me up online, mailed it to me, and wouldn't even accept a refund of the postage.

This novel is dedicated to my grandmothers, but it's in the world because of two women: Karen Stradal, my first reader as a child, and Brooke Delaney, my first reader now. Without your love and support, none of this happens. Thank you for being my family.

J. RYAN STRADAL'S New York Times best-selling debut, **Kitchens of the Great Midwest**, won the American Booksellers Association Indies Choice Award for Adult Debut Book of the Year and the Midwest Booksellers Choice Award for debut fiction. A contributing editor at **Taste** magazine, Stradal was born and raised in Minnesota. He now lives in Los Angeles.